City of Dark

C.H. Dickinson

"Lasciate ogne speranza, voi ch'intrate."

- Dante, Inferno, Canto III
Inscription above the Gates of Hell

"Abandon all hope, ye who enter here."

Paris stands on a void. Before the city could be built, the earth first had to be gutted. The stone blocks of the Louvre and Notre-Dame came from underground quarries below the city. Material was torn from the city's bowels to erect churches, administrations and homes.

Today, 300 kilometers of underground tunnels pay tribute to a millennium of urban expansion. Popularly known as the catacombs, *this huge network of quarry tunnels is situated at a depth of roughly 20 meters below street level. It is illegal for any unauthorized person to enter the catacombs, and most entry points in the city center have been sealed. Nonetheless, an estimated 15,000 people manage to gain access and visit this subterranean world every year.*

The most avid visitors return regularly and are known as cataphiles. *Their freedom of movement is hindered only by the constant patrols of* cataflic *police, who ensure the area is kept safe. Likewise, engineers from the quarry inspectorate oversee the structural integrity of the network, which is under threat both from inevitable signs of erosion and wanton acts of malice. Their work is essential. After all, if the tunnels were to collapse, the land above would sink into the ground and the most beautiful city on earth would instantly turn to rubble.*

STREET MAP OF PARIS
5th ARRONDISSEMENT

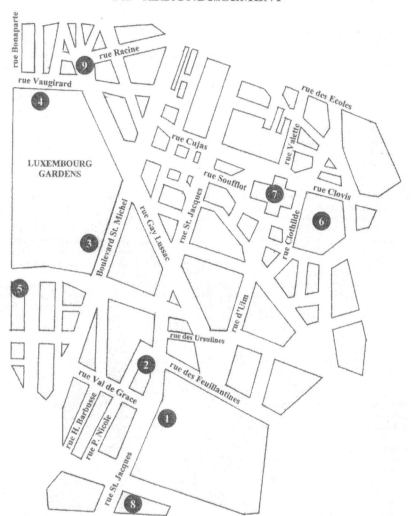

1. Val de Grace
2. Student Residence
3. Toni's University
4. Luxembourg Palace / Senate Building
5. Montaigne High School
6. Henri IV High School
7. Pantheon
8. Cochin Hospital
9. Odeon Theater

EMPTY QUARRIES UNDER PARIS
5th ARRONDISSEMENT

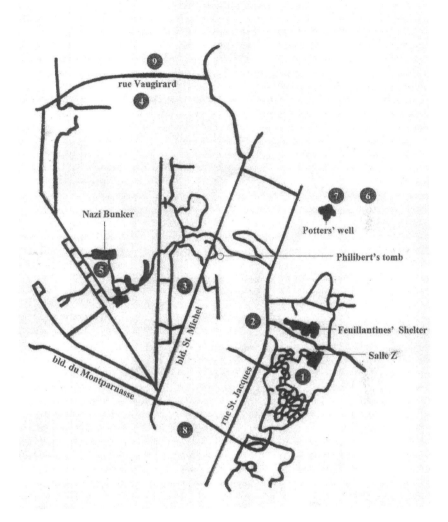

Prologue

Tuesday afternoon, 2 PM, Paris catacombs

The temperature in the stone shaft was unbearable. Philippe's hands slipped on the metal rung as he used the last bits of strength left in his arms to pull himself a few inches higher. After dragging himself all that way through the pitch black labyrinth, his leg exploding with pain, he was still going to die. He wasn't going to make it to the surface. Heat, exhaustion and dehydration would get him first. For Christ's sake, there was no way he could go much further. His strength was gone. He couldn't even feel his right leg anymore. He clawed upwards, using his remaining good leg for support. Grabbing hold of the next rung he hoisted himself up, then hooked his left leg into the lower one. How long had he been climbing like this? Minutes? Hours? He'd lost all sense of time. How deep were the catacombs here? Twenty, thirty meters? It felt like he'd been going for miles. Once again, he stretched upward and dragged himself another foot higher.

The tiny rays of sunlight piercing the darkness from the grate at street level failed to register on his line of vision. Thirst had broken his hold on reality. He'd lost his bag of provisions at some point in all the madness. In any case, the snacks and drinks had only been meant to last one night. He knew he'd been underground for much longer than that. And his last sip of water had been ages ago.

The combination of dehydration, hunger and the growing infection in his leg were blurring his senses. Was this reality or just some agonizing nightmare? Were Quentin and Quartz really dead? Or had he got reality mixed up with one of the old stories he'd read about the catacombs? Was there a man after him? A green devil? Where did the reality end and the insanity begin?

1

Le Monde, Wednesday evening edition, dated Thursday June 20th.

Arnaud de Chanterelle to undergo surgery

Wednesday morning a government spokeswoman announced that Prime Minister Arnaud de Chanterelle would be admitted to hospital this evening to undergo surgery for a small inguinal hernia. At a press conference, Colonel Marc André, the surgeon who will be performing the operation, explained that it was a straightforward procedure lasting about 30 minutes and that the Prime Minister was expected to be back on his feet within a day or two.

During the Prime Minister's hospitalization, the President has asked Jean-Yves Grafferi to take over all priministerial functions.

2

Thursday morning, 5:15AM, corner of rue St. Jacques and rue des Feuillantines

The worst place to be during a heat wave is on the top storey of a badly insulated building. Unfortunately that's exactly where Toni Corrigan was. To make matters worse, someone on the military base across the road had been calling out orders and just generally bashing around like bad neighbors since before dawn. And now the cops had joined in with a concert of sirens. This might be the end of her love affair with Paris. She dragged a pillow over her head.

Toni cultivated the image of the perfect grad student. She got up late, worked late, ate at anti-social hours and associated mainly with academics. She'd been up working on an article until after three – waiting for the temperature to drop to a bearable level. So she wasn't pleased about being woken this early. True enough, she happily got by on much less than the standard eight hours of sleep, but two hours was cutting it short, even for her.

Then again, it was way too hot for self-suffocation.

Chucking the pillow to the floor, she rolled out of bed. Even though nobody in the building across the street was likely to notice her walking around naked this early in the morning, she grabbed her sheet and draped it over her shoulders before heading for the window.

What she found outside was the street ablaze with the blue glare of police strobe lights. Not in itself an earth shattering event. If you judged by the wail of police sirens, Paris constantly sounded like it was on the brink of meltdown. She was pretty sure most of the time it was probably just cops looking for a power rush. Bang on the siren, make the world think you're doing something important. Even if you're only headed out for coffee.

Having said that, there did seem to be some real problem today. There was a surge of activity in the courtyard of Val-de-Grace church that was completely out of sync with the early hour. A large tarpaulin had been raised around the far wall, and from her 7th floor window Toni could glimpse over the top of it. Clearly the fuss was over a message that had been smeared on the wall. If it had been up to her, she would have written "Soldiers are morons" or at least "GIs who make noise before 9 AM are morons". From what she could make out, the real message was more poetic. She leaned forward to get a better view. The topmost line was almost completely obscured by the tarpaulin. All she could see was: S SERVANT. But the next line down was an entirely legible bright red scrawl:

FROM THE DEPTHS OF DARKNESS

If there were more lines beneath, they were too far down for her to see.

She leaned against the window frame, staring absently at the scene. True enough, it was strange that someone on a military base would go around spraying graffiti. And it was even stranger that the graffiti should be accompanied by this dense police presence. But whatever. Maybe some soldiers had gone on a drunken spree and done something stupid. Or maybe some local kids had broken into the grounds then crowned their stunt with a tag. Either way, she could have done without the dawn chorus.

It took her five paces to cross from the window to the shower-room cum toilet where she opened the medicine cabinet and pulled out one of the few toiletries she kept: a packet of cotton wool. It was only three paces from there back to her bed. The room was actually smaller than her bedroom closet back home in Montreal. Twelve square meters. With furnishings that were squalid at best: the bed was the thinnest of mattresses on a shaky wooden frame. And there was no closet, just a minuscule wardrobe barely big enough to store her winter coat and a quilt. This being entirely inadequate, there were bits of clothing piled around the room and under the bed.

Flopping backwards onto the mattress, she let the sheet waft onto her body before stuffing two pieces of cotton into her ears. She stared at the ceiling and contemplated the effect of the improvised earplugs... Almost nil. Combined with the heat that was already sweltering, she had no choice but to surrender.

There was no way she was going to get back to sleep. She might as well get up and do something. Normally she would kick off her day with a jog around the park. Today it was already too hot for that. The quarries would be cool and peaceful. It was time to go catawalking.

3

Thursday morning, 5:15 AM, Val-de-Grace military hospital

As he drove along Port Royal Boulevard, Sadiqi counted at least 30 squad cars stationed silently, their strobe lights piercing the early morning haze. High security had just become extreme security. The Vigipirate terror alert level across the city had now shot up to peak at "Urgent: Attack Imminent".

He pulled up at the security barrier and brought the tiny Renault to a halt. Not only was the boom barrier down and the gates locked around the base, but behind the iron fence, a soldier wearing a bulletproof vest stood with a machine gun firmly grasped against his chest. Two clones were standing just inside the gatehouse, looking like wax statues. Not that any of this was surprising in itself. Ever since 9/11 machine guns had become fairly commonplace in central Paris; police stations were guarded by officers sporting semi-automatics and armed soldiers patrolled the streets. What was more unusual was the man in the gatehouse with the grey hair and the four gold stars on his red epaulettes. A general. Medical corps.

Aware that there were two machine guns pointed at him and that the soldiers were probably more than a little edgy after the night's events, Sadiqi kept his right hand on the steering wheel as he leaned out the window. *"Inspecteur Général Sadiqi, Unité de Coordination de la Lutte Anti-terroriste."* His tone was businesslike and contrasted with his appearance. Although he'd been part of the counter-terror brigade for most of his career, Sadiqi remained very much the plain-clothes cop. *Un flic.* Jeans. Black t-shirt or sweater depending on the weather. A leather sports jacket in the winter to cover his SIG Pro pistol and an unbuttoned shirt over the t-shirt on days like today when it was just too damn hot for the jacket.

The cop drew a small plastic card out of his shirt pocket and offered it up for what turned out to be the Mother of All Security Checks. It took them so long to run his name through the computer, they must have been reading his entire life's history. Not that it really mattered. Sadiqi had nothing to hide and his profile spoke for itself. Born in Paris in 1974, a degree in Arabic studies, military service with the navy, then a Master's in political science before being recruited straight into the counter-terror unit. Almost twenty years of outstanding service, so far – which probably explained why the careless smile on the old ID was seldom present anymore. If the general wanted to get fussy about ID, that was fine. But maybe, just maybe, these guys should have been worrying about security earlier in the evening. That way the Prime Minister might still be alive.

Sadiqi reached for the nicotine candy on the seat beside him, popped one out of the aluminum and crunched it between his teeth. The expression on his face was a perfect blank that hid what he was really thinking: *These guys had screwed up momentously and now they were scrambling to deflect guilt. Pull the cops out of bed. Call over counter-terrorism. Do anything to make sure the press didn't cast blame on the military for letting this happen.*

Probably the most irritating thing about being called to Val-de-Grace was the total lack of any obvious link between the Prime Minister's murder and counter-terrorism. Sadiqi felt this case should have been someone else's headache. This had nothing to do with terrorism. Terrorists targeted civilians. That was the whole point. One dead prime minister was NOT terrorism. Momentous, yes. It was political assassination. But that wasn't his problem. *Quel merdier.* In fact, the only reason Sadiqi was here at all was as a personal service to Dukrin, who wanted to be sure she had someone she could trust on the case. As inspector general, he was far too high-ranking to be running field cases. But as Dukrin had so accurately pointed out, they couldn't exactly send in a clown like Podesta to cover the Prime Minister's assassination.

Then again, if he was going to run this case, there was another headache in the making: the question of jurisdiction. This was a military base and Sadiqi was a police officer. In other words, a civilian. It wasn't yet clear whether the brass in charge here would actually let him do his job without interference.

At least there was one glimmer of hope in the morass of uncertainty. Somehow the generals had managed to keep the news of the PM's death out of the media – social or otherwise. There hadn't been so much as a tweet off the base, which was a near miracle. That definitely wouldn't have been possible in a civilian context. Apparently there was indeed an up-side to military secrecy.

Sadiqi was still brooding when the commanding officer cast a final sceptical glance at the ID before marching to the car. If the cop's unbuttoned shirt and three-day stubble didn't mesh with the general's idea of a counter-terrorism investigator, he kept his thoughts to himself as he climbed into the passenger seat.

"*Médecin Général Lalanne*," he said, extending his hand.

"*Sadiqi, Inspecteur Général, brigade anti-terroriste.*" The cop shifted the car into gear. "So what've we got?"

"Other than a dead Prime Minister?" Lalanne growled. "We've got one fuck of a mess." The only indication of his stress level was the tiniest movement of the zygomatics as he clenched his jaw.

The cop felt a measure of sympathy. As the general in charge of the facility during a major security breach, Lalanne's career had just reached the end of the line. He might as well retire now because he sure as hell wasn't going to get any more promotions. Then again, as general in charge of the biggest military hospital in France he probably couldn't go much higher.

"So what happened?" Sadiqi asked heading the car up the driveway.

"Carnage. The security cameras caught the whole thing. A monumental snuff film." If it weren't for the note of disgust ringing in his voice, the general's composure would have been perfect.

"A man in a balaclava shooting the PM," Sadiqi suggested.

"A man in a balaclava shooting everyone," the general corrected. "Eight guards and one nurse."

Suddenly this was sounding a lot more like terrorism. 'Collateral damage' was the aseptic term usually trotted out to camouflage the horror. An attack on a prime minister was an attack on the symbols of the nation. An attack on hospital staff was a human drama. The news triggered a now familiar reaction in the cop: a wall went up in his mind, steeling him against the all-too-bloody reality he was about to enter.

"How many assailants?"

"One."

Sadiqi tried to visualize it. One man, alone, in a secure military facility, sails in, kills ten people, then disappears. How the hell was that possible? And who the hell had sent him? This couldn't be a lone wolf; the attack would have entailed serious logistics.

"Anything helpful on the CCTV?"

"Not really. There are plenty of pictures. The footage is clear but..." the general shrugged.

"But a man in a balaclava is a man in a balaclava," Sadiqi offered. That wasn't a lot to go on.

* * *

A few minutes later the two men were marching across the parking lot to the hospital building, the cop rolling an orange armband with the word 'POLICE' onto his sleeve.

"He got in over there," the general said, signalling to a window that was now roped off with security tape and guarded by two soldiers. "It's a nurses' office. Cardiology. Lucky for them they were tending to a patient when the assailant climbed in."

Lalanne spoke sparingly and moved quickly. He only came to a halt on the threshold of the hospital long enough for them both to don Tyvek suits before continuing into the hospital. "He came out of the nurses' office over there and shot the two men guarding the main entrance over here."

Sadiqi's eyes swept around the hallway, memorizing the layout and considering the circumstances. One thing was clear. Although the Prime Minister's surgery had only been announced the previous day, the assassination had been planned for much longer. This hadn't been improvised at the last minute. The assailant had known the hospital's layout. He'd known exactly where to go and what security to expect. He might even have known where staff would be posted. With all that skill on his side, it seemed overly optimistic to hope that he'd been careless enough to leave behind forensic evidence.

"Has the scientific team found anything?"

"They've not even started down here yet. But they should be down soon. They're almost done upstairs."

The scientific team had already finished in the PM's room, Sadiqi thought. *How long could they have possibly spent there? Maybe an hour.* Speed like that meant one of two things: either excellent efficiency or gross incompetence. The cop wanted to know which he was working with. "Who came from forensics?"

The general hesitated, trying to recall the name. "Fourchier? Fondriet?"

"Foutriquet?"

"Yes, that's the one." Lalanne lowered his voice: "Looks like a clown, talks like a madman but he seems highly competent."

That was about the best description Sadiqi had ever heard of his favorite forensics specialist. Foutriquet was the best. If there were clues here, he'd find them.

Feeling slightly more optimistic, the cop followed Lalanne down the hallway listening to the rest of his report. "The cameras caught the guards being killed," he said, pointing at the device above their heads. "So the bodyguards on the 4th floor were braced for an attack." The elevator doors parted and the two men stepped inside. "They knew the assailant was in the elevator. The problem is he stopped the elevator on the second floor, exited, then continued on foot." General Lalanne took a short breath before nodding to his right. "The stairway is just beside us. When the elevator reached the fourth floor, the bodyguards were waiting in front of the doors." The general turned and signalled a few bullet holes in the elevator's back wall. "That's when the killer jumped out of the stairwell and shot the guards instead."

As if to illustrate, the elevator doors slid open and the two men found themselves in front of a blood splattered wall. "That was the first guard," Lalanne said looking at the reddish-brown stain. "Then two more around the corner here." The bodies had been removed leaving just the bloody traces.

The general headed down the corridor past a small office. "The killer sheltered behind the corner of that wall to shoot the two guards in front of the PM's door. Then he came along the hallway and shot the nurse who was hiding under the desk here."

"Which left him free access to the PM's room," Sadiqi finished.

Snapping to a halt, Lalanne pivoted to face the cop. When he spoke, the words were factual, yet the tone was one of disgust. "Most of the victims received a single bullet, either through the head or the heart. The assailant didn't even empty his magazine to do this."

That was definitely not what Sadiqi wanted to hear. Ten people dead and no stray bullets. One thing was obvious: "The assassin's a better shot than the bodyguards."

"The men stationed up here were the Prime Minister's own personal bodyguard. Elite police division. The men downstairs were military – equally well-trained."

"I don't doubt it. But the killer's well-trained, too."

As murky as the facts were, one thing was clear: The person they were looking for didn't fit with the standard profile of disillusioned youth getting involved in terror via the internet. Whoever had done this had arrived on the job with more than just a few hours' practice on a shooting range in some desert. The assailant had managed precision shots while under attack from a battery of men with special ops training. Not a lot of people could do that.

This whole thing was turning out to be much worse than Sadiqi had expected. In fact, this was starting to feel like one of those moments he dreaded – when his nightmares morphed into reality. Not a feeling he enjoyed, but one he'd felt too many times before. Like watching the youtube video of a colleague murdered point-blank on the sidewalk after *Charlie Hebdo*. Or wading through the carnage of the Bataclan theater attack.

These were the fucking watershed moments, when the new trends arrived.

And 'new' was never good in the world of terror.

4

Catacomb visitors who aren't satisfied limiting their subterranean explorations to the official ossuary museum at Denfert-Rochereau have to run a major obstacle course to access the real quarries. This involves climbing through manholes, crawling under bricked-in walls, deciphering incomplete maps and dodging cops.

But unlike 99.9% of quarry visitors, Toni didn't have to worry about any of those things. Thanks to her choice of university, she was part of the privileged 0.1%. *FranceTech* was one of France's leading universities for civil engineering and mining techniques. Fittingly, the land below the school represented the world's most extensive urban mining pit. There was a door in the university basement that opened directly onto a Cartesian stairwell spiralling down to the heart of the underground network. And she had the key.

This was where civil engineering met urban spelunking.

In fact, all the land around the southern end of the Luxembourg Gardens, where *FranceTech* now stood had long been the center of the quarry network, starting with a group of commercially minded monks in the 13th century. Not only had the Carthusians provided the city with fresh fruit from their orchards, they'd also spent considerable time working underground. During the four or five hundred years the order spent in Paris, they hollowed out most of the area below their monastery, selling the stones they quarried to the booming construction industry of the day and using the space they excavated to store their homemade wine. It wasn't until the Revolution came and ecclesiastical property was confiscated by the state that the land was sold to the university. By installing its premises above the Carthusian quarries, the school had provided its Parisian students with a legacy of first hand mining experience. And Toni was one of the heirs to that legacy. Her research had taken her around the world but this was the crowning glory. This was what she'd been working towards for years – a post-doc in Paris.

Because, while underground structures were her general field of expertise, the Paris underground was her true passion. Toni could remember exactly when she first learnt about the Paris quarries – or the "catacombs" as she'd called them back then. It had been during her second year as an undergrad. Like most people, the first inkling she had of them was limited to the ossuary – the underground gravesite where the bones of millions of dead Parisians had been relocated in an effort to clean up the city's overcrowded cemeteries. Later, in her third year at McGill, she'd had the good luck of meeting a French exchange student who told her about his extensive cataphile experiences. Toni had been fascinated by the world he described. Underground parties, sleeping in hammocks in the World War II bomb shelters, fording subterranean rivers. Even though with hindsight she realized that the self-proclaimed cataphile had probably been nothing more than a cata-tourist, at the time his stories had sounded amazing. He was the first person to explain to her that the ossuary represented just three kilometers of tunnels within a network of several hundred. Beyond the limited confines of the tiny burial site, there was a vast network to discover. That detail had caught her imagination. After three years of non-stop undergrad maths and physics, the catacombs had provided the promise of fun in the barren wasteland of civil engineering studies. All of a sudden her field of expertise had taken on a new dimension.

As an engineer, she'd started by wondering about the possible effects of anarchic medieval mining techniques on the contemporary urban landscape. After all, a void under an urban area ran the risk of generating sinkholes. But she soon discovered that although collapsing quarries had been a problem in the past it wasn't much of a threat anymore. There'd been a city-wide panic in the 1700s when several streets had been swallowed by sinkholes, so before having his head chopped off, Louis XVI had created a special bureau to save the city. The bureau was called the IGC and its job was to keep an eye on the quarries, build surveillance tunnels and fill unstable galleries. Two hundred and fifty years on, the collective opus of its army of engineers was an underground landscape of carefully masoned dry stone walls that reinforced and connected the endless old quarries of deep beige rock. It was a world suspended in time, where you could still see the trace of the chisels used by the workmen who had extracted the blocks of limestone five hundred years earlier.

By coming to pursue research at *FranceTech* Toni had earned herself the chance to visit those beautiful quarries in total freedom. Not only did she have her own access key, more importantly, she had official authorization to move around underground delivered by none other than Pierre Caron. As the person at the top of the quarry hierarchy as well as a staff professor at *FranceTech*, Caron was the obvious research director for her and when he'd accepted to take her on as a post-doc, she'd been elated.

The euphoria hadn't lasted long. After about ten minutes with the man she'd realized he was just as dry as the books and articles he wrote. Not to mention the fact that he seemed to have made it his mission in life to shut down as much of the network as possible. Which made her task, all the harder. After all, she was convinced that the network represented an opportunity rather than a threat. Her research constantly sparred with Caron's.

Not that she was going to let that bother her this morning. At least she could still enjoy the tunnels. Jogging down the spiral staircase on a direct line to the heart of the network she knew she was lucky. Her link to Caron set her apart from all the city's other cataphiles who were forced to trail across miles and miles of tunnels before attaining this central point. They had it hard; she had it easy.

Then again, it depended how you looked at it. From most other points of view Toni had it hard, while the average Parisian had it easy. After all, being a foreigner in France was a problem in itself. The

French were wary of anything not home grown and they had a particularly critical eye for anything North American. Anyone who couldn't manipulate the French language with the dexterity of Molière or Mitterand was somehow considered subnormal or certainly inferior. This set Toni at a disadvantage in intellectual circles. Despite her near perfect mastery of French there was always someone on hand to tell her that she'd forgotten a subjunctive or confused a masculine with a feminine. Some people would have shrugged off the criticism or turned it around. Pointed out the Gallic incapacity to distinguish between "a beach" and "a bitch" or "a sheet" and "a shit". But Toni preferred to avoid that sort of clash. After all, she'd been raised in a country where being nice was practically part of the genetic code. So she continued working to fit in as well as possible, polishing her accent and doing her best to appear more typically French. She'd even grown her chestnut hair – and she made a point of tying it in artistically messy ponytails and buns like the other students. But ultimately her complexion was too fair to be French, and her eyes too intensely green. And no matter how much she aspired to appear French, she drew the line at hobbling around on four-inch stilettos or taking up smoking to create the illusion.

That was another reason why life underground was so appealing. In the quarries, she didn't have to worry about looking like the perfect Parisian. No heels and lipstick. Underground she wore the cataphile uniform: bluish-grey workman's coveralls, rubber boots and a mining helmet. After all, the quarries were essentially disused mines, so it made sense to dress like a miner. Rock and dust surrounded her in all directions. And boots were necessary to ford flooded corridors. Inundation was particularly common in the deepest parts of the quarries, closest to the water line, but it could happen anywhere, especially in the tunnels under parks, where rainwater seeped through the soil unhindered by the usual layer of urban cement. Not that she was likely to see much flooding today; it hadn't rained for over three weeks.

Of course, officially speaking, although Toni looked like a cataphile, she wasn't one. She was a research student specialized in structural weakness or, to be more precise: "Subterranean structural weaknesses and their consequences on urban planning: The case of Paris in the Twenty-First Century". At least that's what she claimed when she went to interview IGC inspectors or give presentations at engineering conferences. In actual fact, she was probably one of the biggest cataphiles the city had seen in a long time. She knew the map of the left-bank network by heart and had read every book on the subject in the extravagantly well-furnished *FranceTech* library. She had also read all the popular coffee table books as well as every novel or short story that so much as mentioned the catacombs. Her knowledge of subterranean Paris encompassed everything from the geological make-up of the rock strata to the final destinations of the limestone blocks extracted from the various pits throughout history, not to mention all the best parties ever held underground. She'd been through every card catalogue, research engine and cross-reference available. She lived and breathed the quarries, past, present and future.

Not that the theoretical knowledge would have been worth much without the hours of hands-on experience she'd racked up. Zipped into the coverall that erased the thin, athletic body, Toni raced down the spiralling staircase as fast as her rubber boots would allow, the light from the cap lamp bouncing off the curved stone shaft.

One of the most basic rules of quarry exploration was to always bring a good supply of light: for the neophyte, this meant two or three flashlights and a large stock of batteries. For the more experienced explorers, the fashion was acetylene miners' lamps combined with a halogen cap lamp on the forehead. The acetylene lamps gave cataphiles a nostalgic aura – turning a walk through the quarries into a walk through time. But Toni wasn't into trends. And in any case, she found the stench of burning acetylene nauseating. She preferred diode lights that were both powerful and long lasting. And she was always sure to have the necessary stock of batteries on hand. That was essential. Because no more batteries meant no more light. And no more light meant no more hope. There was no sunlight underground, and no electric plugs anywhere. So a cataphile with dead batteries was a dead cataphile. Without a flashlight, it was impossible to read a map or recognize any of the tiny but essential landmarks that distinguished an exit from an endless blind alley. Explorers who ran out of light were stranded, unable to move until someone wandered by and saved them.

Toni had never run out of light herself; but she had rescued the occasional castaway. Once, while exploring some of the smaller galleries just north of the ring road, she'd come across a couple of goths cowering in the dark with their pet ferret – all three of them pitifully awaiting death by starvation. Faithful to catacomb legend, the teenagers had misread an over-simplified map and their flashlight batteries had died after several hours wandering in circles. Until Toni arrived, they hadn't stood much chance of ever seeing the surface again. They'd been pretty happy to see her. Then again, they probably would have been happy to see anyone; they would have been happy to see the cops.

But it was unlikely Toni would run into anyone this morning. It was barely 6:30 when her foot hit the bottom step of the stone staircase. Definitely bedtime for the common nocturnal variety of cataphile. She would have the entire network to herself.

There were good things in life and there were bad things. But the bad in no way diminished the enjoyability of the good. Caron might be fighting the opposite battle to her, but at least he'd given her the keys to this place.

5

A block west of the Trocadero, the Art Nouveau apartments of Passy Heights blushed in the pink caress of dawn. But, watching from his library window, Pierre Caron couldn't have been less moved by the spectacle if he were blind. The only pleasures he found in nature this morning were the sparse breaths of air wafting between the curtains at a mere 27° Celsius.

Installed in a tower below a domed roof, his library had the strange peculiarity of being circular. His wife complained that an engineer should have more sense than to keep a library in a round room. She said it was a waste of space. All those books squeezed into position along their spines with their pages fluttering around at the back of the shelf.

The comment annoyed Caron. There was no way he was going to let her transform his library into some cozy den where she could host her coffee mornings. The books weren't going anywhere. Some things weren't meant to be tampered with. The books, like the apartment, had been passed down by Caron's parents. They were a family legacy that needed to be respected. Very much like Caron's profession, which was also a family affair. And had now become the cause of his sleepless nights.

Peering out at the early morning, with no cars yet prowling the streets, Caron imagined that the neighborhood must have looked almost identical when his grandfather still occupied these rooms. Gilles Henri Rivé, the man who first introduced him to his life's vocation, had been one of the most voracious explorers of subterranean Paris ever. The man had spent most of his free time travelling the passages under the city with the rapacity of a hunter let loose in the African savannah. And from his grandson's earliest age, Rivé had shared that passion lovingly. Before Pierre had even turned ten, there had been expeditions through the abandoned remnants of the 1900 World Fair's exhibit below the Trocadero, with its reconstructions of the necropolis of Sakkara and Agamemnon's tomb. Stone blocks harking back to the tunnels' glory days.

So for Pierre Caron, the underground was part of his most intimate understanding of the city. Not only did he feel at home there. He felt a sense of proprietorship over the land. It was his world. He had become the gatekeeper of subterranean Paris. As director of the *Inspectorat Général des Carrières* – the General Inspectorate of the Quarries – he oversaw quarry safety for the whole city, as well as lecturing to the new guard of engineers at the university. Caron controlled the network. His grandfather would have been chuffed had he still been alive.

Well. Perhaps not entirely. There were a few things his grandfather would definitely not have appreciated about Caron's job. For starters, Rivé had been a historian, enamored by the quarries and driven by a desire to uncover everything there was to know about the object of his love. Caron's ambitions were less romantic. He was an engineer. What he wanted to do was modernize the tunnels. And, of course, in this day and age, that meant downsizing. As far as he was concerned, the underground network was yet another relic preventing Paris from developing into a truly modern city. Anyone with half a brain should realize that the bubble-gum structure of the catacombs threatened construction projects on the surface.

It was all very simple really. And if his grandfather had still been around, Caron would have forced him to see it his way. The construction of apartment blocks and businesses on the surface could only happen if the ground they were built on was sufficiently robust. Multi-storey buildings couldn't be erected above multi-storey quarries. The pock-marked earth of subterranean Paris was likely to collapse under the weight of those enormous modern structures if something wasn't done to reinforce the tunnels. So building permits could only be granted to lots where the space below ground had been properly reinforced. As a general rule, that meant cement needed to be injected into the ground to plug the endless kilometers of tunnels that created an obstacle to new buildings going up.

Caron poured a lot of his energy into making sure those injections happened. In any other major city in the world, it wouldn't have been a problem. Business would have taken precedence and administrators would have done their job. Unfortunately, of course in France, what should have been a clear-cut engineering problem had become a basely political issue, which was why it annoyed Caron so much. As was far too often the case, decisions about technical specifications weren't made by engineers but by politicians. The question of cement injections had been torn out of the hands of civil engineers and thrown to the politicians, who pussy-footed around the issue of the quarries' historic value. Anytime anyone dug a hole in Paris, you could be sure a dozen associations would come tripping along to complain that the work was an assault on the nation's heritage. Which meant apartments didn't get built, shopping centers never got a chance, and office blocks were relegated to eternal blueprints.

It was infuriating. Unlike his grandfather, Caron didn't care for history. He didn't like redrafting plans because a few square feet of land had to be preserved to please a handful of voters. He envied the power wielded by Baron Haussman in the 19th century, steaming ahead ripping out insalubrious old buildings and erecting new ones. Wrenching the city into the modern age. Like Haussman, Caron liked to think of himself as a practical man. A modernizer. And the quarries desperately needed modernizing.

It was ridiculous the amount of energy that had to be thrown into something that should have been so simple. After all, commercial construction was in everybody's interest. New businesses. New jobs. But Caron seemed to be the lone voice providing the construction industry with the support it so desperately needed. Approval of cement injections under the land targeted for these projects was only every agreed after a monumental struggle with multiple administrations.

Fortunately there was one up-side to all his efforts. His associates had been generous. Real estate prices had more than doubled in Paris over the past fifteen years so businesses were enthusiastic to see new land become available for their projects. In return for his services, Caron received what his wife jokingly referred to as *the sweetener* of his job: consulting fees.

But that wasn't enough to reassure him today.

Leaning out the window, the professor felt his chest tighten. Already, the rare breaths of fresh air were retreating behind the day's nascent inferno. He cursed the heat. He cursed the city. Drawing the shutters closed, he decided to try again to get some sleep.

Of course, if he were honest with himself, he knew it wasn't the heat keeping him awake. It was Clavreul. That was the real problem.

Senator Jacques Clavreul.

How had Caron let himself get caught up in this?

Again the answer was simple. It was ambition.

Caron's ambitions to modernize the quarries had brought him face to face with this man of power and influence. Charismatic and outspoken, Clavreul was willing to address the problems head-on. All of them – even the darkest. If anyone could breathe new life into the debate about the urgency to renovate the quarries, it had to be the senator.

It was this intoxicating proximity of his dream's fulfillment that had made Caron careless. At the time it had made sense. He had believed Clavreul was trustworthy. Sharing information had seemed like the best way to pursue their shared objectives.

But now he suspected he had gone too far.

6

Inside the PM's room, the décor was just as gruesome as the blood-splattered walls in the hallway; except here, there was no sign of a struggle. The Prime Minister, or what was left of him, was lying serenely in bed, his arms outstretched on top of the covers – a picture of tranquility. Unfortunately most of his head was now missing and the usually white sheets were soaked a deep crimson that was starting to veer to burnt sienna as the blood dried.

Obviously de Chanterelle had slept through most of the excitement. If the noise in the hallway had woken him, he hadn't had time to climb out of bed or move to a safer location. "A clean shot between the eyes," Sadiqi observed.

"Plus one through the heart, for good measure," the general added.

At the sound of the voices, a small round man popped his balding head over the top of the bed. Evidently he'd been crouching on the floor checking something. "*Inspecteur Général Sadiqi*," he smiled, as if this were some long awaited social visit. "I don't often get a chance to see you these days. You're usually behind a desk, not doing the grunt work."

The police officer nodded in recognition and stepped forward to shake hands with the doctor. Below the polyethylene protective clothing, Sadiqi knew there was a greying polo shirt and worn flannel trousers that would compose the perfect image of a masterly sloven. "*Docteur Foutriquet.* I could say the same about you."

"It's not every day I'm called in by the Prime Minister." The doctor had always had a taste for dark humor. No doubt it went with the job.

Sadiqi turned back to observe what was left of the once-Prime Minister's face. He had never met the man when he was still alive, but had seen pictures of him probably every day for the past year. The lower face was still intact, with the familiar jaw line. The usually pursed lips were now relaxed. "What have you got for me?"

Foutriquet opened his eyes unnaturally wide and took a deep breath, rubbing his palms together nervously. "I'm afraid there's not a huge amount of information I can add to what's on the CCTV. At roughly four o'clock a man came up the stairs and shot everyone. As you can see, there's not much doubt about that." The doctor's eyes fixed meditatively on the blood-soaked sheets.

"No hair? No clothing fibres? No DNA?"

"We're still looking," Foutriquet chirped, optimistically. "Maybe the bullets will tell us something."

Lalanne spoke up: "He used a PA MAS G1. With a silencer. You can see it on the video. All the victims were shot through the head. Except a few where he administered a shot to the throat as well, to make sure they were good and dead. And the nurse – who got it through the heart. He knew she wouldn't be wearing a vest. I'm guessing he did all this with less than 15 bullets."

Sadiqi was mildly impressed with the general's *sang-froid*. The man hadn't got where he was by pushing paper. The mayhem he'd seen tonight hadn't shaken him. And the information about the weapon was interesting. That was a 9mm pistol heavily favored by the French military. A licensed Beretta; not necessarily the easiest type of weapon to find illegally. It fit perfectly with the rest of the attack. Sadiqi had never seen anything like it before. Sure, he'd seen plenty of victims sprayed randomly with blanket fire from AK-47s. But never this type of laser precision.

"If you knew where the killer was, if you had him covered by CCTV, why wasn't security there to stop him when he left the building?"

The general's face was impenetrable. "They were," he answered calmly. "We had all the exits covered... Except he didn't use any of the exits."

Sadiqi was puzzled. The man couldn't still be in the building; the hospital would be under siege.

Lalanne provided the explanation. "He went straight out the window…"

"Abseiled down like Mummery," Foutriquet chimed, with characteristic incomprehensibility.

"Used the bed as an anchor. Rappelled down," the general confirmed.

Sadiqi's exasperation was beginning to overflow. "You've got to be kidding."

"Unfortunately not," Lalanne shot back. "Nobody saw him enter or leave either the building or the grounds. But we do have a shot of him on one of the security films. A shadow running into the trees over there."

The inspector looked out the window. While the southern edge of the base housed the state-of-the-art hospital, the western edge was formed by Val-de-Grace Church and the historic buildings of the 17th century hospital.

"He must have left by rue St. Jacques," Lalanne continued. Despite his decisive words, the general sounded sceptical. "We have a dead security agent in the gatehouse over there. Also with a bullet between the eyes."

The more he heard, the stranger it sounded to Sadiqi. Of all the ways to access the base, using rue St. Jacques struck him as the most difficult. The western entrance was an open square protected by 12-foot high iron gates. It would be almost impossible to scale those gates without drawing attention. And even if someone had managed to climb over, the fence was several meters from the gatehouse. In other words, any intruder would have to cross an open floodlit square under the constant gaze of surveillance cameras.

It was outrageous.

Or was it?

Alarm bells were getting louder and louder in the cop's head. The assailant had got on the base without being noticed, avoided most of the surveillance cameras then found his way around without a hitch. He was also a crack shot with a pistol. All these factors could mean many things but the simplest explanation was an inside job. "If nobody saw the killer enter the base and no one saw him exit, maybe security was somehow reconfigured to make him invisible."

The general's arms folded tightly across his chest. "You're insinuating the killer's one of my men."

Sadiqi's eyes wandered to the bed where the corpse lay. He couldn't run the risk of not pursuing a possible lead simply because the Ministry of Defense wasn't going to like it. "Judging from the killer's movements he must have had detailed information about where security cameras were positioned. And the PA MAS is a military weapon." Try as he may to sound diplomatic, Sadiqi was giving an order not making a request. *"Mon Général*, I want to question your personnel."

Before the inspector could say anything more, General Lalanne pushed past him and out of the PM's room. "I'll do whatever you think necessary," he called over his shoulder. "But you should see the western entrance before you start jumping to conclusions. This guy may have kept himself under the radar, but he left us a message."

Sadiqi breathed a sigh of disgust. Just what he felt like. A message.

Ever since *Charlie Hebdo*, killers had been leaving taunting messages in the wake of their rampages, gleefully claiming responsibility for the bloodshed. It used to be that you had to hunt for the killers. Nowadays they left calling cards and ID, complete with photos, home addresses and political affiliations.

Bravado terror. Cocky, self-annointed apologists of hate. They made him sick.

7

As he made his way back to bed, Caron thought back to his contacts with Clavreul. He had first met the senator about three years earlier in the lead up to the Senate building's renovations. The Senate, at the foot of the Luxembourg Gardens, contained extensive underground apartments, some of which opened on to the quarries. As director of the IGC, Caron had been asked to ensure that changes planned for the underground rooms didn't open any security breaches with the quarries below.

Official consultations regarding national monuments cropped up fairly regularly in Caron's job. The basements and cellars of Paris were the city's intimate treasures. Some of the deeper, bunker-like basements were so close to the quarry network that there was always a risk cataphiles might try to break through. So it was part of Caron's job to make sure the two domains remained separate. He knew more about what lay below ground than anyone else in the city. He caught glimpses of the restricted areas of all the most majestic palaces and private hotels. And the Senate basement was definitely one of those jewels. The renovation work he had eventually sanctioned stood as a monument to the recreational aspirations of aging men of power: reading rooms, conference center and salons, not to mention a ping-pong room and a hundred-seat cinema, all leaning heavily towards traditional/luxurious standards and tastes.

But Caron's consultation work at the Senate had been more than just a chance to discover a new building. It had been his link to Jacques Clavreul. At the ripe old age of 84, the senator had the look that French voters preferred – that reassuring paternal look, with respectably grey hair and classically tailored suits. Yet despite his mild-mannered appearance, Clavreul's reputation had preceded him. The Senator was often targeted by the left-wing media for his extremely conservative views on homeland security and family values. Crime statistics and immigration levels were the senator's sweet spot. And that gave Caron something he could work with. He'd come up with a plan to make Clavreul's agenda square with his own projects in the quarries.

Initially Caron had met the senator in his capacity as senate quaestor. Basically, Clavreul had been the head of a committee overseeing the renovation work. Not that the senator had been down on his hands and knees checking that the parquet flooring was properly scrubbed or varnished. No, he was well above that. He was simply the interface between the senators and the companies carrying out the renovations. But it wasn't Clavreul's administrative duties that interested Caron; it was his political influence. Caron knew he could offer the senator what he desired most – a menace to brandish in front of French voters. In return, the professor would get what he had been battling to accomplish for years – approval to shut down the network. Or as much of it as possible.

So after reviewing the Senate's security needs together, Caron had taken the opportunity to broach some wider-reaching quarry issues with Clavreul. Most notably the quarries' greatest flaw: the fact that they constituted a massive potential terrorist soft target.

The IGC man had detailed the underground menace. The quarries provided hidden access routes to government buildings and powerful individuals. Equally importantly, if any of those tunnels were to collapse, huge sinkholes would appear on the surface. In the past the network had provided refuge to smugglers, outlaws and revolutionaries. In the twenty-first century they were both a potential den and a potential target for terrorists.

Caron had explained the pure scale of the problem to the senator. The underground network was too extensive. The manpower currently assigned to upkeep and policing was rudimentary yet modernization was financially unthinkable. There were only a handful of police and engineers responsible for overseeing the security of over three hundred kilometers of tunnels. It was a losing battle. With the trend towards increased government cutbacks, it would be almost impossible to finance satisfactory levels of policing. The needs were too vast, the vulnerabilities too complex. Small improvements were useless – just band-aids holding together a collapsing barrage. A complete waste of money. Downsizing was the only realistic solution. A few particularly renowned quarries could be kept open to placate the inevitable groups of whiners intent on preserving the city's "underground heritage", along with the strategic surveillance tunnels. But hundreds of kilometers could be neutralized very easily – namely by injecting cement. It would only take a few months to get the work well under way.

It was an issue Caron had attempted to harness with other politicians and civil servants in the past. But Clavreul had gone for it, hook line and sinker – his sights firmly set on opposing the terror threat facing the nation. The questions the senator had asked went straight to the heart of the problem. He wanted to know where access points existed, how they were accessible, which government buildings were situated above tunnels. In response, Caron had produced maps, explained the buried grid of underground streets and given details of structural weaknesses.

Much to his satisfaction, it had all paid off; the senator had been won over. He had asked Caron to write a concise report on the major underground dangers, and he had promised to explain the findings to some of his eminent colleagues. Better yet, he had promised to make sure the President himself received a copy of the report.

Vindication! Caron had leapt at the opportunity. Writing the report had been one of the greatest pleasures of his career because it meant that things were finally moving. And the senator had been just as enthusiastic. Hell, Clavreul even talked about creating an office to oversee quarry modernization and naming Caron to head it. The crowning glory of a brilliant career, giving him almost total power over the quarries to fill in any gallery or tunnel he chose.

And that's why the senator's current change of mind seemed so incomprehensible. Caron had been within spitting distance of his greatest ambitions and then somehow the whole thing had collapsed. Because on Tuesday, Clavreul had basically said he didn't want to hear anything more about the project.

It had all happened at the cocktail party held to celebrate the official reopening of the Senate's renovated rooms. For two hours, Caron had sat in the Salons Boffrand in the Luxembourg Palace, sipping champagne and watching people fan themselves with their programmes as the mirrored walls reflected the parched gardens outside. But when the speeches had finally finished, and the IGC director found himself face to face with the familiar smooth features of Clavreul, the senator's dark eyes had refused to hold his gaze.

Clavreul had brushed him off. "I've spoken with several colleagues about your recommendations," he said slowly, "and unfortunately I've not been able to make them see things your way. The consensus seems to be that the dangers aren't as great as you suggest."

That was it. End of story.

Caron had found himself staring at the sharp cut of the senator's Stark & Sons back panel.

It was unfathomable.

Never trust a politician. Caron was smart enough to know that. Still, the blind ignorance of these men astounded him. He'd gone for the hard sell in the report, detailing the worst nightmare scenarios he had been able to come up with. Yet nobody was going to pay attention to those warnings until something terrible happened. Only then would Caron be vindicated and the senator would be the one looking foolish and short-sighted.

But even that daydream wasn't enough to cheer Caron up. Because deep down inside he knew he was fooling himself. It wasn't really Clavreul's rejection that was bothering him. It was his own misjudgement. The indiscretions he, himself, had committed.

During his meetings with the senator, Caron had shared a huge amount of information. Not just facts about the quarries' layout and structural weaknesses. Much more. He had answered all the senator's questions, even the most detailed. Even the ones that touched on classified information. For God's sake, he had told the man things he had never even shared with his closest colleagues.

He felt a fool.

The muscles in the back of his neck knotted together with the same sense of unease that had been keeping him awake for the past two nights. The weight of regret pressed against his shoulders. Ambition had made him careless. Not only was his professional conduct questionable, more importantly, he had betrayed the Brotherhood. He had broken his vow of silence. He had disclosed lore that should have been kept secret.

What he had done was inexcusable. And indefensible. He had made a mistake. He knew that. Try as he may to convince himself that it wasn't important, he knew it was.

8

As he and Lalanne covered the ground between the hospital and Val-de-Grace church Sadiqi tried to get his head around the case. It wasn't going to be long before he had journalists breathing down his neck. The combination of dead prime minister and counter-terrorist investigation was going to have the press light-headed and reeling with excitement. "What have you told the media?" he asked.

"Nothing," the general clipped reassuringly. "Only the President's office, the Minister of Defense and the Minister of the Interior know about it for now. The President's due to hold a press conference here at 09:00. Until then we have an information blackout."

Sadiqi knew what that meant. The news had been kept from the media to give the government time to get their story ironed out before feeding it to the public.

"Only the officers cleaning the fourth floor know what's happened. Everyone else on the base is just guessing," Lalanne added. The two men were now in a baroque passageway in a much older building. A few steps in, they paused in front of a tiny office containing eight surveillance monitors. Another bloody tableau. Most of the screens were covered with a dark red film. But other than the blood, there was no sign of life. "This is the check point for the west wing where we lost a security officer." Lalanne observed the scene coolly before starting down the passage again. The gatehouse had been a target, but that wasn't what the general had brought Sadiqi to see. It was the front courtyard that was more worrisome.

Unlike the deserted back passageway, the area out front was buzzing with personnel. Lalanne waved his hand in the direction of the towering iron fence that cut the base off from the street beyond. "The gates were sealed as always at 20:00. And the key is still in the guardhouse. After 20:00, the only way off the base is through the south entrance, where we met earlier."

"Maybe he escaped over the fence?" Sadiqi said, shooting a glance at the arrow tipped ends of the twelve-foot high iron bars separating the churchyard from the street.

It didn't sound likely. "We've not found any trace of a man going over the bars," Lalanne said. "But then we've not found a trace of a man going anywhere. This guy's fucking Houdini."

"He did have mountaineering equipment," Sadiqi said.

The general frowned. "That just doesn't make sense. Pissing around, trying to avoid emasculating himself while he tries to make a quick escape. It's too messy." He hesitated a moment before adding, "But then whoever we're dealing with seems to have a taste for risk." The general moved towards a canopy of white plastic sheeting that had been improvised along the south wall. He pulled back the entrance flap.

Entering the makeshift tent, Sadiqi's eyes were immediately drawn to a huge scrawl of red spray paint, written in letters about two feet high.

HE SENDS HIS SERVANT
FROM THE DEPTHS OF DARKNESS
INTO LIGHT

Merde. This wasn't what he'd expected when the general said there was a message. He'd figured on an email or something pointing to the authors of the crime. Not this.

The two men stood silently side-by-side transfixed by the message. *What the hell was that supposed to mean?* Sadiqi wondered as the words looped through his mind. *He sends his servant.* The *servant* reference sounded ominously evangelical. And what about that first word. Was it supposed to be "*he*" or "*He*"?

"Is it from the Bible?" he asked, hoping Lalanne's team might have had time to figure it out.

The general shook his head. "According to my men, it's from the Quran. That's why we called you."

Sadiqi's jaw didn't exactly drop but some of the muscles loosened. Up until a second ago he'd figured the "terrorist" tag had been put on the investigation mainly for effect. To add extra value to the PM's death. The whole operation looked more like professional assassination than terror tactics aimed at a civilian population. At least it had until now. But the graffiti added a whiff of fanatical ideology completely out of sync with everything else. "Anyone stupid enough for this kind of bullshit, shouldn't be too hard to trace." The words echoed with more confidence than he felt.

Quite frankly, Sadiqi was baffled. Every minute seemed to lead him further away from his initial certainties. He was less and less sure what exactly he was looking for. The profile incoherencies introduced multiple unknowns.

"I certainly hope you're right," the general said, tearing his eyes from the message just long enough to send Sadiqi a glance filled with more challenge than compassion. Then he rotated 180° on his heels. "Get a team in here. I want this gone before rush hour," he barked out to a young soldier on the far side of the tent, waving toward the spray paint.

Instinctively, Sadiqi protested. "You can't remove this."

Lalanne's jaw tightened again. He wasn't used to having his orders questioned, certainly not by a younger man and most definitely not on his own base. When he spoke, he used the slow, hard tone of someone not likely to budge. "Inspector, I've received orders from the Minister of Defense to remove this. I was told to wait until you'd seen it, but not a minute longer. The message has to go. In an hour's time there'll be rush hour traffic running down this street. The ministry wants this gone."

A combination of outrage and exasperation rose from the pit of Sadiqi's stomach. "That's ridiculous."

"I have my orders. The message has been photographed and treated by your scientific team but now it has to go."

Seething at the herd of young subordinates already assembling cleaning equipment Sadiqi wondered how the hell he was supposed to take control of the case if someone else was giving the orders. "Do we at least know whether the message was left before or after the assassination?"

He never got an answer. Lalanne had turned his full attention to a breathless colonel who had just dashed into the tent. "General, we've found something new. You're going to want to see this."

9

The colonel led Sadiqi and Lalanne into a small courtyard framed between the walls of the baroque church and the Museum of Military Medicine. The damp, confined space contrasted with the majestic dome towering above. This was the dirty back alleyway of grandeur. They were now standing in front of something that looked strangely like a stone vespasian. The metal door on the battered oval kiosk was ajar and a quick glance at Lalanne told Sadiqi that this, for some reason, was cause for alarm. The cop reached into his shirt pocket for his nicotine candy.

"I'm taking it, the guardhouse isn't the only way off the base," he said, popping a lozenge out of the aluminum backed plastic and shooting it into his mouth. It was days like this that made him wish he hadn't given up smoking. The little mints didn't provide the same release as a long drag on a cigarette. "So where does this lead?"

The colonel eyed Sadiqi warily then glanced at the general, waiting to be told whether to speak up or keep quiet.

This was the most rattled the general had looked all morning. "*L'escalier Mansart.* It's Mansart's staircase." His voice was quieter than it had been earlier and his hands were clenched nervously behind his back as he stared at the open door. "It leads to the catacombs."

The word "catacomb" made the skin tighten across the back of Sadiqi's neck. Just what he needed. The catacombs were a cop's nightmare. They were an empty, unused void furrowed under huge expanses of the city. But in a city of two and a half million people, no void ever stayed empty for very long… Consequently, the catacombs weren't so much part of the city as part of a parallel world – an underground network Sadiqi knew little about. If the catacombs had something to do with de Chanterelle's murder, the cop would soon be out of his depth – no pun intended. Finding a killer above ground was always a challenge. Finding one underground could prove impossible.

"You're telling me there's a direct staircase from the heart of the country's main military hospital to an unmonitored tunnel network?" The disbelief in his voice was biting.

"Of course not," Lalanne snapped. "The stairway leads down about twenty meters… But the shaft has been walled off from the network for years. Once you reach the bottom, there's a double wall – brick and cement. You can't access the catacombs anymore. The staircase is a dead end."

Man's ability for denial had always been a source of bitter fascination for the cop. "*Très bien.* In that case, there's no problem, is there?" The tone of his voice said the opposite. He pulled his phone out of his pocket and switched on the flashlight. Then he squeezed through the doorway into the stairwell with the general following close behind.

Despite his misgivings, the catacombs weren't entirely unknown to Sadiqi. The police and fire departments occasionally used them for training exercises and he'd participated in a few emergency simulations underground. But the subterranean vision that awaited him under Val-de-Grace was very different from anything he'd ever seen before. To begin with, the wide stone staircase stretching out before him was completely different from the narrow shaft he'd been expecting. His previous experiences of the catacombs had always involved climbing through a manhole then down a long metal ladder before reaching the bottom. Clearly this entrance was much older, dating back to a time when architects placed aesthetics above functionality and kings, not municipal planning boards, distributed building funds. The stairwell was about two meters wide, with large flat steps gently sloping down straight ahead. The ceiling was low so Sadiqi had to duck a few times to avoid smacking his head on the stone arches. Otherwise the passage was surprisingly easy to navigate.

As he penetrated deeper into the darkness, he was uncomfortably aware that his decision to proceed without proper back-up had perhaps been a little rash. The terrain smelled of ambush. His phone only provided a vague glow in the infinite darkness and if, by some improbable chance, the killer was still in the tunnel, the glimmer of light created a perfect target – Sadiqi was visible without being able to see much himself. If he were attacked, the gun he'd now taken out of its holster would be useless. He would be shot long before he saw his aggressor.

The fear was short-lived. A hundred steps down from the entrance it became obvious that no one was poised in the tunnel waiting to shoot. But that's where the good news ended. This day was getting worse by the minute. Sure, the brick wall that had been designed to block any movement between the catacombs and the military base really existed. But now there was a huge gaping hole right in the middle of it.

Shining his light on the void Sadiqi pivoted to see Lalanne. " I believe the correct military term is 'Situation Normal: All fucked up'." Definitely snafu.

10

Both the darkness and the twenty-degree change in temperature between the surface and the network reassured Toni she had left her earthly concerns behind. Surrounded by the cool, familiar beige stone underground, she headed off to the left. The walls of the narrow surveillance tunnel she was now in had been crafted with hewn stone laid carefully, in thick slabs, to support the layers of rock higher up, and ensure the structural integrity of the city above.

Her first destination this morning was Philibert's tomb. If *FranceTech* University was the geographic heart of the catacombs, then Philibert was its soul. Like many of the underground icons, the tomb wasn't much to look at for the non-initiated. Nothing more than a small grotto housing a marble slab with a message carved into it:

IN MEMORY OF PHILIBERT ASPAIRT
LOST IN THIS QUARRY ON III NOV
MDCCXCIII. REDISCOVERED ELEVEN YEARS LATER
AND INHUMED IN THE SAME SPOT XXX APRIL MDCCCIV.

Despite the simplicity of the installation, Toni found herself sighing with reverence every time she came here. Not so much for Philibert himself as for what the marker represented. This was history in a way it didn't exist back home. Nothing was this old in Canada. Toni ran her fingers over the letters forming the date, MDCCXCIII. 1793. Mackenzie had only just made it to Vancouver. Canada was still a British colony welcoming loyalists fleeing the newly established United States. In Canada, nothing was this old. Paris turned her timeline upside down. Everything in this city seemed to be dated in centuries rather than years. Everything around her was part of history.

The marble flickered in the torchlight. The tomb paid homage to a long-dead caretaker of Val-de-Grace, who'd gone on a subterranean expedition to raid the wine cellar of the Charterhouse monks, but had got lost in the labyrinth of the quarries. Above ground, Paris had been too busy chopping off heads and changing regimes to worry about a missing caretaker. All alone, when his candle burnt out, Philibert had panicked and had a heart attack. His body wasn't discovered until eleven years later, despite being only a few dozen meters from the staircase that would have led him back up to daylight. A fitting part of catacomb legend.

But it wasn't the stone that held her attention today; it was the sheet of paper perched on top of the marble. This wasn't the first time she had found messages here. Philibert's tomb was a Mecca for cataphiles, and leaving fliers in the quarries was a sort of replacement telephone system in a world devoid of technology. There was no chance of catching a phone signal this far underground. You were out of range of the cell networks. And any self-respecting cataphile would refuse the idea of defacing the stone walls by posting messages via graffiti. (Ironically, most of the walls were completely covered in graffiti left by cata-tourists, likewise making the walls a useless medium for messages – it would be impossible to pick out a single message in the mosaic of color.) So paper and pen remained the most common way of sending information from one group of explorers to another down here. Since the previous September, Toni had collected over fifty different fliers. Some announced parties. Others were cartoons or poems left for no particular reason other than to leave a mark.

Today's message leaned toward an eerier tone. At least reading it sixty feet below ground, in a remote quarry housing an ancient tomb certainly made it feel eerie. *"Qui a vu Snoopy, Bango et Quartz? Disparus le 15 juin."* "Who has seen Snoopy, Bango and Quartz. Disappeared June 15." The seemingly ridiculous names did nothing to make the message more light-hearted. They were typical of the nicknames used below ground by cataphiles to avoid disseminating real identities that could give the police material for arrests or fines. Frequent visitors traveled under aliases because although one visit to the quarries might be tolerated by the authorities, repeat offenses carried hefty fines.

Toni did a quick count in her head. June 15. That would have been Saturday. Not quite a week ago. Creepy. At least if it was true. But then sometimes cataphiles purposely said creepy things to scare one another; it added spice to the visits. After all, the skull and cross bones were a standard cataphile symbol, intended to give people the shakes. Even so, she would try to remember to check it out when she got back to the surface.

She stuffed the paper in her pocket and set off up the rue St. Jacques corridor towards the Z-Room.

The Z-Room was her favorite part of the network. Come to think of it, it was everyone's favorite part of the network. A dense hub where history bonded with architectural beauty. The Z-Room was huge. It was Paris. Above ground Val-de-Grace church commemorated the birth of Louis XIV. Below ground its clandestine shadow gouged its way upward through the limestone. When the church was first designed, the area had undergone extensive reinforcements to make sure the land would support the weight of the massive stone structure above. And those reinforcements were carried out by the same architect who had designed the church itself – the n°1 architect of the 17th century, François Mansart. The result was a fusion of barren cavern and sumptuous architectonics. There were cupolas, semi-cupolas, arches, intricate stonework walls... all executed to perfection.

But the best thing about the Z-Room wasn't the beauty of the architecture. It was the challenge the dense labyrinth offered the urban explorer. Because its name was misleading; the Z-Room wasn't a room at all. It was a seemingly endless succession of galleries and corridors. It was impossible for the non-initiated to navigate the area without breaking into a cold sweat, even if they were armed with a good map. The first time Toni had gone there alone she'd brought along a ball of string, unwinding it as she went, leaving a trace to follow on the return trip, like Theseus in the Minotaur's den. Maps were all well and good, but the Z-Room was a maze.

Nowadays Toni had outgrown the "ball of string" technique. She still carried detailed maps, but she barely ever referred to them anymore. This was her neighborhood. She was so used to walking around these tunnels it was like crossing the street to get to the bakery. Over the past year, the quarries had become her life. As she made her way along the main surveillance tunnel, her two beams of light leading the way, her mind wandered towards her current research.

In a way it was ironic that she had ended up on a post-doc stint with Caron. Having chosen an engineering specialty sufficiently complex to hold her interest, she had opted to work under a professor who had absolutely no complex notions about the quarries. It was widely known that Caron's goal in life was to scale back the quarries. In fact, if he had his way he would simply inject cement into the entire network and seal it up forever. He had already made massive efforts in that direction. Although many books claimed subterranean Paris covered an impressive 350 kilometers the true figure was probably closer to 200 – and falling. The rapid scaling back was largely Caron's doing. He had been busy dicing up the network, cutting off bits here and there, making it trickier and trickier to get from one end of the Left Bank to the other. Every time Toni noticed a quarry on her map that had ceased to exist thanks to Caron, she shuddered. He pandered to the big real estate developers; filling in quarries to make the surface strong enough to support towering apartment blocks. Destroying French history in order to help a few rich men make themselves a little richer.

Fortunately for the network, France still worried about its cultural heritage and people like him had to face the resistance of historians, archaeologists and popular demand. As Toni walked under rue St. Jacques, her hand caressing the carefully laid stones, she felt a tinge of sadness. She knew that one day the Carons of the world would win. Too few people had ever visited the quarries. People thought that the guided tour of the official ossuary was the full extent of underground Paris. Too few people would ever make a stand to save this monumental network. How could they? They didn't even know it existed.

Lost in thought, she didn't notice the footsteps until she was walking past the tunnels that branched off under the Ursulines. The tapping sound brought her back to reality. Any noise in the catacombs could mean only one thing: another person was very close by. No other noise was possible. There were no machines down here, or animals. No mice or rats; there was nothing for animals to feed on so they stayed away. And since noise didn't travel far in the catacombs, if Toni could hear footsteps it meant that whoever was there, was very close. In other words, she wasn't alone anymore.

So much for having the place to herself. Then again, it wasn't a problem. A lot of cataphiles were good company. They were a docile although sometimes slightly stoned breed. Maybe whoever it was would wander along with her for a while.

She turned and was dazzled by three rays of light edging towards her. "Could you lower your beam a little?" she called out.

The friendly reply she'd expected didn't materialize. The beams were still glaring into her eyes. And worse yet, whoever was down the corridor wasn't walking towards her anymore; they were running at full sprint.

Toni's heartbeat quickened. Of course she'd heard stories about people being attacked in the quarries, women raped – the inevitable legends of wanton violence. Up until now she'd thought those were just rumors and myths invented to dissuade the curious from setting out to discover the network. But maybe the threat was real.

The transition from daydream to self-preservation was automatic. The acceleration instant. She broke into a sprint, feet thumping forward toward some unknown goal.

Yet despite the adrenalin spurt, she could hear the footsteps gaining on her. She couldn't outrun these guys. At least not in the stupid rubber boots. These guys were faster. And most likely stronger. Her only hope was to lose them.

"Hey you!" a harsh male voice called from behind.

Heart hammering, she ignored the call and charged forward, ducking into the tunnel that led to the Z-Room.

But instead of sanctuary, all she found was the end of the line.

As she shot around the archway, she hurtled into a massive torso. Worse yet, the shock sent her sprawling onto the floor, her hands spread open to cushion her fall. And that's when the flashlight fell out of her hands and went rolling down the corridor. Then something reached out and tore the cap lamp off her head. Not having a lamp was the worst thing that could happen. There was no way of escape if she didn't have her own light. She could use her phone to guide her, but that might not last long enough to get her home. No. Not having a light put her at these guys' mercy.

A flood of ridiculous pleas spewed out of her. Clichés she would never have imagined using. "You can have whatever you want. Just let me go…"

11

Sadiqi's investigation wasn't going well. In a moment of uncharacteristic optimism, he had hoped the catacombs would provide an ideal terrain for an investigation. After all, it was a completely restricted area with no civilians wandering around wiping away clues. The truth wasn't quite so rosy.

This was the first time he'd been under Val-de-Grace and it was blatantly obvious that the training exercises he'd been on in the quarries under the Trocadero hadn't given him a complete understanding of the full extent of the underground network. What he'd seen under the 16th arrondissement was half a dozen fairly straight tunnels. What he discovered under Val-de-Grace was incomparable. There were tunnels and crossroads and galleries everywhere. Almost two kilometers of tunnels concentrated into the equivalent of one city block running under the Latin Quarter. Each tunnel seemed to breed new tunnels. Every time he poked his head around a corner, there were two or three more paths to choose from. It was impossible to keep the layout clear in his mind. He'd tried exploring the immediate vicinity beyond the staircase, but after sketching out a map on a piece of paper, he had only dared advance about forty meters beyond his starting point. It was like being in a completely different dimension where streets multiplied magically.

Worse yet, and possibly the nastiest surprise of the morning, his cell phone didn't work in the quarries. It was like stepping into the past. No phone waves. Every time he wanted to give an order or call someone, the inspector had to climb the 103 steps back to the surface to access the network.

By 6:30, he had already made three return-trips to the surface and the wasted time was starting to grate. His first call was to get in sniffer dogs to try to pick up the assassin's trail. The dogs and their handlers had arrived early enough – a little before 7. Initially his plan had been to send them straight out. Why not? It was perfect terrain. Nobody to walk over the footsteps and erase the killer's scent. Except, unfortunately, the handlers were trained to handle dogs, not to navigate caves. They weren't equipped for the quarries and Sadiqi couldn't let them go off without special catacomb guides. The last thing he needed was to be made to look incompetent by announcing to the press that not only did he have no leads on the Prime Minister's murder but the team who was supposed to follow the killer's trail had gone missing somewhere under the city.

So he had called the cataflics – the police brigade in charge of monitoring the quarries – to ask them to send over a detachment. He had had to get belligerent about that, because it was a small brigade and the captain claimed he couldn't make anyone available at such short notice. It wasn't always easy negotiating for help between brigades and the fact that, for the moment, the Prime Minister's assassination was classified information didn't make Sadiqi's job any easier. He had ended up pulling rank to get what he wanted. And that was never a good solution because it got people's backs up. Instead of working as a team, the cataflics might decide to sabotage or, at the very least, slow down his investigation. Sure enough, an hour on, Sadiqi was still waiting for the extra backup to arrive.

The cataflics' leisurely pace reporting for duty had a double effect on Sadiqi. On one hand, he was annoyed that they were so uncooperative; on the other hand, he wished he could manage without them. He didn't like having to work with so many different teams. Only a few hours into his investigation, he could see his work getting bogged down in a combination of too many cops and not enough skills. He didn't have the versatile support he needed. He had cataflics who were trained to arrest illegal underground sightseers but who knew nothing about preserving forensic evidence. Scientific experts who could collect evidence but didn't know how to navigate this crime scene without GPS. Detectives who knew nothing about the catacombs. Dog handlers who couldn't be left to go out on their own.

Basically, there were just too many people traipsing around, destroying evidence, turning his ideal ground for an investigation into Grand Central Station.

And that's when he had climbed to the surface and made his third call, asking his assistant to find some detailed maps of the quarries. If he could get his hands on some good maps, he wouldn't need any of those other squads. Counter-terrorism could work alone. That would cut down on the amount of evidence that was likely to get trampled. More importantly, it would limit the number of rumors leaking out to the press.

Standing in the garden behind the church, the inspector leaned up against his car and glanced at his watch then popped another nicotine mint. Not more than twenty a day. That was supposed to be the limit. It was going to be hard sticking to that today. Especially if Podesta didn't get his ass in gear. The lieutenant had gone out in search of those maps over an hour ago. What the hell was taking him so long? Sadiqi pulled up the lieutenant's number on his phone and waited for the call to connect. It went through almost immediately. *"Qu'est-ce que vous foutez? Where the hell are you?"*

"I'm right here, in front of you, *Chef*," came the answer, entirely unruffled and showing no sign of any need to rush. Sure enough, raising his gaze, the inspector caught sight of Lieutenant Podesta tramping across the lawn.

Unlike Sadiqi, Rémy Podesta's plain-clothed look showed fashion sense. His loosely fitting linen pants, airy raw silk jacket and open-necked shirt, all in tones of white and beige, made him look like he'd just stepped out of the summer edition of *GQ*. The inspector bit into his mint to get the full nicotine rush but it wasn't the vision of sartorial flair that depressed him. It was the middle-aged man the lieutenant had in tow.

As an expert at summing people up Sadiqi knew that the guy headed towards him was going to be nothing but trouble. The man's confident stride and firmly set lips forebode self-importance. The hair greying around the temples might have provided an air of aging respectability if the double chin and oversized belly didn't point to a weakness for gastronomic business luncheons and self-indulgence. Perhaps worst of all, the heavy-rimmed 1980s glasses suggested a hard-line intellectual in the habit of giving orders rather than following them. Overall, it didn't look good.

Without much enthusiasm, Sadiqi ambled towards the two men, holding out his hand to the visitor, trying to keep his facial expression both friendly and determined. "Khalid Sadiqi. I'm in charge of this operation," he said, purposefully omitting the fact he was from the counter-terrorist unit.

"Professor Pierre Caron, Director of the IGC," the man replied. His unfashionable glasses contrasted with his expensive shoes and well-tailored jacket. Probably his wife bought his clothes but hadn't yet figured out how to order new prescription lenses without having her husband present.

"Sorry to pull you out of bed so early, Professor," Sadiqi conceded genially. It wasn't usually his instinct to play the 'good-cop'. A cold, aggressive negotiating style came more naturally. But if Podesta had played the heavy, barging into Caron's life, ordering him to fetch some maps on the double, the inspector would assume the other role: simpering, flattering and requesting. It wouldn't have been his first choice, but it was worth a try. "Actually, we have a bit of a situation here, Sir. I can't go into the details. Let's just say there's been a security breach in the catacombs and we need to carry out an extensive investigation."

The effect of his words was immediate but not helpful. Instead of offering his support, the man started to gripe. "I've been warning people about this risk for years. Nobody listens. Nobody wants to take responsibility for closing down the quarries," Caron said, peering intently through his thick lenses, as if accusing the cop of being personally responsible for any problem he was being forced to deal with.

"Security wise, I think we can say we've hit rock bottom," Sadiqi agreed, still going for amiable and professional. Yet the fawning ring to the words irritated him, even as he poured them out. "And frankly, Sir, I'm going to need your help. We have to explore the catacombs and the quarry brigade isn't sufficiently staffed to meet our needs…"

Once again the man from the IGC cut him off. "I hope you don't expect me to provide you with a detachment of my engineers."

Podesta rolled his eyes; Caron had been yammering like this for most of the morning. "I did tell the professor he didn't have to come here. That you just need maps, not supervision…"

Caron balked. "I can't distribute the maps to just anyone."

Sadiqi took a deep breath in a semi-yoga-like attempt to center his energy. He wasn't much of a talker himself. Listening had always come much more naturally than talking. So he didn't have any patience with self-serving blowhards. And he had forgotten just how much he hated fieldwork, especially this side of it: angling for a lead, gently persuading witnesses and potential deponents to be helpful. Enticing them to do what should have been their civic duty: help solve the crimes. "We're hardly 'just anyone'," he said, pausing to let the comment register. He hated these intellectual types who thought every cop was a high school flunky. "I'm head of my division. I don't usually engage in fieldwork; my presence here is exceptional due to the seriousness of the situation. What I need are detailed maps that will allow me and my officers to work independently."

That last word set Caron off again. "Independently, independently," he echoed. "There are nearly 200 kilometers of tunnels under our feet, *brigadier*, and if you don't mind my saying so, I think it would be very unwise to let any of your men go off by themselves. The maps are complicated and the network is dense and dangerous. As far as the IGC is concerned, my engineers always go out in groups of three. I would recommend..."

Sadiqi had tried toadying. It hadn't worked. On top of that, he didn't like the way this guy had just demoted him out of twenty years' career. This time, he didn't bother waiting for Caron to finish his sentence. "Monsieur Caron, first of all, I am not a 'brigadier'; I'm an Inspector General, which means that I am overseeing this operation from start to finish. Secondly, with all due respect, I *do* mind you telling me how to run my operation for the simple reason that you have absolutely no idea what my operation is. And thirdly, I've asked you to provide maps. Can you or can't you fulfil that request?"

The scolding seemed to call Caron to heel; his eyes lost some of their rebelliousness. Or at least that was the initial impression. It took Sadiqi a second to realize that it wasn't his words that had caused the man's attitude to change. Neither the engineer nor Podesta was paying attention to the inspector anymore. Instead, they were peering over his shoulder at two plain-clothed officers marching a handcuffed prisoner across the courtyard.

For a fraction of a second Sadiqi felt buoyed by the hope that perhaps this was the killer. The illusion faded fast. Coveralls or not, the person being trailed across the garden had nothing like the muscular outline of the man filmed on CCTV earlier that morning. In fact, the prisoner wasn't even male; it was a young woman.

*   *   *

Her dust-covered ponytail screamed: "student" and Sadiqi could see that the dirty coveralls hid a body with perfect poise. Years of dance lessons had gone into that poise. Most likely paid for by mummy and daddy in a not-so-distant past. She couldn't be much older than twenty-five. Twenty-eight max. And between her youth and the hideous overalls, he was willing to bet she was a cataphile who'd been interrupted during a recreational outing. Nothing to do with the PM's death.

The IGC director woke him from his speculation: "*Mademoiselle Corrigan. What's going on?*"

"You know this woman?" The inspector's surprise had less to do with the coincidence of two non-military acquaintances meeting up at Val-de-Grace and more to do with his incomprehension over how Lara Croft in the jumpsuit could possibly have anything to do with this pedantic old gnome.

"She's a student of mine," Caron explained.

"Post-doc," the young woman corrected.

Apparently Caron was in the habit of diminishing the accomplishments of everyone around him, not just the police. And his use of the term *Mademoiselle* was clearly intended to be condescending. Nevertheless, no matter how unpleasant the professor, if he could vouch for the student, this was unlikely to be a serious lead. Sadiqi signalled to the two detectives to release her.

"But she resisted arrest," one of the officers countered.

"I didn't resist arrest." Her voice was determined but calm. "I ran away because you started running towards me with no warning."

"We shouted "Halt: Police.""

"Well you didn't shout it loud enough. Sound travels badly underground." Her gaze moved from the arresting officers to Sadiqi. "I nearly had a heart attack back there... Don't you guys read people their rights in France? No? You just jump on them and slam on the cuffs."

The full weight of the misunderstanding was fast dawning on Sadiqi as he deciphered the girl's accent. Although her French was impeccable, the accent slipped ever so slightly on a couple of words. Some people probably wouldn't even have noticed the lapses, but he had a good ear for accents. It seemed that not only had his officers been a little heavy-handed, they had made the mistake of attacking an American. Which was not going to improve his morning. Americans tended to kick up a whole pile of shit over legal errors. He didn't need that. Not now, not ever. Experience had taught him to play things very cool where foreigners were involved. A diplomatic incident would definitely not help his investigation. "Take the cuffs off. I'll take it from here," he said to the arresting officers, then waved them away.

But, American or not, he was in no mood to let someone barely out of school criticize his team's behavior, no matter how feisty she was. "*Madame,*" he said, opting for the new social convention of addressing all women with the same title. "I don't think you're in a position to criticize the police. You illegally entered a restricted area."

"I never asked to be brought to Val-de-Grace."

"I'm not talking about the base; I'm talking about the catacombs. Perhaps you're not aware that it's illegal to penetrate and circulate underground."

Rather than looking worried, a smile crept into her features. "If you're referring to Article 2 of the by-law dated November 2nd 1955, then yes, I am aware of the stipulations. But it just so happens that I *am* authorized to move around the quarries. And if your officers had asked to see my authorization, I would have shown it to them."

It wasn't the answer Sadiqi wanted to hear. "And just who happened to give you this authorization?" he asked with forced politeness.

"I did." It was Caron who had spoken.

The inspector shook his head. There was only so much shit he could take in one day. "Not anymore," he said. As far as Sadiqi was concerned, any control Caron had over movements in the catacombs had just ended. "As of this minute, nobody is allowed in the catacombs without my personal authorization."

"You can't do that," the director protested.

"I think you'll find that I can." Before Caron had time to protest further, the cop had turned his attention back to the girl, who was now looking less playful than a moment earlier. "What were you doing in the quarries?"

"Searching for a little peace and tranquility."

Chatting in a café, he would have found her self-confidence appealing. Amid all his other headaches it was simply annoying. "You do understand that this is a police investigation and I'm asking you to explain what you were doing near a crime scene?"

The way she lowered her head might have been the tiniest sign of submission, but her eyes held his gaze. "I'm a post-doc at *FranceTech*. I'm paid to do research on the quarries. I spend a lot of time down there. Having said that, this morning I'd still be sleeping if you guys hadn't been making so much noise."

Sadiqi was lost again. "I beg your pardon?"

"All the noise out front."

There was a lull while he digested this comment. "Where exactly do you live?"

"*La Maison des Ponts et Chaussées*." The cop had absolutely no idea where that was. "The student residence on the corner of rue St.

Jacques and rue des Feuillantines. 7th floor with a view of Val-de-Grace church."

The girl had hit home. He knew exactly where she had been that morning and exactly what she had seen. "So how long were you in the catacombs?"

"I left *FranceTech* around 6:30/7."

Sadiqi's lips didn't move, but the word '*Damn*' echoed loudly through his mind. 6:30 wasn't the answer he had hoped for. He'd wanted her to say she had spent the whole night underground and that she had noticed unusual comings and goings. Maybe a man in a balaclava toting a semi-automatic pistol. Obviously a long shot. "Can anyone confirm that?"

The green eyes stared at him with a spark of surprise at the request for an alibi. Or maybe it was just quietly concealed amusement. Either way, she scanned through her morning's movements. "The security guard at the residence saw me leave. And the one at *FranceTech* saw me arrive."

Sadiqi stretched forward and handed her the grey backpack his men had confiscated, along with the two flashlights. "Look, I'm sorry if my officers were a little rough. They mistook you for someone else."

The comment seemed to appease, and her expression softened into a smile. "That's ok. I guess I reacted badly, too." Which is where Sadiqi would have chosen to end the conversation, except the girl was having the opposite urge. "So I guess the message on the wall had something to do with your investigators underground."

Sadiqi fell back on his *I'm-just-a-dumb-cop* routine. "What do you mean?"

"The message out front says something about the 'depths of darkness'. And the staircase your men just dragged me up certainly leads to the depths of darkness. So what's happening down there?"

That was too much. She was annoyingly curious. "Madame," he snapped, "I'm the one asking the questions."

Among colleagues Sadiqi had a reputation for being a fairly scary person. This probably had something to do with the fact that in the line of duty his nature was binary: either irascible or outraged. And his explosive reactions in the interrogation room made suspects quickly realize that he probably wasn't big on anger management. So up until that moment, it had been his experience that whenever his temper flared, people invariably shrank back, and a veil of unease crept into their eyes. But not today. As the threat of anger rippled across his torso, he saw the young woman pause, waiting to see if that anger would explode. But when it didn't, an inviting smile broke across her face. "Then ask."

The intensity of the gaze was strangely hypnotic. He had only ever come across eyes with that depth of green in photos, never in real life. Unfortunately today he had more important things to think about than his witness' self-possession. "For starters, I'll need your full name, nationality, plus a phone number and an address where I can reach you."

"Antonia Corrigan. Canadian. You can find me at the *Maison des Ponts et Chaussées* or *FranceTech*. My number's 06.99.99.99.99. Does this have anything to do with the missing cataphiles?"

The cop didn't look up; he just kept typing the address into his phone. Although her question struck him as strange, he was quite happy she'd asked it – only because it was way off target. A red herring would stop her from making any link to the PM. "Missing cataphiles?" he repeated, his voice non-committal.

The student slid her hand into her coverall pockets and pulled out the folded sheet of paper from the underground tomb. The inspector's eyes glided over the message but once he had read the words he was even more confused than before. "Snoopy, Bango and Quartz? Cartoon characters?"

The ponytail was shaking back and forth again. "No. They're cataphile aliases. Pseudonyms." The blank look on the cop's face told her she needed to explain. "Basically, what the message is saying is that three cataphiles have gone missing."

Sadiqi wasn't sure whether any of this made sense but he stuffed the note into his breast pocket. Not that he was interested in the missing cataphiles. But the Canadian didn't know that. If she was going to believe he was interested in them, then logically he had to hold on to the clue. The less information leaked off the base, the happier he was.

"I take it you're a frequent visitor to the quarries." Not only did the girl nod, out of the corner of his eye the inspector could see her professor nodding, too. "So did you notice anything else unusual while your were down there?"

The nod morphed to a shake of the head. "I was down for barely half an hour."

Unfortunate.

Without bothering to thank her he switched his attention to Caron. Sadiqi had done well to join the police; he'd never mastered the arts of transition and cajoling that were so important in the business world. "And what about maps?" he asked. "Can you get me some?"

Caron snorted. "Of course I can. As soon as you tell me what all this is about."

The cop had no intention of spending his morning negotiating an information trade-off. His strongest ally was silence. The more he talked, the more Caron would protest.

The technique worked. After a few seconds of listening to the quiet hum of the waking city, Caron made his first offer. "If you drop by my office at Denfert around 3PM I can have the maps ready for you."

They were making progress. A wee bit more encouragement and Sadiqi would have what he wanted. "I need them this morning."

"I have a lecture at *FranceTech* at ten. I don't usually go to the IGC at all on Thursdays." There was a pout in Caron's voice.

Sadiqi couldn't be bothered to make the effort to be polite any longer. Especially not with a guy who was doing his damnedest to make life difficult for everyone else. "So you're suggesting I send my officers into the catacombs to get lost, with no maps, just because you hadn't planned on going to the office today." It was time to get things moving. "Lieutenant," he said to Podesta. "Escort Ms. Corrigan off the base then accompany Professor Caron to his office. I need those maps now." Then he reached into his jeans' pocket and pulled two visiting cards out of his wallet. "If either of you think of anything else, make sure you call me."

12

Toni would have preferred to make her way back to *FranceTech* alone but Lieutenant Podesta insisted on racing her back to school at breakneck speed complete with flashing strobe light and blaring siren. And the illegal U-turn he made on boulevard St. Michel, crossing a double white line and stopping in a bus lane, left her convinced beyond the shadow of a doubt that French police had a tenuous grasp on the concept of road safety.

As soon as he stopped in front of the school's main entrance she hustled out of the car and bounded up the steps into the lobby of *FranceTech*. The security officer on duty inside peered out the glass door, watching with curiosity as the car continued on its way to Denfert-Rochereau with professor Caron still tucked into the back seat. Not a conversation she wanted to have; she headed down the hallway instead.

Living up to its reputation as one of the most prestigious engineering schools in Europe, *FranceTech* was housed in what had once been a private mansion in the heart of the Latin Quarter. The actual offices, however, were less palatial than the bronze and marble outer trimmings. The entire interior design was an attempt to reconcile 19th century architecture with 21st century administrative needs. Architectural fusion. A building originally designed to house a dozen students when the school was first created was now the seat of learning for thousands of people, and the teaching machine had adapted. Some departments had left central Paris for the suburbs, or even the provinces, and the students remaining in Paris were obliged to accept a cramped work environment. Elegant high-ceilinged rooms had been diced into small cubicles, piling a maximum number of students one on top of the other.

Leaving the central hallway, with its floor to ceiling murals of French mining regions, Toni turned into a gloomy narrow corridor that looked like it might have been home to the cleaning staff in the mansion's glory days but certainly not to the lord and lady of the manor. The creamy marble of the main hall gave way to a contemporary concrete finish while thick wood paneled walls loomed up on either side. And the office door she pushed open at the end of the passageway was nothing but particleboard with a doorknob slapped on.

Likewise, the "office" wasn't exactly grandiose. Five graduate students and post-docs had to vie for space on a mezzanine above the secretary's desk with very little in the way of basic research materials other than a hexagonal table and five chairs. In principle the mezzanine was an astute way of optimizing floor space under the high ceilings. Below, Hélène carried out secretarial tasks. Above, the students were free to work or read or chat. The set-up worked well for Hélène, who on the rare days she bothered to come in, successfully managed to navigate around her "ground floor" desk area without hunching over. But then Hélène was very petite. The five students, on the other hand, spent most of their time hunched over like Neanderthals. The only upside was that the mezzanine was equipped with a white tube-shaped banister, which at least stopped them from pushing one another over the edge like lemmings.

Some exchange students would have been appalled by the conditions. Toni recognized them as an Old World quirk. Rather than complaining about workstations that weren't up to North American standards, she accepted the fact that space was more precious in central Paris than in downtown Montreal. After all, there had to be some price to pay for the view of the Luxembourg Gardens and the Eiffel Tower – even if she did have to share it with five other people. In any case, the conditions weren't intended as an affront to students in particular; everybody had to accept the limited space constraint. By Montreal standards, Caron's private office was about the size of a phone box.

The way Toni saw it, the essentials had been provided, i.e. telephone and internet access. And that's what she needed now – an early morning surf. This early in the day she had the office to herself so she didn't need to fight for space. She pulled her laptop out of her backpack, revved it up and googled "val-de-grace police". In a blink she had an answer.

> Le Monde: Arnaud de Chanterelle to undergo surgery
> spokeswoman also indicated that there would be an
> increased **police** presence around **Val-de-Grace...** Article
> appearing June 20, 2012...
> www.lemonde.fr/journal/2012-06-19/ - 42k - Cached –
> Similar pages

She clicked on the link and ran her eyes across the article. The Prime Minister was in hospital at Val-de-Grace for a hernia operation.

That made sense. If the Prime Minister was in hospital it was normal that there would be a heavy police presence. Some sort of increased security during a VIP stay.

Except Sadiqi had stated quite clearly that she was trespassing on a crime scene. Which meant that the cops hadn't been on a routine patrol; they'd been looking for someone. So there was more to all this than just extra guards for the PM. There had to be. There had been dozens of cops in the Z-Room when she'd been hustled up Mansart's staircase. The famous gallery had looked more like an archaeological dig than a preventive guard watch. No. The police hadn't been worried something bad was going to happen. Something serious had already happened. And judging from what she'd seen, the quarries had been involved.

Perhaps there had been some sort of death threat? That made sense. Then again, there had been a whole hell of a lot of cops around, combing the quarries and the hospital grounds. Although French police tended to gravitate in flocks rather than isolated pairs, she wasn't convinced the authorities would have called in quite that much manpower just to follow up a death threat.

She really couldn't gauge just how big a reaction a death threat against the Prime Minister would be likely to elicit. It had always seemed excessive to her that the French needed both a President and a Prime Minister. One or the other struck her as sufficient. And although she knew a fair amount about President Tibrac, Arnaud de Chanterelle was an abstraction; she always thought of him more as a figurehead, quietly applying the president's policies. If it hadn't been for her fleeting arrest that morning, she wouldn't have cared one way or the other. But now all that had changed. She suddenly wanted to know everything there was to know about the man.

She highlighted the word "police" in the search bar and typed in "de Chanterelle" instead. The list of answers that popped up featured everything from medical insight to the mentally insane ramblings of conspiracy theorists:

GP's Weekly
Arnaud de **Chanterelle** admitted to **Val-de-Grâce**.
Wednesday 19 **June**... Inguinal hernia ... most common in boys and men (only 10% of cases affect... risk that it will get trapped
www.docweek.com/flash/ index.cfm?=viewflashinfo =817 - 35k - Cached – Similar pages

What is Arnaud de Chanterelle really doing?
Is Arnaud de **Chanterelle** really preparing to undergo surgery at **Val-de-Grace** or has he disappeared to travel to 2003 UB313 to learn new management methods for... **June**.
www.goanywhere.com/offbeat/06/where_is.php - 28k - Cached – Similar Pages

I'm happy, what about you ?
19-06-2012: > After 18 months of driving us mad, de **Chanterelle** is finally going to leave us alone, if only for a few days. Hopefully his surgeon will manage some... **Val-de-Grace**
homefrance.forum.com/im_happy.htlm - 24k - Cached – Similar Pages

But at least one suggestion looked promising.

Retribution will come
He sends his servant...depths of darkness into light.
Arnaud de **Chanterelle**... **Val-de-Grace** this morning. Our struggle against the oppressors continues....Long live

freedom.
chanterelle.blog.liberty.fr/chanterelle/retribution_will.html -
20k - Cached – Similar pages

She clicked on the cached link and found herself looking at a chat room discussion on the merits and shortcomings of Arnaud de Chanterelle's recent policies. Scrolling down the page, she arrived at the "retribution" quote with her key words highlighted in yellow and pink:

> June 20; from Ng
> **Retribution will come**
> He sends his servant from the depths of darkness into light.
> Arnaud de Chanterelle was brought to justice at Val-de-Grace this morning. Our struggle against the oppressors continues. Many others deserve punishment. Long live freedom.

What was that supposed to be? A death threat? Her train of thought derailed into the darker regions of her mind. How exactly had de Chanterelle been "brought to justice"?

She would have liked to believe the comment was meaningless. Or at worst the work of a crank. Yet she couldn't. "He sends his servant from the depths of darkness into light." The words leapt out, circling through her memory where they had been sitting since five o'clock that morning. "SERVANT FROM THE DEPTHS OF DARKNESS". It was the message she had seen sprayed on the wall at Val-de-Grace.

Her fingers raced over the keys, typing in her next search: "servant depths darkness". As soon as she hit enter, the listing pixelized on the page.

The Ideal **Servant** of Jehovah
God's ideal **Servant** was ... Jesse. ... You cannot be "light," in the **depths** of **darkness**, unless you are consumed by the ...
www.biblepress.org/**servant**.htm - 23k - Cached – Similar pages

Rock Lyrics: In **Darkness** lyrics
Lyrics for album Winter In **Darkness**. Tracks: Going Down to Hades, ... **Servant** on the battlefield running to find

freedom in the **depths** ... lyrics.rock.com/lyrics/in_
darkness.html - 12k - Cached – Similar pages

Search Me O God: Cast Ye the Unprofitable **Servant** ...
Cast Ye the Unprofitable **Servant** Into Outer **Darkness**
(Matt. 25:30) ... The real **depths** of suffering need to be
overcome, ...
www.quaker.org/books/cast_ye.html - 10k - Cached –
Similar pages

Qur'an Chapter 57: Al-Hadid (The Iron)
He is the One Who sends to His **Servant** Manifest Signs,
that He may lead you from the **depths** of **Darkness** into
the Light and verily Allah is to you ...
www.uni2.edu/MRI/koran/057.html - 25k - Cached –
Similar pages

It was the fourth listing that caught her attention. "Quran." Her
blood ran cold. "He sends his servant from the depths of darkness into
light." The Quran reference was almost identical to the one she had
read in the graffiti.

13

Nestled under the strange rounded white domes of Sacré Cœur
basilica, Boulevard de Clichy looked like a ghost town so early in the
morning. The hookers, pimps and kebab salesmen had all been chased
away by the already scorching sun and the Nightingale found himself
wandering down the deserted boulevards, where he could compare the
relative merits of various sex shows on offer in the neighborhood.
Perhaps that afternoon he would check one out. For now, he was lying
low. Being discreet wasn't as straightforward as it had been twenty
years ago. When he was a kid, you could hang out in parks, or kill
time in shopping centers. Nowadays shopping centers were equipped
with CCTV so any extended bouts of window shopping could be
picked out by security agents. And thanks to the current pedophile
hysteria, any male sitting alone in a park was likely to be stopped by
the cops and asked for ID.

He hovered in front of the Moulin Rouge and glanced at a display
advertising dancers dressed in black leather bondage belts framing

naked breasts. A familiar warm feeling grew between his legs as he enjoyed the photo layout. He loved Paris. You didn't even have to pay for soft porn. It was on offer free of charge on posters all over the city. But the array of bodies was of nothing more than passing interest, and his eyes soon drifted to his watch. 9:15. Time for coffee. A café was never more than a few steps away in Paris and the Nightingale headed straight across the square, where several tables were arranged the length of the sidewalk.

It was easy for him to blend in with the tourists enjoying *café crème* on the *terrasse*. The Nightingale's face was conveniently non descript. It was difficult to put an age to him. His skin was worn by the elements, but judging from his clothes and the way he held himself he was probably younger than he looked. Certainly under 40. Although his blue Nordic eyes might have appealed to the brown-eyed French girls who crossed his path, they weren't bright enough to stand out in a crowd. And the small ironic upturned mouth might have been considered equally appealing. It projected a misleading impression of friendliness. In reality this semi-permanent curve of the lips was more an ironic sneer at the twists and turns of life than a sign of good humor.

Easily the most distinctive part of his appearance was his red hair. When he was younger it had been a burning red that was almost unknown in France. It had been his trademark twenty years earlier, back in the days when it was four inches long and each morning he plied it with gel to make it stick straight up in the air. Nowadays, the sheen was slightly darker and in any case he kept it trimmed short so it blended quietly with his overall well-behaved look. Comfortable walking shoes, a beige polo-neck t-shirt and khaki chinos. He would never wear jeans; jeans were sloppy. Cowboy gear. He was no cowboy. He was a professional. The chinos looked good, clean. And he liked khaki. He felt safe in khaki. Even in the city, khaki was camouflage, making him invisible in the crowd.

He was just about to take a seat on the *terrasse* when he noticed a TV screen on the wall inside with a red banner across the bottom announcing a special news bulletin with a presidential address live from Val-de-Grace.

It was too irresistible; they were going to talk about his work. Like a drug addict drawn to his next fix he moved inside the café. The dozen or so clients and the staff barely noticed as he sidled up to the bar. Most of the patrons were half asleep, cradling their double espressos and staring blankly at the TV, watching without listening. The Nightingale ordered a coffee and was taking his first sip when the image of a man with light brown balding hair and a slightly simian face stepped up to a lectern, framed between two tricolor flags and wearing a beautifully composed expression of sadness.

President Tibrac was what the French referred to as "Gaullist" – although "well-born conservative" probably would have been more precise.   His poise and dress sense were the product of careful breeding as were his erudition and his blind contempt for any ideas other than the ones he'd grown up with. His aristocratic nose was constantly held tilted in the air as if to avoid an unpleasant smell wafting under it. That unpleasant scent was the stench of the lower and middle classes that continually opposed his policies.

As members of a working class neighborhood, none of the people standing at the bar on boulevard Clichy had much sympathy for the man on the screen and there were muttered insults as the president took a deep breath and began his speech. Looking deep into the cameras and speaking very slowly as if to emphasize the gravity of the situation, Tibrac gave the impression of being a man on the verge of announcing inevitable Armageddon to his countrymen and women.

"It is my very sad duty," he began dolefully, "to have to inform the nation that our esteemed Prime Minister, Monsieur Arnaud de Chanterelle, passed away early this morning. Just as you are, I was shattered to learn of his unexpected death." The President paused here, to draw another breath before continuing. "As you are aware, Monsieur de Chanterelle was scheduled to undergo surgery at Val-de-Grace today. Tragically the Prime Minister had a very severe allergic reaction to the anaesthetic administered in preparation for this operation."   The Nightingale's face moved a shade closer to amusement. He'd been called a lot of things before, but never an overdose of anaesthetic. "None feel this loss as deeply as I. Arnaud de Chanterelle was a dear friend as well as a close associate. His disappearance will leave a void at Matignon, at the Elysée and in the hearts of all French men and women."

While the President was looking grave and talking about how he was certain the entire nation would join him in "transmitting our deepest condolences to Monsieur de Chanterelle's widow and children..." snickers were already rising around the bar. A man in workmen's overalls standing beside the Nightingale nursing his 9AM glass of white wine mumbled to anyone listening, "Good riddance."

A waiter bustling off to deliver tea and *café au lait* to an English couple sitting outside shouted back, "One less politician. Doesn't sound like a bad start to the day."

Far from plunging the congregation into commiserations, the news had brought them to life and a volley of banter started flying back and forth across the bar.

"Dream on. Politicians are like weeds. You cut one down, six more spring up."

"Oh, maybe this time Tibrac will actually find someone who can reach some sort of social consensus."

"Social consensus? When was the last time you heard a politician pay attention to what the street was screaming for?"

"Yeah. They'll get someone just as bad to take over."

The man in the overalls, obviously not on his first glass of wine of the day, was the only one dwelling on the death itself. In a voice loud enough to drown out all the other commentary, he continued: "Val-de-Grace. A military hospital. Who'd've thought a bunch of soldiers were smart enough to kill anyone worth killing?"

The affront shattered the Nightingale's bubble. He wasn't touchy about a lot of things, but he didn't like people shooting their mouths off about the military. Especially rednecks who didn't know their head from their ass. He raised his head to get a better look at the idiot.

Maybe it was the movement of his head. Or maybe the waiter had simply recognized the Nightingale's buzz cut for what it was: the sign of a military background. Whatever the reason, the man behind the bar detected the tension that had sprung into the air. And he knew that if he wasn't careful, he could end up with a brawl on his hands.

"Perhaps *Monsieur* has served?" he asked, turning an interested eye toward the Nightingale and discreetly pushing the other client's glass further along the bar.

The Nightingale didn't answer. The question brought back too many memories; memories that couldn't be transmitted to these civilians by a simple 'yes'. Memories of all the battlefields these guys at the bar had seen flashing across the TV screen as they sipped their drinks while the Nightingale experienced the wars first hand. He had been trained to be an elite fighting machine. He and his buddies had parachuted into the most dangerous combat zones in the world, been left to fight, then the ones who survived had been flown off to the next battle. The Nightingale was one of those survivors. Most of his friends from training hadn't been so lucky.

The redhead stared at the flabby man with his glass of wine. For a fraction of a second, he considered strangling him there on the spot to illustrate the fact that it was not acceptable to insult soldiers. But the urge was gone in a flash. The guy was some dumb fuck. There was no point in getting worked up about it. The planet was littered with human trash. Some you could kill, some you just had to ignore and hope they didn't infect too many other people. The Nightingale drained his cup and slapped a coin on the counter.

Silence enshrouded the bar. The staff and customers were happy to see the back of him.

14

By late-morning Sadiqi was getting twitchy. He would happily have stripped off his shirt and SP2022 and jogged a few laps around the base to evacuate some nervous energy but trampling potential evidence wouldn't exactly help his case progress. Instead, he was pacing up and down the garden between the church and the hospital, popping nicotine candy and waiting for word from the teams he'd sent out.

So far the scientific team had failed to find any useful leads. Just a few threads from the mountaineering rope used to climb out de Chanterelle's window. Excellent quality. Edelrid probably. But then, what climber would risk his life on a poor quality rope? Nothing interesting had come off the corpses either, other than confirmation of Lalanne's theory about the make of weapon. As for Sadiqi himself, he'd reviewed the CCTV footage meticulously but the brief sighting of someone in a balaclava and black pants and shirt wasn't very informative. The man they were looking for was probably about 1m80, muscular build and in excellent physical shape. That hardly narrowed it down.

His last hope lay with the sniffer dogs. But the cataflics had arrived so late they'd got held up in all the security checks surrounding the President's visit so the royal cortège of two handlers and three cataguides left way behind schedule and Sadiqi was still waiting for news.

At least the President's press conference had added a brief note of comic relief to an otherwise bleak morning. The line about de Chanterelle's *accidental* death was pure Mozart. Sadiqi would have liked to see the faces on the guys who had spent their morning mopping up blood; they probably had a pretty good idea all that red stuff hadn't come from an anaesthetic overdose. And what about the relatives of the murdered nurse and security officers? What was the President planning on telling them?

But that wasn't Sadiqi's problem. As far as he was concerned, an info blackout was good news. It meant he wouldn't have to deal with the media. And that would save him one hell of a lot of time and energy.

The inspector was just reaching for another candy when his phone started vibrating. It was his boss' ringtone. Sasha Dukrin. Not only the most powerful woman in French counter-terrorism, possibly the most important person in Intelligence. Strictly speaking, she wasn't really his boss, at least not anymore. She had been, a while ago, when she was still head of counter-terrorism, before getting promoted to lead the DGSI intelligence service. In fact, she had been more than simply his boss; she was the person who had recruited him into the service. She had trained him. Forged him into what he was. Which was why he still thought of her as his *boss*. And having worked side-by-side for over fifteen years in the UCLAT, she still considered it her prerogative to come and ask him for help on cases that didn't fall strictly within the scope of his responsibility. Which was made all the easier by the fact that the DGSI and the UCLAT were both housed in the same building. That was how he had come to be working this case.

His hand changed course and slipped the phone out of his pocket.

"*Un beau merdier ce matin*," he offered, instead of a greeting. "I've got nothing for you. I hope you've got something for me."

"We've got a message claiming responsibility for the assassination," a cool alto echoed down the line.

A breakthrough? he wondered. Someone openly claiming responsibility for the attack would mean a solid lead. Before he could get too optimistic, Dukrin started tearing down her own good news. "The message was posted on dozens of chat rooms and blogs around the world. Mainly on big media websites. Copied on Twitter accounts." Sadiqi silently wished he could go back to the legendary Good Old Days. Modern technology was exhausting; it made everything move so fast while at the same time creating a sea of useless dead ends.

"We're trying to figure out where the post originated," Dukrin continued. "Here. I'm sending it to you now. The first line is identical to the message from Val-de-Grace. The one that was sprayed outside the church." The inspector moved the telephone away from his ear and called up his email on the touch screen. The message appeared.

June 20, from Ng: **Retribution will come**
He sends his servant from the depths of
darkness into light.
Arnaud de Chanterelle was brought to justice
at Val-de-Grace this morning. Our struggle
against the oppressors continues. Many
others deserve punishment. Long live
freedom.

"It could be a copycat. Maybe someone from the neighborhood
was up early, saw the message and did a little deducing," Sadiqi
commented.

"No. The message was posted before the news of the PM's death
was even off the military base. Well before. In fact, these messages
went out around 4:15 AM."

"Lalanne said the quote was from the Quran."

"Cryptography had the same initial reaction but they dropped the
idea almost immediately. They think the reference is purposely
misleading. It's meant to make us think about the Quran and all that
entails." Sadiqi read the words *Islamist Fundamentalists* into his boss'
words. "Perhaps send us off, chasing our tails in that direction. In fact
there's a similar reference in the Bible so there's really no reason to
think this has anything to do with Islam. Especially being as
fundamentalists would have been far more likely to leave the message
in Arabic." Sadiqi nodded even though Dukrin couldn't see him.
Fundamental Islam believed that the Quran could only be read in the
original Arabic; it made no sense to leave a reference to the Holy
Scriptures in a pagan language.

"So you think the message is meaningless?"

"Cryptography is still working on it," she answered non-
committally. "But I'm optimistic IT can get something useful out of
this. They're almost certain the message was sent from Paris. It
transited mainly through French servers. They're trying to trace the
device it came from."

That was good news. A trace on one of the computers linked to
the organization responsible for the assassination could create a solid
path to the murderers. Like houses and apartments, each individual
computer had its own address that got logged on to the server of every
website the computer visited. In other words the computer left behind a
trace of its movements just as clear as a trail of crumbs. If IT could
find the IP address that had sent this message, their teams could track
down the physical computer and its owner.

At least that was the theory. It was just a little hard to believe that whoever had masterminded the break-in at Val-de-Grace had done something as stupid as leaving behind a trail. "Have we got an IP trace?" Sadiqi asked with a combination of enthusiasm and disbelief. The average internet surfer might not worry about their computer being traced over the web. Organized crime, on the other hand, was usually obsessive about it. Avoiding recognition was key to their survival – not to mention a relatively simple thing to do.

"Not yet," Dukrin admitted. "The message came through anonymized proxies and there isn't just one IP address, there are several. A different one for each message."

This sounded more in keeping with the tone of the operation so far. Configuring a web browser to pass through a proxy was simplicity itself, and it meant that any website where the messages had been posted had only seen a fake address that masked the criminal's personal IP address. "They want us to know they're out there but they don't want us to find them," Sadiqi said.

"You got it. They're both visible and invisible. In all, the same message was posted in over thirty media chat rooms and blogs but they didn't spend long online. Each successive posting was made roughly forty-five seconds apart. And for each one, the servers give us a different IP code."

"It would have been a little optimistic to think they'd leave us their address."

"Optimism helps me through the day," she commented with nothing like optimism in her voice. Sadiqi knew the words were her idea of a joke. Dukrin was pessimistic in the extreme about life, the universe and everything. Pessimistic and not at all ashamed to say so. She didn't expect the answers to their cases to come easily. And (with the possible exception of Sadiqi himself) she didn't trust anyone – neither the criminals she was tracking nor the people who worked for her nor the people she worked for. "IT is still working on it, but – as you so kindly pointed out – coming up with an address will be about as easy as finding an honest politician. We do have a second tentative lead, though. The text of the message is in English and it's signed 'Ng'. We're checking whether it's a known pseudonym or code name for anyone we have on file. We're also checking with Interpol. Maybe Scotland Yard or the CIA or someone can tell us who we're looking for."

That didn't sound good. If Dukrin was already checking with her foreign colleagues, she must be low on leads. But before he had a chance to press for details, she was already spiralling away. "I've got someone on the other line. I'll get back to you later." The line clicked off.

15

Sadiqi would have liked more time to consult with his boss but as soon as she rang off, his phone started buzzing again.

This time it was the long-awaited news from the dog handlers. "We're out of the catacombs, Sir. I'm afraid it doesn't look good. The dogs led us to the old railroad tracks behind Montsouris Park. We even managed to follow the scent above ground back to Porte d'Orléans." The man hesitated.

"But," Sadiqi offered.

"But then the target went into the metro and we lost the scent. Too many different trails. Probably took a train. God knows where he is now."

Sadiqi had expected as much. The killer's trail had been pure at first thing that morning. It was probably still pure in the catacombs even now. The problem was, once their target was back above ground there was no way of following him. All he had to do was jump on a metro or a bus and he was lost to the dogs forever. He could be anywhere now. He could be in fucking Timbuktu. They'd wasted too much time.

Sadiqi clutched at the last thread of hope. "Does the station have CCTV?"

"Yeah. We've got a copy of the morning's recording. Chardin's checking it."

That was something. Not much, but something. The killer must have taken one of the first metros of the day and the station wouldn't have been busy that early in the morning. With a little luck, someone at headquarters could compare the footage from Val-de-Grace to the one from the metro and come up with some sort of corporeal match.

Maybe they could put together a Photofit.

16

The half hour spent at Val-de-Grace that morning had provoked a small crisis of faith setting Toni's whole hierarchy of beliefs upside down. Caron's fears about the quarries had always struck her as ridiculous. This morning, she was less certain. First of all, being chased by the police had made her aware of how vulnerable she was down there. She hadn't spent enough time in the gym recently; she needed to fix that in case she got ambushed again down a dark gallery. Secondly, she now seriously believed that the police presence at Val-de-Grace was due to some unprecedented criminal activity involving the underground network. If that was the case, then maybe Caron was right after all. Maybe the quarries really were a terrorist nightmare just waiting to happen.

Having spent over an hour sitting in the empty office, googling cross references about de Chanterelle, Val-de-Grace, retribution and inguinal hernia, Toni was definitely aching to share her thoughts by the time Cédric Trouvé strode into the office.

Although not an expert in her field specifically, Professor Trouvé was closer to Toni's intellectual "ideal" than Caron. Trouvé had written prolifically on his engineering speciality, which was eolian turbines. Yet it wasn't his knowledge of civil engineering that fuelled Toni's respect; it was his overall aura of culture. His books were always full of anecdotes and examples carefully slipped in alongside the pure maths of the case studies. While Caron knew everything there was to know about each crack or low ceiling in the quarries, Trouvé had a well-developed sense of an engineer's social impact.

As always, the professor's "Good Morning" rang out warm and friendly. And the purple reflections in his silk tie brightened the room while the spiky gelled hair harked back to some distant punk past. Standing behind his desk, he began unloading papers from his briefcase. He seldom closed his office door. The time he spent at the school was allocated to his students. So Toni wandered straight into his micro-office.

Not that she had a definite question ready. She just needed to talk. And despite Trouvé's invitation for her to install herself in the chair across from him, it took her a few seconds to formulate her ideas. "I was at Val-de-Grace this morning," she announced, awkwardly.

A smile crept across Trouvé's lips. "I presume you mean *under* Val-de-Grace."

Normally the irony in his voice wouldn't have bothered her, but today it made her defensive. "Yeah, you're right. I *was* underground.

At least until I was arrested and taken upstairs and then ordered to keep out of the quarries. The whole base was crawling with cops." The amusement drained from the professor's face. Without giving him time to think up a simple explanation for what had happened, Toni delivered a run down of the morning's events, ending with a brief description of her interview with Sadiqi.

"Are you sure he was a police officer?" Trouvé stroked his beard. "If he was giving orders at Val-de-Grace, it's more likely he was a soldier."

"You don't see a lot of military officers on duty wearing jeans and two days' worth of stubble. The guy looked like he was straight out of an Eiffel Tower episode of *Law and Order*." The confusion on the professor's face indicated a lack of familiarity with American TV series. "Definitely a cop. In any case, the whole base was crawling with cops. Sirens, strobe light – the whole kebang. Plus, he gave me this," she said, pulling Sadiqi's card out of her back pocket. There wasn't much to it; just the name, number and police crest.

But Trouvé remained unconvinced. "I guess there are extra police reinforcements on the base during the PM's surgery," he said.

"Right," Toni agreed, "but this guy wasn't there doing some routine patrol; he was looking for evidence. Something strange was going on. Just ask Caron."

Toni was often accused by her French friends and colleagues of not being sufficiently Cartesian. Her tendency to skip from one point to the next with no logical order produced a reaction of total bewilderment.

"Caron was there?"

"Yeah. When I was dragged out of the quarries and taken to the head cop, Caron was already there, talking with him." Walking Trouvé through the details made the story sound more conclusive to her. As if to sharpen her conviction, her phone buzzed with a news alert. She took one look at the screen and her stomach churned. "Prime Minister Dead".

She pivoted the screen towards Trouvé so he could see the headline. A measure of concern crept into his features as she clicked on the link to call up the newcast off *France Télévision*. Instantly, an anchorwoman with starched blonde hair and a lowcut sundress that seemed out of keeping with the solemnity of the occasion appeared on the screen. "Good morning," the journalist began with a knell of sadness. "The Prime Minister's death is at the heart of today's news. This morning, President Gustave Tibrac announced the untimely death of his close collaborator, Arnaud de Chanterelle. Prime Minister de

Chanterelle's doctors were unable to resuscitate him when he suffered an allergic reaction to the anaesthetic administered in preparation for the operation he was to undergo."

This rational explanation of the PM's death had a calming effect on Trouvé. "Unfortunately medicine is an imperfect science," he offered reflectively. "A similar thing happened to an Interior Minister about twenty years ago. He spent a week in a coma after an allergic reaction to a curare-based anaesthetic. He was luckier. He pulled through." The professor eased into his chair with a sigh, leaving Toni feeling slightly mad. Or at the very least, she felt she was the last remaining sane element in a world gone insane. There was no way she could play along and pretend nothing unusual had happened?

"Look at this," she said, pointing at the screen. "This is all archive footage; there's no sign of the police cars that are crawling over the base right now. Look! A shot of the front entrance to the main hospital building. A shot of de Chanterelle being admitted yesterday. A shot of a doctor administering an anaesthetic to an anonymous patient. A shot of the President and de Chanterelle at a reception in some undefined past," she reeled off the running commentary as the images flashed on the tiny screen. "But there are no actual pictures from this morning other than a couple of seconds from the President's press conference announcing the death. There's certainly no mention of any police presence. It doesn't make sense," she said. "If the Prime Minister had a heart attack, why was the hospital crawling with cops? Okay, sure. Any VIP visit requires a certain number of bodyguards. And a dead PM plus a presidential visit probably demands a particularly large number of cops. But those weren't bodyguards I saw this morning. Rambo-Sadiqi wasn't standing guard; he was in charge of a police squad searching for something. And when I was handcuffed and dragged through the Z-Room by those cowboys, there were dozens of cops roping off corners of the quarries, picking up beer cans and old candles and sealing them in little plastic bags. I'm not completely stupid. There's no way those guys were patrolling. They were looking for evidence."

"Maybe there were multiple incidents. Perhaps the PM died by accident but there was also something UNDER the base," Trouvé offered.

Toni stared blankly at him. But she wasn't one to stay dumbstruck long. "Sir, with respect, don't you teach a course in advanced probability? You know as well as I do just how unlikely it is that two unrelated incidents took place at Val-de-Grace this morning."

The look of resistance faded from the professor's face, replaced only by thoughtfulness. Toni wasn't sure how to say "cover up" in French. She was pretty sure she was about to find out.

17

Sasha Dukrin reclined into her high back swivel chair, pushed her glasses up on top of her head to clip back her hair, then stared menacingly at the phone on her desk. Her petite figure gave a false sense of fragility but the immaculate cut of the black Saint Laurent pantsuit announced precision, organization and power. The expression on her face was indecipherable. The only clear sentiment was sheer determination. It was a look that rarely left her face. The job she did never got any easier. By definition it was just one crisis after another.

As head of the DGSI, Dukrin coordinated and ran everything from policing to riot control to any number of special services including all the counters: counter-terrorism, counter cyber crime, counter-espionage as well as surveillance of any other potential threats. On a good day she had a hard job. On a bad day, like today, she was expected to move mountains. And instead of lending a supportive hand and helping her to move forward, the President had just installed himself on the opposite side of the mountain and was pushing in the wrong direction.

The hotline that linked her office to the Elysée Palace was supposed to facilitate communication between the country's security service and the President in times of national emergency. At least that was the theory. In practice things worked a little differently. The President did indeed have a direct emergency line to her office. When he had called that morning at 6:30, she had been there, waiting to fill him in on all she knew about the PM's assassination. She, on the other hand, didn't necessarily have an immediate link to the President. If he didn't want to hear the bad news, he ignored her and then complained that he hadn't been properly briefed. Likewise, if he didn't want to give her information, he kept it to himself. That morning, he hadn't even hinted that he was going to cover up the assassination. And now he was ignoring her calls. Ever since she'd watched that sham of a press conference he gave at Val-de-Grace, Dukrin had been trying to reach him. She had now been waiting – not so patiently – for over an hour.

The director snatched a file off her desk and started reading while part of her mind concentrated on willing the president to phone. Tibrac knew she wanted to speak with him. She had left messages with various secretaries not to mention the head of his personal bodyguard and his motorcycle escort team. Fair enough, he was having a busy morning. But having invented a completely unbelievable story about what had happened to his Prime Minister, he could at least have the decency to explain what the strategic aim of his angle was. Because she sure as hell couldn't figure it out. For the moment she was willing to believe that the President had acted on some political imperative. Counter-terrorist investigations were tricky. There were always political interests that needed juggling. But Dukrin had always tried to work harmoniously with those imperatives. The President knew that. So why was he screwing around with her when he should have been facilitating the investigation?

Dukrin pulled her glasses out of her hair and started fiddling with them. Today was an inextricable mess. Not only did she have a dead Prime Minister, cryptic internet blogs claiming responsibility for the assassination and an increasingly substantiated link to the catacombs, thanks to the president she was now overseeing an investigation that didn't even exist officially. How could it exist? Officially there had been no attack so officially there was no terrorist investigation.

The sandy haired commander glanced at her computer screen where the national press agency was relaying images of competing gangs of journalists vying for the best shot of the President standing mournfully outside de Chanterelle's widow's apartment. What a circus! What a load of horseshit! Dukrin watched the President's face as he said something about his sadness over his prime minister's untimely passing. What a show! Who did he think he was kidding? When had Tibrac ever been on good terms with de Chanterelle? Okay, maybe four or five years ago. But certainly not since naming him Prime Minister. Their relations had been fair to middling in the early days before becoming openly conflictual in the past few months.

The president's relationship with de Chanterelle was typical of all his personal contacts. Tibrac was a *homo politicus, par excellence.* All his relations were political, and therefore, all his friendships were tainted by politics and consequently sordid. De Chanterelle was a case in point. He was an old friend of Tibrac's, going back to their days at l'ENA - the elite *Ecole Nationale d'Administration* that moulded French politicians along carefully defined lines, teaching them all the most important skills needed to prepare the country's political and economic future – namely rhetoric and manipulating statistics.

Although they had lost sight of one another for many years, two years earlier the president had named de Chanterelle prime minister in a last ditch attempt to rally support across the widest spectrum possible. After all, rallying support out of thin air was an intrinsic part of Tibrac's political genius.

The president's lifelong career in politics provided a beautiful example of despotic power games, complete with scandals and bad choices. Yet somehow he had always survived the accusations of bribery, shady dealing and illegal electoral financing. He'd managed this because there had always been someone else on hand to get axed instead of Tibrac. There had always been a fall guy. This abracadabrantesque political manoeuvring had resulted in one major drawback. By the time he managed to get elected President, after thirty years of morally assassinating the opposition and close collaborators alike, Tibrac had decimated his entourage from the political class.

This might have proven problematic for a less creative politician. Not for Tibrac. He knew how to turn adversity to his advantage. When it came time to name a Prime Minister untainted by the schemes and intrigues of the past, Tibrac just chose his candidates from outside the realm of politics. During his five-year presidency, he had named three Prime Ministers. None of who were politicians. The first was a high-ranking civil servant, the second was a top businessman and number three, de Chanterelle, was a professional diplomat. They were all people who had served their country in various ways but who had never been elected in their lives. This worked in the President's favor. None of his PMs were tainted by allegations of political corruption.

On top of that, the three men had one other redeeming quality in common. They were all people who would do as they were told without showing too much personal initiative because that was precisely what they had been trained to do: Apply policies decided higher up the ladder. In other words, carry out Tibrac's covenant. And that, of course, was why de Chanterelle had begun to lose favor with the President. Politics had grown on the PM. He had become too autonomous. He had shown too much initiative. He had pursued his own convictions and drawn up his own agenda. In short, he'd been agreeing with rival factions, not sticking close enough to Tibrac's aims.

Dukrin watched as the President gave one final sad wave to the group of journalists and ducked into the back seat of his black chauffeur driven Renault Safrane. Less than a minute later the hot line phone on her desk rang and her hand jumped to grab it.

* * *

Only one voice ever came over that line. *"Monsieur le Président,"* Dukrin said, trying to keep her voice even, hiding the annoyance not to mention the relief at finally catching the man.

"Chère Madame." Dukrin winced. Why couldn't he use her proper title like everyone else? She was 'Madame le Directeur Général'. Why did he insist on addressing her as if she were his cleaning lady? Two words from the man and she was already seething. "What can I do for you this morning?" he asked with no trace of the pathos he'd been showing the TV cameras thirty seconds earlier. The man was such a bullshitter. What did he fucking think he could do for her this morning? Come over for tea and homemade cupcakes?

Dukrin didn't like the president. She didn't like his politics, but then she didn't really like anyone's politics. Moreover, she didn't like him as a person. The way he ran the country was bad enough. The way he behaved with her was enraging. She knew he didn't take her seriously. He was constantly sending his Interior Minister to interfere in her operations. Making her redefine policies just when the old ones were starting to show results. He'd never shown the slightest sign of wanting to work productively with her. Instead, he treated her like she was someone's wife who had inexplicably taken over her husband's office and affairs. She knew she wasn't viewed as a proper associate. She was made to feel out of place among the lords of the court. For God's sake, the first time they met, the man had kissed her hand. *Enfin merde!* What century did he think he was in?

The only thing Tibrac understood about gender equality was that it made good press. Being the able media manipulator he was, he worked with that. When he was first elected President, he'd made a big song and dance about naming as many women as possible to senior posts in the government. Ministers, spokeswomen, heads of commissions. You name it. He brought in the skirts. Then he held a huge press conference to inaugurate his broad-minded initiative. Photo shoots of Tibrac with his harem. The photos had been pasted everywhere from *Elle* to *Paris Match* to *Le Monde*. Huge double-page spreads of a congregation of well-dressed powerful women. It was a good photo op that stuck in the minds of voters – as it was supposed to. The truth of the matter was that within six months of his election, he had replaced all but two of those thirty-eight women with men. Four years on, Dukrin was the only one still standing.

As much as she disliked the man, the head of intelligence remained cool as an April morning whenever she spoke with Tibrac. Today was no exception. She was just as disposable as the other thirty-seven female ministers and advisors who had been discreetly dismissed before they'd had time to accomplish anything. If she didn't want to end up like them, she had to hold back the anger erupting inside. That was not a problem; she'd had years of practice at hiding her emotions. She hadn't got where she was by tearing into powerful men. Success demanded a clever combination of determination and fawning. If the president was going to beat around the bush, she could play the understatement game, too. "I was a little concerned about the information you gave the media this morning, Mr. President," she said meekly. "Not to mention the order to remove evidence from the wall at Val-de-Grace."

"Ah?" Tibrac breathed with carefully constructed surprise. Dukrin could hear the sarcasm in his voice. She would have liked to send him a spoonful of arsenic for his morning coffee.

"You've put us in a delicate position, Mr. President," she continued, using the same cautiously compiled calm.

"How so, *Chère Madame*?" If there had been a hidden camera in her office, the president would have seen her scowling at the phone base, shaking her head. Dukrin hadn't expected him to apologize for inventing the story about the overdose. She knew better than to expect him to apologize for anything. Apologies weren't part of his social makeup. He was the kind of person who would tread on your foot at a cocktail party, then snarl at you for having your foot in the way. Apologies were unheard of. But from there to pretending he didn't know what she was talking about was quite a distance. He was trying his damnedest to make a fool of her.

What she ached to say was: *"You gave the media false information about the Prime Minister's death. Not misleading information. Blatantly false information."* As it was, she swallowed her pride, as she did every time she spoke with this bastard, and laid out the facts in the most diplomatic way she could think of. "Mr. President, this morning I sent an officer from the UCLAT to Val-de-Grace to start investigating. Four hours later, you held a press conference and announced that the Prime Minister's death was accidental rather than criminal. That puts my officer in an extremely delicate position. It means I have, in a sense, asked him to carry out an investigation that doesn't exist. How can we search for clues if there's not been a crime? How can we ask witnesses to come forward without telling them what they're supposed to have witnessed?" She wanted to add, *"How can we ask hospital staff to clean brain tissue off the walls if there hasn't been a murder,"* but she reined herself in before any irreversible damage could be done.

"Mais Madame," Tibrac answered, falsely bewildered. "I was simply doing what you asked me to do."

All the rage that had been rushing around Dukrin's mind instantly dissipated. Sh'd been ready for just about any explanation except that one. Her train of thought derailed and she found herself struggling to remember what she had wanted to say next. The only sound she was able to produce was a choked "Mr. President?"

Slick as ever, Tibrac was ready with his repartee. That was what Dukrin hated most about the man; he always had the upper hand. What he did best was manoeuvre. And what he was doing now was manoeuvring admirably. If they gave out medals for the most imaginative, twisted lying, Tibrac would win the gold. The words rolled off his tongue as if he were discussing something as banal as dinner arrangements. "During our conversation this morning you appealed to me to keep any information about what had happened as discreet as possible. You asked me not to mention the possible link to the catacombs in order to avoid panic. You said you wanted your investigators to be able to act freely, without hindrance from the media or the military." The Director General of Intelligence was still grappling to figure out what the president was implying. She remembered their conversation perfectly. She'd appealed for discretion, but surely she hadn't told him to lie.

"Yes," Dukrin answered. She could hear her voice faltering. Losing some of its conviction. "What I meant was that I wanted my investigators to be able to proceed unhampered to carry out the investigation at Val-de-Grace. I didn't want trouble from the military over jurisdictional issues." Dukrin had just wanted to hustle the investigation along without getting stuck in a quagmire of in-fighting.

"Yes, well the military versus police jurisdiction is the key problem, isn't it?" said Tibrac, a little too cryptic for Dukrin's liking. She knew the President well enough to realize he was trying to make a point. She just couldn't figure out what the hell point it was.

"I would have thought that military jurisdiction was a minor problem compared with the PM's assassination," she said.

Something vaguely resembling a laugh or a cough came down the line, quickly followed by Tibrac's response. "I'm referring to the catacomb issue, Madame Dukrin," Tibrac purred. "It's a little embarrassing, isn't it?"

Dukrin was still drawing a blank. The catacombs were a complication. Not an embarrassment. "I don't know why it should be," she said. "The quarry brigade does a good job with limited means. We should be able to…"

"I wasn't referring to the quarry brigade. I'm referring to the opinion you gave on the *Clavreul Report* a few months ago." Red flags started going off in Dukrin's mind as they did every time she heard mention of Senator Clavreul. But her failure to come up with any immediate reply summoned Tibrac to continue. "*The Clavreul Report on Subterranean Safety.*" He paused for effect. "It went into great detail on the pressing need for increased security below strategic buildings – Val-de-Grace, among them."

Dukrin sat bolt upright. She had just understood what she was up against. Like a hare cornered in a field of hunters, her muscles tensed as she began translating each veiled threat uttered by the President. Because that was exactly what he was doing. He was threatening her. Their conversation was no longer about a police investigation at Val-de-Grace. It was about their careers – hers and his.

The details of the *Clavreul Report* came flooding back to her. Back in December, during the annual ritual of civil unrest, student riots and worker protests in the run-up to Christmas, Tibrac had sent over a report asking her to read it and give her opinion. The document had been a near hysterical treatise on the strategic danger posed by the catacombs and their potential use for terrorist activity. There had been seemingly endless pages listing key danger points and drawing doom-filled prophecies claiming that the police were helpless to enforce law and order underground. It had been exactly the kind of tripe she expected from a report with Clavreul's name on it. Demagogic scare mongering.

The solutions proposed in the report had been two-fold. First: fill in a major part of the old quarries by concrete injection. Second, put the land below Val-de-Grace under military jurisdiction to be patrolled as part of the war on terror. The latter suggestion had naturally annoyed Dukrin. Although she liked to think she always put her professional responsibilities ahead of her personal ambitions, she had worked damn hard to get where she was and she didn't like to see her powers cut. Handing over responsibility for the catacombs, and by extension everything under the city, would have undermined her powers considerably by shrinking her sphere of influence and action. Because that's what would have happened. It would have started with Val-de-Grace. Then they would have extended military powers to the entire subterranean network. The catacombs, the metro, the reservoirs, the canals. It would all be put under military control. And she wasn't about to let that happen while she was in charge of security and intelligence activity.

In any case, the report had been too outrageous to take seriously. That was her personal opinion. It was also the opinion of the two specialists she'd contacted for feedback. Fair enough, one of those specialists had been Captain Ferry who, as head of the cataflics, didn't have what you could call an objective take on the situation. If the report had been angling for extra manpower for the police, he might have supported it. But being as the aim was to get the military involved in policing the quarries, he had disregarded it, not wanting to see his powers lessened either. The other expert she consulted had been a civil engineer with no stake in the matter. Of course she hadn't been able to share all the information in the confidential report, but the expert had been convinced that the general tone was obsessive and not worth following up. So she had sent a message back to Tibrac saying that the cataflics could be counted on to oversee security in the catacombs and that the question wasn't worth pursuing.

She was now living to regret her refusal to give up some of her power.

"I take it you're holding me responsible for what happened this morning," she said, picking up a pencil and tapping it nervously on her desk.

"Not at all. No," Tibrac's voice rallied encouragingly. He was obviously pleased she'd caught on so quickly. "You're an important team player. We wouldn't want to lose you," he said. "It's just a shame we've got into such a sticky situation." The geniality was slipping from his voice as quickly as it had arrived. Each word sounded more ominous than the previous. "Bad decisions have got us into this mess. Clearly the *Clavreul Report* should have been acted upon. It wasn't. I have a letter from you stating your opinion that the issue didn't need pursuing." That was just like Tibrac. Hold on to every memo and letter that could reduce his responsibility. Dukrin listened carefully. Waiting for him to divulge whatever it was he had up his sleeve. "If the press were to make a link between your failure to act on the report and what happened to de Chanterelle, they would hold a lynching." Dukrin felt bitterness burning in her gut. *Her failure to act. Her failure to act.* Who the hell was the head of the armed forces? Whose job was it to ensure national security? The bloody president's, that's whose. Her opinion was nothing but that: an opinion.

But Tibrac was smooth. He would know how to make all this look like it was her fault. Make no mistake. She had to do exactly what he said or else she would be taking early retirement.

She listened intently as the President continued his explanation. "On the other hand, if the media don't know about the assassination, then they won't know about the catacombs and therefore they won't be talking about a security lapse."

Before she could disagree, Tibrac had already begun ironing out the pitfalls. "Of course, sooner or later, the press will discover the truth. But by holding back that information for a short time, we can make the situation work to our advantage instead of against us. The main thing is to find the murderer quickly."

Dukrin couldn't believe she was hearing this. "That may be so. Unfortunately the conditions you've set up for us won't make catching the criminals any easier."

"What are you talking about?" Tibrac snapped, no longer making any effort to sound suave. "I've arranged things so that you won't have anyone interfering. The fact that the press is reporting an accidental death rather than an assassination leaves you total freedom to act. The journalists are busy writing unforeseen obituaries and questioning the safety of curare based anaesthetics. There won't be anyone tripping up your men or slowing them down asking too many questions. At least not for a few days. They're too busy combing the halls of all the local hospitals looking for anaesthetists to interview."

Although Dukrin didn't always get on with the media she wasn't ready to pretend they were brain dead. "That's not entirely true, Mr. President. My phone's been ringing all morning with calls from *France Presse*, *France Télévision* and a couple of the big newspapers. There are already rumors about assassination. The news is out."

"Of course there are rumors. There always are. They're easily brushed off. The internet is rampant with conspiracy theories. All you need to do is deny them."

The head of intelligence wasn't so sure. A mistake could, in some cases, be pardoned. Outright lying was harder to get around. Tibrac wanted to lie because afterwards he could pin the lying on her. She, on the other hand, would just dig herself in deeper if on top of ignoring the *Clavreul Report*, she now started fiddling the facts. "I'm ready to assume responsibility for my decision on the *Clavreul Report* if it's the only way to ensure a transparent investigation for my men," she offered.

"I'm not."

There it was. At least she'd got him to say it. He wasn't trying to protect her career. He was setting her up to fall if the truth about the assassination came out too soon. He was protecting himself. It wasn't her fault the *Clavreul Report* hadn't been acted upon. He should have made the decision himself. So he was setting her up as the scapegoat. Their political necks were on the line and if someone had to take the chop, Tibrac wanted her to go first.

"And in any case," the President continued, "transparency is perhaps not the best approach in such a delicate case. May I remind you of the issue you raised with me after the Courneuve affair."

Once again Dukrin found herself floundering on the edge of dumbstruck, protesting politely. "Mr. President, I don't know what you're referring to."

"I think you do. The Courneuve round up," Tibrac's voice answered with a mocking undertone. "Your concerns about a possible leak between some of your own operatives and criminal groups."

The Courneuve round up, she repeated to herself. She had almost forgotten about that. Eight or nine months back she'd been uneasy about the results of a sting operation. A team had been sent out to arrest a group of militants with links to terrorist organizations. The round-up hadn't netted as many people as anticipated. Only about half the projected number. There had been concern about a possible leak. Collusion between the police and the militants. She'd mentioned it to the President during a routine meeting. But nothing had ever come of it. All subsequent operations had gone smoothly so she'd put it out of her mind.

Tibrac hadn't. It was precisely the kind of useful titbit he squirreled away in case it came in handy later. The kind of information that helped make other people look incompetent, other services responsible for screw ups. But once again, Dukrin couldn't follow the president's reasoning. "I fail to see what that has to do with the current situation."

"I would have thought it was obvious," Tibrac cooed smoothly. "The fewer investigators informed about the full details of the case, the less chance we'll come up against another leak." Tibrac waited for a moment, giving Dukrin a chance to gauge the full depths of his twisted reasoning before doing his summing up. "Madame, I expect you to keep all information concerning this case on a strictly need-to-know basis. Do you understand?"

She understood perfectly. She needed to find the perpetrators or else her head would roll. She had shown bad judgement on the Clavreul report. Following the assassination, she had asked the president to lie in order to cover up that bad judgement. And to top things off, her services were incompetent and infiltrated by criminals. It was her third strike.

If the truth about de Chanterelle was uncovered too soon, the script had been written to make her look like the weak link responsible for the death. The only way to survive was to make herself and the services in her charge look competent. What mattered now was solving the case and doing it fast.

Yet again, Tibrac had astutely manoeuvred himself into a position where his political future was ensured. If anything went wrong, if the investigation didn't provide satisfactory results, she would take the blame both for the Prime Minister's assassination and the police's failure to bring in the killer.

Tibrac had to be one of the biggest bastards she'd ever met. And coming from someone who had met all of the most loathsome murderers in the country over the past thirty years, that was saying a lot.

"It can't be that complicated, Madame," he concluded patronizingly. "How many groups have the skills and the capacity to break into Val-de-Grace?"

Twelve hours ago, Dukrin would have answered that question with a resounding "None". As it was, that was no longer a choice.

She needed results and she needed them fast. She estimated that it would take the press about forty-eight hours to get a clear take on what had really happened. If she didn't have a credible suspect before then, her career was over. She would be selling kebabs from a portable stand this time next year.

18

The Seine River flows from east to west through the center of Paris separating the city into the Left and Right Banks. Pinpointed at the heart of this bisecting line the *Ile de la Cité* marks the birthplace of the modern city. At one end of the island, Notre-Dame Cathedral whispers to passers-by of the role of Art, Literature and the Church in the construction of modern France. At the other end, the *Palais de Justice* towers regally over land that was once home to Roman governors and Merovingian kings. And tucked in the courthouse's southern-most wing along the Quai des Orfèvres, the French judicial police have their headquarters. This is where interviews with suspected criminals take place. This is also where Sadiqi had come to get a photofit on the de Chanterelle killer. Unsuccessfully.

Against the backdrop of Gothic spires the inspector was grappling with a sense of impotence. His shoes hammered out his frustration as he stomped across the courtyard towards his car. His investigation was going nowhere. He had no suspect, no witness and no hope.

Despite all the modern technology available, it was impossible to produce a portrait of a suspect without some good old-fashioned witnesses. Unfortunately that's precisely what was lacking – witnesses either human or virtual. True enough, the video footage from Porte d'Orléans metro station had provided a glance of the person who was his most likely suspect. Wearing both sunglasses and a fishing cap pulled down over his eyes, not to mention too many clothes for a 30°C morning, Sadiqi had singled out his Number 1 suspect amid the mass of morning commuters. That was about the full extent of the information he'd been able to draw from the footage.

There was no way of producing a photo portrait of the killer because they didn't have enough data to work from. The video technician had given it her best shot, trying to extrapolate something from the limited info on the recording. Except there was too much extrapolation and not enough fact to build on. The finished portrait was entirely useless unless the suspect was stupid enough to spend the rest of his life walking around Paris with the same cap and Raybans.

The wasted time was problematic. Fair enough, getting the photofit done was just standard procedure. The problem was, this wasn't a standard investigation. In any normal investigation, Sadiqi would have made a public appeal for witnesses from Porte d'Orléans station to come forward and give details about anyone they'd noticed behaving suspiciously that morning – details about the suspect's appearance, anything special about his behavior, information about where he had got off the metro... Although that was still possible, it was a lot trickier in this non-investigation.

Sadiqi had been told that Tibrac had a way of disregarding specialist input; doing whatever he damn well felt like. Until today the cop had never had to deal personally with the man's whims. Not that the president had ploughed ahead unthinkingly. He had thought it all out; he just hadn't consulted anybody before acting. According to Dukrin the aim of the cover up was to assist the investigation by confusing the criminals. Cut them off from the possibility of following the case in the news. Far from aiming to isolate the counter-terrorist brigade, the president had encouraged Dukrin to mobilize extra investigators to round up suspects from the underworld and hold them for questioning. Discreetly. That was the key word. All this was to be done away from the prying cameras of the media.

The investigator took a deep breath in a last ditch attempt to strengthen himself. It didn't work. The president's strategy was full of shit. It was all well and fine wanting to limit the case's visibility, but it might have been a good idea for Tibrac to check with Dukrin before testing his theory. This wasn't the 1950s anymore. The public demanded transparency. Twisted tactics often produced twisted results. Fair enough, journalists waiting for the latest feedback on an investigation made a lot of phone calls and stuck microphones in your face a little too often. On the other hand, journalists who unearthed a cover-up were far more dangerous. Of the two options, the first was a safer long-term strategy.

Not that Sadiqi had much information worth sharing. In fact, if he had to call a press conference this second, he would have absolutely nothing to say. He didn't have any leads and worse yet he didn't have any great brainwaves about what to investigate next.

Crossing the parking lot, he could feel the late morning sunshine radiating off the cars around him. And when he pulled open the quasi-molten metal door of his little Renault, a blast of sweltering heat erupted from inside. Sadiqi would hardly have noticed if the plastic seats started dripping out onto the sidewalk. He leaned into the furnace and opened the passenger door to get some air circulating.

While the car was breathing, the cop took a step away from the oven and grabbed another nicotine candy.

He'd made his way back to the parking lot, not because he needed to go anywhere (quite frankly he had no idea what to check next) but because his car provided a reassuring presence. This was where he liked to come to think. The driver's seat was like a mobile office – a workspace in transit. A place where he could gather his thoughts as he moved from stage to stage of his investigations. Today, the heat made it impossible for him to climb in behind the steering wheel so he stood beside the door reflecting on what he should do next.

He could go back to Val-de-Grace and see if anything new had turned up. (But that would be a waste of time. Lalanne had his number and Sadiqi was confident the general would call if they found anything.) He could go to HQ and check if Dukrin had been holding back any information. (That wasn't a tempting idea either because it meant letting her know that he was working in the dark. That he had absolutely no leads.) The only alternative he felt even remotely enthusiastic about pursuing was to go home and have a shower, which might possibly awaken him from what he hoped was merely heat induced torpor and not terminal brain malfunction.

He was within grasping distance of opting for the shower when his phone buzzed.

"*Sadiqi. J'écoute,*" he chanted.

"*Salut Khalid, c'est Alex,*" a genial voice boomed down the line. Sadiqi reflected that this particular voice had no right to be so cheerful. Alexandre Trémont was a colleague; a fellow investigator from the counter-terror brigade. He should have known that the Val-de-Grace case was a headache and that Sadiqi was the one with the migraine. "Dukrin told me to call you."

"To harass me?"

"To help you. I've got some news that might be linked to Val-de-Grace."

Sadiqi bit into the candy and let the pleasant effects of the nicotine course through his body. A whisper of relief had just crept into his life.

19

The buzz he had been feeling for most of the morning was fading and the Nightingale was starting to feel the need for sleep. The timing was right. He was used to a stop-and-go rhythm. Charging ahead for hours then lying down to rest wherever he happened to be. Now he was about to get two hours' beauty sleep. Which was more than enough for him to recharge until the end of the day.

The place he had come to for his break was a cinema – chosen for its faults rather than its qualities. The Nightingale wanted a foreign-language film so that the dialogues wouldn't keep him awake. And it had to be a small, low budget cinema – no surveillance cameras and no one to notice him. The resulting choice was an artsy cinema, with one lonely employee doing everything from selling tickets to changing film reels or dvds or whatever the hell they used to project films these days. The movie playing was some Danish garbage that, according to the poster on the billboard outside, was all about the human condition.

Whatever that was.

It didn't matter. As the Nightingale stepped through the swinging doors into the cinema, he knew he'd made a good choice. There were only half a dozen other people in the place. Not a roaring success.

The fact that anyone at all wanted to watch this brand of intellectual masturbation amazed the Nightingale. He wasn't much of a film buff, but when he did go, he wanted something entertaining, and full of action. Then again, perhaps he wasn't the only one who had paid to come in for a lunchtime nap in an air-conditioned room. Between the inevitably classical soundtrack and the boring voices of upmarket culture, the Nightingale expected to be asleep within a few minutes of the opening titles.

But there was something he had to do first.

The entrance doors opened onto the back of the cinema but instead of making his way to one of the tattered red armchairs, he headed straight for a door halfway down the aisle. Two large carrier bags rustled against his pant legs as he pushed open the door with the luminescent "toilettes" sign above it. Once locked in the cubicle, he started stripping off his polo shirt and chinos.

When the stores had opened that morning, the Nightingale had transformed into quite the busy shopper in one of Montmartre's low-budget clothing shops. It hadn't been easy to find something that looked sharp in the forest of polyester wedding gear. Fortunately his athletic build played in his favor. Everything looked good on him. And it wasn't as if he needed something that would still look sleek in a week's time. He just needed it for one afternoon.

A couple of trailers followed by some mindlessly sexy ads for coffee, perfume and ice cream played in the projection room while the Nightingale slipped into his new shirt and suit then transferred his Beretta and silencer from his backpack to a laptop case he'd picked up that morning. The gun fit snugly into the central pouch.

The redhead drew the lock back and stepping out of the cubicle paused to evaluate the overall effect in the mirror. Not bad. But he'd forgotten something. He reached back into the bottom of the pink carrier bag and produced a small package. Reading glasses. At least that's what they looked like. In fact the round wire frames were fashion gear, not vision wear. Plain plastic lenses. In his case, they were disguise wear.

Now fully transformed, the Nightingale took a longer look at himself in the mirror. His eyes hardened with satisfaction. It was amazing how much a pair of glasses and a suit could change a person's appearance.

As the first powdery strains of the movie's title music wafted from the loudspeakers, he returned to the darkened cinema and shuffled to a chair in the back row. A good spot. A comfortable spot. The music drifting out of the sound system was vaguely grating but he was an expert at ignoring noise. Eighteen years of barracks life had seen to that. Hunching down in his seat, he could feel a slight breeze blowing down from the AC, lulling him into total relaxation.

In that state, on the edge of sleep, some people might have found themselves thinking either about the man he had killed that morning or the one he was going to kill later that afternoon. Not the Nightingale. He was both a true professional and a philosopher. He knew better than to question his orders. In any case, he had absolutely no regrets about killing de Chanterelle. The man was a politician. And although the Nightingale had spent most of his life working for politicians (or perhaps because he had spent most of his life working for politicians), he considered the breed no better than scum. This afternoon's target was probably from the same rich scumbag.

Instead of worrying about it, he closed his eyes and drifted off to sleep.

20

Parking in the Latin Quarter was hell at any time, so Sadiqi didn't bother even looking for a *bona fide* spot. He just grabbed whatever space he could find near the *Petite Périgourdine* then flipped down the passenger seat sun visor with the word "POLICE" printed in large letters. With the Pantheon staring down from the top of rue Valette, he stepped nonchalantly through the café's floor-to-ceiling windows that had been opened to provide diners with a little fresh air and a smattering of exhaust fumes from the road outside.

"*Bien joué.* Nice parking job," Trémont remarked, getting up to shake hands and motioning to the car carefully balanced between the bus lane and a flower shop, with two wheels on the sidewalk.

"It's ecological parking," Sadiqi explained, with no sign of humor. "The longer you spend driving around looking for parking, the greater your CO_2 emissions. By cutting my search time, I'm helping to reduce global warming."

Trémont nodded his approval and signalled to his colleague to take a seat.

If anyone in the café had been observing the two men, they would have had a hard time guessing they were colleagues. Nothing in their appearance suggested they had much in common. Sadiqi, with his close-fitting jeans and t-shirt revealing a well-tended body, personified the victory of a steady workout over imminent middle age. Trémont, on the other hand, was decked out in a purposefully casual suit and open necked shirt that was sufficiently loose fitting to hide a burgeoning paunch. Yet, regardless of the physical evidence, the older man radiated an impression of overall good health missing from Sadiqi's tense manner. "You should try sleeping sometimes, Khalid. It would do you a world of good."

"I keep trying, but the phone keeps ringing."

Trémont was shaking his head emphatically. "Nah. You're not trying hard enough. It's all about making yourself less indispensable," he wisecracked. "Performing below capacity is an art that can add twenty years to your life. You'd avoid some of the shit cases. I hear the one Dukrin gave you today is quite something."

"No. Nothing serious. The Prime Minister just had an allergic reaction to his anaesthetic."

"Yeah, I heard that one too. And they say politicians don't have a sense of humor."

"What about you?" Sadiqi asked, pushing aside the knife and fork on the table to make room for his elbows. The tiny piece of particle board that would serve as their lunch table put hardly any distance between the two men, but they still took the precaution of leaning closer together to keep their conversation out of earshot of the other diners. Not that anyone was likely to overhear. The Latin Quarter was so full of foreign tourists it was doubtful any of the people at neighboring tables would be able to understand a word they said even if they were listening. "You said you had some important news?" Sadiqi prompted.

Before Trémont had time to answer he was cut off by a waiter dressed in a black suit and a floor-length white apron, proffering menus.

Sadiqi gave the lunchtime specials a quick once over. The heat favored neither the *cassoulet* nor the *confit de canard*, so he settled on a honey and garlic seared duck breast, accompanied by a glass of Cahors. Trémont overruled the glass of wine in favor of a bottle, and opted for both the *foie gras* and the *confit*.

As soon as the waiter had swept away the menus, the two men returned to business.

Trémont scooped a couple of papers out of his leather briefcase and handed them to his colleague. "Just remember: I said I had stuff that might help you. I never said you'd like it."

Ignoring the ominous warning, Sadiqi plunged right into reading. The first sheet was from Cochin Hospital and the line of type below the letterhead was printed in bold capital letters: CASE SUMMARY FOLLOWING THE DEATH OF MADAME JOSIANE DELATIER, AGE 87. "What's this? Some long lost aunt who's died and left you some money? What's it got to do with me?" he asked.

Trémont had gone back to leafing through his briefcase but mumbled, "Humor doesn't suit you. Just read it."

Sadiqi did as he was told, discovering a report written in a concise professional language.

> Madame Delatier has been a long term patient in the hospital's geriatric closed ward since February 2015. Although she suffered from dementia her physical health was good for a woman of her age until she became ill with flu-like symptoms late on the evening of Monday, June 17th. After showing signs of improvement following the introduction of antibiotics, Mme. Delatier began to have trouble breathing on the night of June 18th. Dyspnoea was accompanied by a grating sound during inspiration, due to upper respiratory obstruction. Thoracic x-ray revealed a widened mediastinum. The patient was tachycardic when admitted to intensive care on Wednesday afternoon, her heartbeat reaching 146 bpm at rest. She went into shock at 8 PM and died at 3 AM on Thursday, June 20th. Signed: Doctor D-T. Nguyen

The waiter arrived with the Cahors just as Sadiqi was finishing the report so the wine tasting was left to Trémont. Ignoring the familiar ritual, Sadiqi skimmed over the second document typed on exactly the same letterhead paper as the first.

> Case summary following the death of Madame Yvette Lebon, aged 43.
>
> Mme. Lebon was admitted to emergency at 5 PM on Wednesday, June 19th, suffering from severe respiratory distress and cyanosis accompanied by generalized myalgia. She was taken to intensive care at 7 PM where she complained of chest pain. At that time, her resting heartbeat was 154 bpm accompanied by diaphoresis. Chest radiography revealed enlarged mediastinal lymph nodes. Her state degenerated throughout the evening. The patient went into shock just after 10 PM and died at 2:36 AM on Thursday, June 20th. Signed: Doctor D-T. Nguyen.

Although Sadiqi wasn't familiar with all the medical jargon, he got the gist of what had happened. He looked up at Trémont who was sipping his wine calmly. The terrorist brigade didn't spend a lot of time hanging out in hospitals. Trémont's presence at the head of the investigation pointed to a limited number of possible causes. The most deadly being the most likely. Stretching towards his colleague his lips barely moved as he whispered: "Anthrax?"

Trémont put down his glass and leaned so close their heads nearly touched. "Pulmonary anthrax."

"You've got spores?"

"You'd better believe it. Someone went around three hospitals last Sunday distributing packages filled with powder: Cochin, the Salpêtrière and Lariboisière. A total of thirty-five patients have been isolated in intensive care with similar symptoms."

"How are they doing?"

"Degenerating quickly. The medical team estimates we're likely to have a 95-100% mortality rate despite antibiotic treatment." Trémont gave his colleague a couple of seconds to absorb this information before continuing. "At least four wards were infected, with three packages left in each. There's a risk there might be more. It's possible the news has been covered up in some hospitals or that certain department heads thought it was a hoax and didn't have the powder tested. As far as we can tell, most of the packages were left in rooms with double if not triple or quadruple occupancy."

Sadiqi's brain started drawing up the scenario. Trying to visualize how the job had been pulled off. "Do we have any idea who left it?"

"No. Not really. Someone just walked in and left presents for people. Boxes of chocolates, books, birthday cards. All laced with anthrax."

"Patients don't just accept presents from people they don't know," Sadiqi protested

"They do if they've got Alzheimer's and don't recognize any of their visitors."

The picture was taking shape. "Not too fussy about who they accept presents from."

"You've got it. And this could get a lot worse. *Premièrement,*" said Trémont, his elbow propped on the table and his upturned thumb waving back and forth to enumerate a first problem, "We've not even reached the end of the incubation period."

"Which is?"

"One to seven days. The cases we've seen so far are just the first. We know the packages were delivered on Sunday – it's Thursday today. In other words, some patients have started to show symptoms of infection but others are still incubating. That's the second thing," Trémont lifted his index finger to accompany the thumb, "overall we're looking at a high number of potential victims. There are the patients themselves, their roommates, any friends or family that visited the room after the package was opened, medical and cleaning staff..."

The number of cases multiplied in Sadiqi's head and one of the first things that struck him was the logistics of keeping the news secret. "How have you kept this out of the press?"

"Precisely because we're still in the incubation period," Trémont said. "Only the lab, the chief hospital administrators and the Intensive Care doctors know about the anthrax. A handful of patients and staff have been asking a lot of questions but we've not given the full story yet – we don't need them handing the news to relatives. People we suspect to be incubating have been put under observation – but they've been told it's to protect them from a possible superbug outbreak."

Sadiqi gave a bitter laugh. "You think they're going to be less scared by a superbug?"

"It's got nothing to do with how scared they are. The fact is that a superbug isn't news. There are outbreaks all the time. Nobody's going to call in the media to report it and even if they do, it's not going to bring in the journalists – they're too busy reporting on de Chanterelle's death and how the hospitals are coping with the heat wave victims."

The waiter reappeared with two heaped plates and the table fell silent. A small metal basket containing two-inch slices of baguette arrived to complete the table setting, then the waiter officially proclaimed the meal open with the magic words, "*Bon appetit*," before shooting off to serve another table.

Trémont picked up his knife and studied his plate before deciding whether to dig straight in to the foie gras or begin with the accompanying fig jam. He decided to mix the pleasures, placing a lump of liver on a corner of bread then spreading a dollop of jam on top. It was a fleeting moment of pleasure but he was fast to get back to business. "The fact is, the truth is going to get harder and harder to hide as more and more people start dying."

"Have fun with that," Sadiqi sympathized as he tucked in to his own meal.

"That's nothing. You've not heard the punch line yet." Trémont put down his fork, reached back into his briefcase and pulled out a third page on the same letterhead paper. "This is the cover letter that Dr.

N'guyen sent to the chief hospital administrator at Cochin along with the two letters you've just read." Sadiqi tasted a mouthful of duck before reaching out to accept the last document. Best to enjoy a little food before reading. Based on Trémont's lead-in, he figured the letter would probably spoil his appetite.

> Madame Blondel,
> Please find, herewith, copies of my reports concerning the deaths of two patients during the night. I think we can surmise that Mme. Delatier died as a result of exposure to the anthrax powder that was deposited in her ward last Sunday. It is for this reason that I am both concerned and perplexed by the death of Mme. Lebon. The symptoms she exhibited were almost identical to those of Mme. Delatier, yet she was not present in the hospital last weekend when the suspected infection occurred. According to her husband, up until early this week she had always been a healthy, fit woman and seldom manifested signs of illness. I leave you to draw your own conclusions and to take the necessary measures.
> Cordially,
> D-T. Nguyen.

When Sadiqi looked up from the letter, another piece of toast, generously spread with the pale ochre *foie gras* was hovering between his colleague's plate and mouth. "The second woman who died had never spent a day in hospital in her life," Trémont explained, "In principle she hadn't been exposed to the spores."

Tilting his head sideways, Sadiqi offered the only explanation he could think of. "So she didn't die of anthrax. It was just a bad flu."

Trémont savoured his *foie* reflectively. "Oh no. She died of anthrax. The question is, where did she come in contact with it?"

Sadiqi was familiar with Trémont's narrative style. He would eventually get to the point. He just liked unfolding facts as if he were some modern day Sherlock Holmes.

"We went to check out her house and her workplace. She was an auxiliary helper at Montaigne High School."

"Cleaning staff, you mean."

"That's right," Trémont nodded, lowering the next piece of toast he had prepared and leaning toward Sadiqi: "We collected three grams of anthrax off the school's kitchen floor."

"I guess she wasn't a very good cleaning lady," Sadiqi joked, trying to avoid the implications of what he'd just heard.

Trémont ignored the awkward humor. "Initial analyses show that both the anthrax from the hospital and the stuff from the school were from the same batch."

"Sounds like a clear link. But I'm still not sure this is supposed to concern me."

Trémont watched Sadiqi as he stabbed the next slice of duck off his plate. In a way it was a shame to ruin his colleague's lunch when he was obviously enjoying it. But business was business. "It's supposed to concern you because of how the stuff got into the school in the first place." He gave Sadiqi time to swallow. Wouldn't want him to choke on his meal. "We found a hole pierced in one of the school's walls."

"Someone injected in the powder from outside?"

"Someone injected in the powder from the *catacombs*."

Trémont watched as his colleague stopped eating and abandoned his fork on the side of his plate. He had known the news would kill Khalid's appetite. That was how the guy managed to stay so trim. For some reason, the bad news always put him off his food. Funny old world. The bad news had the opposite effect on Trémont. He always felt better if he ate.

21

Sadiqi folded his napkin and placed it under his fork. He had just lost his appetite.

This was more than an attack on the civilian population. It was an attack on a school. On children. Every parent's nightmare.

It was only the presence of one reassuring detail that calmed the sense of imminent disaster. "But high school classes are finished for the year. The schools are only open for exams at the moment. There aren't any cafeteria services, are there?" he asked.

"No. You're right. The kitchens have been closed – other than to school staff."

"So whoever did this made a mistake. He wanted to kill hundreds of kids; instead he only got one person."

Trémont shrugged. "Maybe he wasn't trying to kill. Maybe he was just trying to scare people."

"Scare who?"

"I'd say, scare the whole country. It's got all the hallmarks of a scare campaign. Hospitals, schools…"

"One school," Sadiqi corrected.

Trémont was shaking his head. "No, we think we've got a second vector of contamination. We're waiting for confirmation."

The knot in Sadiqi's stomach doubled. He pushed his plate away. "Which one?"

"If you wanted to wipe out the country's elite, where would you strike?"

Sadiqi didn't feel like playing Twenty Questions. "Just spit it out."

"Henri IV," Trémont answered, popping another mouthful of his entrée into his mouth.

As the words sank in, Sadiqi found his thoughts racing up the street to the famous high school barely a block away. Henri IV was the most prestigious school in the country. It moulded the country's most aspiring young minds, preparing them for the Ivy League of the French higher education system. Many of the country's political and industrial elite had been through the school. Parents considered it a great honor for their children to be accepted there; news that it had become a terrorist target would create panic.

"Anthrax spores at Henri IV High School?" Sadiqi murmured.

Trémont nodded. "We think so. We're still waiting for the lab results. What we do have is a very sick employee."

"Another cleaning woman?"

Trémont took a piece of bread out of the basket and smeared it with the remaining fig jam. "No." There was a dark knell to his voice. "The principal."

Wonderful. Sadiqi could see the media circus already. A dead cleaning lady was one thing to keep quiet. A dead principal was something else. Suddenly his day didn't seem so bad – relatively speaking that is. At least one of his colleagues was dealing with an equally inextricable mess. He picked up his glass, as if to propose a toast. "What can I say, Alex. My heart goes out." Despite the words of empathy, a sarcastic smirk stretched across his lips. "The media are going to have a field day when you announce an anthrax outbreak at Henri IV."

Trémont raised his own glass in response and returned the smile. "You mean when YOU announce it."

Sadiqi froze, his glass halfway to his mouth.

Trémont savoured his wine stoically before delivering the news. "Dukrin's convinced there's a major terrorist attack being launched via the catacombs. She said you suspected they were used to access Val-de-Grace. And we're reasonably certain they were used to access Montaigne. She's worried that what we've seen so far is small time and she wants the entire investigation centralized through you."

"When was this decided?"

"Just before I called you. She thought it would be better explained face-to-face rather than over the phone."

The mess at Val-de-Grace was convoluted enough. How could Dukrin possibly expect him to figure out the anthrax investigation at the same time? As always, she asked too much. "Does she have any reliable intelligence linking the two?"

"For starters, we checked with the quarry brigade about any strange occurrences in the catacombs recently. Off the top of his head, Captain Ferry mentioned that the other day his men had picked up a cataphile with a nasty foot wound."

The news left Sadiqi cold. "Kids get lost and injured down there all the time. They twist their ankles or fall down holes. Step on things they shouldn't have?"

"Like a loaded Beretta."

Sadiqi's train of thought crashed into a wall. "It's a bullet wound?"

"Not only that, judging from the kid's babblings, two of his friends have been even more seriously injured – possibly killed."

"And you think that's true?"

"It's starting to look very likely. Ferry confirmed that at least one other cataphile has been reported missing since Sunday."

This news didn't seem all that earth shattering to Sadiqi. Surely a missing cataphile didn't necessarily mean foul play; simply that someone had taken a wrong turn and hadn't found his way out yet. "Kids get lost down there all the time."

"That's true. But this missing cataphile isn't a kid. He's called André Zucchero." Trémont watched his colleague closely, waiting for some sign of recognition. None came. "You've not heard of him either? Nor had I but Ferry seems to consider him a catacomb star. The doyen of cataphiles. He goes by the nickname *Quartz*. He's published books on the subject with prefaces written by prefects and previous directors of the IGC. He knows the catacombs inside out."

"Quartz". Why did that sound so familiar? Who was it who had told him about cataphile pseudonyms? It only took Sadiqi an instant to sift through the morning's memories and then he was reaching into his shirt pocket and pulling out the flier the Canadian had shown him.

"*Qui a vu Snoopy, Bango et Quartz? Ils ont disparu le 15 juin.*" He handed the paper to his colleague.

Trémont looked at the words then half-shrugged, half-nodded. "Yes. That fits. Beside his underground adventures, Zucchero has a busy life above ground that includes a wife and three kids. When he goes off exploring, he lets the little family know when they can expect him back. Friday he headed off to a party in some place called 'the Z-Room'." As the waiter came by to clear away his plate, Trémont stopped to take a deep breath. "His wife reported him missing on Sunday. He'd promised to be back by Saturday afternoon."

"Good of him to provide such a strict timetable."

"He's a serious guy. Has a day job at the Ministry of Finance."

"Let me guess: High ranking civil servant."

"Medium ranking, but yeah, basically. He's also very active in a number of associations promoting subterranean culture – spelunking, catacombs, troglodyte dwellings in the Dordogne, caves in the North."

The picture was clear. It was very unlikely Zucchero had gone missing accidentally. Sadiqi felt a twinge of sadness for the man's wife and kids. Yet another widow. He filed his sadness away in one of the mental vaults he kept available for that purpose. "So that covers two out of three people from the flier."

"It also fits with what the injured kid says – Desjardins. It's hard to get a straight answer from him. I saw him this morning; he's delirious and completely incoherent. He was seriously dehydrated by the time he was pulled out of the catacombs and his foot was badly infected. He wasn't found until Tuesday. From what we've pieced together from the parents, he'd probably been underground since Friday night. And it's possible the injury dates back that far, too. It's hard to tell exactly what happened but it looks like these guys stumbled onto something they weren't supposed to see."

"Like an anthrax stockpile?" Sadiqi suggested.

"No. That's the whole point, isn't it? If they'd just come across a guy with a couple of grams of anthrax in his pocket, nobody would have noticed anything. If these guys were attacked, it was because they saw something bigger. Something much more obvious."

"Like what?"

"That's the question, isn't it? Whatever it was it was something big. Something visible. Something that couldn't be ignored or hidden."

A lull descended over the table, Sadiqi staring out the window, Trémont staring at Sadiqi. It was Sadiqi who finally spoke. "This is bullshit. We've got a few isolated incidents and suddenly it's being blown into a major organized terrorist operation."

Trémont's eyes locked with Sadiqi's. "I spoke with Foutriquet about an hour ago. The bullet that killed de Chanterelle and the one that was in my cataphile's foot were shot from the same gun. These aren't unrelated coincidences."

"You couldn't have started with that?"

"I was curious to see how long you'd try to fight the obvious."

Sadiqi wiped the back of his hand across his forehead. There was a thin film of perspiration. He would have liked to say it was the heat making him sweat, but it wasn't just that. There was danger out in the city and it was closing in. Still, he tried to rationalize it all. "Okay," he said. "So de Chanterelle and Desjardins are related. The link to the anthrax is a bit of a long shot though. Whoever left it didn't get into the hospitals via the catacombs."

"They didn't have to. It was easy enough just to walk in during visiting hours. But we're almost certain they got to Montaigne through the catacombs. Like I said, we found three holes in a kitchen wall pierced through from the catacombs. It needs confirming, but it's almost certain that's how the powder was administered."

"And Henri IV?"

"For the moment, the link to H4 is weak. In principle there are no catacombs under the school. Which would mean that whoever dumped the anthrax just walked in through the front gate. But that's not an easy thing to do. There's only one entrance and it's monitored by a fulltime custodian. Only students and parents with pre-arranged meetings are admitted."

Sadiqi wasn't convinced. "School custodians aren't exactly security guards. How many hostage takings have there been in schools over the past ten years." Off the top of his head, he could remember at least three cases of armed crazies walking into schools, holding children and teachers at gunpoint.

Trémont shrugged. "Well, if you don't like the catacomb theory for H4, it's now up to you to figure out what really happened. Dukrin wants her top guy on this case, and that's you. I don't ask questions, I just follow orders. You are now officially in charge of any trouble even remotely related to the catacombs." He picked up the bottle of Cahors, refilled his glass and took a deep gulp. "If you need me, I'll be hanging around the hospitals interviewing anthrax patients and their families to find out if they've seen anyone suspicious. Sounds like fun, doesn't it?"

Sadiqi noted the lightly veiled bitterness in his colleague's voice. After all, which was worse? Spending your day trying to find a killer in three hundred kilometers of underground tunnel or talking with terminal patients and their relatives? Either way you looked at it, it wasn't the kind of work most people would be willing to do.

Sadiqi raised his glass again. "To Dukrin and her talent for delegating shit jobs."

Trémont had already drained his glass before the toast was finished.

22

When the Senate was in session, the halls of the Luxembourg Palace flattered the Republic's political class with aristocratic pomp and finery. But during the summer recess, the red carpet and gilded ceilings became props without a show. When the senators disappeared off to their country houses so too did the horsetail hats, gold braid and drawn swords of the Republican Guard.

Like most of his colleagues, Senator Clavreul had plans to escape to the country as soon as he'd collected a few papers from his office. Making his way down the hallway, he reflected on how there was something restfully immoral about the way France came to a standstill between June and September. For two and a half months, the weather report took precedence over government policy in the minds and souls of Frenchmen. It was a time when politicians could easily slip legislation through parliament while the citizens lay on the beaches enjoying the latest thriller instead of following the news.

The Prime Minister's death was a perfect example. Officially this was supposed to be a day of national mourning, yet there were few signs that it was anything other than business as usual. Clavreul was certainly the only one who had bothered to don a black armband.

Of course, if more of Clavreul's colleagues had been around they would have found the armband an unlikely addition to the senator's usual wardrobe. Not because it was an outmoded sign of mourning. On the contrary, the senator was well-known for his attachment to old-fashioned traditions. What was considerably more surprising was the fact that the senator should show any sign of grief over de Chanterelle's death. He'd never been a fan of the Prime Minister's cautious politics aimed at social cohesion. When faced with the inevitable clatter of unionists protesting what they claimed was the government's neoliberal stance, de Chanterelle had always been too pliable. While Clavreul believed in a firm hand to rule (upheld by police reinforcements to scatter the mob if government policies proved unpopular), the late Prime Minister had gone in for the bipartisan negotiating tactics that were constantly bringing the country to a screeching halt.

Of course de Chanterelle wasn't the only politician guilty of weakening the country through endless discussions and dialogue. Compromise seemed to be the new plague sweeping the country. The situation in the Senate today was a case in point. At present the Upper House was controlled by the right-wing. Yet for some reason the Speaker had felt it necessary to invite Cédric Trouvé and his band of junior Bolsheviks in to hold their annual powwow in these hallowed halls.

Advancing down the corridor toward his office, Clavreul could hear noise rising up from the *Salle des Conferences* where the 30 VNG conference was planned for the following day. An uncontrollable urge began guiding him away from the staircase and toward the conference room.

On a normal day, the conference room was one of the Senator's favorite spots in the building. Bonaparte himself had overseen the decorating work that had transformed the vast hall into an exquisite example of Empire style. The room shimmered with gold and pulsed with red from the floors to the wall hangings to the moulded ceilings. Yet despite its magnificent size, the warm colors and the fireplaces created a feeling of coziness. Clavreul had spent many hours reading his newspaper in these plush velvet armchairs.

Not surprisingly the love he felt for the room made the dislike he felt for the people now populating it all the stronger. If there was one thing Clavreul hated more than a middle-of-the-road liberal, it was a left-wing intellectual. And if there was anything worse than a left-wing intellectual it was a roomful of left-wing intellectuals.

The massive wooden table in the center of the hall was surrounded by a horde of 25-year-olds who had organized themselves into an over-educated Fordist production line, busily sliding working papers and goodies into bags with the name and date of the conference stamped on the side in garish blue and yellow swirls. God awful freebies. There was probably a key ring and luminescent pen – possibly even a baseball cap for the idiots to enjoy.

Clavreul's eyes ran down the length of the room looking for the ringleader – the egregious Cédric Trouvé. Apparently he hadn't arrived yet. If he had, he would be easy to recognize by his cortege of groupies. The senator had never met the man in person but he had seen him often enough on TV rattling on about one cause or another. A man in a badly ironed suit with too much hair and far too many ridiculous ideas about saving the world. The kind of ideas that appealed to the young. And the people on hand were indeed mainly enthusiastic young hangers-on. Hoping to be initiated into the band. Dreaming of becoming part of Trouvé's clan of boy scouts with their secret handshakes and tireless lobbying.

The Luxembourg Palace deserved better. Instead, the sumptuous room with its gold leaf walls was now home to what looked like a village fête. Any moment now the organizing committee might start hanging balloons from the crystal chandeliers, barbecuing hot dogs in the hallway or taking down the Gobelins tapestries to use as picnic blankets. It was such a ridiculous generation, blind to the beauty around it. Scrambling to put Chinese made pens in Chinese made carrier bags. Pathetic. It was nothing short of an outrage to these sacred halls.

The time had come to end this sort of stupidity. The tide was changing. This couldn't be allowed to last much longer.

Clavreul turned and stamped off, leaving all that was wrong with France behind him.

23

For over five minutes, Sadiqi had been standing in a dingy hospital corridor watching a soap opera unravelling in Philippe Desjardins' private room. A mother and father crying at their son's bedside while the child rambled deliriously. It was a bad play in a tired décor.

The young man lying in the bed was neither small nor frail. On the contrary, he and his parents all looked like good strong members of the healthy, well-fed, organic-eating upper middle class. Exactly the kind of people who were probably most unprepared to survive whatever bad experience this kid had gone through. Despite his physical strength the boy looked wraithlike and haunted. Even as he lay resting in bed, his face muscles were taut and his hands trembled in knotted white knuckles.

Sadiqi had seen this before. He'd even seen a couple of colleagues in this state. Whatever the detailed diagnosis, in layman's terms the kid was having a nervous breakdown.

A tremor ran through the young man's body and the woman standing beside him moved forward to place her hand on his chest, as if to hold him down. Sure enough, a wild explosion followed.

"*Maman, Maman,*" the young man cried, pulling against his mother's restraining arms. His eyes were misted, unseeing, unfocused but the voice brayed out strong. "*Je l'ai vu. Je l'ai vu. Le Diable Vauvert. Le Monstre Vert. Il voulait me tuer. Il voulait nous tuer tous.*" Tears flowed down the young man face and his body seemed to shake from fear – or maybe exhaustion – as he clutched desperately at his mother's waist, causing her to rock precariously on the edge of the bed. Gently caressing the young man's hair with one hand the woman used the other for support, propping herself against the mattress to avoid being pulled over by his hysterical energy.

While Sadiqi's eyes observed the scene his brain focused on the words that had been howled several times over the past five minutes. "*I saw it. I saw it. The Vauvert Devil. The Green Monster.*" It sounded like complete gibberish. *Diable Vauvert.* The Vauvert Devil. The expression was familiar; it meant 'the back of beyond'. But the inspector couldn't understand what Desjardins meant. After all, you could say, "I have friends who've gone to live *au Diable Vauvert*"; I have friends who've gone to live 'at the back of beyond'. But there wasn't actually a devil. Nobody every claimed to 'have seen' the Vauvert Devil. So what did the kid mean? That he'd been so deep in the catacombs he'd lost his way? That he perhaps hadn't known where he was anymore? He'd been *au Diable Vauvert*? He'd been to the deepest reaches of the catacombs? It was a possibility. Not particularly convincing. As for the Green Monster, Sadiqi was at a loss.

Unlike the inspector, the young man's mother wasn't wasting her time trying to decrypt the message. Her full attention was given to rocking and reassuring her son. "He's gone. It's alright," she cooed.

Without warning, a desperate surge of energy washed over the young man as he locked her arm in his grip, staring wildly into her eyes. "He killed Quentin. And Quartz. They're dead," he whispered inconsolably as if terrified that by saying the words aloud he might bring the same misfortune on himself. "He killed them. The Green Monster."

"It's alright darling," the mother coaxed.

"He tried to kill me."

While the soap opera played out in the room, Sadiqi stopped a passing doctor to check if it would be alright to interview the young man. The doctor shrugged non-committally. "I'm not sure you'll get anything useful out of him. He's been asleep for most of the time since he arrived. That's changing a little now. He's awake more often, but delirious most of the time. His condition is *not* good. He was in an advanced state of dehydration when he was brought in. Not to mention a nasty infection in his foot."

"You said he's delirious most of the time. So some of the time he's okay?" Sadiqi asked hopefully.

The doctor swept back the folds his lab coat and placed his hands on his hips. He was tall and had that strange habit, common in many tall people, of hunching over slightly, as if this somehow made his height less noticeable. "His state has certainly improved. At times he's coherent. It's just that when he's coherent he's far less expansive. He becomes introspective. You're going to have trouble getting any sort of useful information out of him. Most of the time he's either talking nonsense or not talking at all. He's even fallen into catalepsy a couple of times. Just staring at the wall. He's not making the progress we'd hoped."

"But you're confident he's going to pull through."

The raised eyebrows and pursed lips suggested the diagnosis was far from certain. "We're a lot more hopeful than we were two days ago, but I can't promise anything. We're still worried about his foot. I think we've avoided amputation – but only just. By Monday we should have a better idea which way it's going to go. But even if the foot survives, it might be a while before his mental state stabilizes."

The cop hoped the doctor was being overly pessimistic. Desjardins was his best potential lead. He had to pull through. Sadiqi needed his insight. He needed to know what the kid knew

As the doctor headed down the hallway, the inspector turned his attention back to the scene in the bedroom. The seizure had passed and the young man's body was limp again, his eyes fixed on a window that opened onto an uninspiring view of a brick wall. Probably not the ideal landscape for someone with psychological problems. A lovely field of tulips blowing in the wind with bees buzzing around would have been more heartening.

Now that the young man was calmer, his father whispered something to the mother and began gently leading her out of the room. That was Sadiqi's cue.

When they'd almost reached the doorway, he moved toward them and broke into the cop routine. "Excuse me Sir, Madam. Khalid

Sadiqi, *Police Nationale*," he said, flashing his ID. "I realize this is very difficult but I'd like to ask you a few questions…" Trémont had already been in that morning, bothering these poor people but Sadiqi knew his invasion of their space would be tolerated, simply because it brought hope. The parents would be counting on the police to avenge the attack on their son. "I was outside the door a minute ago while your son was talking." 'Rambling' would have been a better word, but Sadiqi was doing his best to sound positive. "He mentioned two names: Quentin and Quartz. Do you know who they are?"

The man answered without hesitation. "Quentin's his best friend. I don't know about Quartz."

That was good news. Sadiqi already knew about Quartz-Zucchero: the star cataphile. This other guy, Quentin, was the one he needed to find out about. "Can you confirm whether or not anything has happened to Quentin? If he's missing?"

The two parents shot one another a glance before dropping their eyes to the floor. It was the mother who spoke. "No. I know all those things Philippe said about Quentin sound awful. But it can't possibly be true that he was killed by a monster, can it?"

Sadiqi didn't answer. He just moved to the next question. "Do you know the other boy's family?"

Again the woman shook her head with a sort of desperate realization that she'd been so worried about her own son that she hadn't considered the possible disappearance of another woman's child. "No. I don't even know his family name. I don't think he's from Paris."

"I think he's from the Pyrenees. Or maybe it's the Jura," the father offered. "The mountains."

That would explain why he hadn't been reported missing, Sadiqi reflected. He was from out-of-town. No parents following his movements. Someone would need to follow up and confirm that the kid had never come back from his night in the catacombs. "Does your son have an address book where I could find Quentin's phone number?"

The father was already shaking his head. "No. Just his phone. And that got smashed in the catacombs."

Not surprising, Sadiqi thought. If the kid had been running around, crashing into stone walls in the dark, the phone would have taken a beating.

But there was still a vague chance that the information in the device's memory might be accessible even if the screen was broken. "Do you still have the phone?"

The father nodded unthinkingly then went back into his son's room. A moment later he handed the device to the cop. "I hope it tells you something," the father mumbled. Plainly he couldn't care less about the phone. What he wanted was his son back. The phone without his son made no sense.

24

Once the parents had left, Sadiqi headed in the opposite direction, mulling over what he'd just learnt. Perhaps what struck him most was what he hadn't learnt. What was all this gibberish about a Green Monster killing Quentin and Quartz? Sadiqi needed to find Desjardins' companions – or whatever was left of them.

With a couple of swipes on his phone he got Thomas Ferry from the cataflics on the line.

"Khalid Sadiqi, here. UCLAT. We spoke this morning." His tone was businesslike but not overbearing. It was true, he had been unyielding when he ordered Ferry to provide him with a team to help with the sniffer dogs. The silence down the line told him that the captain hadn't forgotten. "I'm working with Alexandre Trémont on the Desjardins case. I'm trying to track down the two people the kid claims were with him on Friday night…"

"I can confirm that one person is missing," Ferry's said. Sadiqi was pleased to hear him sounding vaguely amenable.

"Yes, Trémont said. André Zucchero."

"That's all I've got. We don't have any other reports of anyone missing."

So much for helpful. Sadiqi could feel Ferry itching to hang up on him, so he pushed forward as quickly as possible. "Yes, I understand that, but I might have a lead. If I give you a cataphile pseudonym can you match it to a real person?"

There was a slight pause on the other end of the line. "Possibly," Ferry said, sounding a little annoyed at not being able to end the conversation. "It depends whether or not we have him on file – which depends on how many times we've picked him up."

Sadiqi pushed the front door to the hospital wing open and was instantly submerged in a sweltering wave of heat. The temperature in the cement parking lot made the badly air-conditioned hospital seem icy in retrospect. "I've got two possible names: Snoopy and Bango.

If you can match the nicknames to a real name that would be good. If you can give me a profile or any other information, that would be great."

The chief cataflic said nothing but Sadiqi was encouraged by the sound of typing in the background. Ferry was running the names through a computer. This was confirmed by an interjection of "*Merde. Damn machine.*" A few more clicks down the line and Ferry was back with his first answer. "Yeah, I've got Snoopy. It's Philippe Desjardins. That's the kid we picked up."

"Yeah." *Not much use,* Sadiqi reflected. "The second name is Bango."

There was more typing quickly followed by an answer. "Yeah. I've got him. Quentin Asselin."

Quentin. Delirious or not, that confirmed what Desjardins had said. Sadiqi felt a combination of hope for his investigation and regret for the young cataphile, who seemed slightly more real now that he had been baptized with a complete name. "Anything else on him other than the name?"

There was a click of keyboard then Ferry read off some more information. "He's a student. Living in residence."

"Do you have a phone number?"

Ferry reeled off the number before offering his own opinion. "It doesn't sound good. Desjardins was rambling about his friends being killed when we picked him up."

Although Sadiqi agreed entirely, he didn't want any rumors running through the quarry brigade. "Ah, come on. This was supposed to have happened nearly a week ago. I'm sure your men would have turned up the bodies by now if these guys were really dead."

"There are a lot of tunnels down there. Plenty of places to hide a body or two." Before Sadiqi could respond, Ferry had managed to slide in a couple of questions. "So what exactly are you guys investigating? Since when do they call in the UCLAT for a disappearance?"

Sadiqi had been hoping to avoid that question. Now all he could do was trot out the old clichés. "I can't discuss that for the moment. I'll fill you in as soon as I can."

"Yeah sure," Ferry scoffed. "I'll probably see it on Twitter before you get back to me."

Sadiqi knew just how true that was. The leaks would be out long before colleagues were briefed. The whole situation might be a farce if it weren't so pathetic.

25

Follow-up on the missing cataphile was delegated to Podesta. Sadiqi couldn't be bothered wasting time investigating something he already held as truth. The sinking feeling in his stomach told him they weren't going to find Quentin Asselin alive. The kid's days playing in the catacombs were over.

What interested Sadiqi infinitely more were Desjardins' rantings. It was just possible that there was something more to this Green Monster and Vauvert Devil than delirious babbling. A catacomb specialist might be able to shine some light on the question. And he knew just where to find one. In any case, he needed to talk with Caron about those maps he'd sent over.

Two quick calls and a quarter of an hour later the cop was surrounded by the nauseating blend of linoleum flooring, rotted wood panelling and 1970s furniture that characterized *FranceTech*. Office C-11 bore witness to the Parisian knack for squeezing a maximum number of people into a minimum amount of space. The chairs piled up in the corner suggested that at times the population density of the room could reach alarming levels. However today there were just two students in the main office: a young man, who was so absorbed in whatever he was doing he only glanced up briefly, and the Canadian from Val-de-Grace, who rose from her desk and leaned up against the mezzanine railing.

"I'm looking for Professor Caron."

"And there I was thinking you'd come to restore my quarry privileges." The smile was wry but at least it was a smile. Too often young people expressed complete sectarian dislike for the police. At least she wasn't doing that. "Just knock and go in," she said pointing a finger towards one of the doors opposite.

He followed the instructions and pushed opened the door, only to be welcomed by an icy glare from the professor. "Do you always barge in without waiting to be asked?"

"Madame Corrigan told me to knock and enter."

Caron harumphed. "Pfff. Americans aren't exactly renowned for their good manners." Of course, what annoyed him most was the lost opportunity to be rude first. The professor made a point of keeping people waiting. He never answered when people knocked; whether it was students at the university, colleagues at the IGC or his wife at home. (And that was precisely why Toni had told the inspector not to bother waiting for a reply.)

The cop ignored Caron's rudeness in the same way he had ignored the student's frosty welcome. He wasn't here to play games. He offered a cursory handshake before opening the cardboard tube he'd been carrying and sliding out a roll of documents. "I was hoping you could coach me quickly on how these maps work," he said spreading the pile of broadsheet pages across the desk. These were the maps Podesta had brought back from Caron's office that morning but this was only the second time they'd come out of the tube. The first time the inspector had seen them he'd instantly decided they were too complicated to entrust to any of his men.

If there had been any doubt up to that point whether Caron planned to be helpful or not his answer to the cop's request settled it. "Surely you know how to read a map, *brigadier*," he sneered.

Years of experience had taught Sadiqi that nobody has much respect for cops – special ops or not. But he could really do without witnesses talking to him as if he were some sort of moron. At times like this he wished he could just perform a nice little scorpion kick to knock some sense into people. Today, as always, he controlled the urge. Instead, he pulled himself up to his full height, put his hands on his hips and drew back his outer shirt to expose his SIG Pro in its holster. It wasn't a subtle message but it was effective. "If I'm a *brigadier,* then you must be an undergrad," he said slowly, his voice straining. "And yes, I do know how to read maps. But these are a little unusual." He flattened out the pages, clipping the corners under books to keep them from rolling up then leaned over the desk and stared at the intricate dovetail of colors adorning the sheets.

The gist of the maps was easy to follow. Roads and buildings above ground were marked with black or brown lines while colored shading marked what lay below the surface. It was precisely the complexity of that color scheme that disturbed Sadiqi with its array of solid colors, striped shading, polka dots and blank white spaces. Clearly the maps were designed for engineers with special geological training, not amateurs.

Caron didn't come to the rescue. "Surely it's not that complicated. The yellow shading represents limestone deposits. The other colors are either supporting pillars, dry stone walls or other reinforcements used to fill in unused galleries."

"I sort of realized that. What I was hoping for was some pointers on how best to navigate the area."

"Take a guide," Caron snapped.

"I specifically wanted the maps so that I wouldn't need a guide."

The professor threw his hands in the air. "Then open your eyes and use the legend at the bottom of the page." His hands were poised on the desk and his mouth soldered in a mute insult. "Everything you need to know is on those maps. *The Atlas* is a perfect representation of the quarries. All of Paris, whether above or below ground, is marked on there."

"Everything?" Sadiqi asked.

"Everything," Caron replied crisply. "That's what we do at the IGC. That's my job. That's our business. We survey the quarries, look for trouble. If we find any sign of wear and tear, we mark it on the maps then we fix it. We know where every cracked tunnel ceiling is. Every hole in the ground. Every potential danger caused by aging. Not to mention every measure taken over the years to reinforce past weak spots. Any change we make is carried onto *the Atlas* which precisely represents the entire subterranean city in the most rigorous way possible."

The strains of this conversation wafted through the open door to the outer office where Toni and her Italian post-doc friend couldn't help overhearing. Realizing the new arrival was a cop, Marco listened distractedly for a few moments. But he found the talk less interesting than he had hoped and he quickly returned to his research. Toni on the other hand, was attentive and within a couple of minutes she was bristling at Caron's little game. It was a habit with him to speak in half-truths then wait to see which students would pick up on his abridged version of facts. Over the past months, she'd learnt to play the game, constantly checking the details that her director set in front of her. Calling something a quarry, when it was really a surveillance tunnel; saying something was built on gypsum when really it was built on limestone. The game seemed even more perverse when played with a police officer investigating a crime – even if he hadn't been very clear what that crime was. Either way, the claim that everything below ground was strictly represented on the maps made her feel like running into the office to clarify. It was one of the subjects she was ready to split hairs about.

The window to speak, however, was lost because Sadiqi had already pressed on with his next question. "How do your engineers access the quarries?"

Caron unclasped his hands and shrugged. "The IGC has access points."

Getting information from Caron was as easy as growing organic veg in a toxic dump. If Sadiqi wanted a specific answer, he would have to ask a precise question. "Where is there an access point in the Latin Quarter?"

Caron couldn't avoid an answer. "At the top of boulevard St. Michel by the Luxembourg RER station, or Escalier Bonaparte," he replied grudgingly.

"Where's that?"

"Rue Bonaparte," the professor drawled with a tone meant to emphasize just how stupid the question was. The man's condescension was seriously getting up Sadiqi's nose. If Caron wasn't careful, he might discover that martial arts kick after all. "Could a member of the public access that entrance?" he continued.

"The public?" Caron sneered, yet again. "The quarries aren't open to the public. There are no public access points."

Sadiqi leaned across the desk so that Caron was forced to raise his head to look him in the eyes. "Professor Caron, you're not being very helpful. You know, I didn't come to see you simply because I'm bored and have nothing better to do with my time." He spoke the first words so softly they stayed locked in the tiny office but as he continued his voice grew in volume and intensity. "I'm here because it looks like the quarries are being used for criminal purposes. And somehow I don't think the criminals bothered requesting official authorization from your Office." Sadiqi locked Caron's gaze, morphing the physical aggressiveness into visual form "So tell me, Professor, are there any entrances that members of the public could access if they were sufficiently motivated."

Caron didn't look any more ruffled than he had a minute earlier. "In principle, no. In practice, yes." Sadiqi's eyes bore deeper into the director, willing him to expand on the subject. After a short pause, Caron elaborated. "It used to be possible to get into the GRS from a number of points across the Latin Quarter…"

"The GRS?" Sadiqi interrupted.

"*Le Grand Réseau Sud,*" Caron explained. *The Great Southern Network.* "It's the official name for the network on the Left bank that stretches from the Luxembourg Gardens to the southern edge of the city."

The cop registered the definition and signaled to the director to continue.

"Thirty years ago manholes used by the phone and the electric companies linked up with the quarries. It was relatively easy for anyone to penetrate underground if they were strong enough to pry open a manhole. I'm not teaching you much when I say the quarries were a secret haunt to generations of students. They were used for parties. For a little excitement." Caron seemed to lapse into a dream for a moment, deciding what he should and shouldn't say. "Then in the 80s things got out of hand. There was a long series of problems. Skinheads fighting punks, young women getting raped. The authorities were forced to step in. As you probably already know, that was when the police Quarry Brigade was formed to patrol underground – although *brigade* was a rather grand term for the two-officer team that made up the whole force at the time." Sadiqi waited for the man to stop complaining and get to the point. "In order to make the brigade's job easier, all the access points that weren't officially necessary for the IGC or police were soldered shut or equipped with special entry locks to keep out unauthorized visitors. In principle."

"In practice it doesn't work," Sadiqi suggested.

"A couple of moderately strong young men with crowbars can do what they want." The shrug that accompanied this statement showed disappointment. "On top of that, there are still a few historic access points in the city center, but none of them are directly accessible from the street. You have to enter a courtyard or a building to get to them and you need a key to open them. The IGC would have preferred to wall in most of the access points but we were refused authority to do so for cultural reasons. I'm sure you can imagine the difficulty of permanently shutting a spot that's considered to have historic value." Caron's face had shrunk into a grimace, as if he had a bad taste in his mouth. "Nonetheless the entrances are beyond the reach of the general public. Escalier Bonaparte is locked. As are all the other entrances in the city. You need a key to open them."

"And who has those keys?"

The question seemed to irritate the professor. "The IGC has keys to all the entrances it controls – like rue Bonaparte. City Hall has copies of most of them as well. Plus other essential administrations."

"What about Val-de-Grace?"

"Val-de-Grace has been military land for centuries. The armed forces are in strict control of their own material."

Sadiqi considered this. Although the wall in the middle of the staircase leading up to Val-de-Grace had been sledge hammered, the door at the top of the staircase hadn't been forced. It had been opened using a key. And Sadiqi didn't like that. He would have preferred to be told that there were several keys floating around, some in the possession of the military, others in safe keeping at city hall or the IGC. If what Caron said was true, whoever they were looking for had obtained access to Val-de-Grace through military channels. And finding out if a key had gone missing from military safekeeping wasn't going to be easy. His disappointment came out in an impatient rant. "*Merde.* Why aren't the catacombs properly sealed? They're a disaster waiting to happen."

Caron heaved his shoulders into the air. "I couldn't agree more. The problem is the politicians. They seem to have countless excuses for not intervening: It would be too expensive to close them. We would be ruining part of the national heritage." He stared angrily at the officer as if all this was his fault. "Monsieur Sadiqi. I'll be frank. For years I've been warning about the dangers generated by the quarries. On a human level, they're a danger to young people who go down there looking for thrills. On a strategic level, they pose a danger to the nation's capital. This city is covered with important buildings. Some of those buildings are perched on top of quarries. Government buildings, like the Senate. Medical facilities like Cochin hospital, scientific institutions like the Observatory and military facilities like Val-de-Grace. There are old quarries everywhere. The land below Paris is hollow. The buildings on the surface were built with stones taken from beneath their very foundations. Six storey buildings built on three storeys of emptiness. Most of southern Paris from the Luxembourg Gardens right back to the Ring Road could be mined with explosives bringing the whole city quite literally crumbling to the ground. As Louis-Sébastien Mercier said, you wouldn't need a very big shock to return the stones of Paris' buildings to the place from which they were so laboriously quarried."

The quote was impressive. If Sadiqi had been alone with Caron he might even have been seduced by this apocalyptic vision. As it was, for the past ten minutes, the professor's words had been spiralling across the office up to where Corrigan was sitting. The shoddy description of the *Atlas* had been bad enough. Misrepresenting classic quarry literature bordered on sacrilegious. Most French students would have let it slide, too embarassed to confront their professors. But Toni had been brought up to speak her mind, and she was now going to give her opinion. "With respect, Sir," she called from the outer office, "it might be worth mentioning that you're quoting an author who's been dead for 200 years".

Sadiqi turned and saw the young woman leaning down from the mezzanine. Her skin flushed slightly. "I didn't mean to interrupt. It's just a little misleading to apply words that were referring to underground decay 200 years ago to the risk of terrorist activity today. Mercier is an author from the time of the French Revolution. He was referring to possible implosion not potential explosion. His aim was to convince the king to extend consolidation work." Toni noticed that her professor had turned visibly red. Caron hated it when she questioned his arguments and this time she'd definitely said too much. But there was no turning back. "As for the question about why nothing has been done to close down the quarries, there are several reasons. First of all, it's impossible to completely fill the quarry void. Erosion would continue to happen even if cement were injected into the whole network. Rainwater trickles underground and erodes stone. If the surveillance tunnels were filled in, it would become impossible to keep an eye on that erosion, and the consequences would be disastrous. Secondly, the risk of a strategic terrorist threat is limited because the ground under sensitive buildings has already been isolated from the wider network. Most entrances from public buildings have been soldered shut for over thirty years now. Walls have been built under Cochin Hospital and the Observatory to isolate the ground below those institutions from the rest of the network. Passages under the Senate are guarded by military police."

This forceful rebuttal was more than Caron could take. "The danger is real," he protested. "It's nonsense to pretend that the quarries don't present a risk."

"Zero risk doesn't exist whether it's in the quarries or your local grocery store," Toni shot back.

Sadiqi could see that his interview was moving from an information gathering session to a public speaking exercise. Still, once again he was impressed with the way the girl stood up to the pompous Caron. She seemed to know what she was talking about. "What about schools?"

"Schools?" Toni repeated.

"You've mentioned some of the important buildings situated above catacombs. Val-de-Grace, Cochin, the Senate. What about schools? Are there schools above the old quarries – or accessible from the catacombs?"

"Of course," Caron harrumphed, trying to regain his position of primacy. "There are several high schools: Montaigne, Lavoisier, Racine. Plus some universities: this one, of course, the faculty of Pharmacy, parts of the Faculty of Fine Arts. Large parts of the Latin Quarter are above the old quarries along with many of the country's most prestigious institutes of learning."

"What about Henri IV High?" Sadiqi asked.

Caron's face fell. Just when he was about to ram home his point that the strategic security of the Left Bank was quite literally undermined by the quarries, the cop had produced a counter-example.

"No. Henri IV and Louis-le-Grand are off the grid. People used to think there were quarries under H4, but when the Pantheon was built, extensive excavations were carried out around the area. All that was found were some small potters' wells. No real quarries."

Sadiqi noticed that the professor was still glaring at his student as if this counter-example had been her doing. Thinking back to university, the cop could remember professors and students sparring at conferences. It was done with a smile. It was considered intellectual gymnastics rather than outright disagreement. But Caron wasn't smiling; this was more than an abstract intellectual debate for him.

"What about the term *Diable Vauvert*. Does that mean anything to either of you?"

The professor was curt. "As it does to you. *C'est au diable Vauvert*. It's at the back of beyond, the ends of the earth."

Sadiqi turned to the Canadian. There was a definite look of amusement on her face. "There's a little more to it than that."

26

The Canadian's smiling disrespect for her mentor brought a spark of life to the interview with Caron. Not only did she have the confidence to disagree with her professor, she did it in the most innocent way possible – as if there were nothing more natural than casting doubt on the man's knowledge. Even more surprisingly, Caron let her get away with it. Like a peacock, the professor responded to the student's prodding by preening himself intellectually. "There's the etymology, of course," he snapped. "The legends. If you go in for that kind of thing."

"I take it you don't?" Sadiqi said.

"No I don't. I'm an engineer, not an anthropologist or a historian. I'm not a fan of today's fashionable *pluridisciplinary* approaches." Caron spit out this term with an intensity designed to wound, causing a shadow to quiver across the student's face. Pleased with the affront he had managed to administer, the professor decided to demonstrate his full superiority. "Like all Parisians, I know the general story."

Sadiqi was born and bred in Paris. "I don't know the story."

The look on Caron's face showed nothing but contempt for this cultural ignorance. His impatience was palpable as he began reeling off information in a fast monotone. "From the Tenth to the Twelfth century Vauvert Castle stood where the Luxembourg Gardens are today. At the time, the land was outside the city walls, on the main road leading to Orleans. The castle was abandoned relatively soon after it was built and the grounds soon earned a reputation for being haunted – or inhabited by the Devil. People generally tried to stay away from it. It was considered an area to avoid." Sadiqi waited for the professor to elaborate. But he appeared to have finished. As if his short narrative were self-explanatory.

"And a thousand years later we're still talking about *'au Diable Vauvert'* as a place not worth visiting? Because of some deserted old castle?" The inspector wasn't satisfied. He couldn't see how this tied in with Desjardins' mumbling about Vauvert.

Corrigan was still leaning over the metal banister of the mezzanine. "Professor Caron tells the story very badly," she smiled. "There's more to it than that."

"Is there a link to the catacombs?" Sadiqi asked.

"Oh yeah." There was a warm glow in her words, as if she were just waiting to be asked to elaborate.

"Yes, why don't you go and talk with Corrigan," Caron muttered, gesturing towards the student. "She loves fairy tales. A true champion of pluridisciplinary nonsense."

Although Caron was trying to get rid of Sadiqi, the inspector wasn't in such a rush to leave. Instead he signalled to Toni to come down and join them in the professor's office. She didn't need to be asked twice.

"So what can you tell me about the Vauvert Devil… and the Green Monster, while we're at it?" the cop prompted, as the young woman installed herself on the small chair in the corner of Caron's office.

"A fair bit. But I'm not sure what use my nonsense is likely to be to your investigation." Her eyes brushed defiantly over the professor but Caron had pulled up his email on his laptop and was pretending to ignore the two of them.

All told, Sadiqi had only spent about ten minutes with the professor and already he disliked him; the poor student probably had to put up with endless stupidity from the man. The cop felt a measure of sympathy. "Nor do I. But I've heard the term used recently so maybe you can help me figure out whether or not it's relevant."

That was all it took to get her started. Intrigued, Toni turned her full attention back to the cop. She could tell that he was using this time to sum her up in exactly the same way she was using it to analyze him. She also noticed that although he pretended to be very patient, he was tapping his fingers on the edge of the desk. There was a nervous core scratching against the calm exterior.

"So. The Vauvert Devil." A twinkle came back into her eyes. "I don't know how well you know the quarries but I guess you realize there's no natural light down there. Their main defining feature is darkness. That's why the quarries have always been associated with the Prince of Darkness... the Devil. The quarries are Hell on Earth and that's exactly how they're perceived by popular culture. If you've ever seen Gustave Doré's illustrations of Hell in the *Divine Comedy* you'll know what I'm talking about. Labyrinths of impregnable stone. Walls opening onto endless chambers each consumed by inescapable darkness. To quote Joseph Méry, the quarries are 'A city of streets without houses, like the capital of Hell'."

Who the hell was Joseph Méry and what did the *Divine Comedy* have to do with any of this? Sadiqi remarked to himself that maybe it hadn't been such a great idea dragging the student into this, after all. Caron hadn't been forthcoming with information but it looked like Corrigan was going to buttonhole him with hours of catacomb trivia. The cop might have asked her to cut to the chase except he really didn't want to side with Caron, who was making a song and dance of his disapproval, mumbling, "God help us" under his breath.

Which was enough to call Corrigan to order. Her features hardened slightly. "Like Professor Caron said, the story of Vauvert goes back to the end of the 10th Century and the reign of Robert the Pious. It's one of those archaic royal stories about finding an heir to the throne. Robert's first wife had failed to provide him with an heir, so he took a second wife. Unfortunately for him, he did this without the Pope's consent – which you just didn't do in those days."

"Ex-communication," Sadiqi suggested, in an attempt to hustle the story along.

"Exactly. So there he was, with a lovely new bride but nowhere to go because the old wife was still living in the conjugal palace. What to do?" the girl asked, then answered her own question. "Robert was rich, powerful, with plenty of land. So he had a new house built. Vauvert Castle. The mansion was put up just outside what in those days were Paris city limits. In contemporary terms, that would be roughly where we're sitting now. Not only was the site conveniently close to the old palace, but construction proceeded surprisingly fast because it turned out the site was located above extensive limestone deposits so the stones used to build the castle were dug straight out from below the grounds."

"No time lost transporting the stone across the city."

"Right." Toni thought for a moment, making sure she didn't stray too far from the subject. "Anyway, you have to remember that all this was happening at the end of the 900s. Europe was suffering from Millennium fever. Everyone was sure that the Messiah would be returning soon and that the end of the world was nigh. So Robert started getting jumpy. He decided it wasn't a good time to be stranded outside the Church, where he ran the risk of being one of the losers on Judgement Day. It was time to get back into the fold. Back onto good terms with the Pope." The strands of hair framing Corrigan's face blew backwards every time the fan on Caron's desk rotated in front of her. She seemed to be enjoying herself, the corners of her mouth had turned upwards in quiet amusement. "Strangely enough, he managed this by taking a third wife. It's a little complicated but basically his first wife had died in the interim, so by repudiating his second wife (who was his cousin, so not a good choice for marriage) he was free to remarry whoever he wanted as far as the church was concerned. Once he was happily attached to Wife Number 3, he was allowed back into the church, and also back to his old palace. He didn't need Vauvert anymore. The castle that had been home to the illicit love affair was abandoned and left to fall into ruin."

The girl was a better storyteller than her professor but Sadiqi wasn't convinced her information was any more helpful. So far, the only potentially useful thing he'd managed to learn was that Vauvert referred to an area located on the present site of the Luxembourg Gardens. "How does this link to the quarries?"

"Easy. The castle and grounds remained abandoned for centuries," the student continued. "At least they were abandoned by the King. But like any well-placed unoccupied property, they were soon taken over by squatters – mainly thieves and highwaymen who lived in the deserted castle and its underground quarries. Which might sound like an unimportant detail but it isn't. You have to visualize the scene. Anyone looking at the castle from the nearest road would only have been able to make out a dark shadow covered in thistles and ivy. In the winter or late in the day, smoke would come billowing out of the ground in places where the thieves were sitting around campfires in the quarries. You'd be able to hear their dogs howling at the moon from behind the castle walls. All this, combined with the stories circulating about people being attacked in the area after dark – not to mention the old legends about a previous owner being ex-communicated – would have given the spot a major evil aura. Especially being as the road running beside the castle wasn't yet called *Boulevard St. Michel* but *rue d'Enfer*."

"The Road to Hell." The link between the story and Desjardin's experience seemed weak, but Sadiqi kept listening, hoping that at some point a connection would fall into place.

"Exactly. At least that's what it sounds like. In fact, the name comes from the Latin meaning *inferior*, in other words 'the road leading out of the city to the south'. But to the people who saw smoke coming out of the ground around a castle associated with sin and danger it would have seemed like the road to Hell. Either way, the effect was the same. Over time the castle became known as a home to ghosts and the devil."

Caron couldn't stand to see his student getting all the attention. "Miss Corrigan, I'm sure if Inspector Sadiqi wants a historical romance, he'll go and buy one. Perhaps you should stop embroidering."

The student winced visibly. She'd been brought up being encouraged by teachers. She still hadn't grown used to this French technique that consisted in insulting students. In France, she'd discovered a society where professors mastered the arts of taunting and mockery. Where encouragement was seen as coddling.

Apparently Sadiqi wasn't a fan of the Old World approach either. No matter how far off topic Corrigan was taking him, he wasn't going to side with Caron. "That's okay, Professor. My tiny brain can handle all this information." Then he encouraged Toni to pick up where she'd been cut off. "So posterity inherited the expression *Diable Vauvert* even though the castle didn't survive?"

"Not exactly," she corrected. "The castle survived in one form or another for a while but it's true that the royal family hated the place. Nobody dared live there after Robert's death. It wasn't until two hundred years later that King St. Louis decided to get rid of the property by giving the land to the Carthusian monks to build a monastery. Only a holy order was considered strong enough to banish the castle's diabolic presence. According to legend, it took the monks three days and nights to cleanse the land, wrestling with the devil while thunder shook the castle and a dark cloud of sulphur hovered over it."

"In short the thieves left."

Toni's eyes sparkled mischievously. "They moved. They went to Montsouris, which was a little deeper in the countryside. But the Vauvert Devil remained part of popular culture. To this day, any self-respecting cataphile would know the basic story."

"And what about the Green Monster?"

"It's basically a derivative of the same story. The Green Monster was the Devil's son. According to a story by Gérard de Nerval, the Devil took on the appearance of red wine..."

"He what?"

Corrigan scrambled to clarify. "The Carthusian monks brewed wine and kept it stored in the cellars under Vauvert. According to the story, one night the Devil entered the cellar and put his evil essence in one of the bottles. The wine from that bottle was drunk by a young woman on her wedding night." Sadiqi's eyebrows must have been rising higher and higher because the student broke off. "Look, you were the one who asked. I'm just telling the story."

The cop had heard a lot of crazy stories throughout his career. This was no worse than some of those. And at least Corrigan knew that what she was telling him was a fairy tale. "I'm still listening. Keep going."

Toni decided to cut it short. "So as a result of letting the Devil into her body through the wine, the young bride conceived the Devil's child – the 'Green Monster'. After living among humans and ruining his parents' life, the Green Monster eventually left his mortal home and returned to the bowels of the earth where he'd been conceived. In other words, he went back to the quarries. There are several similar stories. There's the *Ghost of Montsouris*, who's supposed to be gifted with unusual agility. He knows all the tunnels of the quarries like the back of his hand and can see perfectly in the dark and..."

It was as if a synapse had clicked into place in Sadiqi's mind. Suddenly a note of clarity was calling out to him from among all the gibberish. "... He can see perfectly in the dark," he echoed.

Corrigan nodded. "Yes, and there's the Green Man, who's a cross between a devil and a ghost, complete with tail, horns and hoofed feet. Supposedly he surfaces through wells or cellars and brings bad luck to anyone who sees him. Same as the Green Monster. Whoever sees *him* is supposed to die in the upcoming year – or lose a close relative."

Sadiqi's eyes were resting on Toni, but she wasn't sure he was really looking at her. His thoughts seemed to be elsewhere. "They're great stories," she offered. "Quarrymen were notoriously superstitious. They lived hard lives. Worked in harsh conditions. Many of them became very ill and died as a result of their rotten work conditions. I suppose you could say the legend of the Green Monster helped rationalize their high mortality rate."

"They didn't die because of harsh work conditions, they died because the Green Monster was after them," Sadiqi summarized.

"Which is why I maintain that Miss Corrigan should have become an anthropologist rather than an engineer," Caron broke in.

Toni glanced at her professor. Sadiqi had difficulty placing her expression. Was it disgust or embarrassment?

"Apparently I talk too much," she apologized. "Sorry. I guess this isn't very helpful for whatever you're working on." And having decided that she'd done enough talking, she attempted to switch roles with the cop and get him talking instead. "So what got you so interested in the Vauvert Devil?"

On an ordinary day, the inspector might have said that that was classified information. But today he needed allies. His own personal knowledge of the catacombs was incidental; there were many things he needed to learn before his investigation could progress. He needed good sources of information about the underground city. Caron was too miserly with his knowledge. Corrigan was probably a better potential source.

And, in any case, he liked her. He liked her intelligence. He liked her humor. He liked the way she stood up to her professor. Without leaking any classified information, he could enlighten her a little. He wanted to keep her close. Reward her for the help she'd offered in case he needed to come back for more later.

Unfortunately everything linked to the investigation was basically confidential. He rooted quickly through his brain and pulled out the first bit of tempting yet useless information he could think of. "You know that flier you gave me this morning?" he asked.

"The one about the missing cataphiles?"

Sadiqi nodded. "Well, we've found one of the guys named on it. He was pulled out of the catacombs a couple of days ago, injured and delirious. He's still in hospital. Still delirious. I went to see him earlier today and he was rambling about the Vauvert Devil and the Green Monster. He said he'd seen them."

The cop had expected Toni's jaw to drop in disbelief. Instead a wry smile danced across her lips. "He'd seen the Green Monster... Every cataphile's dream. To become part of catacomb legend. What better way to go than carried off by the Green Monster?"

Sadiqi could almost see the image painting itself in her mind. He watched her sitting there, the image of well-balanced youth. Motivated by her studies. Building a career. Yet somehow completely submerged in an alternate world. "Is that the dream? To be carried off into oblivion."

Corrigan held his gaze. "Not oblivion: immortality." Although the impression was fleeting, for a moment Sadiqi thought he could see something dark in the depths of those beautiful green eyes. Then it was gone. She placed her hands palm down on the desk and adopted a pose of perfect professional respectability. "But, I'm not a cataphile. I'm an engineer." She was staring straight at Caron.

27

Sadiqi found himself holding on to the image of Corrigan as he wandered back to his car. You did whatever you had to do to get through the days. Life was funny that way. In the midst of this damn investigation, the young woman at least provided a reminder that not everything in the world was rotten.

It wasn't until he had climbed in behind the steering wheel of his makeshift office and pulled out his phone that his mind switched back into professional mode.

Using his car as an office wasn't a setup universally appreciated by everyone. The technologically minded Dukrin was constantly reminding him that the whole point of having a smartphone was to be able to do your work anywhere. In all fairness, Sadiqi usually did take his calls and messages whenever and wherever they arrived. But he thought more clearly and processed information more thoroughly if he was sheltered from the distractions of the street. If he couldn't work from his real office, he preferred to make important calls from the privacy of his car. And checking in with HQ fell into that category.

As he swiped in his boss' number with one hand, the other strayed toward the Zippo lighter lying in the tray under the handbrake. There was no lighter fluid left. There hadn't been lighter fluid for nearly six months. But he still liked the feel of it in his hand. He only had time to spin the flint wheel once before the familiar *"Allo"* picked up. Dukrin's voice never gave anything away. Despite all these years he'd known her, she remained the only person whose mood he couldn't gauge during a two-minute exchange.

"You've spoilt me today," he said, leaning his elbow out the window. "Is this supposed to be cop-Nirvanah? Both the PM's non-assassination plus the shit in the catacombs."

"It's all shit in the catacombs," Dukrin corrected, no trace of emotion, as if she were commenting on a patch of grey cloud that had somehow appeared in an otherwise blue sky. "Two attacks launched the same week using the catacombs would be too big a coincidence."

"Yeah. It's just I haven't found the link yet. I don't know who I'm looking for."

"I'd say you could start looking close to home," she answered. Sadiqi recognized the intonation as one of Dukrin's lead-ins to an update. "I've just had the lab report on the anthrax spores." On the other side of town, she flipped through the document lying on the desk in front of her. The political implications of what was written in those pages were colossal. "There's a good chance the anthrax is home grown. All the samples tested were identified as coming from the same batch... And the batch's molecular make up is identical to spores produced by the CRSSA in Grenoble."

Sadiqi had no idea what the CRSSA was. His countrymen's love of acronyms was a major pain in the ass. Every branch of anything had an acronym. It was impossible to keep track of them all. "What's the CRSSA?"

"*Le Centre de Recherche du Service de la Santé des Armées* – the Research Center for the Armed Forces Health Service."

He might not have heard of the CRSSA before, but the mere translation of the initials clarified a lot. They weren't looking for some dabbler who had downloaded an anthrax recipe off the internet. They were up against some fierce professionals. "You mean it's weapons grade material?"

"You got it. Pure as uncut cocaine. But much more deadly."

Sadiqi watched out his window as a woman crossed the road in front of his car pushing a tiny baby in a stroller with one hand while coaxing a toddler to stay on the zebra crossing with the other. Ignorance is bliss. And it was days like today that made Sadiqi wish he could drown in a pool of ignorance instead of having to hear this kind of shit. It was bad enough foreign terrorists killing Frenchmen. But French terrorists killing Frenchmen with weapons produced by the French military... It was, depressingly, an all too familiar story. "I thought we'd signed the Bio-Weapons Convention. I didn't think we were producing that stuff anymore."

An unsmiling chuckle rippled in his phone. "That's what I love about you Khalid. You're efficient, competent. You live with shit every day. Yet you still manage to cling to the illusion that we're the good guys. Come on. Wake up and smell the napalm. Okay, we've terminated our bio-weapons programme and destroyed our stockpile. So what? We've also signed the nuclear non-proliferation pact and promised to stop nuking the natives in the south Pacific but that didn't stop a certain President we both know and love from getting his little power surge by pushing the red button the very same week he was voted in."

Dukrin whacked the file in her hand against the desk and took a deep breath to curtail a wild rant. This was no time for polemics about why the anthrax existed. It existed. There was nothing else worth saying on the matter. No point turning it into a big deal. "If you want the friendliest scenario, I'll give it to you. The CRSSA needs anthrax for research purposes. There are still countries that haven't renounced biological weapons, therefore those of us who have renounced those weapons need to protect ourselves against potential aggressors. If we stopped doing research, we'd be putting our citizens at risk. We have to try to find an antidote or at least some sort of viable treatment in case anthrax is used to attack France either in a military or civilian context. In order to carry out that research, our scientists need to have their own live spores to work on." The monotone voice she used suggested she was reeling off an official note someone had stapled to the report rather than providing her own personal angle on the matter. "Unfortunately our scientists are too outstanding for their own good. The stuff they've made is exceedingly powerful. Powerful to the extent that there have already been accidents." That, on the other hand, was authentic Dukrin.

"I don't remember hearing about that."

"Oh come on, Khalid. You wouldn't have. Nobody heard about it. News of it was disseminated on a purely need-to-know basis."

"Until today we weren't need-to-know."

"You got it. Anyway, when the center was testing the original spores, there was an accident in the lab. A container got knocked over and smashed. The scientists carrying out the experiments cleaned up the mess but apparently they didn't do a good enough job disinfecting the area. A couple of members of the cleaning staff were infected." Dukrin stopped. Maybe to catch her breath, maybe because the words got caught in her throat. "They both died within five days of exposure in spite of being hospitalized and given immediate preventative treatment."

There were no limits to the depths of depravity nor the height of stupidity. Sadiqi's anxiety level was rising dangerously. He rubbed the back of his palm against his lips before dropping the lighter back into the tray and reaching for his nico candy. In the past, smoking had been the habit he called on to hide all his other nervous ticks. Now he was becoming a walking candy dispenser. "Unforgiving batch," he said in a sigh mixed with a crunch of candy. "And you're sure the samples from the hospitals were produced in Grenoble; the molecular structure couldn't have been copied?"

It was a reasonable question but not one Dukrin wanted Sadiqi worrying about. "I'm working on that but I'm not holding my breath for an answer. Foutriquet was only able to trace the molecular makeup back to Grenoble because any legally produced molecule of that type appears on an official list. The information was available. Finding out how part of that batch disappeared from their research center is going to be trickier." *If not impossible*, Dukrin thought to herself. She knew how the military worked. If they could possibly keep sensitive information out of the civilian domain, they would. And she, unfortunately in this case, was in the civilian domain. Missing sensitive material was the kind of info that military high command preferred to deal with itself. If a nuclear bomb went missing, the generals *might* mention it to the President, although even that was unlikely. They certainly wouldn't pass on the news if they could avoid it. It was the same for the anthrax. Getting them to own up to a mistake of this magnitude wouldn't be easy. She had one good contact at military intelligence. Her own personal back channel. She had reached out to him and been promised that he would try to find out what he could. Perhaps make a few inquiries into whether any members of staff had left precipitately or gone AWOL recently. It was the best she could hope for but she certainly wasn't expecting a straight answer.

The implications of an undeclared disappearance were, nevertheless, obvious to Sadiqi. "If we don't get confirmation that the anthrax was stolen from Grenoble, then we don't know how much went missing. We can't tell if the packages left in the hospitals last weekend used up the entire supply or if there's still more floating around out there."

"In the absence of an official answer, I'd suggest a working hypothesis. My guess is that there's more out there. We need to keep our eyes open. All the most sensitive targets need to be protected. I've already taken measures to get reinforcements into the catacombs under hospitals, schools and other key buildings. I've also posted officers outside catacomb access points in central Paris. Just keep your eyes open and your mouth shut. It'll all come together," she said with a voice that was too reassuringly optimistic to be natural. "Follow up the catacomb link. Check out the high schools. See if anything was left behind at Montaigne. Figure out what H4 has to do with this. Check if there's a catacomb link there or not." She sighed, unable to think of a fiery inspirational speech. "Just find whoever's behind this. Or at least try to find some sign of operations being carried out down in the catacombs."

Just find them, Sadiqi repeated to himself. What a joke! "What do you think I've been doing since four o'clock this morning. Fucking around. The catacombs are clean. Whoever's behind this has been careful not to leave any signs lying around."

"How do you know that?"

"Because the scientific team scanned the entire area under Val-de-Grace. I had sniffer dogs down there this morning. They didn't turn up anything. There's nothing down there. I've checked with Ferry. Other than a slightly demented kid who was picked up at the beginning of the week, nothing unusual has been reported. If the quarry brigade can't find anything, why would I?"

"Because you know what to look for." The words were no longer designed to be encouraging or comforting. It was pure fact. Sadiqi was the best officer on the counter-terrorist force. Hell, he was the best cop. Period. "Ferry is used to tracking students having unauthorized picnics underground. Not looking for signs of terrorist activity. I want you down there. Not Ferry, not sniffer dogs, not any of your lieutenants. You go down and look." Her voice hardened as she said her final words. "Figure out who's doing this and what they're working up to. Christ. Cut them off before they kill anyone else. I want to know who's behind this and what they want. Fast. We're holding a ticking bomb."

Once she had hung up, her hand continued to cling to the phone, her eyes closed as if in prayer. Sadiqi was the only person she knew she could trust with her life. Things weren't quite that bad yet. But today she was certainly trusting him with her career.

28

Somewhere east of the Eiffel Tower a taxi turned into a tiny street and slackened its pace. The Nightingale peered over the driver's shoulder to see what was causing the slow down. Driving through Paris was like getting blood to flow through clogged arteries. The road they'd just turned into barely provided enough room to drive comfortably under normal circumstances. At this particular minute, there was a double-parking issue making the situation worse.

The taxi driver leaned on his horn but the hulking black SUV in front made no sign of budging. Reeling off a list of obscenities, he reached out his window to squish down his side-view mirror before putting the car into gear and inching forward. As they glided past the SUV, the Nightingale estimated the distance between the taxi and the waiting car. If the side view mirror had been left in place they wouldn't have made it through the passage intact.

"*Pas mal!*" the Nightingale complimented.

"*C'est le métier, Monsieur.*" *Just doing my job.*

"I've seen drivers with a couple of feet more than that on either side hesitate."

The driver laughed appreciatively. "*Oui.* You wouldn't believe some of the rotten driving I see."

"Oh I would. Some people shouldn't be allowed on the roads."

"Most people shouldn't be allowed on the roads." He shot a smile into the rear view mirror. "You 'ave an accent. You are English?"

"Gad No. Irish," the Nightingale corrected in his distinctive brogue, strongly denying any such repellent association. He had long ago realized that while the French hated the English and the Americans, they loved the Irish. There was a Gallic bond, fed by a shared religion and a common dislike of the English.

"*Ah l'Irlande.* They say eets a beautiful coontry. My seester went last summer. She says the Irish are wunderful. And the whiskey. Very good," the driver rhapsodized, giving a thumbs up sign. His reminiscences were second hand, passed on to him by family members who had wanted to make the point that their hard earned savings had been well spent on a worthwhile summer holiday. But the Nightingale's souvenirs were hardly more personal. He hadn't been back to Ireland for nearly twenty years but that didn't stop him from spending the rest of the ride recalling the green hills of his youth. Actually, the green hills of his youth were a vacuous fabrication. They didn't exist. He was from Ulster. Belfast. Far from being raised on the green slopes of Tipperary, caring for horses and the land, he'd been nurtured on urban squalor and sectarian violence. But there was no way he would share those memories with anyone.

When the cab turned into the driveway of the Novotel hotel five minutes later, it was overflowing with invented memories of a time and place that bore the happy shades of illusion. Loving parents and grandparents, a farmhouse complete with cows, sheep and cats, not to mention a rich community spirit including a kindly priest and a caring school master, Irish dance lessons and Feis. In short, it was a world

invented to fit the Nightingale's needs. That was one of his strong
points. He adapted to his surroundings and to the people he was
speaking with. He knew how to blend in. The friendly small talk was
perfectly matched with his suit and laptop bag designed for his role as
the out-of-town businessman.

Yet by the time he'd stepped out of the car and into the air-
conditioned hotel foyer he'd already forgotten the congenial exchange.
He was now preparing for his next role. He would go into the bar to
have a drink and pretend he was waiting for a colleague, like your
average foreign businessman on an afternoon abroad. He would hang
around for half an hour. Maybe read a couple of newspapers. Then
he'd go for a little walk to enjoy the good weather.

And that's when his real role would begin. He would head across
the bridge to the heights of Passy. Caron would be home by four
o'clock at the latest.

He would be dead by half past.

29

Certain environmental conditions are more conducive to work
than others and Toni was definitely experiencing a day "without". Her
encounters with the police had frittered away her usually excellent
powers of concentration while heat and lack of sleep had pitched in to
make her sluggish. An electric fan sat in the middle of the desk,
rotating back and forth between her and Marco, providing flitting
whispers of relief from the increasingly oppressive weather. With
each passage, the breeze ruffled the papers in front of her but
accomplished little else as it struggled hopelessly against the hot air.
At the start of the hot weather, the thick walls of *FranceTech* had kept
the office cool. After ten days of heat wave, the stone was beginning
to act as a furnace rather than a cooler.

As if that wasn't enough distraction, now Caron and Trouvé were
bickering, which was unusual in itself. Toni had never heard the two
professors being anything less than cordial to one another but the
voices coming from the office were downright angry, even if an effort
was being made to avoid a shouting match.

"This is ridiculous," Caron's voice flowed with indignation.

"How can you say that?" Trouvé cut in. "You've compromised
us."

"Don't be ridiculous! None of this implicates P & E."

"Do you seriously believe the Brotherhood will turn a blind eye?" Trouvé retorted. "You're not helping the city. You're following your own ambition."

"That's not true. Nothing was done for personal gain."

"I find that hard to believe," Trouvé spat back. "You've pulled the Brotherhood in with you. It's a glaring transgression."

Toni tapped on her desk to catch her Italian colleague's attention. When he looked over, she held up a scrap of paper with three dots on it forming an equilateral triangle.

The crisp lines of Marco's handsome Mediterranean features pulled momentarily into a frown of displeasure followed by a shrug of indifference. Then he ran his fingers through his long bangs, and whispered, "Boys will be boys."

When she'd first arrived at *FranceTech*, the gradual realization that Freemasonry was an almost constitutional feature in the school had made Toni think she must have tumbled into a parallel universe. It was Marco who had explained the origins of the connection to her, detailing the link between the time honored traditions of Freemasonry and stonemasons and hence *FranceTech*.

"Even though stone is no longer worked by the Freemasons," he had said, "they have held on to the tools of stonemasonry as an allegory for the belief that a better world can be built on the foundations of Brotherly Love and Truth." Of all the people she knew in Paris, Marco was the only one who ever spoke English with Toni; he said it was Europe's lingua franca and therefore the correct language to use with academic colleagues. His English was near flawless, although too formal, with a pronounced tendency to avoid contractions and choose Latin roots over Anglo-Saxon ones. But the foibles of his English only added to its charm. And in any case, whatever he had to say was invariably worth listening to.

But on that day, Toni had balked as she listened to his summary of how the tools and symbols of stonemasonry had become the tools and symbols of Freemasonry. Like the square and compass. Or the way the fraternity divided themselves into the ranks of medieval masons: Master, Fellow, Apprentice.

Stonemason. Freemasons. Building the Temple of Humanity. The underlying parallel between architectural construction on the one hand and the abstract aim of building a better world, on the other. That was how a civil engineering school had become a central link in the dense tissue of French Freemasonry. Everyone at *FranceTech* knew about it and although the visiting Canadian student hadn't been officially initiated into the Craft, she understood the mind-boggling truth. Here, in Paris, in the 21st century, in a renowned institute of higher education, her professors were bickering about something as esoteric as Freemasonry. It was like schoolboys fighting over Pokemon cards.

As a fellow foreigner, Marco seemed to find the ambient Freemasonic atmosphere almost as annoying as Toni. Today, in particular, there were other things he needed to be doing rather than listening to the Brothers bickering. "I wish they would finish so that I could get to the Senate. There are still many things to prepare for tomorrow. But I promised I would help Trouvé carry over some material." He tapped on his watch. "If we do not go soon, we will never get everything ready."

"*You want that I go knock on the door to get Trouvé*," Toni asked, imitating her friend's accent. His English might be excellent but that didn't stop her from occasionally teasing.

"Yes. *I want*," he answered, purposely deforming his own sentence structure. But before she had time to get up and perform the service, Caron stamped out of the office, slamming the door behind him.

"Problem solved," Toni commented. "And yet again Caron demonstrates that he was probably raised by wolves."

The young Italian was always diplomatic but after spending over a year at the mercy of Caron's whims even he had to agree. "At least he is more assiduous today. It is already 3:30. That might be a record for him. It's maybe the first time I see him still here after lunch." The lilt of Marco's accent added theatricality to the exaggerated irony.

Caron's superiority complex *vis-à-vis* the academic world in general and his students in particular was public knowledge. He gave one lecture a week at *FranceTech* and was paid to spend the rest of the day on the premises contributing to research projects. The truth was that you'd have to be a pretty good hunter to track him down once his mid-morning course was over. More often than not he left the school before lunch. And if he did hang around, there was seldom a Becquerel of time devoted one-on-one to any of the students.

Trouvé, on the other hand, was the alter ego, always willing to provide his students with the attention they needed. In return, those students were anxious to serve him. When he emerged from his office, balancing two cardboard boxes filled with brochures for the conference, both Toni and Marco rushed down from the mezzanine to help.

"Let me take those," Marco said, reaching for one of the boxes.

"We'd better get going." Trouvé slid the remaining box onto the secretary's desk. "God only knows what last minute hitches we'll need to deal with."

For months Toni had been hearing about the conference Trouvé was organizing at the Senate but she wasn't involved with it. Marco was the right-hand man on the project. "I can give you a hand schlepping stuff across the park," she offered.

"Thanks, we could certainly use the extra arms," Trouvé agreed. "I'll get my jacket."

When Trouvé ducked into his office, Toni flipped open the top of the box and reached for a brochure. The pale blue cover displayed a logo in the shape of a terrestrial globe shaped out of the letters "vng" with "30" imprinted like a watermark on the background. She was familiar with Trouvé's pet project. The group was a sort of closed virtual forum made up of dynamic and out-spoken under-30s. Most of the time their research and discussion took place online; this was the first time they'd actually organized a meeting in the real world, beyond the bounds of their web forum. More importantly, the organization had direct links to one of the big French think tanks, GRF, which Trouvé was also a member of. And which, according to Marco, also had implicit ties to the Masons.

Old Europe was a strange and mysterious place.

Toni had followed the conference project from a distance but never been tempted to join. Her research concerns were more concrete than Trouvé's. The title of the forum was a little too conceptual for her: June 21st: *Challenging Global Ignorance: The quest for sustainability.* She flipped to the first page:

> In spite of vast improvements in the quality of education and the democratization of access to information in recent decades, the course of history remains unchanged. Suffering caused by culturally motivated conflict is visible both at inter and intra-national levels, the divide is growing between rich and poor while environmental damage draws the planet towards crisis. So why have information and education failed to guide mankind to a harmonious way of life based on reasoned global policies? Although the developing world has benefited from progress in education, too little has been done to accomplish the parallel goal of making the members of the middle classes aware of their global responsibility, namely recognizing the limits of consumer led unilateral growth at current unsustainable rates. This lack of awareness of the true challenges facing the global economy bears witness to the

need to differentiate between information and knowledge. In a world where a weekday edition of the *New York Times* contains more information than the average Englishman in the seventeenth century was likely to access in his entire lifetime, the urgency to educate people on how to evaluate the worthiness of information sources has become essential. Only when applied correctly can information have meaning and influence. The 30vng conference will explore innovative ways to foster global responsibility and awareness.

"Whew," she whistled. "Quite the programme. But I guess it's nothing more than a little light conversation for you guys."

"We should have some incisive debates; we are expecting a good turnout," Marco said. "The list of attendees is at the back." Toni flipped to the end of the programme and skimmed through the names. She only recognized two of them: Cédric Trouvé and Marco Bellini. The short descriptions beside the other names showed that there was a heavy preponderance of university lecturers and doctoral members of research labs. No doubt that meant there might be too much intellectual debate and not enough practical discussions.

A final sentence completed the page. "The closing ceremony and concert at the Odeon Theater will be attended by President Gustave Tibrac of France."

Although not involved in the conference, over the past months, Toni had listened to Marco's worries and complaints about the organizational hurdles. "So you got it all ironed out. Tibrac is really going to be there."

Marco had just emerged from Trouvé's office with another box of programmes. "Somehow I'm not expecting Tibrac's talk to be the most enlightening," he said, heading for the door.

Toni found that easy enough to believe. In fact, she had no idea why Tibrac was associating himself with this conference that was overtly linked to issues like sustainable development. The president had always struck her as one of those politicians who called loudly for France to become richer, more consumer oriented, grabbing a bigger piece of the pie. And if France had a bigger piece of the pie, the way Toni understood fractions, it meant that someone else would get a smaller piece – namely those who already had nothing but crumbs. Go figure politicians. It was probably just some PR stunt to make Tibrac look good in the eyes of people who really cared.

Unless, of course, it had something to do with the Masons again.

30

Montaigne High School was nothing more than a footnote on Sadiqi's long list of priorities. Perched on the southwest corner of the Luxembourg Gardens, it had been an easy stop for him after *FranceTech*. The custodian at the entrance hadn't wanted to let him in, but things had gone smoothly once the vice principal was called. She was both efficient and helpful, despite being more concerned about getting her students through their baccalaureate exams than helping the police.

Trémont was right, there wasn't much to see inside the school. The hallways were silent while a few classrooms were packed with thoughtful seniors hunched over their finals. The only spot of any interest to Sadiqi was the kitchen, where, he was shown a whitewashed wall darkened by grease stains and punctured by three small holes.

"On the other side of this wall, there's a staircase leading down to the catacombs. Or so I'm told," the VP said, fanning herself with a manila envelope and checking her watch. She needed to get back to invigilating exams.

"There's no door?" Sadiqi raised a fist and rapped on the off-white mess. It rang hollow.

"No. There was. But it's been sealed closed."

He rapped again. "This is just plaster on particle board."

"We have a limited budget for upkeep and renovations."

"There's just a layer of plaster separating you from the catacombs?" That sounded outrageous.

The VP shrugged but seemed more worried about her exam schedule than any risk created by the quarries. "I'm not sure. Maybe there's more to it than that. I've not been here for very long, so I wasn't around when the work was done. I can't really say. Maybe there's an iron door under the plaster, too."

Sadiqi was sceptical. It sure didn't sound like an iron door when he rapped. "An iron door. Perhaps with an iron key?"

The VP looked at her watch again. "If there's a key, I don't know who has it. I've certainly never seen one myself."

The cop ran his hand over the wall. It wouldn't take much of an effort to kick down the layer of plaster. But being as the wall was still intact, it was probably better to leave it that way. He would, however, like to see it from the other side.

It was definitely time to head back underground.

31

As he walked up the red carpet of the Honor Staircase, Trouvé readjusted his tie no less than five times. Tie touching was his anxiety tick. And there was certainly plenty to be anxious about. Hindsight was a terrible thing. He wished he had either programmed this bloody conference a week earlier or arranged to hold it in a less prestigious spot.

At the top of the stairs, he paused, both to compose himself and to get his bearings. The growing barrage of organizational hurdles facing tomorrow's conference was daunting. This was the culmination of over a year and a half's work. The conference was supposed to provide an opportunity for the world to listen to the younger generation's most brilliant minds expressing their hopes for the future and formulating new ideas on how to get the global community running in a more sustainable way. There were exciting ideas out there about how to make the ecological footprints of Europeans and North Americans smaller without endangering growth. The aim had been to create an intellectual fiesta. Only now, at the last minute, the whole thing was having the life kicked out of it by a security nightmare.

After spending the past ten minutes talking with the Senate's chief security officer, Trouvé didn't know whether he should be annoyed or worried. Security had been an ongoing concern ever since Trouvé had received confirmation that the conference could take place at the Senate. But now there were last minute complications, made all the worse because of the high profile special guests who were attending. Although the VIPs would have their own bodyguards, the Senate was obliged to enhance security for them.

This had all happened because following some undisclosed incident, the Latin Quarter was now on maximum alert level of the Vigipirate anti-terrorist warning system. Nobody would tell him why this was, but based on what both Caron and Corrigan had told him that morning, Trouvé could make an educated guess.

Not that he was concerned about a terrorist threat. He'd lived in Paris all his life and had seen plenty of terrorist threats come and go. High level, visible security measures were nothing new. Camouflage clad soldiers routinely patrolled train stations and tourist spots toting machine guns. Parisians were used to opening their handbags and backpacks to security agents whenever they entered shopping malls, museums or public building. The fear of getting blown up had never kept any of them cowering at home.

No. As the official organizer of tomorrow's conference, Trouvé was far more worried about the problems caused by over-intrusive security than by the actual attack risk itself. The new measures the security team had just laid out were absurd. Not only would everyone entering the building now have to undergo a spread eagle metal detector test and a detailed bag search, but the mobility of conference attendees was going to be restricted. Security didn't want people wandering in and out of the building whenever they felt like it. They wanted arrival and departure times to be limited to a specific timetable. Talk about a mess. Sealing the conference might reduce security risks but it wasn't going to help Trouvé run his conference smoothly. Invitations had been sent out months ago, confirmation weeks ago. And there certainly hadn't been any mention that participants absolutely had to be in the building spot on time at 9:30. On top of that, there was the problem of lunch. Trouvé had only organized lunch in the private Senate dining room for the keynote speakers – everyone else was expected to fend for themselves. There were plenty of nearby cafés where you could grab a sandwich or a quick meal. But if the participants weren't allowed back in the building after, this was going to be a fiasco.

Taking a deep breath Trouvé readjusted the knot of his tie again then started down the corridor. With each step, his preoccupations grew.

If something went wrong, he would be the one held responsible. If people missed debates because they'd been held up entering the building, there would be complaints. Some attendees were travelling halfway around the world to be here.

And then of course there were the logistics of the closing events, which were an added source of anxiety. A gala evening had been planned to wind up the conference. Tomorrow was the summer solstice, which also meant it was the *Fête de la Musique* – a day when the whole country was invited into the streets to dance and sing and play or listen to music all night long. To fit in with the musical theme, the conference organizers had decided to finish with an opera. *The Magic Flute,* staged next door at the Odeon Theater, would provide the conference goers with an evening to remember. Each attendee had received an invitation for two, plus a number of personalities from both academia and the arts had been invited. If they were renting the whole theater, they might as well fill it.

It had seemed like a good idea a year ago when it had first been floated. Now the theater was surrounded by cops, the artists were having trouble entering the building for their dress rehearsal and

Trouvé had been told there would be sniffer dogs and uniformed *gendarmes* on duty both inside and outside the building during the whole evening. That was sure to lighten people's spirits.

And what about the buffet? It was very likely that at ten o'clock tomorrow night the caterers would still be locked out on the sidewalk by police guards scared of having knives and other sharp objects in the near vicinity of President Tibrac.

That was the worst of it. Tibrac. Trouvé had never been in favor of inviting the president to play any part in the conference events, but now he wished he'd been more forceful in his opposition based on practical considerations rather than ideological ones. Making sure Tibrac was properly guarded was going to be a major headache.

Organizing an event of this scale was always a nightmare. This wasn't the first conference Trouvé had ever put together, but it was certainly the biggest. He knew exactly how these things worked. When an event went smoothly, you didn't notice the work that had gone into it. It was only when things went badly that people noticed the organization (or lack of it).

Having hit this stress high point, the professor took another deep breath and told himself to get Zen. If he thought about it objectively, the increased security measures weren't really a problem. A lot of people felt reassured that increased security meant increased personal safety. And the new measures in place at the Senate were by no means outlandishly harsh. The heavy police presence was unlikely to dampen spirits. People were used to this kind of thing.

With these reassuring thoughts in mind he entered the conference room. As he passed through the gold-leaf doorway, he felt his confidence growing. In a way it was a good thing that the conference was being held in such a wonderful venue where the *gendarmes* on duty were career professionals used to dealing with high security alerts. They knew what they were doing. They would go about their business without disrupting events. And the conference would carry on.

Yet a quick glance around and his stress level peaked again. The sheer amount of work remaining to be done still worried him. Despite the team of twelve grad and post-doc students, who were helping with the logistics, he could see that it was going to take the rest of the afternoon and probably a good part of the evening to get everything set for the morning. If there was negative feedback following the conference, he didn't want it related to anything he had done – or left undone. There was no way he was going to leave the building tonight until all the hitches were ironed out. Which meant that his appointment with Caron was not going to happen.

The professor sidled into one of the immense window brackets that stretched to the ceiling several meters above and observed the students huddled together working on the various projects he had set them, chatting and laughing.

Once he and Pierre had been that close, too. Attending conferences together, debating politics, discussing everything from their courses to how best to save the world. It all seemed such a long way away. How long had it been? Twenty-five? Thirty years? A small pile of calendars that represented half their lifetime. And now they had both collaborated in destroying that tie. Even the most solid friendships hung by a thread.

He reached into his pocket for his phone and swiped in Caron's number. The line switched directly to voice mail. Trouvé would have preferred to catch Pierre personally rather than leave a message, but he wasn't going to waste his afternoon endlessly calling back. Knowing Pierre, he'd probably turned off his phone on purpose and was filtering calls precisely because he wanted to avoid him. A message would have to do.

"*Pierre, c'est Cédric ici.*" The words came out in a glacial tone that Trouvé immediately regretted. He would have preferred to sound friendlier – less ruffled. Wash this under the bridge like all their previous disagreements. Yet he knew that couldn't happen this time. Pierre had gone too far. It was impossible for Trouvé to keep the disappointment out of his voice. If Trouvé had been face to face with Caron, or even talking to him personally over the phone rather than dealing with his voice mail, he would have paused to make sure he got the tone of his message right. But if he paused now, the machine would most likely cut him off. So he laid out the facts bluntly. "I'm phoning to cancel our meeting at the *Petit Suisse...*" he began.

32

On her way back to school from the Senate, Toni raised her eyes to take in the façade of the *FranceTech* building.

This was where Marco had first shown her the school's visible symbols of Freemasonry. This is where she had learnt that for many people codes and rituals were still an important part of life – even in intellectual circles where she would have expected a more rigourously scientific approach.

This revelation had come quite soon after her arrival the previous fall. One evening, as they were heading home together, Toni had commented on how she loved the carved caryatide of the elephant head on the side of the building on rue Auguste Comte, across the street from the university. That's when Marco had spun around and told her that it was the carvings on *FranceTech* that fascinated him. That was it. He was off. And her eyes were opened.

Although she'd often looked at the university building, she had never truly seen it until he gave her the walking tour. He was the one who had explained that the three women in Greek robes carved into the building's pediment were more than a generic 19th century façade. They were the symbols that announced to the initiated that they were entering a realm deeply attached to Freemasonry's ideals. Toni's eyes fixed on the building as she remembered her colleagues words. "The three women symbolize the three forces revered by Freemasonry: wisdom, force and beauty. The two columns standing behind them are central to Freemasonry. You'll find them in any lodge: they mark the passage from a familiar place to a world yet to be discovered. The book the woman in the center is holding represents knowledge."

Toni thought of the other carvings that adorned the school's northern façade. A few rings encircling representations of mining tools. Not particularly surprising at an institution that had initially been specialized in the field of mining.

Except, again, Marco had pointed out symbolic details in the carvings. "The mallet and chisel are the stonemason's tools. He uses them to impose his will on stone – to create a shape that resembles what he imagines. The chisel is poised and ready to act; the mallet symbolizes the will to act. They form a pair. They are inseparable; they cannot be used individually. They represent the Freemason's will to influence the construction of a better society."

Toni had a hard time believing the carvings were anything more than a reference to mining. But once Marco pointed out all the other Masonic symbols on the building, the idea had become much harder to ignore. The leaves surrounding the mallet were oak and acacia. Oak represented all the qualities associated with old age – sometimes even immortality. Acacia was one of the supreme Freemasonic symbols – the sign of the Master Mason – because it was the desert plant that the Masons saw as being linked to death and rebirth.

Of course, Toni would have liked to dismiss everything Marco had said. It seemed ridiculous to claim that *FranceTech* was a

Freemasonic hotbed simply because of a few sculptures. But then Marco had explained that Freemasonry was deeply attached to iconographic symbol. Their lodges, their aprons, their sashes, even the glasses and plates used at special lodge dinners were all covered in symbols. The symbols were there as a constant reminder of their aspirations. The symbols were not coincidence; they were the visible testimony that the Pythagoras and Euclid Lodge that was based at the school was one of the oldest and most venerable in the world.

Although the university was brimming with Masonic symbols, Toni liked to think that most of those symbols were also just every day symbols from European tradition. Even Marco had been forced to concede this point. "Yes, it's true it is hard to tell the two apart," he'd said. "You're right; there are allegorical carvings like these on most public buildings in France. Is the inspiration Masonic or simply rooted in a wider European symbolism? Does *FranceTech* have deep links to Freemasonry or is the existence of the local lodge just a detail?" It was the next part of his comments that had astounded Toni. "It's a question that raises its head often in France – particularly in French politics. How deeply rooted in Freemasonry is the Republic itself? You realize, the national motto – Liberty, Equality, Fraternity – was a Freemason motto long before the French Republic even existed."

Toni had baulked. "You're telling me the Freemasons were behind the French Revolution."

"Who knows? Some people think yes. Others no. It's impossible to say. In any case, some people claim that Freemasons have been behind most of the political turmoil and war of the modern age. Opponents accuse the fraternity of plotting to take over the world; scheming to hold the reins of power."

"There's nothing like a good conspiracy theory."

Marco couldn't have agreed more. "Yes. But this particular conspiracy theory is made stronger by the fact that individual Freemasons have been incredibly influential in western politics for centuries."

"Like who?"

"Washington, Churchill, the Bonapartes, most of the generals at the battle of Trafalgar on both sides. They were all Freemasons."

Toni found the list unimpressive. "Those guys are all dead and buried. To get elected today, it's more important to look good on TV than to be a Freemason. Who's left in the Freemasons nowadays? A few professors like Caron and Trouvé?"

Marco couldn't miss an opportunity to be provocative. "It's still important in France. Many of Tibrac's advisors and ministers are Masons."

Toni mulled over the memory as she climbed the front steps. Most of the time, she didn't even think about the school's links to Freemasonry. It all seemed like just another example of Old World social stratification. An obsolete club, rife with exclusiveness and secrecy, letting a few people in, just so that they could keep many more out – all the women, for starters. After all, the key term here was "brotherhood". Trouvé was a member. Caron. Even Marco had been asked to join, although according to him, he'd turned down the offer... But nobody had ever invited the little Canadian girl to join.

Whatever. She wasn't interested in living in the past. Even though the Masons annoyed her, she had other more important things on her mind. Namely a call she'd been meaning to make to that very 21st century cop with his very 21st century problems.

33

Like any self-respecting Frenchman, Sadiqi had a tendency to over dramatize and ignite situations. Diplomacy was not one of his strong points and so the atmosphere on boulevard Arago was tense.

The counter-terror inspector had come to cataflic headquarters to request Captain Ferry's aid. Not surprisingly, the more insistent Sadiqi became, the stronger Ferry's refusal.

"Just reassign the men you lent me this morning," Sadiqi said as he prowled back and forth across the room, like a caged tiger.

"Believe it or not my men do have to sleep."

"*Enfin merde*, it's only 4 in the afternoon," Sadiqi growled, all signs of his good intentions to gently inveigle the division captain into providing his support evaporating. "They haven't exactly been up all night."

Sadiqi's angry reaction only made Ferry feel like winding him up more. "They already did overtime this morning. They were in at 7 to help you – after spending most of the night carrying out routine surveillance. They'd been on duty since 21:00 last night." This wasn't strictly true. Only one of the men had served a full shift the night before, but Ferry had a point to make and he wasn't going to let anything as trivial as the truth get in his way.

"I was up at 4," Sadiqi countered.

"That's not the same thing, *Monsieur l'Inspecteur Général*," Ferry said with a drop of poison-laced honey in his voice. The captain's insistence on Sadiqi's little-used but correct title was intended to point out that as one of the bosses, he was expected to do overtime. It was part of his job description. It was not, on the other hand, a demand that could be made of patrolling officers.

Suggesting that any civil servant should be forced to work overtime wasn't something Sadiqi would have done under normal circumstances. Bureaucracy couldn't be rushed. Far be it from him to ask anyone to carry out work that went beyond the statutory stipulations set by their trade union. Yet the extraordinary circumstances weighing on the city demanded an equally extraordinary response. "Fair enough," he said, trying to sound compliant. "But all I need is one officer. I'm sure you can find someone."

The arms crossed on Ferry's chest formed a human shield against Sadiqi. "No. My core line-up is already working double overtime and my backup squad has just been requisitioned. I don't have anyone to offer you."

The body language was deafening. Sadiqi couldn't believe what he was hearing. "Who requisitioned your men? I'm requisitioning them back."

The smug expression that formed on the captain's lips told the inspector that he wasn't going to like the answers. "I got the order from Dukrin half an hour ago. I was told to put full-time guards on all major underground sites around the Senate. I'm using my emergency roster," he said, pointing over his shoulder to the grid timetable on the wall.

The lack of urgency in the captain's voice contrasted with the words. He seemed to view an increased security threat as an administrative hassle rather than a sign that anyone's well-being was actually in peril. "We're on full alert," Ferry added with the same emotion he might have used to say 'We're watching paint dry.' "I have people under Val-de-Grace, the Senate and all the hospitals. We're completely overstretched. I don't even have enough men to ensure a normal patrol around the rest of the network. All I've got are two teams that I'm rotating in eight-hour shifts." A little emotion was finally starting to creep into his voice, but it was anger at being overworked, not apprehension over the city's future.

Ferry showed the full confidence of a civil servant who had performed his duty faultlessly. No less than was expected of him. No more than was expected. That was the key reference point. Never do more than you have to. Never be polite if you can get away with being rude. Never be helpful if you can get away with being unhelpful.

It was an attitude completely foreign to Sadiqi who was consumed by his job. He took his work home with him. He took it to bed with him. Terror and crime accompanied him every minute of the day. He knew how the criminals worked. And he knew how the anti-crime machine worked. So it followed that he knew damn well that Ferry was sure to have other backup officers tucked away somewhere. There were always officers trained to help out when things got rough even if they weren't permanently attached to a given division.

Any atmosphere of team spirit had deserted the room long ago. The two men were glaring at one another, arms folded across their chests.

"In any case, this morning you told me you were planning on checking things out on your own. You said you had a copy of the *Atlas*." Ferry's self-satisfied sneer screamed out to the world that he knew damn well why Sadiqi wasn't setting off on his own through the quarries. Generations of cataphiles had ventured underground looking for Saturday night thrills. Sadiqi knew that part of that thrill was the danger of not finding your way back out. And having the *Atlas* didn't alleviate that risk. Those maps were hell to figure out. If he set off with nothing other than those damn maps to guide him through the network, there might not be any city left to save by the time he found his way out again.

Sadiqi missed smoking. He missed the ritual of opening those small cardboard pouches and selecting a cigarette. The feel of the diaphanous paper forming the slender tubes. The scent of the tobacco. The first drag. For thirty-two years smoking had been a useful ritual in tense moments like these. Six months was nothing like long enough to lay the habit to rest. Staring at Ferry while he popped a nicotine candy out of its aluminum wrapper just didn't occupy the space in the same way.

Fortunately, the tense silence didn't last long. Not because Ferry came up with a proposal, but because Sadiqi's phone began to shiver in his pocket.

Without wiping the peeved look off his face he slipped into the limbo world of phone calls. The ethereal lilt with the light accent that came down the line was easy to place: *"Bonjour Monsieur l'Inspecteur Général."*

The call came as no surprise. Lots of people followed up their interviews with extra details. Some were helpful. Some weren't.

Either way, Sadiqi never beat around the bush on the phone. His policy was to get whatever news the caller was delivering and then free the line for the next call. *"Madame Corrigan. Re-bonjour."*

"I'm sorry to bother you. It's just something Professor Caron said earlier. I wanted to clarify," she began cautiously. "I meant to mention it before but it slipped my mind when we were talking about the Green Monster. It's not all that important. It's just a detail really." Sadiqi paced slowly back towards the desk, wishing the student would stop apologizing and get to the point. "It's about the *Atlas*. *The Underground Atlas of Paris*. Earlier today Professor Caron said that the *Atlas* provided a complete layout of everything underground. And that there are definitely no tunnels under Henri IV High School."

"Are you telling me there *are* tunnels under the school?" Caron had struck Sadiqi as less than forthcoming. The detective wasn't rattled by the suggestion the slippery old bastard had been lying. But if there were tunnels, he needed to know more.

"Well, no. Not necessarily."

Wonderful, thought Sadiqi. A yes/no answer. "Give me the condensed version," he said, anxious to get back to his negotiations with Ferry.

But the student was taking her time with her choice of words. "Well... As you know, the *Atlas* was started when the IGC was first created. That was over two hundred years ago," she said, sounding too much like a lecturer for Sadiqi. "The engineers made detailed plans of all the underground quarries. The ones they filled in as well as the surveillance tunnels they created."

"Yes. I know that," Sadiqi interrupted. "I've already had the history lesson, Ms. Corrigan. I understood the first time round. The *Atlas* provides a perfect representation of the quarries."

The steamroller brashness was a little worse than Toni had expected; she hesitated. But ultimately, she wasn't going to let a little rudeness stop her from sharing her thoughts – otherwise she would never get a word in edgewise in this darling country. "No. That's the whole point," she corrected, being careful to keep her voice polite. "The Atlas *isn't* a perfect representation of the quarries. You probably think I'm nitpicking, but the fact is that a lot of historic details about underground Paris have been lost – particularly the information concerning the network running under the Latin Quarter. That's where the earliest reinforcements were carried out."

As impatient as he was, Sadiqi was attentive to detail. And the girl's statement contradicted what the IGC director had said. "No trace was kept of the earliest reinforcement work?"

"Oh yeah. The *Atlas* was made from the start. That's not the problem. The problem is that back in the old days, before the age of photocopiers and scanners, very few copies of official documents were made. *The Atlas* is a complex document. Not the easiest thing to replicate by hand. So basically there was one master copy of *The Atlas*, then a few other partial replicas. The master copy was kept at Paris city hall – *l'Hôtel de Ville*." Toni stressed these last words, certain the inspector would immediately catch on.

He didn't. An expectant silence ran down the line.

"The *Hôtel de Ville* burnt to the ground in 1871," she prompted. "All that was left standing was a stone carcass. The wood interior was entirely destroyed. As were thousands of administrative documents. Decades worth of certificates and registries were lost in the fire. Along with countless other important documents. The *Atlas* was one of them."

Sadiqi had got the message but not the point. He couldn't make out whether what he was being told was important, incidental or useless. "So what are you telling me? That the *Atlas* doesn't really represent the quarries? That Caron was lying?"

"Not exactly. No," she wavered again. *Lie* was too strong a word. And she certainly didn't want to get Caron into trouble by claiming he had lied to the cops. "It's true that the IGC makes sure the *Atlas* provides as perfect a representation as possible of the quarries. It's constantly updated. But a certain amount of information from the original *Atlas* was lost – is missing. The original *Atlas* was based on the state of the quarries at the time of the Revolution. That was the starting point. The initial version traced and reported every single hole that existed under the city at that time. It also monitored when each hole was filled and how that work was done. But the original historic reference was lost in the fire."

Sadiqi listened carefully. In his line of work, the problem wasn't getting information; the problem was sifting through the endless piles of useless information to pin down the important stuff. And this presentation on the history of the *Atlas* didn't seem to come anywhere near the pertinent mark. Yet Corrigan kept insisting there was some point to it all.

"What I'm saying is that huge amounts of detail concerning the original extent of the network were lost. The new *Atlas* put together after the fire represents an imperfect history of the quarries. It shows what remained of the quarries after 1871. A few additional historic details were pieced together from the personal memories of certain IGC engineers and the few surviving pages of the original *Atlas* that were recuperated here or there. But basically a hundred years' worth of information disappeared in the fire." Toni paused again to emphasize the importance of what she had just said. "Data concerning dozens of kilometers of tunnels were lost. Quarries that were hidden behind mortared stone surveillance tunnels disappeared from memory forever."

"What you're telling me is that there might be a filled in quarry that existed 300 years ago that's no longer visible on the *Atlas*," Sadiqi summarized. As far as he could tell, this seemed fairly trivial compared to everything else he was dealing with today.

Toni could hear the uncertainty in his voice. "Inspector, I don't think you understand the implications of what I'm saying. Basically, what I'm trying to explain is that the *Atlas* is up-to-date, but historically incomplete. It shows the surveillance tunnels and reinforcements that were still visible after 1871. But what exists beyond those reinforcements is largely unknown. There are chambers down there that can be reconquered without carrying out heavy engineering work. There are spots on the *Atlas* indicating solid limestone deposits that are really empty quarries that have been filled in with rubble and loose stones. There are tunnels that exist that nobody knows about – or at least that the IGC, in its official capacity, doesn't know about."

Although Sadiqi's eyes were fixed on Ferry scribbling away on his roster, his thoughts were now focused on Corrigan. He had just got the message. "Basically, what you're saying is that Caron could be wrong about Henri IV. It's possible that there *is* a tunnel leading to the school. A tunnel that was filled in hundreds of years ago, but that someone might have rediscovered."

Smiles can be heard over the phone even if they can't be seen. "Yeah," Toni sighed. "That about sums it up. I mean, I'm not saying there *is* a tunnel for certain. In fact, most people would tell you that Caron's right; that the network doesn't stretch that far."

Sadiqi ignored the backpedalling. "And if someone somehow learned about or found one of these old quarries, they'd be able to access it?"

"Stranger things have happened," she said. "Cataphiles who come across a blocked passage or a filled in quarry are more than likely to start digging. There's nothing a cataphile likes more than the opportunity to dig. And even creating new tunnels isn't completely unheard of."

"So it wouldn't surprise you if someone tried to dig to the high school?"

"No. Not at all. Especially if part of the tunnel passed through a previously existing quarry." There was a brief pause before she added: "I'm not saying it would be easy. Emptying an old quarry would still mean a lot of work. Stones would have to be carted out and dumped somewhere. But putting a forgotten quarry back into shape would mean a lot less work than building a tunnel from scratch."

"It's an interesting idea," Sadiqi muttered. What he was really thinking was, *It's a worrying idea.*

Far from finding the idea worrying Toni was toying with the dream that someone might have come across a long lost tunnel and uncovered something that time had forgotten. She was also pleased to hear the cop taking her seriously.

"Thank you, Ms. Corrigan. You did well to call me."

The friendly tone in his voice sparked her on. "Oh, and one other thing, Inspector. I caught a glimpse your maps..." Once again she searched for the best way to give the news without getting her professor into too much trouble. "I think Professor Caron may have made a mistake. The ones he gave you are out-of-date. I'd say they're at least fifteen years old."

Once again this detail of quarry engineering left Sadiqi indifferent. He certainly didn't care whether he had a spanking new edition of the maps or a slightly older one. "So what? The quarries are about a thousand years old, aren't they? A decade here or there won't change much."

Toni asked herself why she bothered. The world of the quarries was a Neverland that Sadiqi just didn't get. Not everyone did. Once again she would have to spell it out. "Subterranean Paris is constantly evolving. Above ground old buildings are torn down and new ones constructed. Underground, weak quarries are sometimes walled off and filled in. Things are created and things are destroyed. Every year dozens of tunnels are sealed off and injected with cement and sand. A set of fifteen-year-old maps are virtually useless. Too much has changed during that time. There are passages marked on your maps that just don't exist anymore. You'll think you can get from one point to the next but in fact you won't be able to. At best your officers will come up against dead ends. At worst, they'll end up lost."

Across the room Ferry continued to scratch away at his work. *He* would have up-to-date maps. Which simply confirmed the fact that Sadiqi was going to have to postpone his investigation until the chief cataflic decided to squeeze him into his roster... Unless...

The idea slid into Sadiqi's mind quite innocently, but once it was there he couldn't shake it.

The student was a catacomb expert. She certainly seemed to know the history of the network; if her practical knowledge was anywhere like as extensive as her historic knowledge she could definitely help. Okay, it wasn't a very professional option. He might be putting her at risk. But today he couldn't see any other choice.

"Madame Corrigan, I have a favor to ask. I need to inspect the quarries, but nobody from the quarry brigade is available to escort me. I was wondering if you could show me around." Across the room, Ferry looked up from his scribbling. Sadiqi was pleased to see a look of shock on the captain's face.

Similarly, down the line, Toni was taking note of the Inspector General's ability to improvize unexpected solutions to his problems. Even if it meant behaving inconsistently. A few hours earlier he'd officially told her the quarries were a no go area. Now he wanted her to be his guide. He wasn't easy to follow. Without meaning to be unpleasant, she couldn't resist making a small jab. "We'd better meet soon, then. Before you have time to change your mind again."

34

Caron unlocked the door to his apartment and was hit by a waft of boiling air. Like most Parisians, he had never bothered installing air conditioning. So with each day of the heat wave the temperature in the building had increased a little. For the past ten days he and his wife had been working hard to regulate the apartment's thermodynamics. They kept the shutters and windows tightly sealed all day long, only opening them in the evening once the sun had set. Yet now even those good intentions didn't seem to be having much effect. If the hot weather kept up much longer he'd soon be roasted alive in his own home.

Once in the library, the professor made a beeline for the fan propped on the corner of his desk. This was the only source of fresh air left in the apartment and he switched it to the highest setting before slipping off his jacket and tossing it onto the windowsill. Even though he would have been more comfortable sitting outside in a shady park, he would spend the afternoon working from home. That was written in stone. Caron was a man of habit. Thursday afternoons were always spent writing up research at home.

He stretched across the desk, clicked on the lamp and reached into his briefcase for his cell phone. It had turned itself off. The battery must be dead. He pulled open the desk drawer and started rummaging around for the recharge cable. It wasn't where it was supposed to be. Which meant Sandrine had been going through his things again. He knew he had charged the phone the previous morning and he was sure he'd returned the cord to its rightful spot. Sandrine, on the other hand, didn't understand the first thing about organization and was constantly misplacing the cord to her own phone. And while she hadn't the sense to systematically return her cord to some safe spot between recharges, she knew exactly where to find his.

Caron slammed the drawer shut. His temper was rising. The missing cable was just an excuse to blow off steam. The slammed drawer had more to do with the morning's events than his phone. He had been strung out all day, driven from frustration to elation and now down to worry.

Although he hadn't appreciated being pulled out of bed at crack of dawn after a sleepless night, his fatigue had dissipated at Val-de-Grace. There, he had seen new hope. The police presence all over the Latin Quarter and the removal of his own personal privileges in connection with the quarries indicated that whatever had happened to the Prime Minister, it didn't have anything to do with his hernia. The quarries were the source of the problem.

That had been worth celebrating. Not that Caron had anything against de Chanterelle. It was just that his death meant that the government could no longer ignore the strategic dangers posed by the underground network. Sure, there would be a period of beating around the bush. There always was. But ultimately it would become evident that the usual law enforcement method of mobilizing a huge number of police on the ground wouldn't work in the quarries. There wasn't enough trained manpower available. What were they going to do? Post individual police officers to stand guard over manholes. That would solve nothing. There were just too many entry points into the system. So the logical conclusion would soon gain momentum: if the quarries couldn't be patrolled satisfactorily, they would have to be closed down. It was inevitable.

If only the pleasure of that moment of insight could have lasted he would still be planning his future at the head of the soon-to-be-established Ministry for Urban Subterranean Reinforcement – or whatever they wanted to call it. But the joy hadn't lasted. Not even until the end of the day. Trouvé had seen to that.

Caron could kick himself for always being so transparent with Trouvé. He was incapable of being anything less than totally frank with him, invariably giving way to a stream of ridiculous adolescent enthusiasm that seemed to come welling back every time he spoke with his colleague. It was a throwback to youth. The problem was that their friendship dated back to their student days. Before becoming colleagues at *FranceTech*, they had been students at *FranceTech*. They had known the same professors, written the same exams. They had picked up girls together. Discussed politics, from de Gaulle to Mitterandism then on to Macron. They had grown into adulthood together and stood side by side as the world changed.

And then they themselves had changed. At least Caron knew that he had changed. Perhaps that was the problem. He had changed while Cédric had remained the same. Idealistic. Naïve. Yes. That was the heart of the problem. Cédric lived life by principles and those principles were too rigid. He wasn't practical.

That was why Caron had always downplayed his relations with Clavreul whenever he was around his colleague. He had always known that Cédric wouldn't understand. That he couldn't understand. Not that Caron had lied about anything he had done for the senator. No. He had simply been... what was the expression? ... sparing with the truth. He had told his colleague about his meetings with Clavreul. He had told him about the report he wrote. He had even shown it to him (or at least most of it). What he hadn't told him was just how much information about the quarries he had shared with the senator unofficially. Bits of conversation he'd had with Clavreul but that he hadn't put in the report. He had kept those details from Cédric because he knew he wouldn't understand. And he had been right to keep them to himself. The little he let slide today had sent his colleague into a fit.

Caron shook his head as he thought of the things said earlier. Leave it to Cédric to imagine that anyone not on the same side of the political spectrum as himself must be trying to overthrow democracy. It was ridiculous.

Caron dabbed at the sweat on his forehead with a cotton tissue. The justifications kept circling through his mind like a mantra designed to keep out the sound of Cédric's recriminations. Because although he didn't want to admit it, deep down Caron regretted his many indiscretions with the senator. He should have been less forthcoming. He had certainly said more than had been strictly necessary to make a convincing case.

The professor shifted in his chair. *Stop the self-flagellation*, he thought. Between fidelity to the Brotherhood and modernizing Paris, perhaps modernizing was more important. What mattered was to get the ball rolling – or at the very least, to get the cement mixers churning.

The fan blew back across the desk dislodging a sheet of paper propped up against the telephone and uncovering the flashing red message button on his answering machine. The light made him relax. Sandrine was always telling him that he spent too much time working. She would take him to concerts and the theater to open his mind to other thoughts. And she was right to do it; the change of pace helped relieve the jumble of every day concerns piled up in his mind. Likewise, the light on the machine was a promise of distraction. It announced news from the outside world. Just what he needed to clear his head. A complete change of subject. He stretched over and pressed play.

A loud beep sounded, followed by Sandrine's voice: *"Chéri*, I'm out with Elise and Sarah this afternoon. We're going to the Dior exhibit at the Arts Déco. There's no point in joining us. You'll just be bored with all the girl talk. I'll be back about 8. Chloé's out this evening. It's just the two of us, so think about where you're going to take me for dinner. *Bisous.'"* The carefreeness of a devoted window shopper laying out her plans for the day was soothing. His wife. Bringing a shot of lightness to a day that had been too heavy.

Caron leaned back in his chair and glanced towards the living-room door. In Sandrine's absence, Hiro Hito was standing at attention in the doorway, guarding her domain. Apparently its mistress' voice had woken the bony black cat from its usual afternoon nap. Or maybe it was just the heat stopping it from sleeping, like everyone else.

Another beep before the next message: "Monsieur Caron. *Je m'appelle Frédéric Volnay.* I work for *France Aube."* A journalist. And the voice sounded intense, like he was particularly excited about a new story. "I tried to reach you at the IGC but your secretary was kind enough to pass on this number. Our paper received a tip this morning concerning the PM's death. My sources tell me the official line regarding the death is incorrect, to say the least. Those same sources say the death was not at all accidental but an assassination, carried out using the catacombs. They also tell me that the catacombs have been used for a second attack. Some sort of biological weapon used on Montaigne High." The muscles that had just relaxed down Caron's back tensed like a bowstring. While he had half-expected the questions about de Chanterelle, the reference to the high school was a smack in the face. "I'd like to know if you can substantiate these claims. I'll try to catch you later this afternoon, otherwise you can reach me at…"

Caron remained glued to his chair, staring at the red button on the machine as if it might explode. A biological attack on Montaigne High School. Was it possible? Not just one attack on the quarries, but two? The same day?

He didn't need to think very long to remember where the document was. His hand shot to a side drawer in his desk and pulled out the *Clavreul Report* flipping quickly to the chapter entitled "Worst case scenarios". Opening the report was superfluous. He knew the document by heart. Chapter 4: The culminating chapter whose pages laid out in detail the true devastation that could potentially be wrought on the city via the catacombs. The director's eyes scanned over the words hoping that perhaps the information on the page might have changed since the last he looked. Instead what he saw was what he remembered. The primary targets he had defined were still the same: Val-de-Grace military hospital and Montaigne High were top of the list. And sure enough political assassination and biological weapons infiltration had been detailed in his list of terrorist possibilities.

He took off his glasses and massaged his eyes, a sense of imminent cataclysm shooting through him. A cluster of black spots appeared in front of him and he could feel a pounding in his ears. His blood pressure had just gone off the charts.

Although he had already suspected there was more to the PM's death than an anaesthetic, the rumors about Montaigne were distressing. They made the whole thing sound less like a random attack and more like an exact replication of the scenarios he had laid out in the report. If that were the case, if his brief was being used as the strategic plan for a multi-pronged attack, he would be responsible for the most widespread devastation ever aimed at the city. Far from protecting Paris, his report could spell the end of the city. The director flipped through the pages in a daze. It read like Revelations – starting with isolated incidents, the report then evolved towards something more spectacular. Quarries exploding, making the earth shake and city blocks fold into the ground in a crash of thunder. The nightmare scenario. Half of Paris swallowed up. A metropolis-wide Ground Zero.

His hand trembled ever so slightly as he reached into his briefcase to pull out the transparent folder containing the paper Cédric had given him. He smoothed his hand over the plastic and reread the words that had seemed so nonsensical such a short time ago:

June 20; from Ng
Retribution will come
He sends his servant from the depths of darkness into
light.
Arnaud de Chanterelle was brought to justice at Val-de-
Grace this morning. Our struggle against the oppressors
continues. Many others deserve punishment. Long live
freedom.

Caron slammed his hand down on top of the paper. Cringing, he
mumbled to himself: "What have I done?"

35

Although Caron's gut feeling told him something was seriously
wrong, his mind raced to find someone else to blame. Even if
somehow some terrorist group had got their hands on the *Clavreul
Report* and was carrying out the threats described in it, surely there
were people in the police trained to track them down and stop them.

There was no way he was going to blame himself for what was
happening. All he had done was transmit his concerns to the higher
authorities. He was doing his job. Fair enough. He hadn't used
official channels. He had bypassed the usual hierarchy. But that
didn't matter. What mattered was being heard at the top of the
pyramid. It certainly wasn't his fault if the men at the top had ignored
his warnings. Had they listened to him, they wouldn't be in this mess
now.

At least that's what he wanted to believe. Yet despite all his
efforts, there was a voice gnawing at him, repeating that he was the
one who had unleashed the furies. Never mind Cédric's concerns
about the Brotherhood's secrets, Caron had formulated plans about
how the greatest potential havoc could be wrought via the quarries.
Then he had written down those ideas in minute detail and handed
them to a man he barely knew, blindly accepting his promise to make
sure the report made its way into competent hands.

The eyebrow above Caron's right eye twitched nervously. Up
until now, he had taken it for granted that the report had made its way
straight to Tibrac via Clavreul. That the president had seen the report
but refused to act on it. It suddenly occurred to him that perhaps that

wasn't the case. Perhaps the report had followed a different circuit. Perhaps the rumors about Clavreul's extremist connections were true. Perhaps the senator had leaked it to some right wing radicals. Or perhaps he had shown it to the president, but after his refusal to act on it, the report had somehow gone astray. Landed in the wrong hands.

Both possibilities were entirely plausible. Both seriously worrying.

Caron grabbed his jacket off the windowsill and pulled out the slightly withered visiting card with the *Police Nationale* crest on it: Khalid Sadiqi. There was nothing else written. No address. No brigade name.

The thought of calling the police officer didn't inspire Caron. The man hadn't exactly made a good impression. He was rude, pushy and clearly proletarian. Despite all these objections Caron stretched over and grabbed the phone.

The number barely had time to ring before it was answered by an unpleasant monotone: *"Sadiqi, j'écoute."*

Caron felt the irony of reaching out to this man for help after spending most of the morning sending him running in circles. But it was too late to worry about that now. In any case, this wasn't a social call. Everything he had to say was purely factual. "Inspector. This is Pierre Caron speaking." He decided that measured understatements were best. "I'm calling because I'm a little concerned about what's happening in the quarries. If indeed something is happening." There was no sign of encouragement or otherwise from down the line so he continued. "I thought you should know that I wrote a report recently that deals with the possibility of the underground network being used for terrorist purposes. The report was ordered by Senator Clavreul. I don't know if you've read it."

Caron could almost hear the other man sizing him up. Trying to figure out why there had been this about-turn, wondering why he was suddenly offering help after spending the rest of the day making the police officer pull every strand of information out of him with great effort. Not surprisingly, there was a hint of suspicion in Sadiqi's voice when he answered. "No. This is the first I've heard of it."

"I probably should have mentioned it earlier, but it slipped my mind," Caron offered feebly. This wasn't so much a lie as a prefabricated excuse that he used whenever he was feckless, whether it was a case of not letting his wife know that he wouldn't be in for dinner or more serious circumstances like today. "The report might interest you. It contains a lot of information about quarry infrastructure – access points, areas that display sub-standard consolidation work, zones close to public buildings that don't get enough police surveillance." The director attempted to drive home his point. "I'm talking about little known information. Information that's not in the public domain."

Having provided this tantalizing introduction Caron paused expectantly, waiting to be urged to continue. Begged for more. Instead, when Sadiqi finally spoke, he sounded sceptical. "Can you be more specific?"

Caron couldn't believe anyone would be so thick. Did he really have to make things any more explicit? "I've heard rumors today," he snapped. "Rumors about crimes that have allegedly taken place via the quarries in the past hours. Crimes that bear a striking resemblance to potential risks outlined in my report."

Sadiqi had the IGC director classed as a 'Grade A' paper pusher with a serious superiority complex and no concept of the value of anyone's time. Still, it was just possible that having been given a couple of hours to mull things over the professor had decided that it might be a good idea to help catch whoever was fucking around in the catacombs. "Okay. So tell me more."

The change of tone allowed Caron to ease back into his usual smugness. "The report was destined for the President. In fact, he was one of the few people ever to see it. It was highly confidential. Only a limited number of copies were circulated, mainly among the intelligence services. The aim was to outline risks without making the information public."

"Because the material was too sensitive?"

Being alarmist was one of Caron's favorite pastimes but having failed to mention the report earlier, he didn't want to build it into anything major now. "There was a certain amount of information that pointed to the weakest links in the chain. Too wide a diffusion would have increased the chances of the information leaking out."

"And when was the report circulated?"

"About six months ago."

This time Sadiqi was quick to react. "If the president saw it six months ago, why haven't any measures been taken to correct potential weaknesses?"

This was what Caron was waiting for: the chance to push responsibility for whatever was happening onto someone else's shoulders. The chance to repeat that he was the lone voice calling for action in a witless wilderness. "It would have been quite easy to correct the problems underlined in the report. Unfortunately, President

Tibrac chose not to do anything. I presume he acted on recommendations from the police and intelligence services."

Throughout his career, Sadiqi had listened to people telling him he wasn't trying hard enough, that he wasn't getting the work done. It was a pain in the ass. He, personally, had certainly never seen this report. If the damn thing was as important as Caron claimed, then it must have passed over Dukrin's desk. On the other hand, if she hadn't taken it seriously then how important could it be? Maybe Caron was still screwing with him. If this guy had given him out-dated maps he might be planning on handing over some out-dated report that would send him on a wild goose chase. It was hard to gauge whether or not Caron's change of direction was sincere.

But either way the cop was going to have to find the time to parse through the damn thing. "Where can I get a copy of this report?"

Caron was pleased to note the concern in the inspector's voice. "As I said, very few copies were made. I could lend you my personal copy."

"Sounds good. When can I pick it up?"

"I'm at home now," Caron offered with uncharacteristic haste.

"I'm busy right now," Sadiqi countered. "But we could meet later."

Under normal circumstance, keeping other people waiting was one of Caron's greatest pleasures. Despite having quite a flexible schedule, he loved pretending he was too busy for anyone else. But today he wanted to get this over with as soon as possible. "I'll be back in the Latin Quarter later this evening. I can meet you at *le Petit Suisse* at 7?"

Sadiqi grunted his agreement. He knew the *Petit Suisse* – not the kind of place he usually chose to hang out. It was a small café overlooking the Luxembourg Palace with the décor straight out of the 1940s. All wood and shiny brass banister. *Après guerre, café littéraire.* Sartre, de Beauvoir, Hemingway. It would be crawling with upper-class students and foreign tourists.

The cop sighed and glanced at his watch. Speaking of upper-class foreigners, it was time he got going. Ms. Corrigan would be waiting.

36

Boulevard Arago was well-known to all cataphiles, usually figuring at the top of their list of spots to avoid. Definitely a no go area unless you wanted to be arrested before your evening of fun had time to get started. It was a question of simple mathematics: As the main police access point to the quarries, it was the spot in the network where you stood the greatest chance of running into a cop.

And there was certainly no lack of cops today. From the top of the block, Toni could make out Sadiqi sitting on the curb, a page of the *Atlas* spread open at his feet. The dark shirt and jeans he'd been wearing that morning were now covered by a pair of greyish blue overalls. Without actually being able to see the back of the outfit, she knew they were emblazoned with luminescent tape arranged to spell the word: "P O L I C E". And like most young people nurtured on the popular belief that authority figures were rarely good company, she would have liked to think, "Dumb cop," and discard this man. But she couldn't. Somehow he projected an aura of disquiet that was both disturbing and strangely fascinating.

As she approached, he sensed her presence and rose to greet her. "So what's the problem with my maps?" he asked, holding the sheaf of paper out to her. The student wondered if there wasn't a hint of amusement in his eyes. Perhaps the vague idea that he took her for a dopey kid with nothing better to do than hang out.

"You don't believe your maps are out of date? You want me to prove it?" Without waiting for an answer she plucked a roll of papers from a tube poking out of her backpack. Flicking through the sheaf, she found a page that looked identical to the one Sadiqi had been studying and rolled it out on the ground at their feet alongside his. "These two maps are both supposed to represent the same area." The background of each one was made of yellow and white continents with intricate seas of aqua blue and vermillion red dots. Superimposed above was a grid of interlocking black and brown lines.

"Look at this, for example," she said, the tip of her index finger hovering above a black rectangle filled with the occasional dot of blue and a smattering of yellow against a plain white background. "This quarry was filled in last year to stabilize the land above and make way for a new apartment block. What it should really look like is this," she said, pointing to a brown and yellow rectangle on her map.

If Sadiqi didn't immediately grasp the significance of what he was seeing it was partially because the young woman's skin tight t-shirt and jeans were absorbing most of his attention. His eyes wandered over the sharp curves of her shoulder and hips before making their way to rest on the map. "What's the difference in real terms?"

"Everything." Understanding the colors was essential to reading the map successfully. "A white space is an open quarry; a room or a tunnel you can walk through. A brown space is an old quarry that's been filled in. In practical terms, it's just solid rock. The spot I've shown you is now nothing but sand and cement. Instead of having an open corridor to walk along..." She ran her finger along a weaving white line on the cop's map: "...you come up against a solid wall of concrete."

The message was unequivocal. Caron had been messing with Sadiqi by handing over the older maps. "My copies are useless."

"Perhaps not useless. I can think of a lot of people who would be happy to have them," Toni said, thinking of some of the dangerously over simplified maps cata-tourists had shown her in the past. "But I'd say you've probably got an extra 100 kilometers of tunnels on your maps that don't exist underground anymore." When she peeked sideways to see what effect this revelation was having on the Good Inspector, his mouth was clenched so tight his lips had almost vanished. Under the immobile façade, he was probably trying to figure out how to make Caron pay for this without actually getting himself charged with professional misconduct. "Don't take it personally," she shrugged. "Caron thinks it's part of his birthright to trip people up. He does it to everyone."

The cop tossed Corrigan a pair of grey cataflic overalls and ordered her to suit up. There was no point in dwelling on Caron's stupidity. While the professor was a pain in the ass, perhaps the student would turn out to be a guiding angel. Her speed at zipping herself into the formless outfit and tossing the helmet on her head only served to emphasize just how commonplace catacomb outings were for her.

"So what can I show you? The old headquarters of the FFI Resistance? The unofficial ossuary?"

In contrast with her initial professionalism, the playfulness was a rude reminder that he was placing his life and his investigation in the hands of a student. What had seemed like the only practical solution back in Ferry's office now struck him as a wanton leap of faith. The reversal made him abrasive. "We're here on business; not a tourist visit."

She turned the enthusiasm down a notch. "So seriously," she droned, forcing herself to sound like the bored guide the inspector seemed to want, "Where would you like to go?"

"Montaigne and Henri IV high schools."

Toni was curious to hear these two spots mentioned again – these schools he had asked Caron about earlier. But she knew better than to ask too many questions. Instead she commented professionally. "Montaigne High is easy. No problem. Henri IV is trickier. Like Caron said, the quarries don't go that far – at least not officially. And if the aim is simply to get as close as possible, there are probably several different points roughly the same distance from the school. "

She was too busy adjusting her flashlight to notice Sadiqi's quiver of impatience. He wasn't looking for an academic jousting match. He just needed a scout. "If you were going to build a tunnel from the existing network to Henri IV where would you put it?"

"Like I said, there are various possibilities."

"Well, then we'll just have to check them all."

If that had been meant as a threat – a punishment of extra hours of work and searching – then clearly Sadiqi clearly hadn't grasped just how much Toni liked being in the quarries. If she had to spend the whole afternoon and most of the night down under, that was just fine. "I hope you're a good walker then," she said as she ducked into the tunnel and began bouncing down the stairs. "Because this could take a while."

37

Once they turned the first bend in the stone staircase, all signs of daylight from Boulevard Arago died out leaving Toni and Sadiqi with only the light from their helmets and flashlights. The heat also dissipated magically and by the time they reached the bottom, they were both starting to feel more alive than they had done for hours.

Which was all well and good but as far as Sadiqi was concerned, it wasn't enough to cancel out all the negatives. On top of not being able to take his call, the terrain felt foreign. The light from his helmet penetrated only a few meters into the darkness, bouncing back and forth off the suffocating walls until it faded a few paces further along. Despite the hundreds of kilometers of tunnels unwinding in all directions around them, all he could see was the crushing proximity of the stone walls. Like a stifling crypt.

Toni, on the other hand, was in her element. She'd had the opportunity to use this entrance a few times before and was well acquainted with the surrounding network. It was a spot of key interest to her research. This was the neighborhood where she'd got all her best photos of gaping fissures and collapsing ceilings. The tunnels near Denfert represented one of the densest spots in the network reaching a total depth of nearly forty meters below street level, with the metro and sewers squeezed in above. It was a feat of pure engineering genius that the area was still standing. But she knew that not everyone shared her enthusiasm for life underground. And judging by the way the cop took a deep breath, like a visitor to a new planet, testing to see if the atmosphere could support life, she suspected that far from appreciating the immense genius of engineering around him, all he could see was the claustrophobic aspect.

This was a fair assessment. The only upside Sadiqi could see was that although the proximity of the walls on either side of him seemed stifling, the air was surprisingly fresh compared with the heat and fumes on the boulevard. The downside was the deeply disturbing succession of gaping cracks running the full width of the stone ceiling. "Do the tunnels ever collapse?"

"Only at midday or midnight," Toni joked, quoting a famous stonemason's adage. The scholarly reference didn't get a smile from the cop. "Don't worry about the ceilings. The IGC keeps a close eye on decay."

"Yeah, well, I hope you're right. That's rock up there. If it falls, it's not like a piece of plaster coming off your ceiling at home."

Toni looked up at the crack a few centimeters above her head and reached out to rub her palm across the cool stones that still showed the marks of the chisels that had worked them hundreds of years earlier. "Roughly 2000 kilos a cubic meter," she said, reminding Sadiqi that she probably knew the catacombs better than she knew the streets outside.

Although she didn't share the cop's apprehension, she did understand it. The Unknown was always a source of stress. A lot of people were nervous about the quarries. Happily, reactions evolved. Toni had been down often enough with friends to know that either people became increasingly nervous or increasingly relaxed as they navigated the network. Either they felt the walls closing in on them, or they sensed the immense possibility of exploration expanding outward.

It would take a few minutes to figure out which way it would go for Sadiqi.

"Let's start with Montaigne," she said. "At least that's a straight-forward destination. H4 will be slightly more complicated to figure out."

The cop fell into step behind.

* * *

Marching along, single file, with Toni leading, Sadiqi remarked how the girl's flashlight produced a strangely, poetic effect, transforming her into a vague outline sketched in a cloud of light. A sort of ethereal guiding genie. Without even glancing at her maps, she was able to navigate confidently. And this, in turn, gave him the confidence to let his attention shift to the landscape around them. He began noticing a complexity to the tunnels that contrasted with the simplicity of the endless stone monotony. His eyes were drawn to the deep layers of graffiti, the frescoes that followed one after the other, the tags and scribbles that seemed to cover almost every inch of stone. And when his gaze fell on the beaten earth ground, he spotted the occasional hand-sized hole opening into a void.

"Am I dreaming or are there more tunnels below us?" he asked.

Always quick with quarry trivia, Toni was happy to explain. "Back in the days when the stone was being extracted, each quarry was defined by a perimeter on the surface. That perimeter was accessed by a well. Quarrymen used the well to go down – and that's how they sent the stones up. But once all the good stone had been removed from below that perimeter, owners had two choices: either they could close the quarry and pay to open a new perimeter further along or else they could try digging down deeper under the same perimeter to see if there was another layer of good quality stone lower down. If it turned out there was, the city ended up with an extra level of underground emptiness."

Toni could sense the cop's unease at her answer. He didn't understand that this wasn't a realm separate from Paris. It was part of Paris. Part of the city's history. Part of its economy. Its architecture. She needed to make the quarries sound fascinating instead of disturbing. After all, she had more than a vague impression that this guy wasn't just an ordinary cop. It was possible he had some influence over the network's future. Some role in deciding whether or not the old quarries were a dangerous part of the Parisian infrastructure. And she didn't like the idea of him taking Caron's side and lobbying towards having the whole thing cemented in. "Look," she said, pausing to shine her flashlight off to the side. If she hadn't done this, Sadiqi would have missed what they were passing. The tunnel had opened out to the left and a magnificent stonework archway leading to a secondary passage with a three-meter high vaulted ceiling had become visible. The cop did a double take. The vision seemed more in keeping with the gothic churches of the city above than these old quarries. "If you follow the beam of light you'll see that the ground slopes down. Not all quarrying work was carried out using wells. This old ramp was used for hauling slabs of stone up from the level below by cart. Look at the stonework. Isn't it beautiful? Twenty meters under ground and builders still had a feeling for aesthetics in those days."

Despite his urge to get where he was going Sadiqi found himself contemplating his guide's motives. The girl was obviously some sort of warped romantic. Here she was, a foreigner in the City of Light. She could fall in love with the pearls of western culture: da Vinci at the Louvre, Monet at the Orangerie, Picasso in the Marais. Instead, she'd come here to crawl around underground, studying construction carried out by a few obscure public works engineers from the Ancien Régime. He glimpsed her profile in the light of his helmet and wondered. There was humor in her face. Maybe she realized the strangeness of her passion.

Strange passion or not, he was quite happy to listen to her as they wandered along. This might not be a tourist visit, but understanding the quarries and the way they worked would help him figure out how the tunnels were being used by the assailants from Val-de-Grace and Montaigne. "Are there many areas where the quarries go down this deep?"

"This is nothing. There are parts of Paris with triple layers of quarries. Albeit filled in."

"Well warn me when we get there because I really don't feel like falling an extra twenty meters."

"Don't worry. The triple levels aren't around here. They're up in the northeast part of the city – around the Buttes Chaumont Park." If Toni had meant to be reassuring, she failed miserably. The first rays of relaxation that had begun to surface in Sadiqi evaporated.

"I hope you're joking."

"No. Why?"

"Because that's where I live."

"Oh, I wouldn't worry about it. It's all perfectly safe."

"It'd better be. I've just bought an apartment, with a 20-year mortgage. I don't need my life's savings swallowed up by a sinkhole."

"Relax," she said, with a lack of conviction that indicated she wasn't even thinking about what she was saying. She was too young and mobile to have ever even considered buying property. "It's not as bad as all that. To begin with, any building that goes up has to have foundations that reach down to the deepest part of the quarries underneath. In other words, your building isn't built on emptiness; it's supported on pillars by the solid ground at the base of the quarries. That's why the big property developers are always lobbying City Hall to have the quarries filled in with cement. It would cut costs for them. They wouldn't have to spend so much money on foundations. They wouldn't have to dig down below quarry level themselves every time they wanted to put up a new building." Toni paused just long enough to catch her breath. "I figure that's why Caron is so gung-ho about filling in the quarries. I think he's probably getting baksheesh from the big developers."

The suggestion left Sadiqi cold. He'd grown up in the working-class part of Paris so being wary of upper-class snobs like Caron came as naturally to him as eating or breathing. He knew all too well how politics, business and the civil service all dovetailed together. If the huge construction companies could convince politicians to fund their next expansion projects, Sadiqi had no doubt they would. Yet, at the same time, only a few minutes earlier Caron had called to tell him about a detailed report on terrorist dangers in the quarries. Which suggested that perhaps Corrigan's obvious love of the catacombs blinded her to the hazards. "I thought Caron was worried about security risks. Terrorist scenarios. That kind of thing." The cop tried to sound as off-hand as possible. He didn't want her jumping to any conclusions about his investigation.

He needn't have worried. Toni had grown up with 9/11 and November 13th. Terrorism was part of her generational heritage. "This is Paris. You can't escape the terror risk if you live in a big city. I mean, obviously I don't know what's happening at Val-de-Grace. I don't know what exactly you're investigating. But whatever it is, you sort of have to contextualize any risk associated with the quarries."

A flashback of the morning's carnage shot through Sadiqi's mind. The blood and body parts smeared on walls and bedding. "Contextualize what?"

Toni heard the exasperation in his voice, but that wasn't going to stop her from making her point. "Well, Caron likes to make it sound like the quarries are a brand new target for the world's terrorists. But that's just not true. The quarries have always posed a potential threat."

"So you agree they could be used for terrorism."

"Of course. Zero risk doesn't exist. The quarries are part of the city. A part that's definitely less well policed than the train stations or the airports. So they're naturally a potential danger." Although the words suggested impending doom, her tone was breezy.

Because most people had no idea what Sadiqi did for a living, he often found himself in this type of situation, listening to various non-specialists sharing their uninformed opinions on terrorism. Babbling in abstractions. "What you're saying is that they're probably not at the top of any terrorist target list?" he concluded for her.

"Yes. But more importantly, the risk is nothing new. The quarries have always been a hub for illegal activity. Like the stories of smugglers around Vauvert I told you this morning. Or contraband. For years the tunnels provided a way of smuggling merchandise and people in and out of the city to avoid paying municipal taxes. Or soldiers escaping execution during the Terror or the Commune." Once the words were out, she sensed how lame that sounded. She grabbed for another, more convincing story. "Or more recently, under the Occupation. The Nazis used the quarries to plan violent attacks against the civilian population. Hitler wanted to destroy Paris to slow advancing Allied troops. In 1944, the Nazi commander, Von Choltitz, filled the quarries with U-boat torpedoes. If he had ordered their detonation, the city would have been blown to smithereens. It was only his eleventh-hour decision to disobey Hitler's orders that saved Paris from the same fate as Warsaw."

"Yes," Sadiqi agreed. "I know the story."

"Even the Resistance used the quarries."

Sadiqi had majored in Poli Sci in university and although that had been many many years earlier, he knew enough history to fill in the blank. "I know. Colonel Rol set up his Resistance HQ in the tunnels under Denfert."

"That's right. The Nazis were perfectly aware there was an air raid shelter there. They had copies of the *Atlas*," Toni explained. "They even posted guards at the entrance to the shelter. Four of them. All from the French police, who were still carrying out their duties under the Occupation. But what the Nazis didn't realize was that the guards they had chosen were also members of the Resistance. The Nazis thought the guards they'd hired were patrolling to keep out potential troublemakers. In fact they were lookouts for the Resistance – keeping the Nazis out. The Nazis also failed to realize that along with providing access to the quarries, the air raid shelters offered a direct link both to the metro and the sewers."

"So that's what made it ideal for the Resistance," Sadiqi said. "They were safely hidden from the Nazis, plus they had unhampered access routes to key points across the city."

"Exactly."

The inspector waited for Corrigan to make a connection between what she'd just said and Caron's fears of terrorism, but it didn't happen. Instead he found himself pointing out the incoherence in her reasoning. "But the Resistance weren't terrorists. They were heroes. They saved Paris."

"The Resistance, Che Guevara, the IRA," Toni lowered her voice in a verbal shrug. "The 'terror' label is subjective; it depends where you're standing. Obviously we think of Colonel Rol and the men and women working under him as the Resistance. The Nazis, on the other hand, thought of them as subversives."

Sadiqi had heard this type of bleeding heart crap often enough. He was just a little pissed off the student was pulling it on him. After all, she might not know he worked for counter-terrorism, but she did know he was a cop. "Okay. So we're doing the terrorism/sedition amalgam thing." He paused for a moment before adding the logical conclusion. "But however you look at it, Rol and the Resistance were carrying out clandestine activity. Which basically means Caron is right. The quarries are a potential hotbed for terror."

There wasn't even a pause before her rebuttal. "In a city the size of Paris there'll always be areas that can't be policed." Sadiqi was pleased to note the embarrassment in her voice, be it ever so slight. At least she had some sense of just how demented this sounded to him. Yet still, she kept going. "I mean, a lot of people think there aren't enough police patrolling the streets above, let alone the quarries. Right?"

Right? There it was. The limited resources argument. He had to agree. "True. There aren't enough police to monitor every S-fiche or juvenile delinquent."

"And there's no infallible way of guessing where a terrorist might strike any more than you can figure out what house a burglar will rob next," she added.

Again, Sadiqi could see where this was going and summarized the theory in the form of a question. "Why would terrorists waste their time designing a complex attack using the quarries when they can walk into any major department store on a busy Saturday afternoon and kill countless defenseless civilians completely off guard?"

"Exactly," she agreed. "Caron says the quarries make it possible for criminals to move from one point to another without much risk of being stopped by the police. That's both true and false. It's true because there are very few people policing the underground galleries and so anyone down here is unlikely to run into the police. There aren't many cops per kilometer of tunnel. On the other hand, anyone underground who does happen to run into the police is sure to be stopped, fined and have their identity checked – possibly even get arrested if they have a good tan and a black beard..."

Sadiqi finished the sentence for her: "... Whereas, the same person walking about above ground *might* be stopped, but not necessarily. They're less visible in a crowd."

Toni nodded. "I believe it's what you call 'offender profiling'."

There was an edge to her voice and Sadiqi could tell by the way she stressed the two words that she saw no difference between profiling and racism. He didn't appreciate the dig. He liked it all the less because he knew it was completely true. He'd lived through it himself. Back in his student days he used to get stopped by the cops in random spot checks several times a year and asked to produce ID. Yet as a cop himself, he'd learned to defend the procedure. "We all indulge in profiling all the time. I'm profiling you right now. You're probably profiling me. We see people. We get impressions. We stretch those observations to assumptions. You're a graduate student, in your mid to late twenties," he said, demonstrating the technique. "Most people who pursue their studies that far come from upper-middle class backgrounds. Your name is English..."

"Irish actually."

"Okay. So Irish. Irish Canadian. I don't know much about Canadian social stratification, but your European origin again confirms that you're probably not from a social category likely to be engaged in overthrowing the establishment; on the contrary, you're part of that establishment. You're also working in a field where women are chronically under-represented. So, maybe you had strong male role models. I don't know. Older brothers who made you compete with them."

"Or maybe I was an only child, brought up by a widowered father who made a point of making sure he came up with a lot of sporty, outdoorsy activities to keep me busy." The sudden iciness of the tone told Sadiqi she was correcting his statement rather than suggesting an ironic alternative hypothesis. He realized he'd gone too far. And he would have apologized. Except she didn't leave him the chance. "Okay. What about you then?" Still marching along, her beam of light and her gaze were both focused in the distance. "Khalid Sadiqi. Let's assume that's North African. Odds are Moroccan. Clearly well integrated in French society. So, given your age (what? late thirties, early forties), probably second generation immigrant family. Judging from our conversations, probably a Master's degree, if not higher... but doing a shit job. So probably the victim of a broken social ladder. Hence the chip on your shoulder..."

Sadiqi had heard enough. He may have misstepped with his profile of her, but that didn't mean he had to listen to this. The young woman was very good at getting under his skin. Her confidence fell only a hair's breadth short of arrogance. Possibly not even. "Of course the danger is that bad profilers end up with caricatures instead of dependable leads." The comment defied the fact that Corrigan's profile had struck very near the mark. That's what made it so irritating.

But he certainly wasn't going to let her know that.

He didn't mind the polemics, but if they were going to keep up this wrangling while they navigated towards Montaigne, it was better to steer the conversation back to more professional ground. A few moments ago Corrigan had simultaneously admitted the quarries were dangerous and argued there was nothing that could be done about the problem. He couldn't let that slide. After all, it was his job to make the city safe. "How much longer til Montaigne?"

"Maybe ten minutes."

"Okay, then. My turn to tell a story."

38

As they trudged along the stone corridors, Sadiqi bit into a nicotine mint to call to mind the details. "So, a few years back, I was in a brigade based in the 16th arrondissement. We used to do training exercises in the catacombs. Just across from the Eiffel Tower. So we're jogging around in the tunnels and after a while we come across a big tarpaulin stretched across a gallery with a sign hanging on it that says, *Building Site, No Entry*".

"Strange place for a building site, 25 meters below ground." Despite the comment, the look on her face was amusement, not confusion. But walking behind her, Sadiqi missed it.

"That's right. But we ignore the sign and go check it out... And what do we find? A security camera filming anyone trying to enter. Our arrival also triggers an audio recording of dogs barking – designed to scare away unwanted visitors. Then a little further along the passage there's a tunnel that opens onto a huge gallery that's been transformed into a cinema, equipped with a full-sized movie screen and a big selection of films on tape."

"Doesn't exactly sound like terrorist equipment."

Sadiqi was frustrated to see the Canadian had heard so many outrageous tales about subterranean Paris that he couldn't even get her mildly worried. "Madame Corrigan, you're very disingenuous. You've not heard the end of the story. How do you know the films weren't for terror training...? Or a sect? Or a paedophile ring?"

Toni ground to a halt and spun to face him. She had the distinct impression he thought she was some wide-eyed innocent who didn't appreciate the potential dangers that could be lurking in the network. And she really didn't like that. "Inspector, I'm willing to believe that you know a shitload more than I do about policing and crime in Paris. But let's get one thing straight. I know the quarries better than you do. The incident you're describing has nothing to do with terrorism. Okay. I wasn't there, and you were. But that doesn't mean I don't know just as many details as you do. In fact, I probably know the details better than you. The episode took place in September 2004. And it wasn't linked to a sect or criminal behavior of any sort. What you're describing was simply a clandestine underground cinema. Some form of movie-buff slumming. None of the material was offensive or banned. Mainly old black and white movies from the 1950s plus a few recent thrillers." Toni even knew the complete list of all the films that had been found. "Far from raising concerns about terrorism, the story would tend to prove my point: it's impossible to carry on clandestine activity in the quarries, no matter how harmless, without being noticed by the authorities. Yes, the installation was illegal but, more importantly, it didn't last very long. The police found it and shut it down. You know that. You were there. You and your colleagues rounded up a lot of cataphiles that Ferry had on his books. It's part of catacomb legend because some of those poor film buffs were even sent over to the anti-terrorist brigade for questioning. The people who were interviewed are still joking about it today."

That was more than Sadiqi could take. "Well they sure as hell weren't joking about it when we interviewed them. They were shitting bricks."

That's what Toni had been looking for. *When we interviewed them. We. We, at anti-terrorism.* All day long, Sadiqi had been pretending to be some vague, generic cop. Now she had confirmation of what she'd sensed from the beginning. It was a blast of reality that left her sobered. The previous five minute's conversation spent winding him up suddenly seemed childish and petty. "Okay." She shrugged apologetically. "So there it is. Why didn't you just say you were from counter-terrorism? Why all the secrets?"

The watchword for this investigation had been to keep everything discreet – to let nothing into the public domain. Yet, somehow the girl had got under his skin enough for him to let slide the information that this was a terror investigation. Having made the mistake, Sadiqi decided to own it. He ignored her question, heading instead for the moral high ground. "You talk as if it's normal for people to run around breaking the law for fun. But basically that whole story just proves that things are out of control underground."

As much as Toni knew she should be listening to the terror expert, she couldn't let him get away with talking garbage. A breath that was half-sigh, half-laughter echoed down the corridor. She started marching down the tunnel again. "I spend a lot of time in the quarries. A lot. So I know that's just not true. In fact it's absurd. I've never seen anything illegal happening down here."

"Just *being* in the quarries is illegal," Sadiqi insisted.

Toni brushed away the comment with a wave her hand. "Being in the quarries is illegal in the same way that parking on a pedestrian crossing is illegal. You might get a ticket; you won't get thrown in prison. At least not unless Captain Ferry is in a foul mood and feels like scaring cata-tourists."

"And you've never witnessed substance abuse in the catacombs? Drugs? Pot, cocaine, whatever."

"Jesus," she laughed. "You must be short on arguments if that's the best you can come up with." His failure to think of any solid examples of illegal activity underground gave her the opportunity to revert to her monologue. "You know, with the exception of the way your colleagues roughed me up this morning, I've never had any problems with violence down here at all. I can't see any reason why, in the name of protecting the city, we should target the catacombs more than anywhere else. Once you start doing that, where do you stop? The quarries aren't the only underground network that suffers from limited policing. Should we seal up the metro, as well? Shut it down as a potential hazard. Cement all the tunnels."

"That's not the same. The metro is already patrolled by the police as well as private security companies. You can't shove it into the same category as the quarries."

"I'm not talking about the metro stations," Toni countered, "I'm talking about the actual tunnels themselves. Fourteen different metro lines and nearly 200 kilometers of rails, most of them underground." She had a point. "Should we cement in the sewers? Both the sewers and the metro network provided access routes for the Resistance when they were trying to get around the city without being noticed by the Nazis. There are even stories about the sewers being used by the communards to escape back in 1871."

"So we should preserve the quarries as part of our national heritage?"

His tone was annoyingly patronizing. "That's a completely different issue," she shot back. "If you ask me whether or not the catacombs should be injected with concrete and ash and closed down as a safety measure, my answer is 'No'. Not for sentimental reasons; for practical reasons. Firstly because they're no more dangerous than many other parts of Paris; I'd much rather walk around the quarries on my own than certain parts of the suburbs. And secondly, as I've already explained, most of the quarries serve an engineering mission."

It was the same argument she'd made earlier, during her sparring session with Caron, but Sadiqi wasn't convinced. "Your logic's sketchy."

"Sketchy?" As her head shook back and forth, the beam from her cap lamp danced from one wall to the other. "You're free to disagree with most of my arguments, but not that one. That one's not opinion; it's fact." Drawing to a halt she swung her flashlight beam down a small secondary corridor that branched off to their left. "Look. Do you see that?" Towards the end of the beam the inspector could make out a pile of rubble blocking the tunnel. "If the IGC were to seal up the tunnels, far from making the city a safer place, the threat level would increase. Not because of terrorism but because of erosion and decay. Reinforcements don't last indefinitely. What you see down there is a collapsed dry stone wall. Whether you build stone walls or inject concrete into the tunnels, the IGC has to be able to access the network to make sure the reinforcements remain in good condition. Water seeps into the quarries. Over time gypsum and limestone erode. So does the concrete that Caron uses to fill in the tunnels. That in itself is a problem. Just look at any low-rent apartment building; the concrete walls start cracking a few years after construction finishes. Concrete isn't a long-term solution; it's a dirty bandage that festers. If the entire southern network were filled in with concrete, including the surveillance tunnels, there would be no way of monitoring structural wear and tear. That would create a potential for disaster worse than any terrorism. It would be a return to the situation in the 18th century when nobody had any idea of the state of the underground network. The quarries would be hidden from view. Everyone would forget about them. Then in ten or forty or a hundred years' time, the concrete would start to crumble and the quarries would begin to collapse. But the dilapidation would be hidden from sight so nobody would know about it until one day, a sinkhole would appear and a street or a school or an 8-storey building would collapse into the ground."

"Doesn't Caron know that?"

"Of course he does. But injecting cement is less expensive than building dry stone walls. And closing up as many galleries as possible is what his business interests want." There wasn't much more she could add. She wasted enough time fighting with Caron. She didn't feel like doing it with this guy, too. Lowering her voice, she broke into step again. "Filling in the quarries would be just another example of bad quality contemporary engineering. Far more dangerous than leaving them open to the occasional cataphile."

The only sound was the crunch of her footsteps as she stamped off down the corridors.

Toni didn't have anything else to add. If Sadiqi found her views excessive then they would just have to continue this visit in silence.

As he watched her recede, nothing could have been further from his mind. Even though some of the things she said were desperately naïve, her presence was growing on him. She was sharp. She was knowledgeable. And she was intense. "How the hell does a Canadian become a Paris catacomb specialist?" he called after her.

The question came as a surprise. And his curiosity a relief. Maybe he wasn't as closed-minded as she'd been starting to think.

She stopped and turned to wait for him. While he caught up, she drew a deep breath, forcing her voice back to its usual calm level. "I've been interested in tunnels since I was a kid," she said before breaking into stride again.

"What? A wonderful kindergarten teacher who showed you slides of the greatest wonders of the underground world."

"No. Nothing like. In fact nothing to do with school; it was all about the holidays."

"Summer vacation in Paris, visiting the catacombs at Denfert? Troglodyte holiday homes in the Dordogne? The Cabinet War Rooms in London."

"Wrong again." Toni had never been taken on a European vacation as a kid. "My dad's a big spelunker. He used to take me anywhere he could find a cave."

"He sounds like a five-star vacation planner."

She shrugged. "It got me interested in the whole thing. The idea that there was a world underground. And in any case, it wasn't all bad. One year he even sold the idea by telling me we were going to California. I thought I'd died and gone to heaven. I told all my friends I was going to Hollywood. Tell me about it. We flew to LA, picked up a rental Jeep and drove straight into the desert. I nearly strangled him." The smile she flashed over her shoulder was winsome. "But in retrospect it was actually a lot of fun. Especially the ghost towns. I mean, you see those places in old TV series and stuff, but they're really quite amazing. During the Gold Rush entire towns sprang up over night just for mining gold and silver. I'm not talking about villages. I'm talking about small cities with populations of 10.000. But when the mines ran dry, people just picked up and left. So now you have these huge towns full of empty buildings but no people." They'd reached an intersection. Without even hesitating to get her bearings, she ducked down the pitch-black tunnel on their right. "Anyway, while we were travelling around we went and visited an old silver mine. Truly amazing. It made me realize just how dangerous mining is. Mine shafts, cave ins, bad air, rotted timber. And that's when I decided that's what I wanted to do. I wanted to work making underground structures safer." She shot another glance over her shoulder. This time the smile was almost conspiratorial. "Some of the places my dad took my were pretty iffy."

Sadiqi was both amused and impressed. Amused by her humor. But impressed with the way she could pinpoint the precise moment when she made this important decision: when she decided who she was going to be.

She was quite something. If he was going to have to spend all afternoon walking around the catacombs, Sexy Librarian was certainly better company than Captain Ferry.

His eyes glided over the slim figure. Not even the shapeless overalls could obliterate the fact her body was in perfect shape. Her student timetable clearly left plenty of time for the gym.

"We can get this done faster if we change gears. How about we jog for a while?" he suggested.

The glance she cast over her shoulder was neither furtive nor demure. It was an overt assessment of whether or not she considered this a serious offer. "Okay," she said. "But make sure you watch your

head. Sometimes the ceiling is very low. You've gotta keep bounce
to a minimum and your head down. Otherwise, I'm game if you are."

Yes. Somehow that didn't surprise him.

39

It wasn't until they'd reached a crossroad that Toni spoke again.

"Montaigne is this way," she said, not bothering to take time to
catch her breath before ducking into a corridor that looked completely
different from the larger one they'd just jogged down. While Sadiqi
had found the solid stone blocks of the first tunnels comforting, he felt
slightly less reassured by the crumbling aspect of the walls in the dug-
out they now entered. And that burgeoning uncertainty grew worse
when Corrigan stopped in front of a shattered red brick wall. 'Great. A
dead end,' he thought. 'She put on a good show, but that's it. She's
lost. Now we're going to waste hours trying to find our way back.'

Except she didn't. All she said was: "This is why we need the
jumpsuits," and before he had time to ask what she meant, she'd
scrambled up the wall and burrowed into a small hole about four feet
off the ground. It was like watching the white rabbit disappear into
Wonderland. Sadiqi hadn't even noticed the hole until she was gone.
It had just seemed like one more sign of the wear and tear that
surrounded them constantly down here. Just a vague cleft of shadows
puncturing the bricks.

More impressive than the girl's departure was the sudden
darkness that engulfed the corridor once she was gone. When she
slipped away, Corrigan took with her two-thirds of the light they had
been sharing up until then. She had been in charge of their only hand
held flashlight in addition to the Petzl lamp on her helmet. The
ghostly beam from Sadiqi's own helmet now provided only the tiniest
island of light in the vast sea of darkness.

The catacombs might be growing on him but he certainly wasn't
going to hang around contemplating the blackness. He wanted his
guide back.

Running his hands over the wall, he was amazed by the wide
choice of holds and perches available. This was a well-worn path.
Apparently generations of explorers had blazed this trail. He lifted his
right foot into one of the wall brackets and grabbed the sides of the
hole, imitating the movements the student had made. His gestures

were less graceful than hers, but he managed to stretch his arms into the shaft and propel himself forward onto the ledge above.

As he snaked along, like some land-locked swimmer, he discovered a moon-like landscape of beaten sand and small pebbles. The main difference with the moon being that he was squished onto his stomach, sandwiched between uneven sandy ground under his chest and the solid stone ceiling a foot above. Corrigan's crash course in sub-Paris history helped him to understand where he was. He was crawling across the top of an old quarry that had been filled in with sand and small rocks. Part of that filling had been removed to create a connecting shaft allowing visitors to penetrate into whichever chamber lay beyond.

Sure enough, a few feet ahead, there was a glow from an open chamber alight with the beams of Corrigan's two lamps. Sadiqi wriggled across the remaining distance and jumped down off the shelf, landing beside the young woman.

The *Alice in Wonderland* impression was now reinforced by the surrounding scenery. Like the previous tunnels, the ceiling of this quarry had been chiselled directly out of the rock mass. But that was the only remaining sign of natural stone. Major parts of the walls around them were now made of cold grey slabs of cement, as was the ground. And straight ahead, at the far end of the tunnel, was an iron door whose once-white paint was now flaking and tainted with rust. It was like being in an ancient underground cell block. Perhaps what made the scene strangest of all were the words stencilled on the walls; black letters printed on white rectangles: *Ruhe* and a little further along *Rauchen verboten*. German.

"Welcome to Nazi occupied Paris," Toni announced.

The cop nodded in quiet amazement. The Nazi bunker. This truly was a piece of history. A legendary catacomb hotspot. Even Sadiqi knew the basic story.

In the lead up to the Second World War, the French had built air raid shelters under strategic parts of the city with the aim of providing protection for civil servants. One of the shelters was housed under the Luxembourg Palace, where the Luftwaffe set up its headquarters when the Nazis moved into the city. As their occupation deepened, they turned most of the land under the park into a massive bunker.

"You have to give them an 'A' for effort but a 'D' for aesthetics," Corrigan said, throwing a ray of light onto the wall beside them. The beam struck a slab of cold uniform cement, lacking any of the beauty of the vaulted archways or the expert stonework of the first part of their trek. "Before the Nazis, this was nothing but a set of huge empty quarries. The oldest quarry in the city. What the Nazis did was isolate their complex from the rest of the network by building the protective brick wall we've just passed through. They also put up a whole whack of orientation signs," she added, running her hand over a large rectangle filled with gothic script that had been carefully stencilled on the wall 75 years earlier.

Sadiqi turned to get a better look at the markings. Until Corrigan had pointed them out, he had thought they were graffiti, like in all the other tunnels. Now he saw them for what they really were. There were three arrows of differing lengths pointing either left or right. Colored arrows on a white rectangular background. Black arrows pointed the way to Notre-Dame and rue Bonaparte, green to St. Michel and red to "Hinterhof". Toni flashed her lamp down the tunnel letting it bounce off the walls wherever a secondary tunnel crossed the main tunnel. At each corner, a new stencilled sign on the walls provided directions to the nearest exits. Looking at the multitude of signs along the tunnel the cop felt a grudging sympathy for the anonymous soldiers who'd been sent down to work in this maze. "I guess they didn't feel too comfortable down here."

Corrigan nodded before setting off again. "Nowadays this is a big subex hangout. The heart of the network. Cataphiles on long treks come here to cat nap. They bivouac. Hang hammocks." There were no hammocks today, only walls covered in the spray painted code names of people who had passed through. "Incidentally, at the Liberation of Paris, Montaigne High was one of the last spots to fall. This is why," she said, moving her arms in a circular motion that encompassed the landscape around them. "The Nazis had their bunker under the school. When the Liberation got underway, they locked themselves in the school and put up a fight. Then when it became obvious they weren't going to win, they escaped underground, slipped into civilian clothes and climbed out of the quarries back into the city disguised as honest French citizens."

"So we're under the school?" the cop asked.

She flashed her light at the rusty iron door at the end of the tunnel. "That's Montaigne."

Sadiqi followed her beam. The exit she was pointing to looked like a prop out of an old WWII movie. The overall effect was reminiscent of a ship or submarine hatch, with prominent rivets around the frame and a wheel in the middle designed for locking and unlocking the door. But the grey military paint was now chipped and reddened with rust. Souvenirs from the past.

Toni grabbed hold of the wheel but before she had time to open the door, Sadiqi caught her arm.

"Put this on first," he said, pulling a white surgical mask and a pair of silicon gloves out of his backpack.

She stared at the objects as if she'd just been handed a dead rat. "Tell me you're kidding." But she reached out to accept the outrageous offering.

"Just point me in the right direction," he said once he'd slipped on his own mask and gloves. "You stay here."

Toni remarked to herself that the now masked man in front of her could easily be an insane Dr. Jekyll hiding in his underground laboratory. But there was no mad laughter. His eyes were cold sober. Whatever he was searching for, was deadly serious.

Edging past him, she placed her hands on the metal ring in the middle of the hatch then leaned her full weight into the heavy structure. "It's right up there," she said, pointing up the staircase that appeared in the glow of their lamplight. "When you reach the top you'll be just outside a wall that leads into the school kitchen."

It crossed Sadiqi's mind that it was strange she should know that the staircase led to the kitchen. But then perhaps that as well was just another drop in the pool of cataphile general knowledge. If she knew that piece of trivia, then whoever had squirted the anthrax in had presumably known as well.

Sadiqi slipped into the stairwell and headed upwards taking the steps two at a time. The equivalent of about six storeys up, his pace slowed until the top ledge came into focus. As Corrigan had announced, the staircase led straight to a door.

To his complete disgust there was no sign of the metal barrier the school's VP had mentioned. The only things that seemed to be separating the door from the catacombs were three planks of wood and a baseboard that had been nailed across the entrance. As far as security systems for keeping the nation's children safe, it was dangerously primitive. No self-respecting squat would use such uninspiring security. Anyone with a hammer could pull out the nails and the door would give way with a good whack from a sledgehammer. Sadiqi wondered when his country would catch up with the times. If it's not broken, don't fix it. In other words, you wait until some lunatic squirts anthrax through, or until a terrorist gang breaks in and takes the whole school hostage before you consider making the barrier resistant. Never use preventive medicine until things get really bad.

The cop brushed these thoughts aside and got straight to work. He kept a careful distance from the top landing, leaning forward to get a better view without actually touching the space that the poisoner had most likely occupied to mount his silent attack.

In spite of these precautions, Sadiqi guessed that not disturbing evidence was probably an unattainable goal. Trémont had said that the anthrax attacks dated back to the previous weekend. It was more than likely that dozens of cataphiles had trailed up these stairs since then; and they would have been entirely unaware of the impact they were having on a police crime scene. Sadiqi would do his best, but a real scientific team would need to comb for clues. If there was any evidence left here, it would take serious equipment to find it. The best he could hope for was to figure out how the poisoner had proceeded.

The holes where the anthrax had been shot in were easily visible, with bright beams of light shining into the catacombs from the kitchen beyond. Running his lamp up and down the surface of the far wall there were no other signs of infraction. Just the three holes, about half a centimeter in diameter, drilled into the wall to form a perfect equilateral triangle roughly 1m40 above ground level. The work had been done with care. There were no traces of loose powder sprinkled on the ground or walls. No spores on this side of the dividing wall. At least nothing distinguishable from your basic catacomb dust and dirt. What Sadiqi really needed was a scientific team to go over the whole area for residual traces.

But that wasn't going to be easy. They couldn't come in through the school. That would ruin any potential evidence as they crashed through the boarded up door. On the other hand they were going to have one hell of a time dragging all their equipment down that little shaft he'd just crawled through with Corrigan.

No. He wasn't going to get much help with this. It was up to him to scour the area.

He ran the lamp beam up and down the wall. When he was entirely convinced that only three holes had been made, he crouched down and started examining the concrete slab of the landing. Again, he looped the flashlight back and forth, checking every inch. But he lacked conviction – what the hell could he hope to find?

Yet on his final loop, the rays of light caught something fluttering against one of the planks that boarded the school door. A tiny shadow of strings flickered so fleetingly that at first he thought it was just an underground mirage.

Sadiqi stretched his flashlight closer. It really wasn't much. Just a rusty old nail on the door plank with some threads dangling there.

He rocked back onto his heels and opened his backpack. From inside he produced a Ziploc bag containing a pair of tweezers. The landing was wide. His calf muscles strained slightly as he stretched over and hooked the strands of fabric onto the tweezers then dropped them into the bag. Just a few khaki threads.

He would have to take the sample and count himself lucky. Perhaps a suspect would turn up who happened to have a bag or a pair of pants this color, and maybe the threads would match. But it was also possible that the threads came from any one of a thousand cataphiles who had visited this spot over the past months. What a joke. This wasn't the kind of thing Dukrin had been talking about when she told him he would know what to look for in the catacombs.

As if she'd overheard his doubts, Corrigan's voice drifted up the staircase. "Any sign of what you're looking for?"

"Not really," Sadiqi called back, as he dropped the baggie into his backpack. "I'm just clutching at threads."

40

Years of creeping up on the enemy had taught the Nightingale to appreciate the cloak of darkness. What some people considered the safety of daylight represented a threat to him. The blazing light of the whitewashed stairwell wasn't the type of environment he liked to work in. He preferred night. But if the attack couldn't take place under cover of dark, then the Nightingale knew the best weapon was camouflage. His outfit would make him visibly invisible. Transparent. Forgettable. He rang the doorbell then peeled off his gloves and slipped them into his pocket.

In complete contrast with his cool businessman's exterior, he was pumped. His full concentration was on what was happening around him. His ears were attentive to the tiniest creak. There were voices seeping down from one of the apartments higher up, but other than that the only sound was the crunch of footsteps approaching from behind Caron's door. The banging steps of a heavy set, confident male. The Nightingale knew things were on track. Caron had stuck to his usual Thursday routine and was alone at home.

This was confirmed a few seconds later as the face from the photo appeared at the door, wearing an inquiring but superior expression.

The Nightingale got straight to work. *"Monsieur Caron?"* he waited for a nod of confirmation before continuing. *"Je me présente: Andrew O'Reilly.* I believe Senator Clavreul called to let you know I was coming." The Nightingale knew that the senator had definitely not called to announce the visit, but he also knew that the mention of a high placed contact was a good way to brownnose this guy.

The tactic worked. Caron's face lit up. His ego made him an easy target. If his opinion of himself had been slightly less inflated he might have wondered at the senator's new change of heart.

As it was, Caron greatly regretted having missed the theoretical phone call. Any news from the senator had to be good news. A sign that things were moving again. The thought made the professor almost tingle with happiness. "What can I do for you?"

"I have a letter from the senator," 'Mr. O'Reilly' said, holding out an envelope. The senatorial stamp on the top left corner was well-known to the IGC director. "If you have a moment to spare he'd like a reply as quickly as possible."

The carefully choreographed scene worked. The heavy-set face relaxed. And now the professor recognized something vaguely familiar in the messenger's appearance. No doubt he had run into Mr O'Reilly during one of his meetings at the Senate. Caron drew open the door and ushered the stranger in, then made polite smalltalk as he led the way down the corridor to his office. "You have a slight accent."

"I'm Irish."

"Beautiful country," the IGC director said amiably. "My wife and I have been several times. Our son spent a summer in Dublin while he was doing his graduate degree. So how did you get from Dublin to Senator Clavreul's office?"

The Nightingale had expected this question and the answer was prepared. His accent was something of a giveaway. You couldn't be a civil servant if you weren't a French national. And you couldn't work for the Senate unless you'd passed through the top school for the civil service and knew how to reel off French like a blue blood. "It's a European initiative," he said. He couldn't be a French civil servant but he could be a Eurocrat sent to work in another member country as part of any one of a million expensive bullshit exchange programmes.

Not surprisingly, the explanation washed beautifully. "Oh, of course. Maybe one day Brussels will manage to teach us French something about German punctuality and Dutch practicality..."

Caron happily carried on a monologue while the Nightingale did a quick reconnoiter. The apartment had been shuttered into darkness, which was going to make the redhead's work easier. The sealed windows and blinds left less chance of the sound of voices or a possible scuffle reaching the neighbors. And there was no sign of other people in the apartment.

By the time they reached the round library, the Nightingale knew his job was going to be a breeze. While Caron opened the envelope, 'O'Reilly' made himself sound convincing in the role of senatorial secretary. The script had already been written; all he had to do was reel it off. "There seems to be some indication that recent events in the Latin Quarter are the result of terrorist activity. The Senator would like you to write a letter to the President, reminding him of your expertise, and asking that he reconsider the suggestions made in your report. He feels certain the president would give a positive response this time." Caron ignored the Nightingale's words preferring instead to plunge into the senator's letter. In a way that was a good thing. At least that's how the Nightingale saw it. The fact that this guy was obviously a self-absorbed prick made the job even easier.

He watched Caron read through the letter. Whatever it said please him because his expression evolved from mild concern to self-satisfaction. Then he pulled a block of letter headed sheets out of the desk drawer.

The Nightingale moved nonchalantly toward the window behind Caron. "It's a shame you need to keep the shutters closed against the heat. You must have a beautiful view."

"Let's not confuse beauty with kitsch. It's not exactly in the best of taste when they turn the strobe lights on the Eiffel Tower." Once again, Caron's words failed to endear him to the Nightingale. The Irishman loved the Eiffel Tower, especially during the evening light shows. Every hour after dark, exactly on the hour, the Eiffel Tower started flashing like a discotheque for ten straight minutes. Whenever the Nightingale caught a glimpse of the scene, it reminded him of the long carouses he'd gone on with the lads on leave.

From behind, the redhead watched Caron write the date and begin composing his letter. But the feel of something rubbing against his ankle distracted him, eliciting a reflex kick. Followed by a plaintive meow.

Wheeling towards the sound the Nightingale realized what he had just sent flying across the room was a bony thin cat that was glaring back at him with accusing yellow eyes. A black cat.

"My sentiment exactly," Caron concurred. "The bloody cat's a masochist. Only ever pays attention to people who either hate it or are allergic."

The Nightingale didn't hate cats. But a black cat was a bad omen.

Caron had already gone back to writing his letter and the Nightingale had seen enough. There was no point in drawing this out.

Reaching into his jacket pocket for his gloves, the redhead felt his pulse race and his senses focus. Killing was such a natural high. Even when the job was as easy as this one. All he had to do was grab this eejit under his flabby jowls and give a quick twist.

There was an audible snap, like a drumstick cracking.

That was all it took. The job was done.

But the high never came. The tension never broke. As he lowered the limp head, the feckin cat jumped onto the desk. Automatically the killer batted the animal across the room.

A black cat was poison on four legs. And as if to confirm this, a sheet of paper ruffled in the fan's breeze.

It was the Ng initials at the top that caught the Nightingale's attention.

He grabbed the page: "Retribution will come. From Ng."

WTF?

Someone was screwing with him.

41

By now they'd been below ground for over two hours and Sadiqi was beginning to find the halo of lamplight more monotonous than intriguing. Worse yet, the shallow tunnel they'd entered imposed an annoyingly slow pace as Corrigan claimed that the low ceiling made running unwise.

True enough, the floor was slightly uneven and if they ran they were likely to bounce themselves into a concussion. But what Toni hadn't told him was that the decision to slow the pace had just as much to do with the fact she wasn't entirely certain where she was headed. Leading the way to Montaigne had been a clear-cut task. Taking the inspector to the spot closest to H4 was harder. While the door to Montaigne was a definite location, the border between the quarry network and H4 High School was an abstract point. Before Toni could take him there, she had to decide where, precisely, that spot was. Where would someone start digging if they wanted to get into H4 from the GRS? With all her knowledge, surely it shouldn't be too hard for her to figure out.

Or was it *all* her knowledge that she needed to apply? How much information were Sadiqi's adversaries likely to have? Would they have access to the *Atlas*? Or would they just be working from pirated cataphile maps? Would they know about possible archaeological hurdles? Geological surfaces? Just how well-informed were these people?

Then again, Toni wasn't sure she should be projecting herself into the adversary's mind. What was she playing at, trying to think like a cop? Come to think of it, what was she doing getting Sadiqi's hopes up by telling him that there was a possibility of digging a tunnel to H4. And 'getting Sadiqi's hopes up', might be putting it mildly. Perhaps she was wasting his time.

It was true that new passageways were constantly appearing. Cataphiles were known for emptying occluded galleries. But they never did more than a few meters of tunnelling.

Getting from the main network to H4 was a whole different level of magnitude. There were dozens of meters separating the high school from the closest official quarry. Surely nobody would be crazy enough to undertake such a monumental job.

Having said that, on the other hand, there were plenty of stories and rumors about quarries under the Pantheon and H4. And legends and stories usually had a firm basis in truth. It was doubtful that someone digging from the known network to the high school would have to dig the full distance. There was a good chance there were forgotten quarries around there. Quarries that had been filled in during the earliest reinforcement work carried out by the IGC and lost from memory when the original *Atlas* was destroyed.

There was no doubt about it. From a purely theoretical point of view, the operation was feasible. It was when she started trying to visualize what digging from the main network to H4 would entail that Toni started telling herself the idea was crazy. A few meters didn't look like much on paper. Visualizing the distance in terms of hours spent chipping away at the stone gave it a whole new dimension.

She lowered the beam of her cap lamp to the ground before turning to share her concerns. "You realize all this is pretty hypothetical," she said, hoping her voice didn't sound overly concerned. "Getting from the network to H4, I mean. You'd need a big team to carry out a job that size."

"I doubt very much there's a big team." Sadiqi didn't have the same reflexes as the student; when he turned, he forgot to lower his lamp and a dazzling flash of light hit her full on, right in the eyes.

She stretched her hand up to his helmet and directed the beam to the ground. "Well, it would take a while for one person working alone to create that kind of tunnel. It would be a lot of work. It's not simply a case of cutting away the stone and digging out the backfill. You'd have to move it afterward."

The inspector considered this. Obviously the digging would be heavy work. Yet a big team underground could never have escaped the police's notice. His theory was that he was looking for a small group working over an extended period. "They wouldn't necessarily have to transport the stone outside. They could dump it anywhere in the network."

"You make it sound easy. I said it was possible. Not easy. Getting rid of several meters worth of stone waste would be a massive job. You know, in the 19th century, it took the IGC ten years to link together both ends of rue d'Assas. The teams advanced at an average rate of about three to five meters per month."

The academic reference exasperated Sadiqi. "I'm not looking for some catacomb aficionados trying to recreate 19th century industrial conditions. If someone's been digging, they'll have been doing it with cutting edge tools."

"If you mean someone with a pneumatic drill, yes, that would go a lot faster."

It was hard enough for Sadiqi to figure out what was and wasn't feasible without Corrigan handing him crazy ideas. Her insight was helpful but only if she stuck to realistic scenarios. "Maybe not a pneumatic drill. These people would be careful not to attract attention."

"Not a problem. Documented evidence indicates that loud noises wouldn't necessarily alert the authorities to abnormal activity down here."

The inspector spent a moment digesting the idea that this sort of research was actually being done in universities. "What documented evidence? Please tell me you don't waste your time measuring sound intensity underground."

She ignored the jab and just answered the question. "No. I'm talking about recorded historical evidence. For instance, back in the 1800s, three soldiers stationed at Val-de-Grace decided to check out the tunnels below their base. So off they went, exploring and becoming increasingly impressed with the labyrinth. Quite the maze. In fact so much of a maze that when they finally decided they'd seen enough, they couldn't figure out how to get back to Mansart's staircase. They'd gone too far and hadn't thought to mark their path."

"Not smart," Sadiqi agreed. He was getting a good sense of how easy it would be to get lost down here. For his part, he'd placed full confidence in his guide and there was no way he could find his way back to the surface if she abandoned him. If it weren't for the underground street signs they kept coming across, he would have absolutely no idea where he was in relation to the surface.

"So they must have been pretty freaked out. After a while, their candles went out and they found themselves stuck in the dark, with no idea where to go next. No way of finding their way out. No food. No water."

"You really go in for the ghost stories, don't you?"

"If you'd let me finish you'd see my point."

Sadiqi put his hand on his hips, impatient for the punchline.

"Luckily for them, they weren't completely stupid. They'd been smart enough to warn some of their friends on the base where they were headed. And when they didn't show up for their next watch, their friends informed the commanding officer."

"Sounds like they probably would have been better off starving to death," the cop commented. He'd been in contact with the military often enough to know that disciplinary action wasn't necessarily the easy option.

The girl noted this first sign of humor in Inspector Sadiqi – albeit sarcastic. Perhaps he was human after all. "Anyway, so the commanding officer set off with a team to find them: four soldiers, a bugler and a drummer. While the soldiers marked out their path unwinding a thread behind them, the bugler and the drummer made as much noise as they could to let the missing men know they were there. But despite all that noise, it took nearly a day to find the lost men – and when they did finally locate them it turned out they'd only been a few rooms away from the main entrance – yet they hadn't heard them."

"And this shows?" The cop needed a breakthrough. Not another story.

Toni sighed. "The point is that sound doesn't travel well in the quarries. The pneumatic drill scenario is feasible. It's QED."

It's QED. Now *that* was an expression Sadiqi hadn't heard for a LONG time. It was funny. It should have made him feel old. But wandering around down here, listening to Corrigan's stories, there were moments when he felt as if he were in a state of suspended animation. It could be today or it could be yesterday or it could be twenty years ago. And he was just a student and she was just a student and they were just chatting about nothing and everything.

Except, like all illusions, it was shortlived. And like all student conversations, there was too much guff. It wasn't QED at all. The idea that a drill might not alert the cataflics in a matter of seconds was absurd. "Your voice travels fine. I can hear your footsteps."

"Yes, but that's not the same thing. You can hear the person next to you but sound doesn't travel more than a short distance. Any noise is quickly lost because the tunnels are too long and there are too many bends and turns. An echo will normally bounce off a wall. Down here, there are so many twisting tunnels that sounds don't reflect back. They dissipate. Any sound leaving my mouth gets lost at the first bisecting tunnel. I guess it's a form of acoustic absorption. If there were someone around the corner, they probably wouldn't hear us coming." She decided to make it as Cartesian as possible. "Sound is absorbed by the hundreds of galleries leading in and out of one another, *ergo* whoever you're looking for may very well have used a pneumatic drill."

She had to be kidding. "A pneumatic drill?"

Toni shrugged. "Actually, the logistics of using the thing would be more of a problem than the noise. Those things must weigh a ton. And you'd need a power supply – some sort of generator. Your guy would have to know what he was doing."

Sadiqi had no doubt the people he was looking for knew exactly what they were doing. "So how long would it take to tunnel to the school with a drill?"

The student made a few quick mental calculations but decided not to share them. She didn't want to hazard a definite estimate. The equation had too many unknowns: the dimensions of the tunnel; the number of spots where, instead of tunnelling, they were simply digging out a narrow connecting shaft. "I couldn't say. A few days. A few weeks. Maybe even months. It would depend on a lot of things. Even if they had no trouble carving into the stone, they'd still have to get rid of the rocks. That could take time. They'd have to duck the cops. Which can be tricky. Like I said, they'd have no forewarning from noise. They'd have to keep a careful watch for the light of police helmets. Chances are that by the time your criminals – or whatever you call them – had seen the light from the cops' helmets, the cops would have seen the light from the criminals'. Not easy to get away."

Ferry hadn't mentioned any encounters like that. And Sadiqi knew it wouldn't have been so hard for the people he was looking for to dodge police attention. The cataflics wore helmets and carried lamps. So did the cataphiles. But there was another way. Desjardins had talked about the Green Monster, the Vauvert Devil. Specters that according to Corrigan could see in the dark. And seeing in the dark could just as easily be achieved with technology. All it took was a pair of night goggles. In principle they weren't easy to come by. Their sale and distribution was controlled by the Ministry of Defense. You couldn't go down to your local army surplus store and buy a pair. But no doubt, in reality, a couple of minutes on the web plus a visa number and you'd have your very own pair of glasses delivered straight to your front door.

42

One of the things that made Toni so successful in academic circles was her ability to impress her mentors. For all his bitching, even Caron was dazzled by the sheer extent of her knowledge. Whether people agreed or disagreed with her, she was very good at making them recognize her professional authoritativeness. And right now, she was aiming for that same sort of connection with the cop. So while Sadiqi tried to visualize the Green Monster, Toni was finalizing her decision about where the best route to H4 High lay.

After weighing up all the possibilities, she had now decided to aim for the Ursulines' gallery. It fit all her specifications. Despite being a central feature of the network, it was reasonably far from the major highways cataflics and tourists used. The fact that it was one of the oldest quarries in the network made it a *rendez-vous* point for enthusiasts but not necessarily a "must see" for the average tourist. Another important feature was the dry stone wall method used to reinforce it. The walls weren't made with cement or mortar, but simply with rocks that had been squeezed together one on top of the other. This offered a double advantage for anyone trying to tunnel out of the network: it would be feasible to remove some of those stones, burrow through the sand and pebbles that filled the old galleries on the other side of the wall, then, at the end of a hard day's work, replace the initial entrance rocks without leaving too obvious a sign of passage. Arguably other parts of the north-eastern peak of the network would fit these specifications, but the Ursulines had one other feature that made it the most likely starting point. It was close to Val-de-Grace. Very close. And Toni knew that the church and hospital were the other focal point of Sadiqi's investigation.

"We can try this way," she said, exiting the surveillance tunnel that ran under Boulevard St. Michel and pointing her flashlight down the gently curving corridor that wound off to the right. The cop's face was deadpan as usual. Toni felt a vague annoyance. She was doing her best. "You know, it would be an awful lot easier if I knew what you were looking for," she remarked as she turned into the side gallery and marched onward.

There was no reaction.

She took a deep breath. Sadiqi's restraint made it hard for her to connect. Then again, his laser focus probably just confirmed that whatever he was investigating fell into the 'life and death' category.

Which was pretty worrying.

She tucked away both her frustration and concern. "I mean I can understand a criminal using the quarries to get into Val-de-Grace. Even Montaigne. That would make sense. The tunnels are already there. But H4? Why spend all that time tunnelling when you can use the front door?"

Sadiqi could think of several reasons why someone might not want to walk straight into a school. Particularly if they were loaded down with weapons or other illegal materials. He kept these thoughts to himself, and opted instead for a change of topic. "Are we close to the Z-Room?"

Toni noted the sidestep but answered anyway. "Yeah. It's barely a five-minute walk from here."

"And that's where all the big catacomb parties take place, right?"

If Sadiqi had seen her face he would have noticed a flash of confusion. Toni had expected the mention of the Z-Room to lead to the topic of the PM and whatever had happened at the hospital. If the last question was related to that, the tangent wasn't obvious. "Not really," she said noncommittally. "There are parties all over the network. A lot of them take place near the peripheral ring road." The southern edge of the city had the advantage of being close enough to major access points to make it possible to furnish underground chambers with an electric generator, real stereo equipment and a good DJ. Parties happening in the Z-Room involved more complicated logistics. Getting there from the most widely-used access points along the old peripheral railroad lines meant a four-kilometer hike at best; any sound equipment had to be sherpaed long distances. "Basically you can have a party anywhere. All you need is a gallery with a name; guests have to know where the party's being held. I suppose you could say you need an address."

"There was a party in the Z-Room on Friday night. Were you there?"

Despite the seemingly logical connection between these two questions, Toni didn't much like the change of tack. If she wasn't very much mistaken, the cop was trying to establish if she had any direct link to what he was investigating. "No. I'm not much of a party person." Her voice was slightly colder. "I come down here to get away from the city, not to find myself in an underground disco complete with subwoofers and guys looking for a quick lay. Why do you ask?"

If he registered the hostility in her voice, he didn't show it. "Do you know any of the people who disappeared? The guys named on the flier you gave me?"

Toni ground to a halt and rounded on Sadiqi. "I agreed to play guide. I wasn't expecting to be interrogated. You want to interrogate me, you read me my rights first."

"The guy I'm looking for is about a foot taller than you and probably weighs fifty pounds more. He also walks around with a loaded Beretta. I've not checked your bag, but I'm willing to bet there's no gun in there."

Toni held his gaze for a moment before making her choice. Ultimately, there was no doubt which way it would go.

He was quiet. He was restrained. But he was a good guy. His calm outer shell was a carefully composed fabrication, stitched together with nicotine candies. Below, there seemed to be a whole other level of turbulence. A guarded energy waiting to be let lose. She was curious what would happen when those floodgates cracked. But she wasn't going to test them now. Instead, she moved back into motion.

"The answer's 'yes'," she said, more quietly. "One of them. I've met Quartz. André Zucchero. I knew him by reputation before coming to Paris. Contacted him a few times by email. Since then, I've run into him at some official meetings and conferences about subterranean issues. Long-term cataphiles tend to be upstanding members of the community. I meet a lot of them through quarry related associations or events."

"What do you consider long-term cataphiles?"

"Middle-aged people. Forty, fifty, sixty-year-olds. A catacomb party might be a kickass way to spend your Saturday night when you're 20. It's a little more off-the-wall once you've got kids or grandkids and are supposed to have reached the age of reason. The rearguard tends to be politically invested. There are cataphiles trying to stop Caron injecting the network. Cataphiles trying to get the public to realize that the city's subterranean treasures are being sold out to the big construction companies."

Sadiqi caught something pleasantly familiar in Corrigan's tone. Her anti-big business indignation appealed to the socialism nurtured in him since childhood. Maybe it reminded him of some long-lost idealism. The youthful enthusiasm. Here they were, walking through one identical tunnel after another and yet she had something new to tell him about each bend or turn they came to, tying it in with some incident from the history of the city on the surface. "You really care about the quarries, don't you?"

"Of course I do. The quarries are Paris. It was these quarries that provided the raw material that makes the beauty overhead possible."

If the cop had been asked to give one word that defined Paris, it definitely wouldn't have been 'beauty'. It might have been 'Corruption' followed at a close second by 'Decadence'. Walking around in Corrigan's company Sadiqi felt torn in his essence. Her enthusiasm and her love of Paris contrasted so starkly with his own antagonistic feelings about the city. She thrived on the stories of the city's history while all he could see was the layers of crime he'd been fighting without results for years. He wasn't sure whether to be annoyed or charmed by her disconnect from reality. To be able to notice beauty everywhere. Not to feel the weariness. Not to have death looking over your shoulder all the time. It was strange. They say that opposites attract but that had never been Sadiqi's experience before. He had always been attracted to people like himself. He had always been convinced that to have clarity was to have strength. Yet now he was beginning to wonder whether what he saw as clarity wasn't simply cynicism.

His bleak attitude was a by-product of the job. It came from dealing with violence and the worst human behavior on a daily basis. And now he'd dragged Corrigan into his world. Putting her at risk. He should have left her in her dream world.

Except he couldn't. He needed her. He needed her insight and guidance down here. So instead of regretting the dangers he was exposing her to, he was relieved when she stopped in her tracks. They had reached a fork in the path with one tunnel bending slightly to the left and another continuing on straight ahead. "Here we are. Anywhere around here I'd say we're about as close as we can get to H4," she announced. "If there really is a tunnel, it'll be hidden around here."

"Hidden?"

Toni wasn't quite sure what to say. "I don't know. Probably some sort of shaft like the one we passed through at Montaigne. But maybe with stones blocking the entrance so nobody notices it."

Any misgivings Sadiqi had been having instantly disappeared with this whiff of possible success. Being as they were here, they might as well try to find what they'd come for. He got straight to work running his hands along one of the stone walls, tugging at any outcroppings, hoping to discover a tunnel or a passage lying hidden behind one of them.

Crazy as it felt, Corrigan followed his lead.

But the efforts were useless. The stones held. Each small piece of rock had been here, stoppering the void, for generations. And over the centuries, the weight of the buildings above had slowly pushed down on the layers of stone, millimeter by millimeter, jamming each chunk of rock closer to its neighbor. It would take more than a little tug to get them out.

"Supposing we do find a tunnel, what will you do?" Toni asked, breaking the silence.

"Follow it and find whoever built it. But what I need first is confirmation that it exists."

"What makes you so sure something's going on at H4?" She kept tugging at the rocks. "Shouldn't you have someone guarding the exit from the school if you think there's a link to the network?"

Sadiqi ignored the first question but answered the second. "We do. But if we could confirm there's a passage – then at least we could neutralize one of the unknowns."

Corrigan stopped searching and turned to watch the cop who was still busy examining the wall. "'Neutralize an unknown'. Do you have any idea how many unknowns there are in the quarries? That's why people like me love coming down here. Because we're constantly discovering one unknown after another. Sure, you can check on H4. But what about every other famous building? You should probably have people covering l'Ecole Polytechnique, too. There are passages running between the two schools."

That was just wonderful. What next? Sadiqi was dealing with a rabbit warren. A murderous rabbit.

As if to confirm this multiplication of outrageous and deadly possibilities, the cop found himself standing with a stone in his hand. The largish rock he'd just pulled on had fallen away from the seemingly solid wall.

In a split second his reflexes sent him plunging to the ground, ducking below the level of the newly discovered opening in the wall and knocking the girl sprawling onto the ground.

"*Mais ça va pas?!*" she protested. "Are you crazy?"

The cop placed a finger on his lips to signal for quiet. The stone that had come free had uncovered a tiny passage. There might be someone hiding in or along the tunnel. Sadiqi's hand slipped down to the belt on his coveralls and drew out a pistol.

Crouching beside her, he took off his helmet with the lamp on it and used her flashlight to lift it upwards until the beam was shining into the hole. Toni couldn't believe she was actually watching someone do this routine straight out of an old movie. Waiting to see if anyone would mistake the helmet for the cop's head. When nobody tried to fire at it, the inspector rose to his feet, aiming his SIG Pro into the hole.

Nothing happened. Sadiqi peered into the tunnel. Empty. There was nothing there. In fact it wasn't even a tunnel. It certainly wasn't what he was looking for. It wouldn't lead them to H4. It wouldn't lead them anywhere. It was nothing more than an indentation. A tiny niche.

Yet the space was easily big enough to be a hiding place. The cop's light bounced off something at the far end of the hole. He slipped on his latex gloves, then boosted himself up and reached in to grab the object.

It was a backpack. Dirty-blue with a logo on the side. A popular brand. The same one carried by over 75% of French students. It felt quite heavy. When he unzipped the central pouch, the weight was easily explained; there were three cans of beer along with a bottle of water. The cop closed the central pouch then rummaged through the front pocket. Once again, nothing unusual. Just an ID card. The photo wasn't immediately recognizable because French ID cards were valid ten years and the photo on this one had been taken when the bearer was 12 years old. He was now twenty. The smiling child in the photo didn't look much like the confused, babbling dehydrated person Sadiqi had seen at Cochin Hospital a few hours earlier. But it was the same person. Philippe Desjardins.

What the hell had he been doing hiding in this hole? Several possibilities sprang to mind. He might have left the bag here so that he could explore the network unhampered. But shining his light over it, Sadiqi noticed a dark brown stain on the bottom right corner. When he touched it, the fabric felt slightly rigid. He couldn't be sure, but he was willing to take a guess. It was blood. And if that was true, then there was a more likely explanation what the bag was doing here.

Desjardins must have run into someone nearby. He had seen something that he shouldn't have seen. He had been chased. Been shot. Then he had hidden here to get away from whoever was pursuing him, and kicked the bag to the foot of the hole, where his injured foot bled on it. Possibly even stayed here for quite some time. Which would explain why it had taken him so long to resurface after being injured. When he had finally left, he must have been too exhausted or confused to remember to take his bag.

Desjardins had really seen something.

Sadiqi shot a glance around the gallery. Every wall looked identical. Every surface was the same as all the others. If Desjardins had been chased, where had he run from? What had he seen? Whatever had happened, it must have happened near here.

The cop wanted to keep searching for clues but it was becoming increasingly obvious that something really was going on underground. In his haste to investigate the catacombs he hadn't fully measured the dangers. He hadn't expected to find anything. Now the possibilities were multiplying. If Desjardins had been forced to hide here, it was likely that there was still danger close by. Booby traps, gunmen, more anthrax… Besides, those two missing cataphiles were probably lying dead under a pile of rock buried somewhere behind one of these walls, very close by. If Corrigan stumbled across an improvised gravesite around the next corner, it might put her off her darling catacombs forever.

"Are you okay?" he asked, turning to the student, who was still crouching with her back plastered to the wall, waiting for the all clear. He held out his hand to help her up.

She took the hand and pulled into standing position. "I'm good. Possibly a little bruised," she added as a mumbled afterthought.

Sadiqi strode back to the main gallery and reached into his pocket for a nicotine fix.

His face instantly morphed into panic. *"Merde. J'ai perdu mes clopes."* *I've lost my cigarettes.*

Toni smiled. That was the most emotion she'd seen on his face all day. She slipped her hand into her own coveralls then pulled out the little sheet of lozenges. "They fell out of your pocket when we were crawling out of the bunker."

"…So you slipped them into your pocket…" His tone was amused, not angry. "What? Were you waiting to see how long it would take me to break into a cold sweat and start vomiting?"

Her smile widened. "Something like that." She tossed the plaque across the gallery, aiming slightly off target. His arm shot out to grab it. The lightning movement was there and then gone.

He leaned lazily against the wall, popped out a mint and stared down the tunnel. His lamp lit a few meters of stone before tapering off into darkness. Then his eyes dropped away from the endless labyrinth and fixed on Corrigan. She might not scare easily, but that still didn't justify involving her in this.

He felt beaten. What he needed was a team down here. Proper investigators, not this engineering student. "We're out of here."

The student looked as serene as ever. "It's your call."

It was indeed. This was the only reasonable decision. Maybe they were closing in on what he was looking for. But he couldn't be certain. Maybe they were just wasting time. It was impossible to say. And that's precisely why he preferred to be on familiar ground.

He hadn't read his text messages or received a call for hours now. It was time he resurfaced and caught up with the latest news.

43

The Nightingale stepped out of the air-conditioned flower shop into the afternoon heat clutching a bouquet of red, white and blue carnations.

By the time he reached Passy metro station his black suit jacket was drenched in sweat. This was only partly a reaction to the heat ricocheting off the city; the other part was nervous sweat. His concerns were quite literally of a life and death type. His life and death.

He loosened his tie and followed the steps down to Bir Hakeim Bridge, where he sheltered in the shade of the aerial metro and the street lamps perched like steel lilies of the valley. Once he reached the middle of the bridge he turned left and headed toward the statue decorating its east flank, *La France Renaissante*, where he stopped and placed his bouquet on the pedestal, facing the river at the feet of the contorted horse.

For weeks now this strange statue had been the designated spot for the Nightingale to leave the floral signal that all was well to whoever was running this show. But today, more than ever, he wished he had confirmation who exactly that person was.

Rotating on his heels he crossed to the staircase that led to the island walkway in the middle of the Seine. The car-less island sheltered under an arch of plane trees was populated mainly by old people walking their terriers. The Nightingale had to continue halfway down the path before finding an empty bench uninhabited by hundred-year-old bitties.

He lit a cigarette and gulped down a breath of nicotine then stretched to prop his feet on the fence that protected walkers from slipping off the embankment. A seagull that had been perched a few meters further along ruffled its feathers and cawed angrily at having its privacy disturbed. As the bird skirred away, the Irishman remembered a superstition he had been told long, long ago. Seagulls were the souls of the dead. If that were true and this bird did have a dead man's soul, it might belong to any of the dozens of men he'd killed in the past.

The Nightingale's thoughts circled back to the job that afternoon. Not to the dead man but to the e-mail sitting on his desk. That was the real problem. That e-mail made him worry he was being set up. Just like Caron had been set up.

A passenger barge filled with waving tourists cruised down the river but the Nightingale's thoughts were elsewhere, remembering the past months. Wondering who exactly was behind this contract.

Of course, he knew roughly who he was working for. The Nightingale took a deep drag. This whole thing had been brought to him by Swart. A man you could trust. They'd known one another for years – been in close contact on many battlefields. And although they'd worked for different organizations, they shared a similar vision of the world. So when his brother-in-arms had come to him outlining a job that aimed to strike down all the warbling leagues of liberals, the Nightingale had given the offer his full attention.

The meeting with Swart had been brief. Only long enough to set out the basic proposal. The Nightingale would be one operative in a small team effectuating a multi-pronged attack on the city. In order to minimize the chances of the plan being countered, each operative would be entirely autonomous, with no contact between them.

With his military career ending, this was the perfect opportunity for the Nightingale to carry on the fight. Not only was it a strategic challenge, it was a mission with meaning. Which was better than the battlefield. He was serving the cause. This was moving the world forward – snatching it out of the clutches of the cosmopolitan radicals. This was all about restoring order.

And to make the pact even sweeter, the deal included a million euros as soon as the active phase began, followed by another million on completion.   Given the choice between a whole whackload of money or living off a miserable retirement pittance, there wasn't a lot to think about. The Nightingale had accepted.

But that was the last he'd seen of Swart. Because although it was his comrade who had brought him the contract, Swart was only the middle-man brokering the deal. It was impossible to say who was behind the plan.

Whoever it was, they had money to burn.

And they were good tacticians.

Because the whole scheme had worked like a well-oiled machine. Orders, instructions and equipment had arrived via a private post box in the 5th arrondissement. There had also been the apartment. The keys to it were in the post box one day. And once he had arrived there, he had found all the material he needed, from digging implements to fake ID and uniforms to very real maps. Everything to carry out his mission both above and below ground had been provided.

Everything.

As for communicating with his employers, the messaging channels were narrow. Absolutely no contact with Swart. And only one-way communication to receive instructions. Rudimentary. But it worked: Every Friday, he had to lay a wreath at the bottom of the *France Renaissante* statue. That was the sign that all was well. He had done this without a hitch. Until last Friday. Because last Friday, when he arrived with his carnations there had been another bouquet already sitting there with an envelope marked "Ng". A plain brown envelope. And when he looked inside he found another envelope with the Senate stamp on it as well as a photo and very simple but concise instructions about what should happen to Caron: Give him the letter from Senator Clavreul, then kill him.

Which had also gone fine... Until he saw that email.

That e-mail lying on Caron's desk was a big problem. Because that e-mail carried the exact same message that the Nightingale had been told to scrawl on the hospital wall. And worse yet, the e-mail had been signed "Ng". His signature.

Which made this whole thing feel like a set-up. After all, the Nightingale hadn't sent that message. Why would he? Leaving that "Ng" signature created an explicit link between himself and Val-de-Grace; the 'Ng' could potentially be recognized by friends, buddies and commanding officers. It tied him to the events.

Not reassuring.

The threat that things were getting fucked up made him consider calling Swart to check if he knew what was going on. The idea was there and gone in a flash.

Contacting Swart would only make everybody's position more vulnerable.

Instead, he pulled the sheet with the message out of his pocket and read it again:

> June 20; from Ng
> He sends his servant from the depths of darkness into light.
> Arnaud de Chanterelle was brought to justice at Val-de-Grace this morning. Our struggle against the oppressors continues. Many others deserve punishment. Long live freedom.

The brief re-reading made him relax marginally. What sort of crap was that supposed to be? Objectively, there wasn't any information in there likely to lead anyone to him. Maybe the message was just intended to distract. To confuse. It could even work to his advantage. The cops would be running around, wasting time trying to trace the message. And no internet trace could possibly lead to his current hideout.

There was no reason to panic. Calm was the Nightingale's specialty. The mission was nearly complete and the success of the final stage would make all the sweat and aggravation worthwhile. There was no way anyone could stop him now; not even the people who had organized this. And he definitely wanted to finish this. The last stage was the best part of the plan. No. There was definitely no going back now. In any case, he had taken more than enough precautions. He had followed his orders but he had been smart enough to improvise a few moves of his own. He had long ago abandoned the apartment that had been provided. Nobody knew the location of his current hideout. The command chain had no way of knowing where to find him. There was no way they could stop him. And once he had finished the mission, he would hitch a ride out of the country and into his new life.

The Nightingale took a final drag on his cigarette and flicked the butt at a mallard cruising down the river. The bird ruffled its wings then went back to its lazy afternoon, floating in the shade.

44

Having spent nearly three hours walking through the catacombs at a constant 15°C, Toni and Sadiqi had completely forgotten about the heat wave. It wasn't until they were a couple of meters from the surface that the sweat began trickling down their backs, gluing the mesh of t-shirt and backpack to their skin.

As the heat engulfed them, they cast off their extra layer of clothing. And when Corrigan's shapeless overalls were discarded, revealing her narrow jean-clasped hips, the cop found another equally instinctive reaction taking hold. He liked this woman. During their expedition not only had she been helpful, he had actually enjoyed her company. And the gorgeous green eyes, set off by the dark hair and fair skin, made the attraction all the easier.

Never one to put pleasure before work, he told himself he needed to pick her brain a bit more, just in case he'd overlooked something. "I've taken up your whole afternoon. Perhaps I can buy you dinner to thank you?" As soon he'd said it, he noted the poor choice of words. Surely the inevitable reply to: 'I've taken up your whole afternoon,' had to be, 'Yeah, well leave me alone now.'

Fortunately, she didn't seem to notice. "Sure. Why not?" There was something so relaxed about her. So detached from all the "Yes, Sir," "No, Sir," formality Sadiqi was used to. All social hierarchy and distance dissolved around her. He had very little firsthand experience of North Americans and, until now, had subscribed unquestioningly to the French belief that Anglo-Saxons were invariably ignorant, over-weight and the root of all evil. The preconceptions were starting to crumble. Corrigan certainly didn't fall into the first two categories; he doubted very much she was in the third. And even if evil did come in the form of a captivating underground nymph, he was willing to face it.

The drift towards visions of where dinner might lead was cut short by a beep from his shirt pocket. Having spent most of the afternoon beyond the reach of the mobile phone network, three hours of messages were now filtering through along with an unsettling number of Twitter feeds #dechanterelle that had nothing to do with anaesthetics and were a little too close to home. On top of that, an alarm message was flashing to remind him that he had a meeting with Caron in five minutes. *Merde.*

* * *

Two minutes later, Sadiqi's Renault was charging down Boulevard Arago. He'd taken the precaution of bringing the girl along to make sure she didn't change her mind about dinner. Safely buckled into the passenger seat, she seemed to be enjoying the ride as they bombed along with the blue slap-on/slap-off flashing light blazing and the siren blaring.

Ultimately the racing served no purpose. Sadiqi arrived on time for the *rendez-vous*, but there was no sign of Caron.

While the cop paced up and down the sidewalk willing the professor to arrive, Toni sat in the double-parked car and pulled out her phone to catch up on some of the messages she'd missed. Or at least that's what it looked like she was doing; while her fingers swiped over the screen, her brain was in fact focused on something else.

Ever since she'd been woken by the flotilla of police cars at Val-de-Grace, the day had been one long succession of unlikely events. And now it was culminating in dinner with a cop. A smile spread across her lips. Khalid Sadiqi. He was a little hard to fathom. And she wasn't entirely sure whether dinner was just more police business or an actual date? After all, despite being sort of reserved, the guy was quite hot. He had that whole rugged/power thing going for him – not to mention the tense energy he radiated. She had the impression he was constantly on the point of blowing a gasket. Which sort of appealed to her: the nervous energy. She flipped her phone to the camera and straightened her hair in the mirror.

If Sadiqi could have read her mind he might have been more confident about dinner. Instead, the sight of the Canadian lounging in his passenger seat made him think he was wasting time that could be used more constructively on the investigation. His usual unimpeachable professionalism was slackening. When he was on a case, it was always a 24/7 deal. His relationship with his boss had been built on his complete availability. Yet here he was, using the angle of finding more information as an excuse to take the girl to dinner.

The whiff of guilt made him reach for his phone to check in with Dukrin. Wandering a few feet along the sidewalk so that he was out of Corrigan's earshot he pinned in the number and steeled himself for a beating. Sure enough, the limited success of the afternoon expedition, in the form of the discovery of Desjardins' hiding spot, wasn't nearly enough to satisfy her.

As a general rule, Sadiqi and his boss understood one another almost instinctively. But the nature of their work meant that at times Dukrin was relentless. She wanted him to perform miracles. To wrap up cases before they'd barely started. Today was one of those days. "I've been waiting to hear from you all afternoon, then when you finally resurface you tell me you've found a backpack and a couple of threads. What's that going to tell us? Our assassin's favorite color? Come on. I need more than that..."

And on and on and on and on. It wasn't her fault. The pressure came from above. Terror was high profile. And high profile cases meant there were people all the way up the line pressing for answers to pass on to their bosses a notch higher up. They didn't want to hear that Sadiqi had found a few strands of fabric or that he had visited a spot where he believed Desjardins might have holed up. What they wanted was the Prime Minister's assassin.

Unfortunately, her hounding was counterproductive. Usually Sadiqi would do anything for Dukrin but when she started bitching, telling him that he wasn't doing enough – then he reacted the same way he reacted when any woman in his life complained about his shortcomings. He cut the sound.

While she reeled off a barrage of information, the cop's thoughts turned back to Corrigan. A microsecond later his eyes followed those thoughts. She was still looking at her phone but apparently the temperature in the non air-conditioned car was starting to get to her. She had grabbed some flier out of the side pockets and was now fanning herself. Her cheeks had flushed and a few wisps of hair were sticking to her forehead. Sadiqi felt his impatience rising. Caron had better move his ass because Corrigan wouldn't stay cooking in his car all night. She would get fed up and that would be the end of dinner. He checked his watch again. 7:25. How long should he wait? It had been nearly half an hour already. Okay, so maybe Caron was stuck in traffic. But in that case he should have called. And what was so important about their appointment? What exactly was this report he wanted to show him, anyway?

As soon as the question crept into his mind, Sadiqi realized that perhaps he didn't need Caron at all. After all, hadn't Caron said that his report had been circulated to the counter-terror services? The cop tuned back in to his boss' voice, waiting for a lull so he could cut in. "Did you ever get a report on catacomb safety. Written by someone called Pierre Caron – in collaboration with Clavreul?"

Sadiqi had no way of knowing that those simple words made Dukrin's heart skip a beat. But the coolness of her noncommittal "Yes" was unmistakeable

"What's in it?"

"I can't remember. A lot of insane apocalyptic scenarios."

"Like hit men attacking Val-de-Grace and anthrax being injected into Montaigne High."

The irony elicited a moment's silence from his boss, before she added, "I'll ask Madame Gaudin to dig it out for you."

The short mundane phrase left the cop grasping for something to say. It was so entirely unexpected. Unexpected because it was their safe word; their code. Madame Gaudin was one of the assistants who worked in Dukrin's secretarial pool. Very old school. In fact, so old school she still believed that as a civil servant she had no boss and no obligation to do any work. Whenever she was asked to do something, no matter how small the task, she first tried to avoid doing it. Or, if that failed, she tried to do it incorrectly – so that she wouldn't be asked to do it again. Or, failing that, she would be as impolite as possible – once again, to make sure the boss never asked for help again.

And that was precisely why he and Dukrin had chosen her name as their code. Normally neither of them would ever ask Madame Gaudin to do anything; she was entirely untrustworthy. That's what made her the ideal signal. The innocent name was their code to say that a subject was too delicate to be touched on over the phone. Or that the line might be bugged. Or both.

Now it was Sadiqi's turn not to know what to say. This was truly the day from hell. He leaned up against the wall letting thoughts cascade through his mind. Dukrin was wary of everyone. That was her job. Yet despite all her planned precautions this was the first time she had ever used their code to ask him not to talk over the phone. Which could mean only one thing. The politics involved in whatever was going down in this case ran deep.

The silence on the line had lasted too long. They both felt it but Dukrin was the one to make an effort at normalization. *"Allez Sadiqi.* Find me something I can use," she said, sending him back into battle.

"Yeah," he agreed lamely. "I'll update you later."

"I'll be waiting."

The cop didn't bother stopping to consider what had just passed between them. As soon as he had cut the line his thumb began dancing through his phone repertory down to C for Caron and *connard.* There was still no sign of the professor. Maybe he was sitting in traffic somewhere not far away. But the phone didn't even ring; it just clicked straight to voice mail. All Sadiqi could do was rant as he stamped along the sidewalk.

The cop's faith in the IGC director had never been strong but it was now at its lowest ebb. The man was obviously an asshole; earlier it had seemed he was actively trying to stop the police from finding out what was going on. It was even possible that he had played some role in what had happened at Val-de-Grace. After all, he was in a position to provide potential criminals with detailed information about the catacombs. He had keys and unlimited knowledge of the network. It was worth checking the man's political links and making sure he really was on the right side of events.

Sadiqi called up the second number in his address book: Podesta. He knew his assistant wouldn't be enthralled at the idea of spending his evening checking Caron's affiliations. The lieutenant was a good man but too bureaucratic. He expected policing to be a 9 to 5 job that could be carried out comfortably until retirement kicked in at 55. Sadiqi grimaced as he thought of the number of times he'd had to pull the lieutenant aside to explain that such-and-such an investigation needed to be done immediately – not after lunch, not at 9 the following morning. And, sure enough, today was no exception. Podesta didn't think that 7:30 was a reasonable time to be asked to check out a suspect. "Can't it wait 'til tomorrow, *Chef?*" he griped. Sadiqi resented the fact he had to get nasty before the lieutenant agreed to have a report on his desk later that night. And despite the promise, it wasn't certain the work would get done.

A wave of exhaustion washed over the inspector as he hung up. This was one fuck of a day. A day in limbo. Barely any sleep, followed by hours of running around from one place to the next, one dead end to another. Zero results. Sadiqi slipped his phone into his pocket and headed back to the car. He had a clear view of the girl riding shotgun. Corrigan might turn out to be the day's sole redeeming feature. Yet sadly dinner now seemed on the rocks. He had more urgent things to do. It had been over 17 hours since de Chanterelle's murder. What he needed was a breakthrough.

He climbed back into the car.

"I'm going to have to give dinner a miss. I really don't have time."

"Ah come on. A guy's gotta eat."

It was sweet the way she protested, as if she really cared. "Yeah. But I'm not making any headway with my case and I've just wasted another half hour for nothing," he said, performing an illegal u-turn on the busy crossroad. "Caron didn't show."

"He loves doing that," Toni said, fastening her seatbelt. "He's constantly standing me up." Sadiqi was about to remind her that keeping students waiting was a trivial discourtesy whereas standing up a police officer was tantamount to wilfully impeding the investigation. The words never got out; instead she cut him off with yet another of her disarming remarks. "You're gonna need food to keep going. You look beat. And I'm sure you need a break. You must have been up since before dawn."

Instead of running the red light, he actually pulled to a halt. "You're very observant," he said, turning to look at her.

"Yeah. I'm good like that. I notice a lot of stuff…"

"What else have you noticed?"

The playful smile was back on her face. It seemed to be her default setting; just like the deadpan was his. "You're pretty hermetic. You don't give a lot away. But at times your face becomes very expressive. It's a momentary thing. Almost a micro-expression." She nodded at him. "Like just then. I saw a flash of surprise."

Sadiqi knew that 'surprise' wasn't the right word. What he was feeling was something closer to wonder. For some reason, Corrigan's appraisal of him transcended the purely professional – which moved him all the more for its unexpectedness. The fact that this beautiful young woman saw him as a something more than a generic cop was flattering in itself. The idea that she was watching him – observing his facial expressions – caught him completely off guard. Unless he was very much mistaken, she had just stated that she found him attractive – that she was paying attention to him. *Damn. Green flag.* His brain whirled for a suitable response. The awkward silence was broken only when the car behind honked to signal the light had changed.

At least that gave him an excuse to break eye contact. Shifting into gear, his gaze was now cemented to the road. He'd probably never been so attentive to traffic in his life.

He would have liked to dazzle her with a clever comeback, but repartee had never been his strong suit. It was Toni who spoke first. "So dinner's back on?"

"A guy's gotta eat." He stole a glance sideways. She was smiling out her side window.

Caron, Dukrin and Podesta would all have to wait. After all, some offers in life just didn't come around twice. In any case, if Corrigan was so dazzlingly observant, maybe he really would learn something useful over dinner.

45

Back in her office, Dukrin sat quietly digesting the conversation she'd just had with Sadiqi. She wondered how much Khalid knew about the *Clavreul Report*. She also fumed at the fact that the damn thing was coming back to haunt her. Not that it surprised her. As soon as she'd seen Clavreul's name on that document she'd known it would become a thorn in her side. Some people trailed nothing but trouble. Clavreul was toxic; he turned everything he touched to poison.

She would have to dig up her copy and have another look before sending it on.

46

The heat wave had seriously damaged the great French tradition of four course meals; nobody has much appetite when it's 40° outside. So the restaurant was chosen less for its menu than for its ceiling fans. It was a small place tucked away beside the Cluny museum, with trendy sofas in bright reds and pinks that contrasted with the black walls. And as soon as the waiter with the silver stud through his eyebrow had taken their order, the cop directed his full attention to his companion.

"So was today your strangest day ever in the quarries?"

"Never a dull moment underground. Just when you think you know everything there is to know, something new comes up." Toni took a sip of her kir and smiled. "But yes, getting pulled into a police investigation is right up there with the most unlikely days ever."

"You're not tempted to spend more time topside," he said. "Paris is a busy city. There's a lot going on. Beautiful things to see. Exploring underground tunnels isn't exactly the standard option. Most people prefer the museums and the restaurants to your endless tunnels."

Toni wondered if the cop really meant what he was saying or if he was just trying to get a rise out of her. From what she'd seen today, it seemed pretty unlikely that the Louvre and the Proust tearoom at the Ritz were what kept the man in Paris. But she also knew it was hard for most people to see the beauty of the quarries in a world that had become convinced that clothes, the stock market and expensive cars were the manna of humanity. That was precisely what she liked about her underground world. To use a pun, she found the surface superficial. The fashions, the shows, the restaurants, the politics. "Most people nowadays are too busy worrying whether they've got the right animal sewn on their polo shirt to think about exploring the quarries. I'm not really into consumer society. I prefer the atmosphere below. Life underground isn't about the illusion of appearances. It's raw down there. It's real. You can be yourself."

"That's quite the recommendation," Sadiqi said drily. "And there I was thinking they were just old tunnels." Rather than making himself sound in tune with Corrigan's vision of the catacombs, he seemed to be doing his best to shoot himself in the foot. Maybe that was part of his nature. Where women were concerned, he had a tendency to say the worst thing possible. It wasn't done on purpose. Perhaps it was simply the easy option.

But although the sarcasm hadn't gone unnoticed, the self-sabotage misfired. Toni knew Sadiqi was interested in her, and she was pretty sure it was more than professional. He'd invited her to dinner. She'd seen him looking at her. Which meant that the only logical explanation for the needling tone had to be that he was teasing. And teasing was something she was always happy to engage in. If he wanted to tease, she could give as good as she could take. She certainly had enough ammunition. The inspector's vagueness about who he was and what he was doing laid him open to jabs. After all weren't cops supposed to tell you what they were investigating when they interviewed you? Sadiqi certainly hadn't. He'd been pretty evasive so far.

"Enough about me. What about you, Inspector?" But before she could go further, the word caught in her throat. It had been jarring for a while but now it just sounded ridiculous. "Do I really have to keep calling you 'Inspector'?"

Sadiqi knew that English-speakers slipped quickly into first names. That was fine with him. The stilted language of French hierarchy was a part of his job he was happy to do without. "You can call me Khalid."

She propped her elbows on the tiny table and leaned forward. "And you can call me *Dr.* Corrigan. *Madame* is nice, but '*Doctor*' sounds much more professional." Her tone was anything but professional and the glint in her eye was pure provocativeness. Sadiqi couldn't help but crack the tiniest of smiles. Which was all she was looking for. "Nah. Go on. Most people call me Toni."

"Toni," he repeated, testing the name to see how it felt.

But she was already looping back to her previous question. "So – Khalid – tell me. How did you become a counter-terrorist cop?"

The first shoots of relaxation evaporated instantly. She was so direct. Again he wondered if inviting her to dinner hadn't been a mistake. "That's not a very interesting story." He didn't like talking about himself. Not that there was any official secret about his job. It's just it was a subject he preferred to avoid.

"Come on. What made you decide to become a cop?" she asked, stretching closer.

For some reason he leaned backwards.

"I didn't really choose the job. I guess it chose me." He picked a piece of baguette out of the breadbasket, and tore off a bit of crust. "I was recruited."

His attempt to avoid giving a straight answer had the perverse effect of making him sound more mysterious. Toni went for what she thought was the bait. "Because you had the right profile?" The twinkle was back in her eye.

Sadiqi winced. "I wouldn't exactly put it that way."

Her shoulders hunched closer. "You wouldn't put it that way, but basically I'm not so far off." She cocked her head sideways. "So what is your profile?"

He tossed a ball of bread into his mouth. Not that he was all that hungry; it was just something to do because he wasn't sure he really wanted to go where the girl was taking him. Yet, for some reason he didn't seem able to hold back a condensed version of his resume. "Middle East studies. Political science. As well as growing up in the wrong part of town around people likely to fit in with a strong criminal, if not terrorist, profile." He purposefully omitted mentioning the 148 IQ and the various martial arts.

"In short, you have contacts in the underworld and you speak Arabic." The girl was impressed. "Sounds like you should be a spy, not a cop."

Again, the joke drew the required smile. "There are several much better fronts for being a spy than being a cop."

"Like?"

"Journalist. University professor... Post-doc." If they were going to be ridiculous, they might as well go all out. The girl was having an intoxicating effect. "People whose job it is to be nosy. People who when they get caught by the authorities start whining, 'But I was only doing my job,' so the international media cry out that it's outrageous that a journalist has been arrested for spying or that a poor PhD student has been thrown in jail."

The carelessness in his voice was irresistible. "Maybe I should have ordered a vodka martini instead of kir." She raised her glass. "To the cops keeping us safe."

He raised his. "And to the intelligence services keeping the cops informed."

For the space of a breath, some of the complexity in his life seemed to recede. He would have liked to freeze that instant and occupy it forever. But as easy as she was to talk with, some topics were better avoided. While she was still drinking the toast, he decided to ease the conversation back to her centers of interest and dodge any more questions about himself. It wasn't exactly light flirting, but as a specialist in terrorism, there was one piece of catacomb trivia he was honestly interested in. "Earlier you said you weren't worried about the quarries being used for terror. But what about the *Cagoule?*" He was curious to hear her take on this. "You talked about several past threats on the catacombs. But the *Cagoule* is the only one that, personally, I'd classify as terrorism."

The whole day had been one strange event after the other, so Toni was willing to accept even this topic as normal, especially as the first sips of alcohol were numbingly effective in the heat. "1936," she mused. "Not many Frenchmen who remember that. And the ones who do would usually rather pretend they didn't."

Her assessment cut to the mark. Although Sadiqi's fellow countrymen loved reminding the world how they'd drafted the Universal Declaration of Human Rights, they tended to gloss over the more divisive points in the nation's history. And there were many. The *Cagoule* was one of those dark stories that always made him feel he was part of a country at odds with itself. It was a story that dated back to the inter-war period. The *Cagoule* had been a secret organization, aligned with Franco and Mussolini, which emerged in the shadows when all extreme right-wing parties and associations were out-lawed by the socialist government. "The *Cagoule* organized a *coup d'état.* They wanted to destroy the Republic by overthrowing the government. One of the key elements of their plan was to attack the Senate via the catacombs."

"Sure," Toni replied, seamlessly easing into the new topic. "The Senate sits on a major quarry axis. But the *coup* itself was stopped before it could happen. The *Cagoule* were responsible for various assassinations and bombings, but nothing more. The plot to take over the government was nipped in the bud."

The nonchalance made Sadiqi shake his head. *"Various assassinations and bombings, but nothing more."* Time the great healer. What had happened eighty years earlier could be spoken about as if it were a minor detail, not a human tragedy. "The group was toxic and dangerous and running wild in your darling quarries. The *Cagoule's* attack on the Senate involved the quarries as an essential part of the plan. The group held many of their meetings underground. And they had detailed maps of the network and code names for each of the chambers they used as rallying points. The catacombs weren't a detail; they were the plan," he said, waiting for a reaction. "If it happened then, it could happen now."

Toni was already shaking her head. "No way. We have Captain Ferry to thank for keeping us safe. There were no cataflics back in the '30s. Even if there still aren't a huge number of cops down there today, there's no way anything like that could happen now. Anyone approaching the Senate would be caught almost immediately. That whole sector is actively monitored. And groups holding regular meetings anywhere in the wider network would be noticed in a matter of days."

The cop tried to hold that optimistic thought but couldn't. Maybe it would be hard to get anywhere near the Senate. But he wasn't so sure activity elsewhere in the network could be kept under tabs. It wouldn't be easy to pick out a handful of conspirators in several hundred kilometers of tunnels, no matter how competent the cops. If someone wanted to hide down there, they could.

Ignoring the dish the waiter had just set in front of him, he took another sip of his whisky instead. This case was really getting to him. He needed to decompress. It would help him to see clearer. It was time to move on to lighter subjects. "I think I've had enough of the quarries for one day. You know, in France, food is the only acceptable topic for dinner conversation. During meals, we talk about meals. It's national etiquette."

The announcement of this new change of topic rang out like a mission statement for Toni. "You don't think I can find a tie-in between food and the quarries?" A trace of indignation played in the lines of her forehead, but as she reached for the bread, her hand brushed lightly against Sadiqi's.

"It might be a challenge."

"Have you learnt nothing today? I have catacomb conversation for all occasions. Even food." She picked up her fork as if preparing to root around in her plate for inspiration. Instead she found herself transfixed, watching a smile spread across Sadiqi's face. It had started as little more than a tremble at the corners of his lips, but now it was a full-fledged grin – the first of the day. With the impassive mask gone, Toni felt she'd finally been given a glimpse of the man below the surface.

Sadiqi felt the chemistry, too. His interest in the woman had ceased to be professional long before dinner. Within an hour of entering the quarries, he had been intrigued. When her hand had glanced against his a moment earlier, it had sent a tremor through him. "Just exactly how much catacomb trivia do you know?"

"Enough for every minute of every day."

"What? You spend 10 minutes calculating structural weakness, then 10 minutes reading folklore about the Green Monster and the *Cagoule*, then maybe, if you have a little free time you help your roommate organize your next rave up in the Z-Room?"

"Something like that. Except I don't have a roommate. What about you? What's your mission in life?"

His eyes were fixed on her delicate features, but he knew it was more than just the pretty face and the lithe figure that attracted him. What he liked was her gritty side. The fact she could travel around the catacombs by herself or stand her ground against idiots like Caron. She had ideas; she had drive. And yes, it was true, she was also pretty damn gorgeous. He downed the end of his whisky. "I guess my mission in life is to be a good cop."

Toni knew that was a lie. She could see it in his eyes, and in the way he needed the whisky to commit the lie. Which was puzzling. She wondered what he wanted to hide.

Then again, it didn't really matter. Honesty wasn't everything it was cracked up to be. There were more important things in life – like grit. And tenacity. And the cop certainly had those.

He was tough. And she was pretty sure he would clean up nice. The body was trim. His light cotton shirt showed the sharp outline of his muscles. Toni knew the cop's eyes weren't always concentrated on her face. She'd seen him looking at her. Checking her out... But had he seen her? Measuring the arch of his shoulders. Imagining the strength in his arms. The power of his torso, those abs and thighs.

"You've got limestone in your hair." She stretched her fingertips across the table and brushed the specks of gravel out of the soft waves of curls.

There was no doubt where tonight was headed.

47

A little before midnight Toni found herself lying naked in Sadiqi's arms, pleasantly exhausted.

"What are you thinking?" she asked, rolling onto her stomach, her thighs enmeshing with his. She nestled her head on his shoulder and stroked the handshaped amulet he wore on a silver chain around his neck.

The cop tightened his grip around her waist. The now familiar smile on her lips suggested Corrigan wasn't hoping for a serious comment. "I'm thinking that I'd really love a cigarette just about now."

"Nice to know you'll remember me so fondly." She stretched her head backward and nibbled at his neck. "I didn't think smoking-after-sex was a real thing."

"It's a thing. First time I've done that without a cigarette."

Toni propped herself on her elbow and ran the other hand across Sadiqi's chest. "When did you give up smoking? Monday?"

Sadiqi didn't often feel embarrassed; but today was a day of new experiences. "I'm a little out of practice."

"It doesn't show. If that's the result of quitting smoking, you should have kicked the habit years ago. There'd be more women smiling in the world." She kissed his left nipple then traced a line along the pecs up to his shoulder. "In any case, I don't think you're supposed to smoke if you're wearing a patch." Her fingers caressed the little beige plaster on his upper arm.

He had to make a conscious effort to stop himself from saying the words he'd repeated to his family for years: that life expectancy in his profession was about 7 years below the national average and it didn't have anything to do with the number of cigarettes smoked. It was a statistic that had made him laugh 20 years earlier when he first joined the force. Now that he'd hit 45 those lost years worried him. He brushed the hair out of her eyes and pulled her closer.

Her lips teased his, but then, without warning, she escaped from his arms, somehow rolling away to the bottom of the bed, leaving him to study the arch of her back rising wavelike away from her buttocks.

She then killed the moment entirely by reaching under the bed to pull out her laptop.

"No," he whispered. The word registered somewhere between a protest and a plea. He moved in her direction and lay a kiss on the crest of her tailbone then began working his way up her spine. *Not the computer,* he thought. *Not the return to reality.*

She wasn't listening. The ping sounded and the computer revved up.

The bullshit train was rolling again. He laid his cheek in the small of her back, his eyes focused on the now illuminated screen.

And as soon as the machine had booted up, the moment was lost. The image on the desktop screen took care of that. His face hardened. "What the hell is that?"

Toni did a double-take but the source of the irritation was obvious. The picture on her desktop wasn't the kind of thing you were supposed to go showing to an anti-terror cop. It was out of a video simulation she'd made of the Pantheon building collapsing, complete with cupola hurtling through the roof of the St. Genevieve Library. This was probably tantamount to making jokes about bombings while passing through airport security. It was something you weren't supposed to do. She tried glossing over it. "Don't worry about that. It's nothing," she said, clicking directly on her web browser. "Just something I did for a research project. Just forget it."

"Just forget it?" Some things weren't easily fogotten. Bombs and exploding buildings fell into that category. "Why do you have a picture of the Pantheon being blown up?"

The student raised her eyes from the laptop and shrugged. "It's not being blown up. It's imploding. You know, that *is* my field of research. Subterranean weakness and its effect on the surface, right? If the land isn't secure, the buildings collapse." She made the remark lightly but Sadiqi sensed a drop of how-dumb-can-you-get impatience in her voice. She felt him recoil. "Look I'm sorry. Just let it go." She tore her eyes away from the screen long enough to send him a peace offering in the form of radiant smile then entwined her ankles with his before flipping back to her search engine.

The cop wondered what was hidden behind that fleeting glance. And, more importantly, he wondered just how much he could trust this woman who had gradually vampirized his day.

He watched as her fingers flew over the keyboard. "Have you seen this message?" she asked. Sadiqi immediately recognized the text on the screen and nodded. It was the retribution text. His eyes skimmed over the words that had been in his thoughts for most of the day. But Toni was already a step ahead, reading the next paragraph. "And look, there's another one now."

June 20; from Ng
Retribution will come

All was dark save one glimmering light in the east. To what did the darkness allude? Even to the darkness of death.

She waited for a reaction while he read the second message. None came. Except he reached for his shirt and started rooting around for something, eventually pulling out a nicotine mint. Toni prompted him. "I thought messages like this were a cop's manna."

The idea that this type of post lit up Sadiqi's life was ridiculous. "Messages like that are bullshit. It's some idiot playing cat and mouse with us, trying to make us waste time delving into their pathetic mind."

The answer had the merit of being frank. Possibly the most direct comment she'd heard all day. But Toni was disappointed not to get a more positive response. "You don't think there are clues in there. I mean don't you have cryptographers and people trained to decipher this kind of stuff?"

"Of course we've got cryptographers. They'll be cross referencing the key words. Trying to figure out if there's some original source that inspired the quote."

Toni was on it before he'd even finished his sentence. The words *glimmering, east, darkness, allude,* and *death* had now appeared in the query box. Before either of them had time to say anything, a screen of proposals appeared.

Worshipful Grand Master
... the **light** of a Master Mason is **darkness** visible,... Yet even by this **glimmering** light may you realize the journey that...
www.mason.com/gmaster.html - 33k - Cached - Similar pages

Dalhousie: Hiram on the www: Lectures on the Craft
Answer: All was **Darkness**, save a **glimmer** of **light** in the **East**. Question: To what does that **Darkness** allude? Answer: The **Darkness** of Death...
www.uni_dallaire.ca/freemasonry/master.html - 45k - Cached - Similar pages

Ritual of the 4th and 7th Degree
A **light** in the **East** points to the Grand Master and the rest of the lodge is shrouded in **darkness**... Two pillars standing on either side of...

Toni's eyes digested the information while Sadiqi found himself waiting for the running commentary. The net wasn't usually his concern. Dukrin provided him with messages and information that turned up online; he didn't do the groundwork. The analyses were provided by others. Which explained why he wasn't entirely comfortable deciphering this list of half-sentences. What he did notice was that Toni was no longer racing onto a new page. Something had caught her attention. "Is that what I think it is?" he asked.

"I don't know," she answered cautiously. Her thoughts had circled back to her conversations with Marco, then to the conversation she'd overheard between her two professors. This could either be a strange sort of serendipity or just a coincidence. "I can tell you what I think it is. I'd say the first three entries are references to Freemasonry. And the second one down is a perfect hit. That's your quote."

Sadiqi peered at the screen, trying to make sense of the meaningless short phrases. "You think whoever's leaving these messages is a Freemason?"

"I don't know." A whole range of possibilities presented themselves. "This morning I was willing to believe that whoever had left the message was an Islamist extremist. Now it looks like there's some sort of tie-in with Freemasonry." So which was it? Or was it neither? "Maybe someone's trying to throw suspicion on a whole bunch of different groups. Drawing attention away from whoever's really behind the whole thing. Or – like you said – maybe someone's just playing cat and mouse."

As an intellectual Toni could run the possibilities through her mind and weigh them up in total abstraction. As the head of the investigation, Sadiqi had to make some decisions about what it all meant. And of all the groups in the world to run up against, the Freemasons had to be one of the most elusive.

"What the hell are they, anyway? A club? A frat? A sect?"

Toni's face went blank. "A sect? I'd never heard that before." She was about to add something, but stopped herself before it was out. Given the guy's reaction to her desktop screen, she suspected he was capable of squirreling away some off-hand comment to be used as testimony later. She would have to be very careful what she said if she was going to hang out with a cop.

Sadiqi was too absorbed by the words on the screen to notice her hesitation. He didn't like this kind of case. He didn't like the feeling that he was being pulled into a game and toyed with. And his current state of fatigue was probably not helping him process information.

Toni was still staring at the screen. "What do you think it means?"

"I don't know. And I'm sure as hell not going to guess. Let's hope the cryptographers can do better. That's what they're paid for."

"But can't you use the link to track down whoever wrote it? Trace the IP address. Find the physical person linked to the virtual message. I thought the police were all about cyber security nowadays."

Sadiqi's job would have been much easier in a world where computers were as easy to trace as physical street addresses. "It's hard to get a clear lead from this kind of garbage. The IP addresses are usually scrambled."

If he'd been hoping to dazzle her with his computer savvy he had misjudged his audience. "Of course they're scrambled. Everyone scrambles their codes. Don't you guys just unscramble the scramble? Find back doors, or whatever."

Sadiqi didn't like what he was hearing. Between the apocalyptic image of the collapsing Pantheon on her screen and this comment about hiding IP codes, he was beginning to wonder if he wasn't quite literally sleeping with the enemy. "What do you mean everyone scrambles their IP code?"

"Well, it's true. Nobody wants to be stalked. I mean, I use a VPN all the time."

A look of annoyance had crept into his eyes. "Why?"

"Because I don't want to be traced, of course."

"What are you doing that you don't want traced?"

The student held the very cop-like stare. "I'm not doing anything illegal, if that's what you're worried about."

"Then why scramble your code?"

"Because I don't want to be followed. It's a question of personal privacy. Nobody's got the right to follow me, either physically or virtually. If someone followed me in the street, I wouldn't like it. Being stalked when I'm online is the same thing. It's precisely because I'm *not* doing anything illegal that I should be allowed to exercise my basic freedom of movement."

Sadiqi didn't like the answer. But he knew it was typical of her generation. It was a generation that viewed internet exploration as a universe of free and unbridled movement. No rules. No costs. No limits.

He pushed aside the laptop and walked the three paces to the window. Val-de-Grace rose majestically in front of him. To the left, the Pantheon towered over the Latin Quarter. Everything looked normal. The floodlights for the tourists. The picture postcard. A beautiful girl on a hot summer night. No. More than that. A beautiful, intelligent, adorable woman. Who hid her IP codes and had a photo of an exploding public monument on her desktop.

Something was rotten. The whole fucking world was screwed up. The cop really wished he had a cigarette now. Without the option of taking a drag of nicotine, he breathed in a dense lungful of the city's nitrogen oxide.

"I should be going," he said, gravitating back to the center of the tiny room and pulling his shirt and jeans out from the pile of clothes on the floor. He didn't dare turn his eyes back to the bed. He didn't dare look at Toni. He didn't dare look at her because he knew he would just want to curl back up in her arms and forget about the screwed up world.

She sensed this. "Oh, come on. Stay. Just a little bit longer," she whispered.

There was a moment's hesitation as he slipped into his Levi's. "No. I've got work to do." He buttoned his jeans.

But before he could tighten his belt, he felt the caress of soft skin beside him and a hand loosened the button he had just done up. "Oh come on. It's hot out. Have a shower first." He felt her lips as they teased the crest of his shoulder. "Then I'll let you go. I promise."

48

It was almost an hour before Sadiqi was sitting in his Renault. And sitting was the right word. Not driving. Just sitting in his parked car in the rue des Feuillantines trying to forget about the girl he'd left upstairs and get his brain back around his case. Which wasn't an easy thing to do. He was tired. He'd been up for nearly 24 hours. He needed to sleep. He needed to clear his mind. Clear his mind. That was what Amélie had never been able to accept. His need to be alone to think straight, without interference.

Yet tonight, in all honesty, he would have preferred the interference. He would have preferred to be up there on the seventh floor, with Corrigan wrapped around him. But he couldn't.

He pulled his phone out of his pocket. A few years ago, his cell phone had been his favorite gadget. His link to the modern world. Now he saw it for what it was. His ball and chain. A symbol of serfdom. Turning it off from 10PM to midnight had been nothing short of a revolution. Now he pressed the ON button and tapped in his pin. "You have five new messages." *Merde.* That was all he needed.

He reached mechanically for the Zippo as he stared out the window. Despite the fact that the sun had gone down hours ago, the metal was still unusually warm against his skin. He flipped the lid open and spun the wheel. There was a spark. But no flame. Never any flame anymore. "Message 1. June 20th, 22:06: *Bonsoir Chef. Podesta ici.* I tried to reach Quentin Asselin. No luck. His mobile doesn't answer and according to his phone company he hasn't made any calls for nearly a week now. His parents haven't heard from him either. I ran a check on his credit cards. He's not used any plastic since last Friday. I'd say it doesn't look good. As for Caron, he's got nothing to hide. Never been a member of a banned or subversive group. He's got a few unpaid parking tickets but then who doesn't. Other than that, nothing. The full report is on your desk. *Allez. C'est tout. Bonne nuit.*" The news was neither good nor bad. It was indifferent, providing nothing but confirmation of what Sadiqi already suspected. Bango was probably dead. Caron was probably clean.

The next message followed automatically. "Message 2. June 20th, 22:45: *Bonsoir* Khalid. It's Amelie." Although she was miles away, Sadiqi tensed at the mere sound of the voice. He cut the communication and jumped to the next message.

"Message 3: June 20th, 23:05: It's Sasha. Call me back as soon as you can." Sadiqi recognized the style. When his boss left short messages like that she expected the call to be returned within minutes.

Sure enough, a reminder followed. "Message 4: June 20th, 23:21: 'It's me again. I'm heading home now. I'd like an update.'" The strain in her voice was discernible.

Sadiqi had a fair idea what the next message was going to be. Dukrin again and sure enough her tone had lost a measure of composure. "Message 5: June 20th, 23:43: *Mais qu'est-ce que tu fous. Enfin. Merde.*" *What the fuck are you up to?* Well, what could he say? It was a valid question under the circumstances.

He checked his watch. That message was nearly half an hour old and he knew that her mood wouldn't have improved in the meantime. Given the choice of which person he should call in the middle of the night, he would by far prefer to wake Amélie and tell her to go to hell.

That was pointless. Dukrin, on the other hand, was probably still wide awake and waiting for him to get back to her.

Sure enough, the phone rang only twice and there was no sign of sleep in her voice. "It's about bloody time".

"Complicated day."

The words didn't convince Dukrin; they did appease her. She moved straight to an update. "We've got a new lead on this thing…"

"The Freemasons," Sadiqi offered before she had time to finish her sentence.

Dukrin relaxed ever so slightly. This was why she'd asked Sadiqi to take this case. Despite his absence earlier that evening, now that he'd reappeared he was on the ball. "You've seen the new message."

"Yes. But I've no idea what it's supposed to mean."

Dukrin explained that other than knowing that it was a reference to the Freemasons, they were in the dark. The inspector sniffed at the lack of insight. The Canadian had been able to tell him as much. Surely cryptography should be able to do better than that.

"I was hoping for more to go on. I've been working from scraps all day. Can't anyone give me a clue? I mean, okay, you give me the Freemasons. But what am I supposed to do with them? Is this a Freemason claiming responsibility for de Chanterelle's murder? Is that credible?"

As much as secret societies and gentlemen's clubs irritated Dukrin, she wasn't quite ready to start accusing the Masons of being behind any serious crime. At least not as an organization. "It might be anything. I suppose we could be looking for a renegade. There are nuts everywhere. On the other hand, there's also the possibility that the Freemasons are the target here rather than the perpetrators. You're reading the message as a claim of responsibility. The alternative is that it's an announcement of something yet to come."

"Do you have any reliable information on this, or is it just a hunch?"

"I have enough information to know to take serious precautions. I've reinforced cataflic security in the quarries. I'm also stationing a number of people above ground around the Latin Quarter."

"You realize we're way out of my field of competence," Sadiqi pointed out, remembering the miles of impenetrable darkness below ground.

"What do you mean?"

"We're getting further and further away from the Islamist extremist scenario. It was shaky to begin with. Now I'd say it's non existent."

Dukrin paused, searching for words she could share over the phone but that would convey some meaning. "I would have thought that was good news," she said finally. "This has all the hallmarks of something homegrown, which should make it even easier to figure out."

She was right, of course. Sadiqi could see it coming. It was still only an intuition but he could feel it growing. They were looking for the enemy within. Something parochial. He knew the signs. The homegrown anthrax. Val-de-Grace. The schools at exam time. The catacombs. These were French references. Parisian references. These weren't international targets. This wasn't some attack coordinated by international terrorist groups. This was going to be French against French. There was no outside enemy. This was an intimate enemy.

So what was the next target? Another pinpointed strike? A famous building? A tourist spot? Or something even more massive? Like the Nazis stuffing the catacombs with explosives with the intention of blowing the whole city sky high. Could that be what this was about?

49

Even after the shower, Sadiqi's scent lingered on Toni's skin. Usually late-night/early-morning was her favorite time for getting her research written up. And usually sex cleared her mind. But not tonight. The invisible presence of this very strange and unexpected man who had somehow made his way into her life had broken her concentration. Five minutes earlier, she had started a sentence with "Substratum facturing precipitated by interventional strategies...", but the words were still sitting meaninglessly on the screen. She wasn't even sure what she'd meant to write. She certainly didn't care. Her mind kept wandering back over the day.

It wasn't so much the attraction to Khalid that left her wondering. Quiet guys who marched in and took control of the situation were right up her alley. No. What unsettled her more was the strength of the attraction. She hadn't been on the lookout for a guy. And even if she had been, she definitely wouldn't have expected a cop to make the shortlist let alone fill the post. But then this guy marches in and suddenly she's staring blankly at her computer, wondering when she's going to see him again. It was so unlike her.

Giving up on her sentence, she pushed down the laptop screen, slipped into jeans and a t-shirt then headed for the communal kitchen. The light at the end of the corridor told her she wasn't the only one having a restless night and when she rounded the corner, she found Marco sipping his umpteenth coffee of the day.

"You're up late," she commented, reaching for the kettle.

The young Italian squeezed himself against the counter to make room for company in the minuscule kitchen. "*Ciao, Carina.* Too hot to sleep. And too noisy." If it hadn't been for his crooked smile she probably would have missed his meaning. As it was, the message was clear. Part of what had stopped him from sleeping had been the sounds of sex floating down the hallway, driving him from his own bedroom an hour earlier. The walls of the residence were paper-thin and nobody got much privacy. Learning to turn off other people's noise was a basic survival skill in communal accommodation – if you couldn't turn off the sound, it was best to relocate. "I didn't know you were seeing anyone."

"I wasn't."

Marco had that rare talent, seldom seen outside silent movies, of being able to raise a single eyebrow whenever he was surprised. "Busy girl. When did you find time to meet a new man? I thought you spent all day showing that cop around the catacombs."

"I did," she said, turning off the tap and switching on the kettle before shooting him a meaningful smile.

The look of perplexity on his face was fleeting, washed away almost instantly by a surge of appalled wonder. "No!" With his hands he drew the outline of a strong male figure in the air. "Mr. Policeman?" Then an exaggerated moment of stunned horror. "*Sei pazza?* You are crazy?"

She couldn't stop herself from giggling. "Why crazy? You're just jealous?"

While her friend considered some of the more blatantly libidinous comments he could make, the Canadian let her thoughts wander back to Khalid. Part of those thoughts were about the de Chanterelle case, the other part was romantic. Yet the two were now connected. By thinking about the case, she felt herself drawn deeper into the memory of the man. And that was what she wanted – for that feeling of closeness to last.

"Actually I have a question for you. When I was talking with…"

"…Dirty Harry," Marco offered, with lightning repartee.

She accepted the ribbing with an amused shrug. "Okay, if you like. Whatever. Anyway, he said that Freemasonry was a sect. Why would he say that?"

No answer was offered. Marco was staring. "*Ma sei completamente pazza. You are crazy.* You meet a man. You sleep with him, then you talk about Freemasonry? No. *Non è possibile.* You sleep with him, then you talk about love, art, sex, music, travel... Anything, but, please... not Freemasonry."

The theatrical display of outrage sent her into a fit of giggles. Ever since she and Marco had met a couple of years earlier at a conference in Bologna, they'd enjoyed a deep complicity. Their interests and knowledge were vast so they kept one another charged intellectually. Better yet, the fact that their sexual preferences were non-complementary had allowed them to avoid the turbulence of a romantic entanglement – which only made the friendship stronger. Platonic perfection. No regrets on either side. "Just answer the question, Marco," she said, still smiling but regaining some composure. "The way you talk about Freemasonry, it sounds like some sort of discussion group. A forum for free speech."

Leaning against the counter, the Italian remarked that he could always count on Toni to come up with elaborate discussion topics at one in the morning. She'd barely got her lover out of her sheets and already she was focused on something arcane. Not very romantic, but certainly lively. Taking a sip of his coffee, he surrendered to the inevitable conversation.

"Freemasonry is complex," he said, still shaking his head in amazement at his friend's thought patterns. "It has many spiritual sources. Perhaps that's why some people consider it a sect. Also, other than some irregular lodges, Freemasons recognize the existence of a Grand Architect of the Universe."

Toni pricked up her ears. This was definitely starting to sound more like a sect. She'd come across many names for the Supreme Being, but *Grand Architect of the Universe* was a new one. "You mean God. Or a god?" It wasn't a very precise term.

"God, Allah, Jehovah, Brahman, Vishnu. *Tutti uguali.* Freemasonry does not say which it has to be, just that you have to believe in an original creator."

"Like the Bahai who believe that whoever you worship, it's the same God."

Marco ran his fingers through his hair, brushing it out of his eyes. He suspected there was more to the Bahai Faith than Toni's short summary, but he wasn't going to get into that. "I think it is more of a moral system than a religion. The different gods are not consolidated into one superior being; there is no... *Come si dice 'sacra scrittura'?"*

"Holy Scripture," Toni offered.

"Grazie. There is no Holy Scripture for Freemasonry. Only a moral system that members study through allegories and symbols."

"The symbols of stonemasonry."

"Essenzialemente. But combined with much Judeo-Christian symbolism plus a mystic side, a kabbalistic side, hermetic elements..."

"Hermetic?" It sounded like something Toni associated with Tupperware.

"Like alchemy."

"You've got to be kidding. As in the philospoher's stone and turning iron into gold." She was beginning to understand why Marco might truly have turned down the offer to join Pythagoras and Euclid Lodge. While the discussion forum sounded like it would have been right up his alley, the esoteric side was beginning to sound a little out there.

Likewise, Marco knew how commonplace Toni's disbelieving attitude was. In a world where communication and information were by-words, religion was one aspect of life that seemed to have escaped public understanding. People's knowledge of their own religion was usually shaky, let alone any basic knowledge of their neighbor's religion. So a system drawing on such diverse origins necessarily posed a problem. "Many elements have integrated themselves into Freemasonry. There are many levels to uncover. Freemasons spend their lives studying this 'Craft'. *Si dice, cosi','"* he half-apologized. "So perhaps it is normal that I cannot summarize all this in just some few minutes. On the one hand, you have a link to the stonemasons of the cathedrals." He held out his right hand. "Then on the other hand, there are other symbols that go back much further." He held out the other.

"Like how far?"

"Nobody knows. *Impossible da dire.* The stories accumulated by the stonemasons are very old. Because, stonemasons were very proud of their craft and so they cultivated many folktales from around the world."

"From around the world? I would have thought that back a thousand years ago, the known world was pretty much limited to Europe," she said. It had seemed like a reasonable enough idea when it was still in her mind, but once she'd said it aloud, she realized she should have thought twice before babbling.

Marco was already drawing in a wisp of air through clenched teeth. "Well there were a few little things known as the Wonders of the Ancient World. Architectural details like the pyramids…"

"Or the hanging gardens of Babylon. Of course. I'm sorry. Stupid of me."

He lifted his eyebrows quickly in recognition of both her stupidity and her apology. "Plus some important Biblical references, like the Temple of Solomon. There is much religion associated with the Masons."

If nothing else, Toni was certainly beginning to understand why Khalid thought the Freemasons were a sect but she still couldn't see any link between what Marco was telling her and what was going on in the quarries. "Just one other question. If it's all related to Judeo-Christian legends, then why is *FranceTech* lodge called *Pythagoras and Euclid.*"

The Italian checked his watch. It was getting very late and he was going to need at least some sleep. Trouvé had asked him to be at the Senate at 8AM for the conference. "*Carina,* I do not have the time tonight." The way he paused to make sure he breathed the 'h' was adorable.

Taking his chin in her hands, Toni rubbed his cheeks, pretending she was his Italian grandma. "Marco, *il piu' bello bambino del mondo."* The most beautiful baby in the world. It was no joke. His features were cosmic Roman perfection. "This is need-to-know, Baby. Ya gotta help me."

"You're just messin' with me," he answered, testing one of the many idioms Toni had taught him. But ultimately he knew he wasn't going to be able to avoid her question. Better keep the explanations simple or he would be facing tomorrow's conference with zero sleep. "*Allora,* I think that Freemasonry is more than just an adjunct of Christianity. There is also the scientific side. Construction throughout the ages became a symbol. You have the religious side – Solomon, the Temple, the cathedrals. But construction is not possible without Science and mathematics. So Euclid enters. He symbolizes mathematics within architecture."

Toni had taken a course in the history of ideas way back in her undergrad days. "I guess that makes sense. Euclid was Greek but spent a lot of his life in Egypt, mainly in Alexandria where he taught geometry to budding young architects."

"That's right," Marco agreed. "But he did not just teach his students the mathematics they needed to build beautiful buildings. He also gave them a certain moral structure; he told that they should treat one another as friends instead of servants or competitors."

"Ahhh. A brotherhood," Toni said, aiming for the overview. "Like in Freemasonry."

"*Esatto.* Euclid was more than just a mathematician. He also created the architectural fraternity."

The kettle boiled and Toni went to pour her tea. "I guess that makes sense. And what about Pythagoras?"

Marco couldn't help rolling his eyes. "*Stai scherzando?* You are joking? You are a civil engineer. You must know Pythagoras."

"$a^2 + b^2 = c^2$," Toni offered.

"*Carina,*" he said, slipping back into the thicker accent he used when he was being playful as opposed to collegiate. "You are *summa cum laude.* What they teach you at McGill?"

"They teach us Civil Engineering. Not Philosophy."

"Okay, but we are not talking about some minor philosopher. Pythagoras is only one of the greatest thinkers of all times. *Piu' piu' grande.*"

"Maybe. Maybe not. I seem to remember being told that a lot of the discoveries associated with him were actually his colleagues' work."

The mock outrage dissolved from the face whose elegant symmetry was marred only by a mole on his right cheek that served to focus attention on the razor-like beauty of his bone structure. "*Brava.* So they do teach you something in Canadian schools." For the two post-docs, the comparative advantages of a European versus a North American education had initially been a source of debate, before mutating into a running joke. Basically they'd called a tie. "Pythagoras was born in Greece in the sixth century BC but he traveled to Memphis. In Egypt, not Tennessee, just in case you are wondering," he added, sarcastically. "He stayed in Egypt for years and learned about numbers, symbols, geometry, astronomy and the mysteries of Egyptian religion. *Purtroppo* – Unfortunately for him, while he completed his studies, Egypt was invaded by Persia. Pythagoras was captured and taken to Babylon with other scholars and priests. *Per fortuna* – Luckily for him, servitu' was not so bad."

"Servitude wasn't so bad? Would you care to elaborate a little on that?"

The young Italian was impatient to get to bed, so he tried to reformulate as plainly as possible. "Captivity in Persia gave all these scholars from different religions and countries a chance to mix together. Some of the prisoners came from as far away as India. This in a world before the printing press and the internet. *Un'esperienza illuminante."*

"An eye-opening experience."

"An eye-opening experience," he repeated, probably saving the expression to memory. "Pythagoras would have met with monotheism as well as the Persian belief in dualism, Hindu philosophers and Zoroastrians."

Toni knew very little about any of these beliefs but she got the general idea. "So he was exposed to a wide variety of religious thought."

"Religion, philosophy, metaphysics. All. And when he was finally free, he moved to Italy."

"Because it's the most beautiful place in the world," she teased.

"No," Marco disagreed with mock seriousness. "France is the most beautiful country in the world. But the Italians are the most marvelous people. So Pythagoras goes there to set up a school of philosophy and that is how you get the link to Freemasonry."

Somewhere in the midst of the banter she had lost the main point of the story. She wasn't sure how they'd migrated from Pythagoras to the Masons. "I think I missed something. What sort of link?"

"The initiation process, for instance. The initiation process at the academy of Pythagoras was very similar to the one connected with Freemasonry."

"Based on some sort of ritual."

"*Esatto.* Not just a comparable process. The trials of Freemasonry themselves are almost identical to the ones Pythagoras used. So much so that some people believe the Masonic ritual was taken directly from Pythagoras." Toni made a rolling motion with her hands to encourage him to go on.

"You understand, in the initiation to Freemasonry, the candidate passes symbolically from Darkness to Light. He goes in a small, dark room known as the *Chamber of Reflection* which is filled with many strange objects: a human skull and bones, a piece of bread, a pitcher of water, a cup of salt, a cup of sulphur, a lighted candle and..." He was stuck for a word and took a quick look around the kitchen. He grabbed an egg-timer off the windowsill. It was old-fashioned, with a wooden frame housing a sand-filled hourglass.

Toni nodded. "An hourglass." Time. The countdown to death.

He returned the hourglass to the spot on the windowsill. "Yes. So the hourglass. And the walls are decorated with a rooster – this symbolizes how the neophyte wakes to a new day. You understand, yes?"

"The profane candidate will die and a new, sacred self begins. Gotcha."

"Yes," Marco said, but rather than sounding pleased that Toni had got the point there was a hesitation in his voice. "But for me, it is a little hard to believe that you have never heard of this Chamber of Reflection before."

"Why?"

He searched for some sign she was joking. It struck him as strange that she honestly seemed to be discovering all this for the first time. "I can understand that you know nothing about the history of the Masons. This is because, Freemasonry tries to stay secret. If you do not meet it, there is no reason to look for it. I am just surprised that in all your reading about the catacombs you have never seen stories of secret societies and initiation rituals."

"Of course I have," she said, thinking of her conversation with Sadiqi about the *Cagoule*. "But I never made the link to anything as big as the Freemasons. How do you get from the Freemasons to the quarries?"

"Well, it is the Chamber of Reflection, no? The dark cave represents the passage from death to new life. And there is another element of the Chamber of Reflection ritual that I am sure you can appreciate. To reach the chamber, the Mason candidate is led, with his eyes covered, along a tortuous path that symbolizes a passage leading to the center of the earth. The chamber is dark; it imitates rock. The underground cave. Along with all the other objects in the chamber, there is a ribbon with the letters VITRIOL written on it. This stands for 'Vista interiora terraie rectificando invenies occultum lapidem.'" The Latin rolled off his tongue as if it were Italian. Then he provided the translation: "Visit the interior of the earth, and by rectifying, you will find the hidden stone."

Toni was amazed. "You're making this up."

Marco shook his head. *"Carina,* I never lie to you."

It was more than compelling. It was a first link between the catacombs and the Freemasons. A feeling of excitement grabbed her. "You really think the Freemasons carry out initiation rituals in the catacombs?"

"Perché no? Why not?" Marco was curious how Toni and her new lover had got on to such an odd topic. He had long been convinced it would be a weird and wonderful experience to be a fly on the wall in the life of Antonia Corrigan. But good story or not, he would have to hear it another time. Tonight he wanted to get to bed. "At the very least, even if Freemasons do not use the catacombs today,

I am sure they did in the past. When this Freemasonry started in France (200 years ago when Pythagoras and Euclid Lodge was just created) there would be no lodge buildings. Members would need somewhere to meet and carry out their initiation. The quarries would have made a perfect Chamber of Reflection at that time."

He didn't need to force the point. Toni didn't need convincing. The only thing she wasn't sure about was whether or not it had a link to the Ng message, too.

50

The Nightingale lay stretched out with only a thin foam sheet separating him from the hard ground. The tunnel he used as a hideout certainly wasn't going to get five stars for comfort. In fact anyone used to living in standard modern squalor would have found it unbearable. But as someone who'd spent his life travelling from one war zone to the next and bivouacking on the battlefield, sleeping in a dugout was a standard experience – even if his usual camping spots weren't often in such famous locations. He estimated that the ground he was now lying on was right under the Pantheon. And as there were only a few meters of rock separating him from the building above, he liked to think of himself as belonging to "the Great Men of the Fatherland", interred among France's famous sons.

The thought made him smile. God knew he needed something to laugh about during the endless hours underground. Of course his time amputated from the world above was drawing to a close. And not a minute too soon. Over the last six months he'd spent way too much time underground. Six months. Shit. He'd spent entire days cutting through rock and removing old stone and rubble. He would never have done this if the motivation hadn't been so strong. After all, he wasn't a kid anymore. And the combined work conditions of total darkness and total silence had strained at his nerves. A few minutes' silence was relaxing. Endless days of it was enough to send you loco. No sound at all, except the noise of his own tools. And he had ended up filling that silence with a constant stream of thoughts.

The Nightingale tried to turn off the nagging voice but it was no use. The same worries broke through again. The self-evident truth was hard to avoid: His mission was drawing to a close, but as the end approached, things were getting seriously fucked up.

Like most soldiers, the Nightingale was deeply superstitious and a day that began bad usually continued bad. A week that began bad could be headed for disaster. The cataphiles running through his dug-out on Friday night had been much more than a pain in the ass; they'd been a sign of imminent danger – an omen that things wouldn't go as planned. And that was a big problem. The whole mission ran the risk of being exposed by a group of subterranean boy scouts looking for new crevices to explore; a bunch of kids wasting his time. He'd lost a whole day walking in circles through the deserted galleries trying to find the third kid; the one who escaped. Checking for signs of blood, listening for noises – breathing, crying, snoring, anything, feck it. He hadn't found anything.

The visits to the hospitals hadn't gone as planned either. Okay, things had started fine. Everything had gone smoothly at the first two hospitals he visited. Perhaps that had been the problem. Perhaps he had let the initial simplicity of the work boost his confidence to unsafe levels.

Cochin Hospital, his third target, had tripped him up.

On the surface, Cochin had looked just like any other hospital. A huge number of people swarming around a series of utilitarian buildings. In fact, as far as the Nightingale could see, hospitals were just like factories. Red brick on the outside; reassuringly contemporary on the inside. A vast machine trying to create health out of a writhing mass of human frailty.

When he had entered the hospital, his eyes had whisked over the signs that would point him in the right direction. Cardiology. Gerontology. Geriatrics: Closed Ward. That's what he wanted: the closed ward. The wanderers. The dementia patients who were locked up to stop them from ambling off and getting lost. He'd never been to Cochin before, but it was easy enough to imitate the sad, confident steps of someone who followed the same route every Sunday afternoon, coming to visit a dear old granny or maybe an elderly uncle.

How far from the truth. The Nightingale had been there to bring death, not comfort. As for his ignorant prey, he felt no pity for them. For starters, these people had no right to be in a French hospital in the first place. He was careful to target the scum scrounging off the French taxpayer. Living life at his expense. Well he would teach them that everything in life had a price.

The targets had been easy to define. Dementia patients were ideal. They didn't do a lot of talking. They remained passive when approached. Chronic memory degeneration meant they were used to receiving visits from unknown people; everyone was a stranger for them. They wouldn't recognize him. But then they didn't recognize their own sons and daughters. And nobody believed a word any of those people said. If one of them complained that a stranger had come into his room and left a present for no reason, the staff was likely to ignore the complaint, simply attributing it to a straying mind incapable of remembering the faces of loved ones.

Of course the Nightingale had made his trip during Sunday visiting hours when the nurses were busy writing up files or having coffee or doing whatever it was they did while their patients were too occupied with friends and relatives to buzz to have their pillows rearranged or the sound on the TV turned up. Not that there were a whole hell of a lot of visitors. Advanced dementia didn't bring in the crowds. That's why the Nightingale chose geriatrics; there weren't likely to be many witnesses around. Maternity, his other chosen target, at the opposite end of the spectrum, was a madhouse with amateur parents trying to look calm while their brats screamed down the building. In both cases, once visiting time was over, nobody would be able to figure out where a stray package might have come from.

That theory had worked for most of the day. No problem in the Salpêtrière Hospital. Even Cochin had gone well to start with. He'd left a box of anthrax-laced chocolates for a sleeping woman in the first room. Propped up on her pillow, still wearing her headscarf, she was his perfect target. He'd watched her closed eyes, dreaming her last dreams and he left the gift of death in his wake.

The second target had gone much the same. A boiling bedroom, where an old man had raised empty bovine eyes towards him – the skin an even darker brown than the eyes. Feigning intimacy, the Nightingale had leaned closer, bringing a small envelope out of his bag and placing it on the bedside table. The man in the chair had been no more alert than the sleeping woman in the previous room.

The hospitals were the ante-chamber to death. Much worse than combat. Why did those non-people have the right to be kept alive with nothing left to live for, while he had witnessed good young men shot down on the battlefield? Strong, healthy men who had laughed and joked and fucked, whose lives had been torn away from them in order to protect these human shells. The Nightingale was happy to put this accumulation of withered skin out of its misery; he was doing them a favor, simply speeding up the process. He was re-establishing the natural order of things. Sending the old on their way; making room for the vigorous.

So it had been with no kindness or compassion that he had stepped into the third bedroom. The contents of the room had been unknown but predictable. There was no change in the layout of the four beds or the high backed vinyl chairs at the disposition of visitors or inmates. The only unique feature of the last room was that none of the beds was occupied. The sole tenant had been an ancient looking woman, with a tangle of white hair accentuated by the dark skin. Her hands were crossed on her lap and she was staring at something unidentifiable, perhaps her wrinkled fingers, perhaps the rings given to her by a husband who had snuffed it long ago, or recently. What did it matter? Perhaps she wasn't looking at anything. Just staring blankly because her eyes happened to be open.

What an endless waste of living matter. The world's refuse assembled in France, sucking the country dry. The Nightingale's outrage welled up as he crossed the room, the box in his hand, ready to offer to her. The package was smaller than the one he had left in the first room, wrapped in different paper, containing a book rather than a box of chocolates. A superfluous detail. The essential contents were the same. He sat down on the edge of the bed nearest the woman, close enough to talk in whispers. Far enough away that his knees wouldn't have to touch her stinking carcass.

But this time his presence didn't go unnoticed. The woman raised her face slightly and turned her eyes towards him. "Do I know you?" The inflection gave away her African origins. More importantly, her voice trembled and her eyes shone with a flicker of something the Nightingale recognized. Fear.

And that's when things went wrong.

The fear was irresistible; it excited him. The familiar surge of power made a sneer creep across his lips, identical to the one that had always sent terror pumping through his adversaries. He loved that feeling of control. It made him feel invulnerable. Supreme. And with that sense of moral impunity wrapped around him, he leaned towards the wispy haired woman and whispered, "*Je suis le Rossignol.* I am death."

As soon as he had said it, he knew he had made a mistake. Whether it was the words themselves or the rasp of his voice was impossible to say. Either way, she jumped into life. Drawing herself up straight she let flow a shrill, accusing voice. "Who are you? Get your hands off me!" Her hand moved at a speed incompatible with the listlessness of a few seconds earlier, snapping from her lap to the buzzer on the bedside table.

The Nightingale jumped to his feet and raced across the room to check the hallway. But it was too late. There was already a nurse on her way.

He ducked back into the room and stood waiting beside the door, a million thoughts rushing through his head. If the nurse saw him, he would have to kill her so that she couldn't alert security. The old bitch, too. Then he would have to dump the bodies...

When the nurse stepped into the room, the old bitty screeched. "Nurse, get this man out! He threatened me. Get him out!"

But a quick look at the nurse's face told him he was safe.

She was very young and wore one of those gentle, appeasing expressions halfway between indulgence and exhaustion. The minuscule smile she sent his way before walking over to pat the old woman's hand and give her a sip of water to calm down, was reassuringly detached. "Don't get all upset," she murmured. "I'll ask the gentleman to leave."

When she turned and came towards the Nightingale, she radiated empathy. "Perhaps you should go, Sir. "

He didn't wait to be asked twice. He slipped through the doorway and was already on his way out when he heard the voice behind him. "Excuse me." Turning, he found the young nurse standing there. "I'm sorry," she said, with genuine concern. "I'm afraid you've come at a bad time. Sometimes she's perfectly coherent, then she has moments like this when she doesn't recognize anyone. She's really very sweet; just confused." The Nightingale pulled himself up to his full height and tried to assume what he hoped was a worried, sad expression. Then he turned and walked back down the hallway towards the elevators.

That had been five days earlier. It hadn't been a major failure. The basic mission had been accomplished. A total of fifteen anthrax packages had been left in wards across the city. Even if contamination didn't happen, there must have been some very scared staff when the gifts and cards were opened and white powder poured out.

On the other hand, tactically, the operation hadn't gone as planned. The old woman had not only seen him; she'd heard his name. Although the name had probably been forgotten by a mind confined to long-term memory, he was worried. Perhaps the information could resurface. More importantly, the nurse had seen him. There was nothing wrong with *her* mind. She'd had time to store his portrait in memory for future reference.

Again the Nightingale was able to calm his fears. A cursory glimpse of someone was hardly going to lead to his arrest. The nurse probably saw dozens of new faces every day. If questioned, she would probably describe him as average height, average build with brownish hair.

Yet deep down, the doubt persisted. The Nightingale felt pessimistic. He had been rattled by his partial failure. Just another cock-up, in addition to the treacherous Ng email.

He would have to move very carefully.

Fortunately he was resourceful. He had a contingency plan. That plan was to avoid all the spots that the organizers had told him he could use as escape routes and safe-houses.

He was too deep into this to stop now. In any case, he believed in the cause. It was time to shake up the liberal elite. Time to strike at the heart of the cosmopolitan power nexus. And his efforts were on track to accomplish that. He had done all the hard work. All the digging. All the sweating. Now there were just a couple of loose ends to tie up. Then the final stage in all this. By this time tomorrow, the fireworks would have gone off and punishment would be raining down on those who deserved it.

Stretching out on his back, he pulled his sleeping bag over his shoulders. For now, he needed to sleep. Tomorrow required perfect reflexes. He had to be ready for the unexpected.

51

When he woke, the first thing Sadiqi noticed was the heat.

Then, shifting his head ever so slightly, he caught a trace of Toni's scent, floating up from behind his shoulder or his neck or maybe caught in his hair. And he remembered. And for about three seconds he registered the most powerful sense of happiness. For once in what seemed like a very long time, he was cradled in the knowledge that there was something beautiful out there in the city waiting for him. Something so very very beautiful.

Then he remembered de Chanterelle. Then Desjardins. Then anthrax.

* * *

It had been another short night and Sadiqi wasn't psyched for the day ahead. After making himself a coffee, he stood on his balcony, reflecting that the view before him was entirely misleading. The evenly distributed buildings, with the elegant monotony of their identical height, size and design gave the impression of complete order. A metropolis in control of itself. But it wasn't. Only the filthy color of the sky suggested the poison running through the city's heart. The sun had been up for nearly an hour. Yet instead of piercing blue, the horizon was a dirty yellowish grey color – a visible concoction of unflinching heat and car exhaust.

He drained his last gulp of coffee then cracked his first nicotine lozenge of the day. As he walked back to the kitchen, he could feel the mercury rising. While the temperature was still almost bearable outside, the air inside was already stagnant and balmy. When he opened the dishwasher to put in his mug he was attacked by a stench of stale coffee and whatever he'd had for dinner two nights earlier. The city was reaching furnace point. Hopefully the air conditioning would be working at the office. But there was no air-conditioning in his car and that's where he would be spending most of the day.

This general sense of pessimism didn't lift when he tried phoning Podesta only to be redirected to voice mail. Sadiqi checked his watch. It was barely six o'clock but that was no excuse for the lieutenant not to be answering his calls. Podesta was the only person he knew who turned off his cell outside of office hours. "*Podesta, vous faites chier avec vos horaires de fonctionnaire,*" Sadiqi barked at the answering machine. *You piss me off with your 9 to 5 attitude.* "When you finally get around to listening to this, I want you to get out every file on every cataphile who's been arrested or fined over the past six months. Round them up. Get them in for questioning. All of them. I want to know if anyone's seen anything suspicious lately. New tunnels appearing where they shouldn't be. Violent attacks. Unexpected encounters. Anything. Use your imagination. But get on it." He moved the phone away from his ear and was about to hang up when a surge of temper washed over him. "Oh and one other thing, Podesta. You'd better keep your damn phone on today – or you'll be joining the ranks of the newly unemployed." The tirade helped Sadiqi get rid of some of his negative energy, but it was an empty threat. As a civil servant, Podesta was basically unfireable.

A few moments later the Renault was hurtling down the sloping streets of the northeast district. Paris wasn't a city of early risers. There was always some traffic, but this early in the morning things were flowing smoothly. You were more likely to get stuck in a traffic jam at 3AM than 6AM. And once he reached République, it was a red axis all the way to the other side of town; practically a highway. The traffic flowed easily past the blue and red tubes of Beaubourg then across the island, in front of the Prefecture and Notre Dame, before continuing along the Seine past the Eiffel Tower and on to the heights of Passy.

Although there were probably many more constructive things that he could do with his morning, Sadiqi's first priority was to go and shake up Caron. He suspected the IGC director knew plenty of things about the quarries that could help the investigation. And the cop didn't want to miss out, yet again, on getting that information. Because between providing the outdated maps and standing him up at the previous night's appointment, Caron's crap was getting old. It was time to stop the bullshit.

At least that was the plan. Five minutes later, instead of carrying on an imposing conversation with the head of the IGC, Sadiqi found himself offering his condolences to the man's widow. The cop could feel himself slipping into one of his dark moods. He didn't like death. In fact his dislike of death was what made him so good at his job. He wanted to save people; he wanted to ward off death. An uncomprehending widow and a mourning child didn't exactly get him revved up for a dynamic day – even if the deceased was someone he hadn't liked. It didn't matter. Death created sadness and sadness created desolation. The city's desolation preyed on the inspector. And although the cops who'd been called in to investigate the homicide hadn't made the connection between Caron's murder and Sadiqi's case, Sadiqi couldn't ignore it

He retraced his steps up the sleepy boulevard to where he'd left his car. Even in one of the most beautiful parts of town, all he could feel was dirt and despair. What did he have? De Chanterelle, Caron, Montaigne High School. A mix of everything from the seats of power to the insignificant. Beyond that, he had no idea where this case was going or what the motives were.

All he knew for certain was that Caron wasn't just some unfortunate target who had fallen victim to a random murder. His death had to be linked to everything else that was happening in the quarries. As head of the IGC the professor had been privy to information about the catacombs that no one else had. And that knowledge had cost him his life. That was the bad news. The good news was that whatever Caron had known had probably been in the report he'd mentioned over the phone.

Sadiqi briefly considered running back to Caron's apartment and asking his widow to pull out the *Clavreul Report,* but that would have meant breaking the seals on the crime scene and possibly contaminating the area. Not a risk he was willing to take. Surely Dukrin would be sending over her copy of the report soon.

So instead of going back to disturb the mourning family, he pulled his phone out and thumbed in Podesta's number. The call clicked straight to voice mail. Sadiqi's message was angrier than the one he'd left an hour earlier. "Thanks for the information on Caron. Unfortunately you missed one important detail. He's dead. He had his neck snapped for him yesterday afternoon. So I want you to listen and listen closely. First of all: if you don't turn this phone on soon, I'll have your badge. Second: I want to know everything you found out about Pierre Caron. No. I want more than that. I want to know everything there is to know about him. Who his friends were, who his enemies were, who his family was, where he spent his days and nights. Check all his phone lines. Home, the IGC, *FranceTech*, his cell phone, his weekend cottage. I want a list of everyone he's talked to over the past six months. Every number: who it belongs to, who they are, what their connection to Caron is." Sadiqi reeled off the orders. If he'd been undecided about what track to take a few minutes ago, that was no longer the case. Caron's murder crystallized the catacomb link further. The IGC director had known something important about the quarries and he had died because of it.

And as the ideas sparked and the associations mushroomed, a thought crept into Sadiqi's head. Caron was murdered because of what he knew. But Caron wasn't the only one who knew something. There was also the cataphile at the hospital. Desjardins had obviously witnessed something underground. Something identifiable. If it became known that he was still alive, he might be in serious danger. "I also want you to get a police guard put on the door of that kid at the hospital. Desjardins. He needs protecting. 24/7. Oh. And Podesta. I want to see you at HQ as soon as you've got your ass out of bed."

By the time his one-sided conversation ended he had almost reached his car. But when he passed in front of a newsagent, preparing his kiosk for the upcoming flood of morning readers, the headlines on the stacks of papers stopped Sadiqi in his tracks. The announcement of the PM's death the previous day had come after the morning papers were published. The Obits were today. The covers of *Le Monde* and *Le Figaro* were plastered with stories about de Chanterelle. Nothing surprising in that. But the foreign journalists hadn't been as compliant as their French colleagues. *The Independent* led with bold, 90-point lettering screaming out: "Secrecy Continues to Surround French PM's Death". The headline on the international edition of the *New York Times* was no better: "Elysée Denies Foul Play". And the lead story on the *The Guardian* was downright depressing: "Possible Terrorist Poisonings in Paris Hospitals". As he read through the titles, the cop's stomach tightened. The truth was filtering through to the media and he still had no answers to offer them.

After selecting a smorgasbord of papers, he walked back to his car, wrenched the door open and climbed in behind the wheel where he shuffled to *The Guardian* and started reading.

52

Whereas usually Toni rarely emerged before 8:00, the heat today had knocked her out of bed at 7:00. Despite her late night and a residual sense of fatigue she was sitting on the edge of her bed drinking a glass of grapefruit juice and eating a piece of rock hard two-day-old baguette trying to see her computer screen beyond the blinding sunlight streaming through the curtain-less window.

Her standard morning ritual was to tune into BBC Radio 4 online but today, exceptionally, she'd tuned into the local 24-hour news station in search of more comprehensive coverage of French affairs. She'd been listening for five minutes and her level of disgust was rising with each second; the BBC probably would have provided more complete and critical information on the situation in France than this ridiculous station. Apparently French journalists weren't big on investigative journalism. The headline news was a combination of the self-evident augmented by a few one-line press releases: The top story was the heat wave. Although Toni agreed that the weather was on everyone's mind, it was hardly newsworthy. The newsreader announced that there was a busy weekend projected on the roads as Parisians fled the city for the countryside. Reservation rates at seaside resorts were up 90% over the same period the previous year. *Big deal.* She could have compiled that story herself just by looking out the window. The second story, about some popular festival that was taking place that evening, wasn't any more informative – the *Fête de la Musique.* A sort of nationwide Music Day. As far as non-stop news went, the station wasn't very good.

To complement the dearth of good quality audio, Toni was surfing among online news sites to see what the foreign take was on the situation.

She skipped to CNN and logged "France" in the search engine. A micro-second later the top story flashed. "Secrecy Surrounds French

Prime Minister's death". Her eyes skimmed down the column. "President Gustave Tibrac of France is coming under increased pressure to provide more detailed information concerning the death of his Prime Minister, Arnaud de Chanterelle at Val-de-Grace Hospital. According to the Paris-based *New York Times International Edition*, the military hospital in central Paris has been submerged by an extensive police presence since yesterday and certain sources within the hospital are quoted as saying the Prime Minister died as a consequence of a violent attack. Police cars sporting the insignia of the scientific police have been seen coming and going through the area but details of the incident have yet to be confirmed. Sources within the military zone also revealed that the site is under an information blackout." The article didn't offer Toni any new insight but it did reinforce her suspicions. She hadn't bothered asking Khalid the truth. She figured it wasn't worth the effort; he wouldn't have told her anyway. But at least it was nice to see she wasn't the only one wondering about the contradictions between the officially announced story and all the visible signs.

Buoyed by this first endorsement of reality, she moved on to the international papers. *The Telegraph* only had an obit with political speculation about who would be replacing the dead prime minister. *The Post* and *The Independent* had roughly the same, augmented by a reference to the same rumors as CNN.

But it wasn't until she logged onto *The Guardian* that she found anything truly awesome.

The Prime Minister wasn't even the top story. The big news was a heartbreaking personal account from the paper's Paris cor-respondent: **Deadly Outbreak in Paris Hospital.** As she scrolled through the article, she felt the bile rising in her throat.

> While most people remember the birth of their first child as one of the high points of their lives, for me it will forever be a memory of pure loss.
>
> My daughter, Felicity Jane, was born early last Sunday morning. A solid 3.7 kilos of perfection. The birth went beautifully. Helen, the baby's mother was a vision of happiness. We spent three days in the maternity ward, cuddling the tiny bundle of warmth we'd spent nine months preparing for. Mother and child were due home on Friday. But suddenly, Thursday, everything went terribly wrong.
>
> When I arrived early that afternoon for visiting hours, the entire Maternity Ward was cordoned off. I was told that Helen and Felicity had been transferred

to another hospital several miles away. No other information was given.

Heart pounding, I jumped in a taxi and raced across the city. I would have liked the driver to run every single red light on the way. Perhaps if he had, I might actually have seen my darling daughter alive one last time. As it was, when I finally got to St. Antoine Hospital, all the staff could offer me was one last look at the cold shell of what had once been the most beautiful child in the world. As for my wife, she had been transferred to intensive care where, I was told, she was too weak to see me.

So what could possibly have happened between Wednesday evening when everything was fine and Thursday afternoon when the world was turned on its head? That's what I asked myself as I paced back and forth up the hospital hallways. But as I paced, I realized there were other fathers pacing beside me. And slowly we pulled ourselves out of our armour of sorrow and spoke to one another.

It's very difficult to get a clear picture of what happened because evidently hospital staff have been told not to communicate any information to patients' families. Only one thing is obvious: several, if not all, of the mothers and babies from the maternity ward where my wife and daughter had been staying were infected with a potent virus that left them hanging precariously between life and death. At the very least, it appears that the entire ward is now on antibiotics and the Port-Royal maternity hospital has been sealed for a complete disinfection. We were told little else.

Then, on Thursday evening, the head of Intensive Care finally came out and gave us a spiel about how our loved ones had been hit by a particularly tragic C-Difficile outbreak. Yet surely that's not how C-Difficile works. Entire wards, one patient after the other suddenly succumbing in the space of a few hours.

So if it isn't C-Difficile, what is it?

The rumor among patients' families is that last Sunday evening, packages were found on the ward containing white powder. And then the rumors grew as we realized that somehow, among all those sad people pacing the hallway there weren't just fathers from Port-Royal. There were people whose family had been staying in two other Paris hospitals. There were also people who had nothing to do with hospitals but whose family had somehow developed the

infection at their place of work: an important Parisian
high school.

You will, of course, think I'm exaggerating or I'm
getting carried away in my grief. Maybe that's true.
Unfortunately the French authorities are doing
everything in their power to encourage my imagination
to run wild. The death certificate issued for my
daughter gave asphyxiation as the cause of death but
offered no explanation as to the cause of that
asphyxiation. Even more unnerving, the hospital has
refused to release my daughter's body. I can't
imagine why. Or could it be that there's something
they don't want uncovered by a British autopsy?

A mixture of emotions washed over Toni. On one hand, she felt
for the guy, composing his article as his life fell apart. More
importantly, she had an objective reaction; one of foreboding. That
was quite the story. And it wasn't coming from a trashy tabloid. It
was coming from a serious paper. It was hard to image that someone
on the editorial board had gone crazy and accepted a wild story with
no proof. They must have had some pretty serious facts to back the
claim. On top of that, the reference to the "important Parisian high
school" dovetailed with Sadiqi's cata-visit the previous day.
Suddenly, in light of the reference to "white powder", that ridiculous
surgical mask he'd given her to wear at the foot of the Montaigne
staircase made more sense. Maybe that hadn't been such a crazy
precaution, after all. It fit. And she knew what it meant. It meant
anthrax. Which would also explain why the case had been given to the
counter-terrorist brigade.

She took one last bite of stale baguette doing her best to get
the crumbs to fall onto the floor rather than between the keys of her
laptop. There was one more thing she wanted to check. She logged
on to the chat room where she'd found the messages from Ng.

As soon as the page appeared, a new post popped up.

June 21; from Ng
Retribution will come
There will be fireworks above the Temple on New Year's Eve.
Darkness will triumph over light. The songs will change to
screams.

It was increasingly obscure. And increasingly ominous. It
definitely sounded more like a threat of things yet to come than a
claim of responsibility for something that had already happened. The

reference to screams was especially unsettling. And the fact that nothing credible appeared on the screen when she tried cross-referencing the words was disquieting. What was it all about? How did all these threads weave together? "The Temple on New Year's Eve". Where was there a temple and why the hell was Ng talking about New Year's Eve in the middle of June?

It didn't make any sense. The catacombs, the Freemasons, the temple? This was crazy stuff. And were there really any links to the quarries?

She folded down the computer screen and wandered over to the window. For all the drawbacks of still living in a student residence at her age, she loved her tiny room – mainly because of the brilliant view she had of the rooftops of the 5th arrondissement. When she'd first moved into the residence, she'd lovingly learnt all there was to know about every monument visible from this window. And the two big domes on the skyline held a special place. To her right, Val-de-Grace church, built by Anne of Austria in thanksgiving for God's bountiful goodness when he provided her with an heir to the throne in the form of the future Louis XIV. To her left, the dome of the Pantheon. Originally built as a church dedicated to the patron saint of Paris, St. Genevieve, it was later converted into a secular mausoleum housing the mortal remains of famous Frenchmen.

How very, very strange… Strange. Yet possible.

Pantheon, from the Greek, πάνθειον ιερόν: Temple to all the gods.

France's great secular temple. Fireworks above a temple. And Sadiqi had been looking for a tunnel headed for Henri IV High – a building that stood right beside the Pantheon. There was no way any catacomb tunnel leading from the GRS could get to H4 without passing right under that particular temple.

Maybe it was a crazy idea. But it was the only one she had. The first thing she wanted to do was check whether or not there was some way of linking this temple reference to the previous night's message.

53

Sadiqi was wishing for a gleam of hope. But there were no gleams in his office, figurative or real. On such a bright day, the large window to his left should have let in light, but the outside world had been obscured by a series of wooden slats running the length of the façade, placed there to make it impossible for anyone to spy into the building. It was a thoughtless finishing touch to an already poorly designed building, which meant that even on a boiling sunny day like this one, the offices were dim and the damn neon lights had to be switched on. As for clarity on the case, he wasn't doing much better. Hunched over a deep, dark espresso – the fourth so far that morning – he was trying desperately to get his brain to notice whatever his eyes had missed. Among the battlefield of papers on his desk, one stood out: "There will be fireworks above the Temple on New Year's Eve. Darkness will triumph over light. The songs will change to screams." And always the same title "Retribution will come" and the Ng signature. The posting had appeared online less than an hour earlier and Cryptography hadn't finished with it yet. Hopefully they'd have something useful to say because Sadiqi sure as hell had no idea what it was supposed to mean. But his gut feeling wasn't good. It sounded like it was heralding a bigger attack than the previous ones. He particularly didn't like the 'songs' turning to 'screams' reference; that definitely sounded like collective retribution.

Other than that, there didn't seem to be any new leads to go on. There was a report on the threads he'd found in the tunnels under Montaigne, but nothing useful. They were from a bag or something not worn close to the skin. A nylon and polyester blend. There was no hope of getting a DNA sample off them. They could only be used to prove parentage if the rest of the object turned up. Likewise, the anaylsis of the backpack he'd found simply confirmed that the blood probably belonged to Desjardins.

He was casting the reports into the cemetery of dead-ends filed on the left-hand side of his desk when Podesta rapped on his door. "I've got the phone transcripts you asked for, *Chef*," he said, handing over a thick file. "Caron certainly was a phone fan. He had a number at the IGC, a number at *FranceTech*, one at home and one at his cottage. A professional cell phone paid for by the taxpayer. A personal cell phone." The inspector studied the pages listing the calls made to and from Caron's phones over the past six months. Incoming calls were recorded in blue. Outgoing in red. "I've gone through the list and marked each person's affiliation to Caron in the margin: wife, daughter, colleague, electrician. But there's one number on there I was sort of surprised to see." Podesta paused for emphasis and Sadiqi was forced to look up. "He was in contact with Senator Clavreul."

If Podesta had been hoping to produce a lightning shock with his announcement he must have been disappointed by his boss' answer. "Caron wrote a report for the senator a few months back. That's why we were supposed to meet last night. He was going to give me a copy of it," he said, his attention turning back to the transcripts.

The presence of a politician's name in this case wasn't enough, in itself, to make Sadiqi jumpy. He was so used to the French system of endless *affaires* and scandals that it was quite common to run across big names in his investigations. Yet the presence of Clavreul's name in the case did make his skin crawl. Clavreul was a nasty piece of work. A smudge on the reputation of the French Republic. Some of the senator's more memorable high profile statements included a soundbite about how the Nazi death camps were nothing but a historical 'detail' and a comment on how immigrants stank and were worthless. Sadiqi wouldn't put anything past the guy. His slippery hands easily slithered into any kind of muck available.

Although less pessimistic than his boss, Podesta still sensed something not quite right in the connection between the IGC director and the senator. "Okay. Maybe he wrote the report a while back. But they were still in contact. Caron tried calling Clavreul three times this week. Judging from the length of the calls I'd say he either only spoke to an answering machine or a secretary."

"We'll probably never know which." Sadiqi wished he'd gone to see Caron as soon as he'd called the previous afternoon. Then again, if the forensic report was anything to go by, that might not have done any good. The analysis put the death somewhere between 3PM and 5PM. The cop had spoken with Caron around 4:30, which meant that he had been killed within minutes of their conversation.

"There's something else," Podesta said. The lieutenant's manner had been optimistic when he first came in, but Sadiqi now detected a slight apprehension. "There was a call on his voice mail last night that Caron never heard. This is the transcript." He handed over a sheet.

"Pierre, c'est Cédric ici. I'm phoning to cancel our meeting at the *Petit Suisse.* I won't be able to make it. There's still too much work to get done before the conference. I just wanted you to know that I've informed the Grand Master and he intends to take punitive measures. I thought you should know. I expect

you think I'm being rash. Perhaps I am. I don't really know. I did what I felt I should. The whole situation certainly is regrettable. I'm sorry. I truly am. *Au revoir, Pierre.*"

While Sadiqi was still reading the message, Podesta started providing specifics. "According to the call transcripts, it's from someone called Cédric Trouvé – a professor at *FranceTech*. They worked in the same department." The name was familiar. Sadiqi was even able to visualize the face. Trouvé was a stock personality on TV and in editorial columns. He was a specialist in renewable energies, or something like that. Big on saving the planet and social equality. Sustainable development, fair trade, reasoned growth…

"What's all that shit about a Grand Master and taking measures?"

Podesta shifted uncomfortably from one foot to the other. "It looks like a reference to Freemasonry."

Sadiqi looked up. "Caron was a Freemason?"

"Yes." Podesta's eyes were still glued to the transcript, in an attempt to avoid his boss' gaze.

'Better late than never' wasn't a motto the inspector could get behind. "I asked you to look into all his affiliations. You told me you had nothing, now you tell me he was a Freemason."

"I didn't think it was relevant. It's hardly a criminal offense."

"It's not a question of being an offense, is it? It's a question of knowing what he was mixed up in. What his centers of interest were. When I ask you to do something I expect you to do it, give me the results then let me decide what's important and what's not. I don't expect you to hold back. In any case, if you didn't have your phone turned off all night you might have heard that we've got several references to the Masons already."

"Yes, *Chef.* I saw that when I checked in."

"Any link between Caron and the group is starting to look important."

"Yes, *Chef.*"

Reeling off the speech on acceptable behavior yet again was more than Sadiqi could be bothered to do. With a sigh of disgust he spewed out the morning's orders instead. "Track down Trouvé and Jacques Clavreul. I want to see them both. Today. No excuses. No postponements. I need them now. Not tomorrow."

Instead of heading off to carry out the order, Podesta stood frozen in the middle of the office. "I thought you wanted me to interview cataphiles."

Sadiqi had nothing to add. A glare would be eloquent enough.

But Podesta kept complaining. "I've got a list with over 200 names on it – and that's just the icing on the cake – the repeat offenders. We're already holding a couple dozen of them at n°36," he said, referring to police headquarters on Quai d'Orfèvres."

They were pointless bleatings. The latest orders canceled out the previous ones. The lieutenant knew that. "Send Pecheron and Mueller over. Tell Ferry to oversee the interviews with them. Scaring cataphiles is his line. Let him waste his time. We're not going to learn anything from them, in any case. They think it's a joke if they get hauled in. Trouvé and Clavreul, on the other hand, might actually be able to tell us something."

Podesta shrugged at the change of plans. He knew that this was probably good news for the case. Looking for a specific person at least sounded like a serious lead. As opposed to rounding up hundreds of cataphiles, which sounded like a snipe hunt. The lieutenant turned to leave but his boss called out a second time: "Oh. And Podesta, if you'd use your damn phone, things might get done faster. I want to be able to reach you. No coffee break with your phone off. No lunch break in airplane mode."

Podesta sauntered off to fulfil these orders and Sadiqi sank back into his chair. The unanswered questions were multiplying. That's all there seemed to be in this case: questions but no answers. And when his phone buzzed, he was sure whoever was on the line was going to announce yet another puzzle.

"Salut Khalid, c'est Alex," a familiar voice chanted.

"I thought you were on holiday," Sadiqi remarked sarcastically.

"Hanging around hospitals interviewing terminally ill patients isn't exactly my idea a holiday." Trémont's tone was bleak. "Our anthrax man's been concentrating his efforts on maternity wards. I've got hysterical mothers at death's door or fathers who've just lost wives and babies. Not exactly a barrel of laughs. At the other end of the spectrum, I've got an asylum load of advanced dementia cases. Anyway, you should thank me for doing the donkeywork. I've got something." He waited for Sadiqi to offer some words of encouragement. None came so he just delivered the news. "One of our dementia targets wasn't advanced dementia but early."

"What's that to me?"

"The difference is that in the early stages people still have moments of lucidity."

Suddenly Sadiqi was all ears. "You mean you've got someone who can ID one of the anthrax guys?"

"Possibly. I have a woman who says a man she didn't know came in, spoke with her and left her a gift. (Confirmed to contain anthrax.) Actually she says that he threatened her. I have a nurse to back up the story, who also saw him. Even better than that, I've got a name. He said that he was the angel of death and that his name was 'Le Rossignol'. She also said that he spoke with a foreign accent. Probably English or American."

"Le Rossignol or *Rossignol."*

There was a pause while Trémont double-checked his notes. "She said 'le Rossignol'."

'Le Rossignol,' Sadiqi wondered, after he'd hung up. *An Englishman with a French name.* Then again, names could be misleading. The world had gone global. After all, Sadiqi was a Frenchman with an Arabic name.

But this guy had said 'Le Rossignol', not just 'Rossignol'. The use of *'le'* made it sound more like a title than an actual surname. And if that was the case, he needed to translate that title. What was the English for 'rossignol'?

Although language had been an integral part of his skill throughout his career, Sadiqi's English wasn't as good as his Arabic; certainly not good enough to know how to say something as poetic as a bird's name. He swiped the screen of his phone to pull up his translation app, then typed in *Rossignol.* Instantly the word *Nightingale* appeared.

The moment of incomprehension was short.

Staring at the word, the letters jumped out at him. The N and the G. The first piece of the puzzle had just clicked into place. *Nightingale. Ng. The web messages.*

His lieutenant's phone went straight to voice mail when Sadiqi tapped in the number. Jumping from his desk, he tore open his office door and screamed down the hall: "Podesta get your ass in here! I told you to keep your phone on."

The lieutenant's head popped round the corner of the next office. "It *is* on. I'm talking with Ferry."

"Tell him you'll call back," Sadiqi snapped with a mixture of excitement and impatience as he ushered his assistant back into his office. "I need you to run a check on the names Rossignol and Nightingale. Find me something. Cross reference it with all the calls going through Caron's phones. Cross reference it with everything going through Clavreul's phone. Cross reference news reports about the senator and the professor. Google it. Check for any references with the catacombs or caves in general. Whatever you can think of. Do anything and everything."

54

If Toni had never before bothered to visit the Pantheon, it was simply because it lacked the *sine qua non* of all great buildings; it had no subterranean network. It was a well-established cataphile fact that there were no points of passage between the Pantheon's crypt and the wider quarry network. Yet because it was the building that marked the borderline between catacomb Paris and non-catacomb Paris, she still knew a fair bit about it.

The building had originally been designed as St. Genevieve's church, to house the reliquary of the patron saint of Paris. However, being as its completion had coincided with the French Revolution and the subsequent decision to eliminate all religious orders in France, the church had never been consecrated. If it hadn't been such a colossal structure, the revolutionaries might have just torn it down, as they'd done with so many other holy sites. Instead, they transformed it into a Pantheon – it had become a temple dedicated to the Great Men of the Fatherland. A shrine devoid of any official religion. A house of worship where the object of adoration was the nation's heroes. Not an easy role to fill in the midst of the Revolution's political turmoil. As each regime was succeeded by the next, so the building's status evolved – as did its dead tenants. Each new regime would throw the bodies out of the crypt and fill it with new ones, depending on the political fashion of the day.

It was precisely the current list of tenants that had confirmed Toni's suspicion's that this could be the "Temple" referred to in Ng's messages. When she'd started googling the list of people buried in the crypt she found a definite Freemason link.

Not that finding the background of all these Great Men was easy. Toni had expected the Pantheon to be overflowing with familiar names from the pages of history and the Arts. Instead, what she discovered was a sprinkling of familiar names peeking out from among piles of the obscure – other than Voltaire, Rousseau, Dumas, Hugo and Marie Curie, none of the tenants were household names. Not to mention the fact that it was hardly a place of social diversity. There was only one black man – or one and a quarter if you counted Dumas as *métis*. And there were only three women: Marie Curie, enshrined for her own personal accomplishments, Madame Berthollet, buried alongside her husband who, according to legend had died of a broken heart two hours after his wife expired. And Simone Veil – a recent addition, hurried in when people had started complaining about the derth of women. Other than their white maleness, the tenants' most obvious unifying characteristic was their nobility. The list of pantheonized men included 26 counts, 3 dukes, 3 marquises and a baron plus three cardinals and an abbot. Basically any aristocrat who had managed to avoid being guillotined during the Revolution seemed to be enshrined there. Toni found this a rather curious defining feature of "greatness" in a country so vocal about its republican values. Furthermore, when she started checking the list, she discovered that out of a total of 75 "great men" Google had never even heard of 26 of them. Given the dates of their interments, she guessed that the great unknowns had probably been Napoleonic generals, familiar only to specialized scholars. Of the remaining 49 who did merit internet references, 15 were definitely Freemasons and another 4 were possible Masons (and several others had strong links with the brotherhood through family or professional life). That worked out to at least one in three if not more. So the Freemason link certainly looked tenable.

As she mounted the steps to the massive entrance doors Toni also felt confident that the building could definitely be labelled a "Temple". The question was: Was it the temple she was looking for? And that question was harder to answer because she wasn't entirely sure what she was looking for. Ideally, she hoped for some link to what Marco had said about the Chamber of Reflection. Failing that, she would accept anything that might indicate a shared connection between the building and Ng's three internet messages. Namely more tangible confirmation of the link between Freemasonry, the Pantheon and the quarries.

Her first impression as she stepped into the main hall was the hugeness of the place. It was certainly bigger than any other building she could remember visiting.

But size isn't everything. And other than its size, the Pantheon didn't have a lot going for it. The building was a bulky form rather than an aerial one and despite its massive proportions Toni found the place stifling. It was too lumbering to give any impression of transcendence, either spiritual or intellectual. It was too heavy. Too dark. While she marvelled at the mystique of churches like St. Eustache, where stone had come together to produce something heavenly, the Pantheon left her unmoved. It lacked that ethereal touch.

Not only had the Revolution ensured that all religious statues had been destroyed, but more importantly the spaces for the thirty-eight stained glass windows originally designed to provide light and airiness to the church had been walled in, giving the profane transept a dark dingy feeling. As an un-consecrated church, the Pantheon had lost touch with its muse. The secular fathers who had tried to transform it into a place of national symbols without striving for something beautiful had caused it to become earthbound and heavy. It was a church without spirituality; a work of art without light.

Making her way towards the cupola, she found her gaze drawn toward the huge mural paintings covering the walls where the windows should have been. Here she contemplated the Gallic spirit's boundless capacity for contradiction. If this was a secular temple, why were the walls covered in paintings of saints? There was St. Genevieve loading boats to provide food for the Parisians who were under siege, and praying that the Huns not strike the city. This was followed a few meters further along by St. Joan of Arc bathed in a cloud of white butterflies whispering to her that she had been chosen by God to lead His army to righteous triumph over the English. Joan of Arc: France's favorite symbol of resistance. Toni thought it fitting that the old girl should be enthroned here, officially establishing the anti-Anglo sentiment as one of the defining characteristics of the French nation.

It was in this reflective mode that Toni turned to get a second look at the paintings behind her and instead found her eyes falling on something she'd missed when she first walked in. Lost in her uncertainties about what a crowd of saints was doing in a supposedly secular building, she'd failed to notice the most blatant sign that there was more than a coincidental thread binding the Pantheon to Freemasonry. Framed between two pillars separating St. Genevieve from Joan of Arc was a huge stone monolith representing what appeared to be stoneworkers. Toni took a few steps closer to get a better look.

At the base of the statue two hulking men hoisted a massive stone ark above their heads. The intricately carved sculptures on that ark left little doubt in Toni's mind that the iconography referred to Freemasonry. On the bottom level a troupe of masons was building temples and hauling stones on carts. A second level depicted what looked like women in long robes – each row turned toward a central figure with two pillars and an altar pointing heavenward. And on the top row there was a multitude of angels blowing trumpets and playing harps.

Her eyes raced to the foot of the column to check if the statue had a title, or a donor's name, or an explanatory note. There was no such luck. All that was offered was a Latin inscription. "Aeterni custodibus ignis quorum splendet opus nomen oblivio tenet."

She pulled out her phone and called up a Latin translation app. The crib it offered came out garbled. So she toyed around, rearranging the terms in search of a more comprehensible sentence. She hadn't taken Latin at school; even if she'd wanted to, it hadn't been offered in the rather mediocre state school she'd gone to. But she had studied the language on her own and was familiar with the declension system and the basic vocabulary. Today, the efforts of her intellectual gymnastics paid off: "Oblivion holds the name of the guardians of the eternal fire whose work shines resplendent".

Whether her interpretation was correct or not, at the very least she had the impression that the name of the guardians of that eternal flame was probably "Freemasons". But the message wasn't exactly limpid. The inscription seemed intentionally evasive. Dissembling itself while standing in plain view. The statue had been erected flamboyantly amid some of the most well-loved symbols of France. Yet, at the same time, it was demure in the way it kept to itself – not offering any explanation of what it was doing among the other icons.

Toni suspected she was once again in the presence of what she'd already noticed on the walls of the *FranceTech* building. Signs calling to the initiated and leaving the non-initiated indifferent. The most recognized symbols of the Craft were absent. There were no compasses, no squares, no all-seeing eyes. Yet there was no way she could think of this statue as unrelated to Freemasonry with its obvious references to the stonemasons and their attempts to build a new spirituality.

Encouraged by this first discovery, she turned and wandered deeper into the nave, breathing in the pervasive feeling of mysticism. Freemasonry, Catholicism, esoterism. It was all here. She could feel it with every statue and painting she passed. After Joan of Arc came a painting of Bonaparte galloping on horseback through the skies to heaven with his Great Army. The image postulated a contradiction Bonaparte himself would have appreciated. After all, he'd always been creative when it came to religion, alternately declaring himself atheist, Christian and Muslim depending on what political necessity dictated.

Then, as she made her way down the steps leading from the ground floor to the crypt, there was a huge urn set in the wall, accompanied by the inscription: *Gambetta's heart*. Toni could hardly believe her eyes. She was looking at a relic. Like St. Genevieve's finger in the church across the road. Except it wasn't a saint's heart. It was the heart of one of the founders of the 3rd Republic.

She was about to continue down the steps when a thought occurred to her. She pulled her phone out again and typed in 'Gambetta' 'Freemason'. The confirmation popped up in a flash. Leon Gambetta. Toni raised her phone and took a photo of the urn. A Freemason's heart. And here it was, preserved for generations to come in pilgrimage.

The student laughed to herself. She suspected that anyone who believed that the Pantheon was a "secular" temple had never set foot in the place. Or certainly never looked into the details. It was the genius of French politics. No. Take that back. It was the genius of politicians the world over. Their capacity to say one thing then do the opposite. Promise the country a secular temple, then deliver this building built in the shape of a Christian cross, with a cross on the roof and every painting inside paying homage to Christian mythology in the construction of the French state. Far from representing the defining characteristics of a contemporary secular nation, the iconography seemed to uphold the Napoleonic proclamation that although there was no State religion in France, Roman Catholicism was the religion of most Frenchmen. And yet, a distinct effort had been made to hide that truth. There was a sense that somewhere along the way the caretakers of the Pantheon had killed God only to raise the State as a new god in His place. And this, in turn, had somehow become inter-twined with the Freemasons.

Perhaps that was enough to confirm that this was a link between the Freemasons and Ng's messages. That was what made the Pantheon a possible target for Ng's terrorist whims. As she wandered back up the stairs, enjoying the last tingles of cool air drifting up from the crypt, Toni felt the heaviness of the building weigh down on her. Why choose the Pantheon as the target of a terrorist attack? The answer was simple. The answer was held in the definition of what the Pantheon represented. Not officially, but intrinsically. It was a place of politics. Of white male politics. The representatives of power. Choosing this spot meant attacking the Fatherland – attacking it in its traditionalist strongholds of restored aristocracy, Catholicism and Freemasonry. It was the French equivalent of WASP culture. Except instead of White, Anglo-Saxon, Protestant it was White, Aristocratic, Gallic, Catholic, Freemason. All strangely rolled into one weird and contradictory power base, representing the same combination of privilege and authority.

And a few feet away across the street to the east was Henri IV High – another power base stronghold, the one Khalid had been investigating the previous day – and under the street to the west were the quarries. This had to be the temple the web messages pointed to. It was all here: H4, the catacombs, the Freemasons, the Republic.

55

To anyone in an alert state of consciousness the wall outside the hospital window would have seemed like nothing more than an obstacle blocking the view. As was so often the case in central Paris, the ward window opened directly onto a solid wall. But to Philippe, the red bricks had grown to become a source of comfort. He loved the wall for the way it reflected the daylight. It was a world away from the terrifying Devil of the underworld. Every time he woke, the bricks were still there, reassuring him. Always strong. Always warm. Always bathed in sunlight.

Bolstered by this reassuring presence, he let his mind wander back beyond the Green Monster to the beginning of the nightmare.

He remembered now. It had become quite clear. It hadn't started as a nightmare. On the contrary. He'd been at a party. Sometime between Friday night and Saturday morning. It had been a great party – one of the best he'd been to in months. Parties in the Z-Room were incomparable. It was the ideal spot, and on Friday the general atmosphere had been perfected by the presence of both excellent company and good music. The only point that even vaguely deserved criticism was the sound equipment, which was a little weak. The best the organizers had been able to come up with was a beat-up old stereo system operating off a car battery.

Despite this minor shortcoming, Philippe had no complaints. There was nothing better than a party under the Latin Quarter. Beneath the carefully executed pillars of the Z-Room's vaulted ceiling, the stereo was cranked up to full blast, blaring out a medley of the latest dance songs intermingled with a few golden oldies from Gainsbourg and Boney M. It was the standard catacomb sound he enjoyed. Some cataphiles loved the catacombs because they made them feel like urban speleologists. Others liked being part of a shadow-world, hidden from the surface yet somehow connected to the same city. What Philippe liked was being part of a club.

He sipped his beer and tapped his foot to the music, soaking in both the unique spot and its temporary inhabitants. The people at the party formed a strange variety of nightclub fauna. They didn't look like party-goers anywhere else in the city, probably in the world for that matter. No trendy clothes or cell phones. They wore either old jeans and sweat shirts or, like Philippe, the dingy bluish grey workmen's coveralls preferred by serious cataphiles.

He had to admit that what he liked most about the coveralls and boots was that they set him apart from the tourists, those uncommitted visitors, who came down with a friend of a friend who knew the network. Just killing time, looking for something original to do on a Saturday night. The tourists were amateurs, usually on their first and final visit. Easy to spot with their running shoes and ironed jeans. After over sixteen months' exploring the city's entrails, Philippe had begun to regard the dabblers with authoritative contempt while he thought of himself as one of the pros.

Yet, in all honesty, he wasn't so very different from the vast majority of the partygoers. Most of the people in the room were students. Like many enthusiastic members of the youth cohort, Philippe chose to believe that only young people had the courage to explore the catacombs and risk possible arrest after illegally penetrating the network. The truth was less flattering. Excursions into the catacombs were time-consuming. Setting out from the ring road on the edge of the city and walking in a straight line to the center of Paris took over an hour above ground. The same trek underground took considerably longer. The throughways were tortuous and often inundated with underground streams that needed fording. Some of the paths could only be crossed by flopping on the ground and crawling along like a frontline soldier. As a result, many of the expeditions with Quentin had kept them underground for a couple of days. And the fact that cataphiles had to be free to disappear from the surface, unneeded and unreachable for days at a time meant that students were the easiest population to recruit into the ranks.

There was one obvious exception to this rule of youth: the hardened cataphiles. The over forties who still navigated the corridors of sub-Paris. They'd watched the catacombs evolve from a skinhead war zone, in the early 80s, to the travelling techno party it had now become. They would probably still be around when the rave culture abandoned the dusty corridors to a newer generation, which, in turn, would adapt the catacombs to their fantasies. The doyens would oversee it all. They would know about the parties without receiving invitations. They would gate crash on the merit of their legendary code names alone: Malaria, Quartz, Nebo... Their reputations preceded them while the names they used and the lives they led on the surface remained unknown in the realm below ground. Unlike the standardized youth crowd, the doyens truly were a strange fauna. They had no common defining feature other than their love of the quarries. Some had long unkempt hair and a wild look that suggested they probably lived in their car or under a bridge when they were above ground. Others had a look of serene authority and an ease with words that matched the Ralph Lauren polo shirt most likely hiding under their grey coveralls.

Quartz fell into the latter category. Philippe didn't know exactly how old Quartz was, but he was definitely pushing fifty, possibly sixty because according to rumor, he'd been visiting the catacombs for nearly forty years. He navigated the network without a map, but he always had a notebook and a pen handy to jot down anything unusual, anything new – or anything he simply hadn't noticed before. He'd been to galleries that no longer existed because they'd been cut off and cemented in. He knew any cataphile worth knowing and they all kept him posted on any news worth hearing. His knowledge was extensive. Not only could he tell you about the Great Southern Network; he'd also explored the networks on the Right Bank. He'd been under the Palais de Chaillot and, even more inaccessible, he claimed to have visited the remnants of the cathedral-like gypsum quarries under Montmartre. Which was probably true.

Lying in his hospital bed, these memories of Quartz made Philippe's heart plunge. His eyes flickered before refocusing on the brick wall. The Nightmare had started with Quartz.

All Philippe had wanted to do that night was catch himself a girl. A normal healthy activity to unwind after two weeks of exams. And he had been on his way to success. He'd been enjoying the party, dancing with a very cute blonde who was completely absorbed pulsing to the music. There was a time for everything, and at that particular point in time, he was looking for an instant girl fix. Nothing too serious; his pre-exam fights with his previous girlfriend were still fresh enough to make him not want any kind of new *relationship*. But the blonde was cute. He'd never seen her before. But then there were plenty of girls at the party he'd never seen before. The weather probably had something to do with the turnout. With the heat wave raging outside, the catacombs were about the best place in town to be. A constant 17°C. Natural air conditioning had proven a magnet for people who would normally have preferred the safety of a nightclub on the surface.

The music speeded up and the blonde threw her hands into the air, thrusting her hips back and forth beating time to the rhythm, her hair flying across her face. As she revolved to the beat, Philippe noticed part of a tattoo sticking out above the hip band of her jeans. A snake tail or the stalk of a leaf. Philippe felt a growing desire to find out what exactly that tattoo was and where it led. He moved in closer.

Unfortunately by pressing towards his partner, he also got a better view of Quentin.

That was the end of his dance. And the beginning of the worst.

Of the group of cataphiles they belonged to, Quentin was by far the most passionate, with Philippe a distant second. Over the past year and a half Quentin had put together a sort of library about anything and everything concerned with subterranean Paris. He spent more on catacomb books than he did on textbooks for university. So, rather than checking out girls, Quentin had been using the party as an opportunity to milk the cata-doyens for info.

A moment later, his friend and the famous cataphile were beside Philippe on the improvised dancefloor. "Hey," Quentin said in what should have been a normal voice but that registered closer to a scream in order to be heard above the music. *"Quartz va nous montrer un passage qui mène direct à Henri IV." Quartz says he'll show us a passage that leads straight to Henri IV High School.*

Philippe found that more than just a little hard to believe. *"Ça n'existe pas." There's no such thing.*

"Want to bet?" called Quartz.

* * *

A chair squeaked beside him and Philippe turned his head sideways. His mother's familiar soft features greeted him – with that skin that seemed a little more translucent every time he saw her. Next to her, his father sat looking even more tired and preoccupied than usual. The expression on both their faces was so much graver than anything he'd ever seen during the various mini-crises the family had gone through before. And when his mother leaned forward, Philippe could see her eyes were puffy and her skin red, as if she'd been crying.

"Philippe? Can you hear me? Are you okay?" she whispered, a quiver of confusion glancing across her face.

Of course he could hear her.

He stretched his hand towards her and she threw her arms around him.

56

The room Sadiqi had been ushered into had that touch of aristocratic elegance that so offended his republican principles. Everything reeked of King and Empire. The secretary's desk was Louis XVI, as was the chair the inspector had been directed to occupy. And the carpet cushioning his feet was a deep, regal blue. All that was missing were a few *fleurs de lys*. The overall effect made Sadiqi look like a bagman at a royal garden party. But far from making him uncomfortable, the way his t-shirt and jeans clashed with the elegant backdrop made him feel mildly superior. There was no way he was going to bow to the upper-class pretensions of the Senate. It was all just appearance, illusion – no substance. He enjoyed playing the *sans culotte* in this world filled with the successors of a supposedly banished aristocracy.

The cop's reaction was understandable since the man sitting across the desk from him definitely looked like the heir from a previous regime, specially bred for his current position. Although the two men were roughly the same age, they came from worlds apart. While Sadiqi reclined comfortably into his chair, the man facing him sat to attention. And it wasn't just his poise that intimated careful breeding. His jacket and shirt had been made to measure and his blow-dried hair looked as if it had been starched into place. No element of his appearance had been left to chance. Sadiqi recognized all the signs of the ruling-class. Silk tie, polished shoes, manicure, gold nibbed fountain pen. This was Nicolas de St. Cyr, Senator Clavreul's secretary. Not a typing and shorthand secretary. Something out of a by-gone era. A male secretary. A speechwriter. An organizer. One of France's elite from the political class. It was a class that held particularly bad connotations for Sadiqi, because it was a class that liked to think itself above the Law. No. That wasn't what annoyed him. What annoyed him was that it was a class that had managed to successfully maintain itself above the Law. And that's why Sadiqi was sitting here now.

"What can I do for you, *Monsieur l'Inspecteur Général?*" St. Cyr asked, rolling off the official title without the least effort. Nobody but high-level civil servants ever managed that.

Sadiqi forced himself to hide his innate dislike for this man and what he represented behind a mask of administrative indifference. "I was wondering if you could tell me if your boss is in contact with someone called Pierre Caron," he said, drumming his fingers gently on the armrests of his chair, regretting both the day smoking in public buildings was made illegal and his decision to kick the habit.

A trace of irritation flickered across the secretary's face, barely noticeable. Nothing more than a slight tightening of the muscles around the eyes. "Monsieur, my *boss*, as you call him, is the President of the Republic. I was not hired by Senator Clavreul. I was appointed to work for him." St. Cyr said this with such precision he could have been reading straight out of a manual. The message was crystal clear. Being appointed secretary to Clavreul had just been the luck of the draw. Bad luck, in this case.

Sadiqi's feeling for St. Cyr warmed microscopically as he took note of this expression of dislike. They cooled again just as quickly, thanks to the man's silent refusal to answer the question he'd been asked.

"Perhaps I should explain," Sadiqi said, shifting in the elegant but uncomfortable chair. "Dr. Caron was found dead at his home last night. He was murdered."

The brutal announcement had the desired effect. A flash of dismay sparkled in the secretary's eyes. It was gone again before any noticeable loss of composure set in. "That's most regrettable. However, I fail to see how it concerns the Senator."

Sadiqi hated this type of foreplay. Tiptoeing around his witnesses. Directing them towards the hard facts, getting them to come out with something he didn't already know. "Could you just answer the question please," he said, doing his best to remain polite. "Did Clavreul know Professor Caron?"

The secretary pressed his shoulders against the back of his chair, drawing himself upward like some great sphinx, ready to defend its master. "He and the senator worked together on a report concerning potential terror threats in the quarries."

The cop ignored the vagueness of the reply. "I'd like to see a copy of that report."

"I'm afraid that's impossible. The report is confidential." St. Cyr's reply came with a ring of official impotence.

"I can get clearance to see it."

"Then I encourage you to do so," the secretary replied, with a purr of coolness. "I can't show it to anyone without clearance. It contains sensitive material."

The flat refusal did nothing to deter Sadiqi. He was used to administrative hurdles. He was used to wasting time, sniffing out the right channels. If St. Cyr couldn't provide him with a copy of the report, perhaps at least he could tell him more about it. "Do you know who received copies?"

"Off-hand, I'd say the President, the Defense Minister, the DPSD." Sadiqi's ears pricked up at the mention of the DPSD. The Department of Protection and Defense Security. They were in charge of everything from counter-terrorism to the defense industry. One of their key jobs was to decide what material needed to be classified as an official secret and who should be privy to defense secrets. "And I believe the Interior Minister saw it, as well as some of the intelligence services."

"Why was it considered so sensitive?" Sadiqi continued.

The secretary shrugged and turned his palms upward to indicate ignorance. His true body language was harder to read. St. Cyr had been formatted to use textbook body codes known to reassure and persuade. It was all too well-studied for Sadiqi to find it convincing. On the contrary, he had a good idea what the secretary's body language really meant. He'd seen the signs so many times before. St. Cyr was trying to decide just how much information he should give away. He wanted to get a feel for how smart or how stupid Sadiqi was. How much would he guess on his own? How much needed to be spelled out? The cop knew the game. He'd played it before. Hell, he played it almost every day. It was a game witnesses indulged in constantly. This guy didn't want his boss on his back for giving away too many details. He also didn't want the police accusing him of withholding information. So he would walk the tightrope, carefully dodging questions or leaving answers open to interpretation, saying as little as possible. The aim was to make it look like he was being helpful when in fact he was trying to keep Sadiqi at bay.

"There must be something you can tell me," the inspector prompted.

The secretary took a deep breath. Probably a relaxation technique he'd been taught in some executive coaching programme. "I've not read the report myself. All I know is that it deals with security risks in the catacombs. From what I understand, Professor Caron was a specialist in that field and Senator Clavreul is very receptive to any type of anti-terrorist discourse. He believes it behooves him to root out evil wherever it is."

The description fell in line with Sadiqi's intuition about the senator. Clavreul was an astute politician of the worst kind: a troublemaker always ready to create the evil within to make sure that the real problems were never dealt with. The cop's brief encounters with Caron told him that the two troublemakers had probably hit it off like blood brothers. "Do you know how they met?" Sadiqi asked, personal curiosity mixing with professional interest. "Did Caron reach out to the senator? Or maybe they met socially?"

"No, nothing like that," the secretary answered, confident that nothing he said on this subject could get him in trouble. "The Senate basement was refurbished. Due to the catacombs' proximity to the Luxembourg Palace, the IGC was consulted about the project. Professor Caron was called in to ensure that everything went smoothly. Senator Clavreul was in charge of the internal committee overseeing the work. The two were predestined to meet. What couldn't have been foreseen was that they would have so much to say to one another."

There it was. The bone Sadiqi had been waiting for the secretary to throw him. "So what was so important about what Caron had to say?"

St. Cyr flashed a look of disdain, as if he'd just been asked to name his five favorite TV game shows, or some similar question so plebeian it didn't deserve to be acknowledged. His answer carried a correlated degree of enthusiasm. "I've no idea. I wasn't present at most of their meetings – I attended only a few in the early stages when they were still discussing the Luxembourg Palace. You see, I was only involved in the discussion concerning Senate security. Professor Caron, however, had very few concerns about safety here."

"Enough for him to produce a report."

"No. The risks he wrote about in the report didn't concern the Senate. At least not directly. I believe he raised more general concerns about wider catacomb issues."

Sadiqi considered this for a moment then backtracked. "You said you didn't attend their meetings. Does that mean you refused to be present because it wasn't part of your job or does it mean you were asked to leave?"

A nervous twitch ran down the secretary's arm as he rapped his fingers on his desk. Even before he spoke Sadiqi could tell that St. Cyr considered being excluded from the meetings an affront. This was confirmed a second later. "On a number of occasions I was asked to leave while they consulted. On other occasions they held their discussions elsewhere." The secretary's face fell while he decided just how much he wanted to disclose. Then he added, "You see Professor Caron took the senator to visit the catacombs."

If any news could have surprised Sadiqi, this was it. The inspector had never seen a picture of Jacques Clavreul dressed in anything but a coal-grey suit and tie. He had trouble conjuring up the mental image of the old aristocrat fitted out in rubber boots and an anorak with a cap light on his head. "I'm surprised the senator had such a hands-on approach."

"I know for a fact that they went down. They used passages directly under the Senate basement; I was asked to help get the necessary security clearance." The movement of St. Cyr's lips was the only part of his body breaking the statue-like poise. The stiffness in the secretary's voice made Sadiqi wonder if this guy ever unwound. And his words were defensive. As if he suspected Sadiqi of doubting him.

The cop closed his eyes and shifted in his seat again. If St. Cyr said that Clavreul had been cata-walking, then it was no doubt true. It was just a strange picture. "So they got on well?"

"Yes. Definitely. Caron and the catacombs were the senator's pet interest for several months."

Sadiqi felt uneasy. St. Cyr was being helpful. Unfortunately the picture he was painting wasn't one the cop had expected. In order to find the connector between these incongruous elements, he needed to ask an equally unexpected question.

"Were the catacombs the only thing they had in common?"

"I beg your pardon."

"I mean, is it possible that they knew one another before the renovations began. Perhaps they'd already met somewhere. Is it possible they were both members of the same club or something?"

"The same club?" The tone was condescending rather than confused. "I'm not sure what you're implying, *Monsieur l'Inspecteur Général.*"

The cop's relaxed slouch contrasted with the intensity of his stare. "Is it possible that Senator Clavreul is a Freemason?"

Sadiqi would have been ready for just about any reaction other than the one he got. He'd expected yet another barely perceptible response: a slightly raised eyebrow, a twitching ear... Instead the secretary gave a loud guffaw and showed the first sign of interest in the conversation.

"Given the numerous comments made by the senator against the Freemasons, I would have to presume that he's not a member."

Stifling his embarrassment, Sadiqi pursued the point. "I hadn't realized Freemasonry was one of his pet peeves."

A tiny grimace appeared at the corners of the secretary's mouth. In any normal person the change of expression would have been almost imperceptible; on the secretary's face it was the equivalent of a hysterical fit. "According to the senator, Freemasonry is an abhorrence. As is immigration, women in the workplace – and let's not even talk about homosexuality." Sadiqi couldn't help wondering which of the above taboos annoyed St. Cyr the most. Either way, the secretary was growing on him as he sat to attention, waiting for the next question. Poor slob. It couldn't always be a bed of roses working as permanent secretary to someone who was so vehemently disliked by a huge chunk of society. St. Cyr's probably got teased all the time at his literary salons.

Regardless, even if the secretary hadn't read the report, surely he had to know something about it if it had really been Clavreul's hobbyhorse for months. "From what I understand, the report was written for the President's attention," Sadiqi pursued. "Do you have any idea why Tibrac refused to act on it?"

"No," St. Cyr answered. "It all seemed to fizzle out. There was a big song and dance about it. The senator and the professor were *copains comme cochons* – the best of friends. They were both convinced that the president would jump in and start reorganizing catacomb security as soon as he read their paper. Then all of a sudden it was over."

"What do you mean?"

"The report was circulated – and rejected – and the Senator never mentioned it again."

"He never mentioned it again?" It seemed like an unlikely end to a long collaboration. "Are you sure about that? I mean he and Caron must have discussed the President's reaction. Didn't they have plans to look for support elsewhere if they believed their report was so important?"

"No," St. Cyr said. For the first time during their interview Sadiqi could sense a hint of incomprehension. "All contact ended brutally. Caron phoned again and again, trying to find out whether any positive action was being taken, yet I don't believe the senator returned many of those calls. He certainly asked me not to put through the professor's calls."

"The Senator refused to take Caron's calls." The secretary's delicate head-shaking migrated to a nod. Even though this confirmed what Podesta had said earlier, it still didn't make sense. Why would Clavreul have cut off contact with Caron? You don't collaborate on a project for that long and then just suddenly drop everything. "What was the time scale for all this?"

"I'd say they first met about three years ago. But the report itself only dates back to last year. It seems to me they finalized it in the fall then transmitted it to the President in October or November."

"And when was the last time they met?"

The pause and deep intake of breath was so protracted St. Cyr could have been attempting some yogic exercise to oxygenate his brain. "Perhaps six months ago. I'd have to check the senator's agenda if you want an exact date..." he said, turning to his laptop to call up the required information. But his hands retreated from the keyboard at the last moment. "No. That's not strictly true. I know when they saw one another. I was there. They met a few days ago. Tuesday. There was a cocktail party next door in the Salons Boffrand to celebrate the completion of the renovation work. Professor Caron was among the guests."

"And Senator Clavreul spoke with him."

"Very briefly. The Senator seemed..." St. Cyr tapped his gold nibbed pen on the desk as he searched for the best way to describe the two men's final meeting. "... perhaps embarrassed by the Professor's presence."

"What do you mean?"

"The senator tried to ignore him. When they inevitably found themselves face to face, Senator Clavreul cold-shouldered the professor. Left him standing in the middle of the room – like an outcast. I remember the expression on Professor Caron's face. He was shattered. He obviously had no idea why he was being shut out."

The secretary sat quietly, his eyes riveted on the investigator. Sadiqi ran his palm along the armrest, first across the soft velvet and then onto the gold-leafed wood at the tip. He was having trouble making sense of the senator's behavior.

As he speculated on the reasons for the change of heart, his eyes drifted out the window to the public garden beyond, where a brood of pigeons was fluttering around, fighting for crumbs. Pigeons, birds... That was the other thing he wanted to ask.

"Monsieur de St. Cyr, can you tell me if the Senator knows or if he's met anyone called either Rossignol or *Nightingale*?" Sadiqi clipped the English word out in crisp Gallic syllables.

"An English name?" The secretary frowned. "The Senator doesn't believe in letting foreigners pry into French affairs. Certainly not an Anglo-Saxon. But, I can check." Once again St. Cyr stretched his arm towards the laptop and called up the computer agenda. As the information flashed on his screen, he began shaking his head. "No, I don't have anything. However, this agenda only covers professional meetings. It's not the senator's personal agenda."

"You don't cross-reference with a personal agenda?"

If the atmosphere had warmed over the previous minutes, it now cooled again. "I'm not the Senator's personal assistant." St. Cyr sounded so offended you would have thought Sadiqi had just accused him of collecting comic books or baseball cards. "I'm a permanent secretary. I provide support, attend briefings. I do not make hair appointments or organize *rendez-vous* with his mistress." He slipped his watch out from below his double cuffs in a deliberate motion. His time was too precious to waste.

In response, Sadiqi readjusted his position in the chair and lifted the transparent folder that had been lying in his lap. "I won't take up much more of your time. Just one last thing. I presume the senator keeps copies of all his correspondence." St. Cyr remained bolt upright but gave another minute nod. "Would it be possible to check if he wrote this?" the cop asked, setting the plastic on the secretary's desk. The letter inside was the one that had been found lying in front of Caron's lifeless body, the Senate letterhead visible at the top of the page.

St. Cyr barely gave it a glance before answering. "I can tell you without even checking. It's not his."

The answer would have been more convincing if the man had taken a better look. "How do you know? You've not even read it?"

"I don't need to read it. The Senator always signs in black fountain pen."

Sadiqi checked the letter again. It had been signed in blue fountain pen. Not much of an argument. It certainly wouldn't stand up in court. "What if he was out of black ink and someone lent him a blue pen."

"He wouldn't sign it. He would send someone out to buy black ink. He never signs in blue. He says it's common." The secretary was adamant.

Absurd as it sounded, Sadiqi knew that some people had ticks about how they signed documents. He'd never come across the blue-is-too-vulgar argument, but Dukrin would never sign in anything but blue ballpoint; she said that black could be copied too easily while fountain pen didn't leave a visible pressure mark on most paper. Blue ballpoint was the best way of being certain a signature was an original rather than a copy.

Still, Sadiqi needed more solid proof than that. "Would you mind just checking if there's a copy in the files."

Without a word St. Cyr moved across the room to the filing cabinet and flicked through one of the drawers, a bored look on his face.

But the look of boredom didn't last. As he pulled out a sheet of paper it morphed into an entirely uncharacteristic expression of confusion. "It appears I was mistaken. Apparently the senator did send that letter."

57

Just as he was leaving the senate Sadiqi's phone started quaking in his pocket. It was Toni. "Where are you?" she asked. "I've been doing some research and I think you'll like what I've found out." The cop had no idea what 'research' she was hoping to share with him. He was also a little concerned that the true aim of her call was social rather than investigative. If that was the case, he was going to have to brush her off.

Despite these misgivings, he more or less gave her his GPS coordinates and before he'd got as far as the duck pond, a cry of "Khalid!" told him the Canadian was closing in. He turned toward the voice, but it took a moment to spot her. There was no sign of the androgynous jeans and running shoes from the previous day. In fact, it was her grey backpack that he recognized first. It jarred so violently with the rest of the image: Toni gliding towards him swathed in a billowing dress that danced on the breeze. Her choice of studied feminity only reinforced his suspicions that this was going to be a social call.

So it was something of an anti-climax when, instead of a passionate reunion, Corrigan simply fell into step beside him and began talking shop.

"I think something's going to happen at the Pantheon," she said, with all the passion of a business partner.

The soft muslin gently folding around her body made Sadiqi's heartbeat quicken and his throat tense. It came as a powerful reminder of their night together. Far too short. But a wonderful night.

In truth, that was the real reason he was so uncomfortable meeting with her. He hadn't felt this strong an attraction to anyone for ages. Not the butterflies in the stomach routine. And certainly not this jarring desire to wrap her in his arms and taste her skin on his lips.

The fact that she seemed so detached was more than a minor annoyance; it was distracting. Sadiqi didn't like mixed messages. Did she really like him or had last night just been a fluke? It sure as hell wasn't easy to guess from the way she was behaving. Frustration began to boil his Mediterranean blood, latent passion scratching to get out. He might be out of practice with women but if he remembered correctly, when you met up with your lover you were supposed to throw yourselves into one another's arms, blood pulsing, temperature rising. It should be exciting. None of this, "Hi, how's life" stuff. If this was the new take on love, he wasn't interested. "Thank you Ms. Corrigan. I had figured that out. You know, there are actual police officers working this case."

The coolness of his welcome froze Toni in her tracks. Which only annoyed Sadiqi even more. He had things to do; he didn't need a scene.

But then he caught sight of her expression. The look of total and utter incomprehension. The inability to understand why he was being so curt. She looked fragile, as well beautiful. And the mixture of conflicting feelings that had been coursing through him fused into one single emotion.

He took a step closer, caressed the soft dark hair and kissed her.

When he resurfaced, he discovered things were clearer. He could feel her hands pressed against his chest. And the glint had returned to her magnificent malachite eyes. "You're absolutely right," she purred. "That's a much better start to the day."

Perhaps the old expression that something good could come out of something bad, was actually true. "Sorry. Work's getting to me…" he apologized. He would have added '*I think you make me a little crazy*' if she hadn't interrupted him.

"But this could help."

As much as Sadiqi would have liked to spend the whole day locked away with her, he had a case to solve. When he spoke, it was with carefully composed gentleness. "Look, I already know about the Pantheon. You're simply confirming intelligence I received hours ago." That information had been forwarded from Cryptography earlier.

A silence fell between them and Sadiqi couldn't help throwing a few more words into the void. "The police aren't completely incompetent."

Her smile was slightly more sheepish than usual. "It's just that last night you didn't know about Ng's second message…"

The cop stared at the ground for inspiration. "Well, I *would* have known if I hadn't turned my phone off. There were three messages from my boss by the time I left last night."

Toni pushed closer and he could feel her warmth against him. "I guess that's sort of reassuring. Not only does it mean you like me. It also means that the French police might actually be on top of this."

A weak pun ran through his brain. In fact several. But he ignored them. "So what was it you wanted to tell me?" The reunion was all well and good but he had things to do. He put his arm around her shoulder and started toward the university building at the far end of the park.

"Well, you've obviously seen the latest message about the Temple," she said, falling into stride and hooking her hand around his arm. Sadiqi nodded. "And okay, you've not told me much about what's going on. But your case has something to do with the quarries, right?"

"I really can't discuss that."

The question was rhetorical. She hadn't expected an answer, so she simply ignored the one she got. "And what's the only temple near the quarries?" The Socratic questioning suited the temple theme well. "The Pantheon. Which also links to the second message. And Freemasonry. The Pantheon is plugged as a secular temple, but you could just as easily call it a Freemason temple."

"Why?" While Cryptography had pointed to the Pantheon as the only likely target near the GRS that could be considered a temple, they certainly hadn't come up with a link to Freemasonry.

"There's a lot of Masonic symbolism in there – not to mention a lot of ex-Masons. About a third of the men buried in the crypt are Freemasons. And last night's message pointed to Freemasonry."

Sadiqi nodded. "We also have a dead Freemason."

As soon as the words were out, he realized what he'd done. The news had got away from him. Caron wasn't some random victim for Toni. He was her professor. Someone she worked with every day. The news shouldn't have been thrown at her like that.

"Who?" she asked.

Judging by the tone of abstract curiosity, she was totally unprepared for the shock of the answer. But nothing he could say would make this any easier. "It's Caron."

Again, his words drew her to a halt. And again an expression of incomprehension appeared as she tried to process this bombshell. "Caron? Professor Caron? He's dead?"

When giving bad news, Sadiqi always kept his delivery as short as possible. Give the information, then shut up. That was his motto. He wished there was something he could say to put things right, but there wasn't. "Murdered last night."

Her eyes fell to the dusty path below their feet. She hadn't exactly been close with Caron. Familiarity and informality weren't things he'd ever encouraged. He'd never been either friendly or helpful. But the strange sense of fragility that accompanied the announcement of death still vibrated around her. She was almost shivering despite the heat. "How did he die?"

There was no nice way to put it. "Someone entered his house and broke his neck."

Toni looked at the man who'd just spoken these words. How could he be so calm? There was something ruthless about his composure. It wasn't like he was telling her that Caron had missed a meeting or received a parking ticket. Or even had a heart attack, for that matter. They were talking about murder.

It was only then that it really struck Toni that Sadiqi probably saw a lot of death. While she was working on abstractions, running around the Pantheon trying to put the clues together, Khalid was actually taking the body count. Personally observing the dead piling up.

So if the cop had been able to see into her mind, he might have taken a moment longer to console her or try to make her feel better. Instead, he flipped straight back to business. "That's why I was headed to *FranceTech*. I wanted to check through his office. I'm looking for a document he put together a few months ago. A study of underground security risks he wrote for Senator Clavreul."

Toni gazed at Khalid. It was strange to watch him work. The little bits of humanity she'd seen pierce through the night before had carefully been filed away and she was once again faced with the chill cop. She got the impression that he must spend a lot of time compartmentalizing his life to make it bearable. Build a mind palace. Run to the far end of that palace and find a room where you can lock away the dead. Then throw away the key. Maybe that was what she needed to do, too. She pushed back the thoughts of Caron and hardened herself. "I guess you don't need my help with your homework." She eased away.

This time his reaction was immediate. He caught her by the waist, gently drawing her closer.

Khalid wasn't a natural talker. His strong suit was observation and analysis not words. But right now, he needed to say the right thing. "Look, I'm really sorry about this. About everything. I know it's a mess. All of it. Caron. You. Me. Everything." He was fairly sure he was making a fool of himself. Yet some things were too important to leave unsaid. "But I like you. Really. So when I've got this case tied up I want to get to know you better..."

"...But for now you want me out of your face." Her features hardened and again she pulled away – as if by stepping away first, she could lessen the pang of rejection.

But the cop was shaking his head. He wouldn't have thought the day could get any more uncomfortable. Apparently embarrassment was a bottomless pit. "Actually, no. That was the other reason I was headed for *FranceTech*. I need your professional input."

58

"If he has a copy here, it shouldn't be too hard to find." Toni said as she rummaged through the files in Caron's cabinet. "The thing's a couple hundred pages long."

That sounded about right to Sadiqi. If the report contained every nightmare scenario involving the quarries that had ever crossed Caron's mind, the document would be fairly substantial. "What's in it?"

"What I remember is a whole whack of typical Caron stuff about the danger from below. Nothing that struck me as particularly unusual. Then again, I didn't get a chance to read it properly; I only glanced through quickly one day when he left it lying on his desk. He was finishing it off when I first arrived and he was pretty cagey about the whole thing. He kept going off to meetings with Clavreul. I'm pretty sure they went walkabout in the quarries together, too. But he never let me tag along."

Once again, the cop tried to visualize the lavishly elegant Clavreul dressed in boots and quarry coveralls. The image just wouldn't materialize. So he turned his attention to more practical things instead. While Toni searched through the filing cabinet, he attacked the desk drawer. Unfortunately it put up more resistance than the filing cabinet, which had yielded willingly to his skeleton key. The desk was one of those massive antiques, with solid wood and a sturdy iron lock. Having failed to jimmy it, Sadiqi tried to force it, kicking and yanking, in hopes the wood would splinter and release the drawer.

While the cop carried out his display of police brutality on an inanimate object, Toni closed the top filing drawer and pulled out the second. Her fingers scurried over the documents, reading the file names. To her amazement the file marked *Chemin de la Reine* was followed by one entitled *Clavreul*. "Here we go," she said, hauling the small manila pouch into the air.

Sadiqi turned expectantly but the flimsy folder looked less than promising. Even Toni was baffled by how light it was. Sure enough, when she flipped open the cover she found herself looking at two measly sheets of paper. No report.

The letterhead at the top of the first page meant little until she skimmed over the numbers below. "It's an investment statement." That was disappointing.

Sadiqi moved closer and picked up the paper. "400.000 euros invested in the NTPS last February. Another 400.000 in Fygues." NTPS was a big public works company; they got a lot of government contracts. Fygues was a building contractor. "Any idea why Caron would be interested in either of those companies?"

"NTPS is specialized in anything involving cement. Roads and runways." Her lips tightened. "They're also the ones who inject concrete into the quarries whenever Caron decides he wants a gallery closed down." The cop recognized the quiver of anger that appeared whenever the young woman talked about damage wreaked on her hell-bound paradise. "And Fygues…"

"… puts up the buildings on the surface once the injections are done." Apartments, shopping centers, parking lots. Fygues built them all.

"This is really incriminating."

The cop reflected to himself that where Caron was, it didn't really matter whether the documents were incriminating or not. The professor was well beyond that type of earthly problem. "No crime in buying stock."

"Yes. Sure. But he filed this under 'Clavreul'. He did that for a reason." It struck her as obvious, but maybe it wasn't for Khalid. "This is conflict of interest and insider trading. I mean, let's say, for some reason, the IGC gave NTPS a big contract to fill in dozens of kilometers of tunnels, that could get construction profits soaring for Fygues."

"Yeah." Sadiqi had got the message, loud and clear but it merited little more than a shrug.

"But this is serious," she prompted. "Remember what I said yesterday about construction stipulations. Before you can build anything in Paris, you have to check the underground structures. If there are quarries below the site, the building's foundations have to go down to the deepest part of the quarries. Obviously that has a cost. If, on the other hand, the IGC pays NTPS to fill in all the galleries under potential building sites, the builder, Fygues for instance, has lower production costs…"

"Which means higher profits, higher dividends and higher share prices," the cop finished her sentence. "Caron was looking to make a profit by influencing Clavreul. He had insider info about the market. If NTPS was given a contract to cement in the network, that would drive up their share prices directly, along with Fygues' indirectly."

Toni was glad the cop had caught on but she truly wished her final contact with her professor had been more uplifting. "I hate to say it, on today, of all days, but that definitely sounds like Caron."

The man had been an opportunist on top of all his other flaws. "Yes. It makes sense", Sadiqi conceded. "If he was convinced that his report was going to lead to big changes in underground reinforcements he could have convinced himself there was money to be made. 800.000 euros. That's a tidy sum. Especially if the share price skyrocketed." A final detail crystallized. "Which might also explain why the statements are here rather than at his home. He probably didn't want his wife to know he was gambling their retirement money on the stock market." Sadiqi had another look at the page in case he'd missed something, but there was nothing useful. He put it down and reached for the other one.

"Aren't you going to tuck that away in one of your little plastic baggies?" Toni protested. "I mean, isn't it evidence?"

Sadiqi leaned onto the desk so that he was within whispering distance. She was so sweet. So naïve. "I hate to tell you this, but France has never been very strict on financial crime. Embezzlement and insider trading are fairly widespread in high places. It's the kind of thing that hits the headlines for a couple of days then fizzles out. And it's rare a judge ever calls in a conviction. Nobody would have killed Caron over a few hundred thousand euros, if that's what you're thinking. And nobody is going to want to post-humously shame an otherwise well-regarded civil servant."

Toni was about to object, but Sadiqi was already examining the second sheet so she squeezed in to get a better view. It only took a glance to understand what the grey photocopy on IGC letterhead paper was. She had an almost identical document in her wallet at all times. Except the photo on hers was different. "That's a copy of an IGC quarry access authorization. But I don't see what it's doing here. It should be in the files at the IGC."

"Jean Brune," Sadiqi said, reading the name then squinting at the picture, running it through his memory, trying to think if he'd ever seen the face before. The photo was grainy. It looked like it was probably a black and white photocopy of a color print. But the man's basic features were visible. Very short hair. Light skin. Light eyes. And a small James Dean nose. Definitely Caucasian.

The cop folded the paper and slipped it into his pocket causing Toni to wince with outrage that was only partially contrived. "Are you allowed to just take things like that? I mean, maybe it's not a crime scene here, but if Caron's been murdered aren't you supposed to close off the space and tag everything you take."

"Are you going to teach me my job?"

"I don't really know what your job is, do I?"

"Don't you trust me?"

"It's not a question of trust. I'm just curious how the French police work. I would have thought there were rules or procedures to follow, or something."

"There are… For the regular police."

"But you're not regular."

He kissed her behind her ear. "I thought you'd figured that out." The words rang with the sound of self-mockery rather than brio. "And there is one perk. I'm allowed to break things if it's in the national interest." As if to illustrate this rule, he walked back over to Caron's desk, braced himself and pulled with twice his normal force. There was a crack of wood splintering as the lock broke through the frame and the drawer flew open.

"The victory of violence over reason?" Toni suggested.

"Perhaps the violence of victory," Sadiqi answered, already shuffling through the layers of office paraphernalia inside. There was a fountain pen, identical to the one St. Cyr had had. Black with a white star on the cap. The tasteful work tool of every well-educated Frenchman. Then a box of paper clips and a pack of cookies. Below that a few sheets of paper stuffed in haphazardly, some with telephone numbers scribbled on them, others with Post-its providing messages that would never be answered.

While the cop was reading the names and notes, Toni caught sight of another object stuffed into the back of the desk. More unexpected than the office staples. A small pile of pale blue fabric. She reached in and touched the warm scratchiness of silk. Sliding it out, she could see the stuff was embroidered with the most delicate little roses. Hardly the type of thing she would have expected Caron to have.

The papers had lost their appeal. What Toni had was infinitely more interesting. Sadiqi's hands passed against hers to unfold the strange object, uncovering an embroidered square and compass nestled between the roses. Flipping it over, he discovered a reverse side that was completely different to the gentle pinks and blues of the public side. The lining was a deep black satin. As if in contrast to the roses on the outside, the inner lining was decorated with a pearly skull and cross-bones. "It's a Freemason's sash," Sadiqi said.

A chill of reverence told Toni this wasn't usually for public viewing. She was seeing something secret. And their examination of the sash probably would have lasted longer if the sound of someone clearing his throat hadn't drawn them out of their contemplation.

Framed in the doorway, a man dressed in a suit and sandals stood observing the scene. "Inspector Sadiqi, I presume. My name's Cédric Trouvé."

59

"Thank you for coming, Professor," Sadiqi said crumpling into Caron's chair and waving Trouvé toward a seat. Toni noted with a shudder how easily Caron and everything he represented had been evicted from life.

Trouvé seemed to be having a similar recoiling reaction because instead of taking the chair the inspector offered him, he remained standing. "Lieutenant Podesta told me about Pierre. He said you had some questions." He flashed the student a cold, unfamiliar stare that suggested she had no right to be rummaging through Caron's office. Toni slunk to the back of the room where she could observe without meeting the professor's gaze. Not surprisingly, his shock over the loss of his colleague was discernible. After all, the two had worked together for years; they'd been close.

The cop was the only one not caught up in the human side of the drama. For him, this was just business as usual. He took the sash he and Toni had been admiring and laid it out on the desk. "I understand you and Professor Caron belonged to the same Freemason's lodge."

Whatever Trouvé had been expecting, it wasn't that. "Inspector, with all due respect, that's none of your business."

"Professor, with respect, everything is my business." It would never cease to amaze Sadiqi how people thought they had the right to tell him only what they thought he needed to know. "I realize this must be difficult for you. You've lost a colleague. Possibly a friend. Still, my question stands. There may be a link between your colleague's murder and your lodge."

It wasn't much of an apology given the extent of Trouvé's loss. From the back of the room, Toni remarked that Sadiqi's strong point certainly wasn't his bedside manner. The mention of *murder* seemed to draw the professor inside himself. When he spoke, his voice was frail. "That's impossible. Pierre's death has nothing to do with the Brotherhood. I'll tell you whatever you want to know about me personally, or Pierre, but the Brotherhood should be left out of this."

Sadiqi found himself giving the standard litany. "Professor, all I'm asking you to do is answer a few questions to help me understand who Pierre Caron was and what happened to him." Years of experience had taught Sadiqi that when questioned by the police intellectuals usually fell into one of two categories: either they clammed up or they got completely lost in endless details. So far Trouvé was in the first category.

The cop pulled his phone from his pocket and called up a screen. "Last night you left a message on Professor Caron's answering machine. I have a copy of that message. You said…" and he began reading, using a cold monotone to emphasize the words: "I want you to know that I've informed the Grand Master and he intends to take punitive measures."

Once he'd finished reading the message, he placed the phone on the desk, in clear view. "Now, Professor, could you explain why you threatened your colleague and tell me what sort of punitive measures you were expecting from the Grand Master?"

This was all news to Toni, who noted that the professor had turned a shade paler and seemed to have shrunk, his shoulder bent, engulfed by a look of pure regret. "*Threatened* is too strong a word," he murmured. "I just thought he should know that I'd reported him to the higher offices of the… group we both belong to."

"You both belonged to. May I remind you, your colleague is dead?" It was hard to accept death and too often Sadiqi had seen people trying to protect the reputations of friends or family who had gone on to greener pastures and no longer needed protecting. The sooner Trouvé started talking about Caron in the past tense, the sooner they were likely to make some real progress. "You said punitive measures would be taken. What punitive measures and for what reason?"

Trouvé shifted nervously from one foot to the other and readjusted his tie. "Inspector, I'm sure you can appreciate that the group we belong to… Belonged to…"

"Look, we both know we're talking about the Freemasons so could we stop beating around the bush. What did Caron do wrong?"

Although Toni was curious to find out what the big disagreement was about, she was finding it even more interesting just observing the two men – Trouvé almost as much as Sadiqi. She'd never seen the professor so out of control. Fiddling with his tie. Breaking eye contact. But why? Why didn't he just come clean?

Slowly, the truth began to trickle out.

"Our disagreement concerned the rituals of our Lodge, not the profane world," he finally said. "If Pierre had done something illegal, I would have reported him to the police. As it was, he simply transgressed the internal rules of our society. That's why I reported him to the Grand Master."

"So the Lodge took matters into its own hands."

The professor nodded but after only two up and down movements of his head the motion stopped and his eyes narrowed cautiously. "I'm not sure what you're implying, Inspector."

"Well, I'm not sure what you're implying, either," Sadiqi said. "That's the point. I don't want a lot of cryptic innuendo. What I want you to do is spell it out. Because for the moment, all I know is that a few hours ago you asked the Grand Master to punish Professor Caron and now your colleague is dead."

The accusation struck hard. Trouvé seemed to lose the strength in his legs. He faltered forward and eased himself into the visitor's chair. Leaning against the desk, his words came out in a great sigh of disbelief. "You're not insinuating the Lodge is responsible for Pierre's death? That's outrageous. The punitive measures I was thinking of were more in the nature of a suspension from the lodge. Perhaps a reprimand or at worst expulsion. Not assassination, for God's sake."

"I've heard stories about the Freemasons."

"I'm sure you have, but that's all they are. Stories."

Sadiqi knew how to use a situation to his advantage. He'd shaken the professor. Knocked him off balance. And having administered that jolt, he now expected him to be more cooperative – sort of like a dog that had just received a good hiding from its master. "Could you perhaps tell me what Professor Caron did to deserve this reprimand?"

"Is this really necessary? It's not a legal question, it only concerns the Lodge. It'll seem unimportant to you."

The expression on Sadiqi's face said *Try me.*

The professor was up against a wall. He wasn't going anywhere until the cop got what he wanted. Trouvé was going to have to elaborate. The first sentence was the hardest to get out. "It's all tied up with yesterday's events at Val-de-Grace." After that, the ideas flowed in a sort of confessional catharsis. He explained how the news of the Prime Minister's death had seeped through the previous morning and how Toni had contested the official coverage. "She also mentioned that Pierre had been at Val-de-Grace. It all seemed very unlikely if de Chanterelle had died from a drug overdose. And when Pierre arrived, he confirmed that the death probably hadn't been accidental. In fact he did more than simply confirm that impression, he strutted it round the office."

Sadiqi's gaze bore into the professor. "What do you mean?"

"Pierre was in unusually good spirits. In fact he was downright jubilant. As far as he was concerned de Chanterelle's death was good news for his projects. He was convinced that the story of the anaesthetic poisoning was a cover-up and that somehow the quarries were implicated in the Prime Minister's death – which meant the government would finally wake up to the potential threat posed by the network."

Although Sadiqi couldn't see what was so serious in what he was being told, Trouvé was obviously uncomfortable. "So far I don't see what he's done to harm the brotherhood. Other than being callous."

"So far there's nothing. But you're right, I didn't like his attitude. It wasn't a normal reaction. It wasn't a disinterested attitude, if you see what I mean. When a Prime Minister dies you usually feel mildly happy or sad depending on your political leanings, your political memories of that person. Perhaps a touch of sympathy for the spouse and children. Pierre's reaction wasn't like that. He was ecstatic and I wanted to know why."

Trouvé broke off as if he had just said something of the utmost importance. If he had, Sadiqi had missed it. The cop stared at the professor. Was he going to have to give the spiel all over again about how important his testimony was? Fortunately, the professor sensed that his explanation had been insufficient. He sighed before getting to his feet and motioning to Sadiqi to follow him into his own office next door. Toni ambled along behind, but hung back, doing her best to keep out of everyone's way.

If the inspector had been wondering what could be said in Trouvé's office that couldn't be said in Caron's, his doubts didn't last long. In the next room the professor headed straight for the windowsill, which was almost entirely obscured by piles of thick photocopied documents. PhD theses. Reports. The odd textbook. It was true academic disarray. Sadiqi briefly fantasized that maybe Trouvé would magically produce a copy of Caron's report from the muddle of papers.

To his amazement, that's exactly what he did.

60

After shuffling through the documents, displacing two or three massive volumes, Trouvé pulled out a thick report with the Senate seal stamped at the top of the page and small print across the center reading '*Subterranean Safety in Paris: Strategies for Palliating Security Weaknesses*' followed a few centimeters down the page by the words 'from the office of Senator J. Clavreul.'

Sadiqi had to make a conscious effort to stop himself from tearing the document out of the professor's hands. "This is the report Caron wrote for Senator Clavreul."

"Yes. Pierre spent several months last year on close professional terms with the Senator." There was a definite ring of disgust in the professor's voice.

"You had a problem with their collaboration?"

Behind his beard Trouvé screwed up his face in distaste. "I thought Pierre was treading on dangerous ground by getting involved with the Senator."

"Why?"

"Like most self-respecting people, I don't much approve Senator Clavreul."

"Enough people approve of him to ensure he has a seat in the Senate and his party takes 15% of the votes at most elections."

Now back in his own office, Trouvé had regained some of his scholarly composure. He crossed from the windowsill to his desk and sank into his swivel chair. A slight shrug of his shoulders expressed his impotence to right the wrongs of his compatriots. "We live in a country where double-digit unemployment has become structural. Where politicians born into wealthy families tell people that if they work hard enough, they'll emerge victorious. People don't believe it anymore. They know that jobs are scarce. They know that if they have a job, they're unlikely to get a raise. We're told that inflation is negligible but the official statistics don't take into account the price of fuel, housing or taxes. They also underestimate the share of basic foodstuffs in household budgets. Mainstream politicians have lost all credibility through years of fiddling statistics to suit their own short-term objectives. They've isolated a large chunk of the population that feels excluded from economic growth. In their isolation those people are looking for easy answers. Someone they can point a finger at. Foreigners, immigrants... Clavreul provides them with that. Unfortunately it's just another type of political strategy. He brews up problems based on lies."

The professor spoke with the confidence of someone in the habit of explaining his opinions publicly, even on the most sensitive issues. No doubt he and Sadiqi would have seen eye to eye on matters regarding the senator. But that wasn't why the cop had asked to see him. The interview was drifting too far away from the case. Nothing had been said yet about what Caron had done to offend Trouvé and his Grand Master. "So what happened? Did Caron use the report to uphold views the Masons disagreed with, or something like that?"

"No, not really. The Brotherhood doesn't have any specific political ideology. Brothers are free to think and vote as they choose. However, it's true that Pierre's attachment to the senator struck me as dangerous. Pierre isn't..." The sadness had returned to Trouvé's features. He took a deep breath before correcting himself, "Pierre wasn't a strongly political person. He could be very ingenuous. He didn't understand politics. Not really. You see, he was a practical person. He took things at face value. He knew the quarries by heart and that intimacy led him to the conclusion that they were dangerous, and that network security needed reinforcing. As much as I disagreed with that vision, I respected it because I knew it was based on in-depth knowledge. However, I don't believe Pierre understood that people like Clavreul latch on to his theories for completely different reasons. They're defending an ideology by weaponizing fear. They're dividing society into factions so that they can lead the way for those they consider righteous."

As someone who had seen all the active files on terrorist threats in and around Paris, Sadiqi had a damn clear idea where reality ended and psychosis took over. He was also convinced that people like the senator took advantage of that fracture line to frighten the average guy-in-the-street. "Basically you think Clavreul was trying to exploit popular fear of terrorism in order to reinforce his own power base."

"Yes, I do. And that's why I didn't like to see Pierre spending time with him. I thought he was laying himself open to mishandling. Manipulation."

In light of the investment statements Sadiqi had found he wasn't convinced just how good an analysis this was. Caron hadn't been as naïve as Trouvé assumed. In fact, it sounded as if Trouvé had been blinded by his friendship with the IGC director. "So what's the conclusion then? You have a copy of the report. Was he being manipulated or not? Did he exaggerate the terrorist risk in order to help Clavreul?"

"As far as our lodge is concerned, the problem isn't that Pierre exaggerated the risks. The problem is that he told Clavreul things that had absolutely no bearing on catacomb security." The professor was choosing his words carefully, doing his best to make his statements as understandable as possible. Presumably this meant he was getting to the crux of the matter. "He knew perfectly well that he was behaving recklessly – that he was giving the senator access to information he shouldn't have. So Pierre tried to hide some of that information from me; to keep me in the dark about what exactly he had said to the senator."

"I thought he gave you a copy of the report."

Trouvé made a face like he'd been sucking lemons. "He gave me a copy of the report because he knew he couldn't hide it from me. He wanted to placate me."

"But he didn't succeed."

"Oh, he did. Certainly. At first. When I first read the report I didn't notice anything surprising. It was just filled with Pierre's usual concerns. *'The quarries pose a potential security threat; they should be filled in.'* But yesterday, when I saw him so happy, I got the report out to check exactly what he'd written about Val-de-Grace. I remembered he'd said something about the possibility of a head of state being killed there. And sure enough, that was Scenario 4.4. Head of state undergoes surgery at Val-de-Grace; terrorists access the hospital through the quarries and assassinate him. Inspector, I don't know what happened at Val-de-Grace yesterday. I have no way of knowing whether the rumors of assassination are true or not, but the coincidence struck me as disturbing. It renewed my interest in the report. So I turned to Scenario 4.5 to see what other fears of Pierre's might come true." As the professor spoke, Sadiqi flipped through the document to the next section, his anxiety growing. "It mentioned the possibility of certain schools, most notably Montaigne High School, being the victim of chemical attacks via the quarries."

Hiding his thoughts and emotions was second-nature to Sadiqi. He could look relaxed even when his blood was racing or pretend to have all the time in the world even when he was up against a deadline. But the information Trouvé was feeding him was stretching this ability. He had also noticed Toni, at the back of the room, suddenly snap to attention at the mention of Montaigne being attacked.

"And scenario 4.6?" the cop asked, now glued to the edge of his chair.

Trouvé frowned. "That's the whole problem. That's why I got angry. There was no Scenario 4.6."

The sense of anti-climax was terrible. Sadiqi felt cheated. "I don't understand?"

"Pierre tricked me. He gave me a copy of his report but he left out a part. The chapters skipped from 4.5 to 4.7. No 4.6. You see, Inspector, Pierre knew I didn't like Clavreul's politics. I'd made it quite clear from the beginning that I believed he was on a dangerous footing by working with that brand of politician. So in order to reassure me, he played the open book; he gave me a copy of his report. Only, what he gave me was redacted. You could say censored. There was a sub-chapter missing."

"What was missing?"

"That's what I wanted to know. That's what I asked him yesterday."

"And what was his answer?"

In spite of the way he sank comfortably back into his chair, there was no doubt that the professor was upset. "The chapter dealt with the use of the quarries by unauthorized groups."

This was finally it. What Sadiqi had been waiting for. "And perhaps the Freemasons were one of those unauthorized groups," he prompted.

Trouvé stared at his hands then readjusted his tie. For a moment Sadiqi thought he was going to refuse to say anything more but then he shrugged as if to say that it wasn't going to make much difference. "Our lodge was one of the first Freemasons' lodges ever created in France. It has always used the quarries for part of its initiation ritual. I'm not giving much away if I tell you that part of the rites includes a walk through a dark winding passage. It's supposed to give the initiate the impression he's walking towards his own grave. Then the candidate is led to a room, a place we call the *Chamber of Reflection*, where he's left to mull over what joining the Brotherhood means."

"That's what was in Chapter 4.6?" Sadiqi said, unable to hide his disappointment. It was hardly a nightmare scenario. A few middle-aged men meeting in some pre-designated underground gallery on a Saturday night to consider the human condition. He got up and moved toward the professor, propping himself on the edge of the desk. "That's it?"

The professor stretched back in his chair as if he were trying to distance himself from the cop. "The point Pierre was making was that unauthorized groups can easily access the quarries for organized events – nefarious or otherwise. If you can hold a disco or a lodge meeting underground, you can also hold a terrorist cell meeting."

"And that's why you complained to your Grand Master?"

"Absolutely. You have to understand. The missing section didn't simply make a passing reference to Freemasonry. It gave detailed information about it. Pierre gave the name of the lodge along with the names of some of our high-ranking members. Plus some indication as to the chamber's whereabouts."

Sadiqi wondered if the professor was bullshitting him. Was this all that had been done to merit Trouvé freaking out and going to complain to the Grand Master?

"Now do you see why I said the issue wouldn't interest the police but that the Grand Master had to be notified? All Masons are under oath to keep the rituals of the Craft secret. And to keep the names of Brothers secret. Giving away that information made Pierre unworthy to remain in the Brotherhood. Not to mention the fact that the indiscretion was made for personal advancement. In order to achieve professional aims."

"His professional aim being to close down the catacombs forever under the pretext that they pose a security risk."

"I think there was more to it than that. I think the Senator had proposed that if the President accepted their project, Pierre would be named head of a new commission in charge of redesigning subterranean Paris."

That made sense. Just like insider trading, Caron would have stood to gain a great deal professionally if his plan had been given the go-ahead. All the same, the cop still wasn't convinced that Brother Trouvé had come clean about all the details. "Are you sure you're telling me everything? Are you sure there wasn't something more in the report? Perhaps Caron suggested your lodge was involved in subversive activity?"

"Don't be absurd."

"I don't see what's absurd about it. You said Caron named some specific lodge members. Why some rather than others? Why not name them all?"

"It's got nothing to do with subversive activity. It's just that Pierre loved to name-drop. The names he gave were all people in the public eye. Politicians, academics, celebrities from the world of art and literature."

Although this made sense, it didn't help Sadiqi figure out what the link was between the quarries, the Freemasons and what was going on underground. He circled backward. "Tell me more about this underground place your lodge uses. Where is it exactly?"

That was more than Trouvé could take. "Inspector!" he snapped. "I've just told you it exists. That's more than I should have done. Not even Pierre went so far as to give the gallery's exact location."

"Well, I need to know."

"I don't see what bearing our Chamber of Reflections' whereabouts could possibly have on a murder investigation."

Over the years Sadiqi had sealed himself deeper and deeper into his own world. Focusing sharply on the essentials of an investigation sometimes became an obstacle to communication. Now, it suddenly struck him that Trouvé really didn't understand who he was or what he was investigating. And no matter how hush-hush this case was supposed to be, there was no point in trying to hide the truth from someone unlikely to swallow the official line. "I'm sorry. I think you may be under the misapprehension that I'm from the homicide brigade. I thought Lieutenant Podesta had filled you in: We work for counter-terrorism. We're investigating possible terrorist activity in the catacombs."

The silence in the room was total. It took several seconds for Trouvé's face to migrate through the full spectrum of expressions from adamant to bewildered. "I don't understand. Since when does the anti-terrorist brigade investigate murder cases?"

There were days when life was an uphill battle. Sadiqi hated it when he had to spell everything out – when every single detail had to be explained and annotated for the people around him. "Your colleague is dead. Murdered. At the same time, I've got major concerns about security breaches underground. Unsafe catacombs and yet no head of the IGC to discuss them with. So, was Caron's death a coincidence or was your colleague killed in order to create an information black hole? Are you following me?"

The arms that had been drawn across Trouvé's chest tightened further.

"So where is this gallery?" Sadiqi repeated.

"I can't tell you."

The cop coughed out an unsmiling laugh. "You can make this easy or you can make it hard."

"The lodge has protected that secret for centuries," Trouvé replied with timid determination.

"You said yourself that Caron had committed indiscretions. Perhaps he shared its location."

"I sincerely hope he didn't go that far."

"Two sources today have confirmed that Caron took Clavreul down to the quarries. What makes you think he wouldn't have gone the extra mile and shown the senator your chamber?"

Far from backing down, Trouvé had locked Sadiqi's gaze. "He wouldn't have done that."

But Sadiqi couldn't shake that vision of the senator decked out in catacomb coveralls. And if the senator had been taken exploring below ground, then maybe other people knew about the chamber, too. The inspector had used up all his patience. "I don't think you're listening. I'm increasingly concerned that Caron's report is being used not as a cautionary notice but as a blueprint for terror activity. The current security situation compels you to share everything you know about section 4.6, including the location of your chamber. Otherwise your gallery could become a terror target."

Trouvé was shaking his head in tiny but determined crisp movements. "That's beyond unlikely."

"You just don't get it, do you?" The last words were laced with acid. "You don't realize that people are going to be killed if I don't find the link between Caron's report and what's happening right now in the catacombs," his voice boomed as he brought a fist down on a pile of papers, sending documents tumbling everywhere.

Far from letting himself be convinced to break his vows to the Brotherhood, Trouvé rose and moved towards the door. "I've told you everything I can; now I have to get back to my conference. We're expecting the President later today, and I need to check that everything goes smoothly."

That was one affront too many. It was Sadiqi who told people when their interviews were over; not the other way around. In any case, the cop was more than a little worried the professor was walking him down that proverbial road to hell paved with good intentions. Moving like the wind, he was blocking the door before Trouvé had got halfway across the office. "I don't think you're listening, Professor. If you don't tell me what I need to know, I'll have you arrested for withholding information. Then you really won't be able to enjoy your conference."

Trouvé looked haggard and uncomfortably conscious of his limited space for manoeuvre. "I can't show you the gallery we use for our Chamber," he muttered, as if this statement might actually be the password that would gain him clearance through the door and back to freedom.

"This is absurd. You say your lodge has been using the catacombs for hundreds of years. If that's true, you can't tell me that, in all that time, a few non-Mason cataphiles haven't stumbled across one of your rituals. Letting a few more people in on the secret is hardly going to change much."

"I just can't." The worry lines on Trouvé's forehead might have expressed any number of things: Regret. Powerlessness. A plea for indulgence. Whatever was going through Trouvé's mind, there was only one possible solution. Sadiqi would have called it drowning the fish. Toni would have called it passing the buck. Either way it was the same thing; Trouvé would get someone else to take responsibility for what had to be done. "I think you'd better talk with the Grand Master."

The cop recognized the side step for what it was. It took the briefest of calls for Trouvé to organize the meeting with the head of *Pythagoras and Euclid Lodge*. Confident that he'd finally satisfied the inspector, he reached out to shake hands and leave.

Except the cop ignored the hand floating in midair. "I've not finished, yet."

61

"Would you mind taking a quick look at this?" Sadiqi asked, pulling his phone out of his pocket and turning it towards the professor again.

Trouvé looked at the screen and read the words with an audible mumble: "All was dark save one glimmering light in the east. To what did the darkness allude? Even to the darkness of death. There will be fireworks above the Temple on New Year's Eve. Darkness will triumph over light. The songs will change to screams."

"So what do you make of it? As a Mason," the cop asked.

The professor's face twisted into a frown as he shook his head slowly. The atmosphere wasn't getting any more comfortable. "Not very much."

It looked like Trouvé was going to make Sadiqi drag every single scrap of information out, bit by bit. "No idea what the 'temple' could refer to? Or 'New Year's Eve'?"

The professor raised his hands in a shrug of helplessness. "I could make any number of guesses."

"Which would be top of your list?" Sadiqi wondered what was so damned difficult. It sounded like a straightforward question. "Presumably there's only one New Year's Eve, even for Freemasons."

"Actually there are several, depending on which lodge you belong to. Some lodges recognize the civil calendar year. Others use March 1st or still others Rosh Hashanah in late-September."

"All those dates are far off. I doubt this message has come with three to nine months' warning." Sadiqi didn't need a demonstration of Cartesian dialectic; he needed answers.

"No," Trouvé agreed. "That's why I think the most likely date is St. John's Day.

There was an intake of breath from the back of the room as Toni recognized the looming danger. St. John's Day was the national holiday back in Quebec. She knew the date well. It had marked the first day of summer holidays all through her childhood. It had taken on new meaning now that she was a catacomb specialist.

"When's that?" Sadiqi asked, showing the first sign of noticing the student.

"The Festival of John the Baptist. June 24th. In fact most celebrations would take place on the evening of the 23rd," she said, the words escaping in a flood. "The Patron saint of quarrymen, masons, and – I now assume – Freemasons..."

The deadline hit the cop hard.

This case was already covered in blood. The messages from Ng suggested it was going to get bloodier. Sadiqi had known the deadline was near, but June 23rd was only two days away. Two days and no leads. He needed the case to start falling into place. Immediately. "And what about the Temple? Could it refer to your chamber of reflection?"

Trouvé grimaced. "Our Chamber is just a tiny gallery. There would be no point in attacking it. The Chamber is empty most of the time. There wouldn't be anyone to harm. In any case, it's not a temple. Freemasons don't have temples, we have lodges."

"Well, what would a Mason refer to as a temple?"

"The Temple is an abstract idea for us. We talk about the *Temple of Humanity* as a construct. It's the Freemason's job to make the world a better place. To improve humanity if you like."

Those were laudable aims but Sadiqi was certain whoever he was up against wasn't simply thinking of causing abstract destruction. Someone was planning on very real and concrete murder. "Maybe the message was written by someone who isn't a Mason himself. An anti-Mason who's not privy to all the subtleties of your lexicology..."

"Yes, yes," Trouvé agreed. "And they've confused the terms. In which case the message could be referring to one of the main national lodges. Perhaps the Grand Orient. It's the biggest in France."

"Rue Cadet. The 9th Arrondissement," the cop said sceptically. He knew the place well. A number of high-ranking French politicians were members. But the 9th district was miles away from the Latin

Quarter. "It's more likely the reference to darkness triumphing over Light refers to the catacombs. We've been trying to think of a possible temple in the Latin Quarter. Nearer the catacombs."

Trouvé frowned. "No. There's nothing around here."

Toni felt disappointed that he hadn't spontaneously named the Pantheon.

"No ideas at all?" the cop prompted.

Trouvé shook his head. "No."

The answer was unadulterated lie. Caron had already allowed too many secrets to seep beyond the bounds of the Brotherhood. Trouvé refused to add to those indiscretions. He certainly wasn't going to discuss the 'temple' he was involved with. Besides, there was no point. The dates didn't match.

Sadiqi could sense the professor's hesitation. And he'd had enough of it. Over the years, he'd heard a lot of crazy stuff during interviews. But secret lodges and obscure rituals... He'd seldom had the misfortunate of listening to such a load of garbage coming from someone this erudite. "I'm going to ask you one last time to share any information about either your chamber or the possible interpretation of the message."

Trouvé shook his head.

"The chamber's location?" Sadiqi asked, again.

"I have nothing more to add," Trouvé repeated.

"Then I'm arresting you for obstruction of justice."

A look of horror washed across the professor's features. "But I have to get back to my conference. They'll be waiting for me."

"We're rarely as indispensable as we like to think. I'm sure the debates will go just as smoothly without you." Sadiqi pulled out his phone to request a car to take Trouvé in.

62

It took Sadiqi a few minutes to accompany Trouvé to the squad car that came to take him into custody. When he got back to the office, he found Toni flipping through the *Clavreul Report*. She certainly hadn't missed the opportunity to get her hands on that when it was left on the desk.

But she tossed it back onto the windowsill nonchalantly and followed the inspector into Caron's office, watching as he picked up the blue sash that was still lying on the desk. "I've known Trouvé to be more helpful," she commented.

"What?" he asked, absently caressing the fabric, then gently folding the sash and stretching his arm to push it to the back of the desk where they'd found.

"Do you think Trouvé's Chamber is the temple?"

The cop released the sash then ran his hand over the inside of the drawer to check if there was anything else pushed in there that he'd missed. "I don't know." And this was true. He didn't have any idea what the temple referred to. In fact he didn't have much idea what the Ng message meant at all.

As if she'd heard his thoughts, Toni added: "And the bit about the fireworks? Does that mean gun fire? A bomb?"

"I can't discuss this with you." His voice was distant and now his fingers collided with something small and cold shoved deep in the back of the drawer. He caught the object and drew it out.

It was a key. Old and rusted, made of what looked like iron. It could have been straight out of a children's storybook, designed with two deep bits to open the lock and a huge looping bow, with a brass chain forming a 'B' hooked into it.

Sadiqi glanced over his shoulder at Toni, perched in the sunlight. "Any idea what this is?"

She rocked forward and plucked it out of his hand, gently flipping it over, feeling its weight in the palm of her hand. The tenderness she showed the object could mean only one thing: this again was catacomb paraphernalia.

"I'd say it's the key to the quarry entrance in rue Bonaparte. I couldn't swear to it. I've only used that entrance once. Caron took me; I'm pretty sure this was the key."

She handed it back to him. And this time she didn't even look particularly surprised when he slipped the key into his pocket. Probably because her thoughts were miles away, still focused on her questions from a few moments earlier. "Why are you so concerned about Chapter 4.6? What about 4.7?" she asked, drawing the conversation back to where it had left off. There was a quiver of uncertainty in her voice that made Sadiqi look up.

"What?"

"I looked at the report. You asked Trouvé about Chapter 4.6, but you didn't ask him about 4.7: The Von Choltitz Scenario. If you're sure scenario 4.6 is about to play out then 4.7 can't be far off either."

"Von Choltitz? You mean the risk that someone might somehow manage to mine the quarries with explosives."

"And by doing so, cause a shift in the upper layers of limestone. Which would create huge sinkholes."

And kill hundreds of people, the cop thought to himself. Of all the possible scenarios this was the most horrendous. Which was precisely why he considered it the most likely. It was the plan that would cause the most damage – kill the most people.

"I hope you realize it's not possible. It's just crazy babblings," she continued. "Von Choltitz was able to plan it because the Nazis had control of the city and by extension the quarries. But it couldn't happen today. It wouldn't be possible to mine the tunnels with explosives without someone noticing."

It couldn't happen. It wouldn't be possible. Two phrases Sadiqi had stopped using years ago. He just didn't think in those terms anymore. Experience had taught him that nothing was impossible. The world was a violent place. And people were willing to expend great efforts to carry out depraved plans.

The sun shone through the window so that he could see only her silhouette as she leaned against the windowsill. Despite his best intentions, he couldn't keep away. He got up and strode over, brushed a stray strand of hair off her cheek and attempted to read the expression on her face. Concern for her darling quarries? Concern for potential victims of whatever was headed their way? Fear for herself, young and alone in a country on the brink of Armaggedon? He wasn't sure what was written there.

The world had become such a complicated place.

When he was in university, a student's biggest worry on a Friday night was whether or not they remembered the condoms. Her generation lived with the knowledge that they might be taken hostage in a nightclub and mown down with Kalashnikovs. Or blown to smithereens in a city-wide bombing.

63

The cop shouldn't have been caught off guard by Podesta's arrival. After all, it was Sadiqi who'd given him the address office number at *FranceTech*. Still he was taken aback when the words, "*Chef*! Great news!" rang out behind.

Podesta's look of satisfaction faltered as his boss turned and stepped towards the desk, revealing the young woman standing behind him. The anticipated great news was replaced by silence.

"Would you give us a moment," Sadiqi said to Toni, nodding towards the door. Before she'd made her way to the mezzanine in the outer office, he'd switched back to his usual terse manner with his lieutenant. "So, what have you got?"

Even though Podesta would have loved to find out what the cataphile from Val-de-Grace was doing pushed up against his boss, he knew better than to ask questions. "We've got a possible ID on Trémont's lead." His voice was a near whisper. The news he was about to share was sensitive and he wasn't comfortable with the girl in the outer office. "I got a cross reference using the senator's name. It came up in a press report from the Ministry of Armies' magazine."

Finally some good news. Sadiqi perked up. "Rossignol or Nightingale?"

"Whichever you prefer. He answers to both."

"Stop being cryptic. I get enough bullshit from the witnesses. I don't need it from you."

The boss' words washed over Podesta like water off a duck. He perched himself on the front of the desk and lay his file on the bureau. "Paul Rossignol is a legionnaire."

Toni had left the door to Caron's office open and although Sadiqi's colleague was speaking very softly, she was able to catch most of what they were saying. And if she understood correctly, one of the suspects they were looking for was from the French Foreign Legion. She guessed that might be a first for the two officers who were, most probably, much more familiar with Islamist extremist profiles.

Podesta dropped into the chair where Trouvé had been sitting. Today's suit was pale grey as opposed to the previous day's beige, but just as dapper. "This guy arrived at Legion headquarters in Aubagne in February 1999. His fingerprints were clean, so they signed him on."

Toni was only vaguely familiar with the Foreign Legion. She knew that big efforts had been made to clean up its reputation. The folklore was that the Legion was a mercenary army overflowing with criminals fleeing their country of origin. That had changed. Today, recruits were supposed to provide ID. And theoretically papers and identities were checked. But she also had a pretty good understanding of how French bureaucracy worked and she wasn't so sure that some underpaid civil servant in the outbacks of Marseille would be doing the due diligence on every candidate who wandered into the recruiting

office. After all, not everyone was willing to die for a foreign army –
perhaps the Legion couldn't always be picky about who it accepted.

Back in Caron's office, Sadiqi was reaching the same conclusion.
"So I'm guessing *Rossignol* isn't his real name. It's the name given to
him by the Legion."

While she listened, Toni typed away on her laptop and pulled up a
screen that explained the Legion's recruiting process. What she
discovered was a curious explanation of how recruits were stripped of
their old identity and provided with new names. Apparently joining the
Legion was like being baptized; it was the start of a new life. Scanning
down the page, she was reassured to see that the authorities
fingerprinted anyone who came in and cross-referenced the prints with
Interpol. If it turned out the recruit was wanted for murder or grievous
bodily harm, he'd be turned in to the police. If he was wanted for theft
or traffic violations, he'd get in. A lot of the guys in the Legion were
wanted for petty offenses like alimony non-payment.

Toni's brain lingered for a fraction of a second on the thought of a
fraternity of warriors who preferred to go and face death on the
frontline rather than send alimony payments to their wife and kids. But
Podesta's voice quickly drew her back to the moment. "So John Doe
showed up and spent his three-day test period at Aubagne while the
authorities cleared his prints. During that time he proved what a good
little soldier he was. Strong, resistant, excellent at following orders.
Not only that, he had a speciality: he was a night owl. He wasn't at all
bothered when the commanding officers hauled the recruits out of bed
at three in the morning for unscheduled wargames. He just trooped on.
He enjoyed working in the dark. He enjoyed being out of sync."

"What's your point?" Sadiqi asked.

"Well, don't you see? If Aubagne accepted him, he was going to
need a new identity. His legionnaire name. His fellow recruits gave
him one. They nicknamed him 'Rossignol' – because of his nocturnal
stamina. The 'Nightingale' for his English-speaking buddies. When
Interpol gave the all-clear on his prints, Aubagne kept the nickname. It
was a joke."

Looking particularly pleased with himself, anyone entering the
room would have thought Podesta had just delivered the best comedy
routine of the year. Sadiqi wasn't laughing. He wasn't even smiling.
"N.G. Nightingale / Rossignol. And do we have any idea where this
English-speaking Monsieur Rossignol was really born?"

"Nothing definite although there's some indication he's probably
Irish. Or Northern Irish. In 2005, Scotland Yard requested DNA

samples from a number of legionnaires in connection with bombings in Northern Ireland in the late 90s early 2000s."

"IRA?"

"IRA. Real IRA. Both probably. I don't think he's too fussy who he works for. Monsieur Rossignol was among the names linked to no less than four separate incidents, including one attack that took place on a busy shopping street where thirty people were killed. Anyway, the French government refused to cooperate. They said that Paul Rossignol was a French citizen and that he wouldn't be asked to undergo testing unless the Brits provided conclusive evidence."

"But he's not a French citizen," Toni thought to herself, scrolling down the page. And again the answer pixelized on her screen:

LEGIO PATRIA NOSTRA. The Legion is our homeland. That was their motto and that was the deal. You could come from anywhere in the world. Once you were officially recruited into the Legion, you were part of the family, whatever your roots. You signed on for five years. And if you made it to the end of those five years without getting killed, the French government honored you with the supreme gift of French nationality in return for your blood, sweat, loss of limbs and possible death.

Toni would have liked to think it was insane. But she knew it wasn't. The set-up made a sad sort of sense. It was a system that preyed on the misfortune and poverty of others. Life was tough in a lot of places. There were plenty of people knocking on the door, willing to go to war for a few years if it would buy them a brighter future afterwards. Eastern Europeans who would rather be French than ex-Soviet Block nationals. Africans who'd grown up surrounded by famine and war. Five short years of sweat no doubt seemed like a good deal if that was all you'd ever known. Of course, the trick was to survive the five years because those guys were sent to the frontline. Wherever France had signed up to send troops into serious action, she usually sent in her legionnaires. They were cannon fodder.

As much as Toni was angered by the injustice, she did understand the logic.

As did Sadiqi. "So I'm assuming this guy had got in over his head in terrorist or criminal circuits in Ireland, and was looking to start a new life."

Podesta considered momentarily before offering an opinion. "I think Rossignol was looking for more than just a new identity."

"What makes you say that?"

"Because he didn't just spend five years and then clear out. He did 18."

Toni risked a glance into the inner office and watched as Sadiqi stretched backwards in the late Pierre Caron's chair and laced his fingers behind his head. She could sense the thought echoing through his mind: Eighteen years. That wasn't good. Eighteen years meant this psycho had enjoyed the job. "And what did he get for 18 years' service?"

"A pension," Podesta smirked.

The smirk was easily interpreted. A pension wasn't much of a trade-off for someone who had put his life on the line for 18 years. But the résumé was helpful. It was all starting to make sense. Sadiqi was finally getting a sense of the guy he was looking for. The pieces were falling into place: He was looking for a mercenary. A paid killer, who after serving Ireland then France was now working for someone else – a private interest, presumably.

Podesta opened the blue plastic folder he was holding and started shuffling through it. After about half a dozen pages he came to a sheet with an official emblem at the top that looked like a royal lily but was in fact supposed to be a grenade with seven flames exploding from it. "There's more," he said, scanning down the paper. "He was from the Second Company."

"Which means?" Sadiqi mumbled.

This time Podesta didn't need to refer back to his paper. He'd already set the information to memory. "The Second Company is specialized in providing back-up for infantry regiments in difficult terrain. They do a lot of work effectuating incursions behind enemy lines; blowing up enemy reinforcements. He's seen it all. Macedonia, Ivory Coast, Mali, Afghanistan.

"Afghanistan?"

"That's right. His last posting was going through caves at 7000 meters above sea level, flushing out Al Qaeda. That's my point. The Second Company is specialized in mountain terrain. Working in caves. Working in dark stone environments... Bombing stone."

The thought of a homicidal mercenary wandering the Paris quarries hit Toni like a tonne of marble. The idea of cataphiles being killed by someone with this guy's profile was basically fratricide.

For Sadiqi, on the contrary, each new thread of information, no matter how depressing, lifted a burden from his shoulders and lightened his load. Each new detail brought him closer to getting his enemy's profile. He now knew who he was looking for. He also knew how dangerous he was. This wasn't some self-proclaimed teenage terrorist who'd trained in abandoned suburban lots. This was a professional soldier who had received top training and years of practice perfecting his technique.

"Incidentally," Podesta continued, "if Rossignol is really the same person the British were trying to extradite, he's a bomb specialist." As the information compounded into a coherent portrait, the lieutenant flipped to the next page of his file. "And there's something else. He retired last September. But just after leaving service, he got sick. Came down with some tropical disease – supposedly related to the countries he'd been travelling in."

"Why *supposedly*?" Sadiqi asked.

"Well a stint in a military hospital would have been very convenient if he'd been preparing plans that involved that hospital."

"*Merde!*"

What seemed obvious to the Frenchmen was more obscure to the Canadian. "I don't get it," she whispered under her breath as her fingers whizzed over the keys. And then there it was on the screen: Soldiers get sent to exotic destinations. They pick up diseases that aren't well-known in France. They need specialist attention. The military hospitals were the most skilled at treating tropical disease.

"Rossignol spent 6 weeks at Val-de-Grace late last fall," Podesta confirmed.

An expression of disgust was now chiselled across Sadiqi's features. "I bet he knows the grounds off by heart."

Podesta put the papers back in the file and slid the dossier across the desk before adding, "And probably not so coincidentally, he basically disappeared from circulation as soon as he was discharged from hospital. His last credit card payment was made in Paris on December 18th. A restaurant in the 9th arrondissement. Since then, nothing's come out of his bank account. No rent. No nothing."

Sadiqi rubbed his hands over his eyes as if trying to brush away the bleak sketch that had just been drawn. "Do we have a photo of this guy?" Before he'd finished asking, Podesta was sliding a photo out.

The likeness was nothing less than what the inspector had expected. Sadiqi reached into his pocket for the photocopy of the IGC authorization card made out to Jean Brune. Despite the poor quality copies of both documents, there was no doubt about it. The basic features were easily recognizable: the snub nose, the cold eyes, the hollow cheeks… It was the same guy.

He studied the paper, filing away both the man's physical picture and his biographic profile, placing all the information in the right boxes and scanning for holes in his knowledge. "Anything to link him to the anthrax?"

Anthrax, Toni thought. There it was. Confirmation of what she had read that morning; and scenario 4.5 in Caron's report. What was happening to this city? She was sitting there, watching two men calmly discussing bombings, mercenaries and anthrax.

While the world grew darker, Podesta continued with his next indictment. "It's a hard call, but it looks likely there's a link. Of course, officially, as a French outfit, the Legion doesn't use bio-weapons. But Rossignol was involved in one raid in Afghanistan where French forces were thought to be at risk of a non-conventional attack. It's more than likely his regiment received special bio-weapons training before that campaign – for self-defense purposes. Either way, he's certainly used to dealing with sensitive materials. Not that it really matters. From where I'm standing, I'm quite sure that with the right instructions and equipment this guy'd be able to do basically anything."

"A legionnaire who's survived 18 years of active service would have to be resourceful."

"That about sums it up."

Eighteen years. Sadiqi thought about it. That was about as long as he'd been working in counter terrorism. That was plenty of time to see a whole heap of action and learn a shitload of useful techniques and tactics.

"Like I said. He retired recently. That's how I tracked him down. He received a medal for distinguished service... Which leads to our next point. Senator Clavreul was invited to the award ceremony plus the cocktail party that followed." Podesta shuffled through his file and handed Sadiqi a sheet of paper with a page of internet print-out complete with a photo of their man in full dress uniform shaking hands with the senator.

"When was that?"

"September."

"Anything else to link the two of them?"

Podesta wobbled his head in a yes-and-no motion. "That's where it gets interesting. There's no explicit connection. No party membership. No direct communication between the two. But Paul Rossignol has been active on a wide variety of extreme-right social media for a long time. Nothing recent, but plenty if you go back to last year and beyond. Biological racism. Repatriation of immigrants. Anti-semitism. White genocide theories. The standard litany."

Sadiqi stared at the picture of the two men Podesta had just handed him. He felt more than contempt and anger for both of them. He felt hatred.

It wasn't clear how the whole thing fit together, but one thing was sure: The timing was right. The Nightingale had been decorated for service to the nation. Then he had done an about-face and gone into service against that very same fatherland. He had been beautifully responsive to all the training he had received from the Legion but that elite French training was now being turned against France.

The cop hated the festering clichés that led his country into one cock up after another. The patriotic bullshit. Rossignol might have been one hell of a soldier but he was one fuck of a civilian. Staring at the photo from the file, comparing it with the photo on the IGC card, Sadiqi found himself wondering why the hell Caron had provided this guy with official authorization to roam unhindered in the catacombs. What had he and Clavreul been working towards?

64

The Nightingale slunk confidently along the cavelike corridor, the muffled sound of his footsteps against the beaten earth floor barely breaking the silence. In this land of perpetual darkness, he had a significant advantage over his opponents: he was working with night goggles while the police were still working with flashlights. The few times he'd been near either cops or cataphiles, he had seen the pinprick of their cap lamps well before they sensed his presence, which left him plenty of time to head in the opposite direction or duck down a side passage.

Today, however, he was using his edge to stalk.

There would be at least two guards up ahead. Possibly three. That was the intel. And so far all the intel had been spot on.

As he approached the point where the first guard was supposed to be stationed, he adopted a defensive stance. He took out his pistol and released the safety catch then flattened his back against the wall, letting the color of his dusty desert fatigues blend in with the mottled stone of the quarries. With veteran precision he eased himself along the next few meters, silent as death itself.

It was barely a minute before the first cop came into view. Of course the lighting the officer had been provided didn't allow him to see more than a dozen meters into the darkness. There was no chance he would notice the Nightingale.

Given the choice, the redhead would have preferred to ease up behind the man and bludgeon him. Avoid making things too messy. But the configuration of the quarry made that impossible. There was no way of approaching the guard from behind. No lateral galleries nearby. The Nightingale would have to fire instead. So those shots would have to be pinpoint accurate. It was essential the man was killed outright without leaving time to alert potential backup.

The Nightingale took aim with leisure. His target was wearing a miner's cap and a bullet-proof vest. Two useless pieces of material whereas a helmet might have saved his life.

As if he sensed death's presence the cop peered down the blackened corridor in the Nightingale's direction. It wasn't a good move. He'd just provided the legionnaire with a clear shot. The redhead fired a single bullet, aimed adroitly between the man's eyes.

The form slumped to the ground and the assassin moved forward. Part of the man's head was now missing, the remnants of brain and blood imprinted on the stone wall, the color blending in with the layers of graffiti.

The Nightingale dragged the body a few meters up a lateral dead end gallery where he let it collapse in a corner before returning to the spot where he'd left his backpack. *One down, two to go*, he thought as his hands slid over the straps of the bag that held the material for this final manoeuvre.

With the same stealth, he navigated through the tunnels until two cops were in view, about twenty meters ahead. Once again, their light system left them vulnerable. The Nightingale crouched down, out of sight. His two targets looked bored beyond belief. They had already been on duty for over two hours. These guys were on three-hour shifts. Three hours standing in a dark, empty hallway. Dangerously mind-numbing work. Enough to put anyone to sleep. And after over two hours hanging around with nothing to watch, not even some heels and skirts, their attention would be lagging.

The Nightingale indulged in a little last-minute re-think – just to make this interesting and keep his brain busy. Should he shoot them from here and get blood and brains all over the quarry again? Or should he sneak up from behind, knock them out first? It was a tricky call. Should he keep it easy or make it fun? He decided to make it fun. He turned into a parallel tunnel then threw a rock noisily onto the ground. Down the gallery one of the cops signaled to his colleague that he was going to check out the noise. The Nightingale smiled at the man's enthusiasm. After two hours doing nothing, the guy was happy for any distraction. At worst, he would be expecting to come face to face with a snot-nosed catacomb explorer he could frighten. He certainly wouldn't be expecting what was really awaiting him.

As the footsteps drew nearer, the Nightingale lifted his gun into the air, poised for the blow.

65

Until today, Rémi Podesta had always considered Sadiqi a faultless investigator. His attention to detail was systematically vindicated and his dedication to the service went beyond exemplary – it was basically mythical within police circles. Not an easy person to work for; but the right guy to have your back. More importantly, when tough decisions had to be made, Sadiqi could do it. Not everyone could think clearly when they were up against a gang of extremists with Kalashnikovs. Not many people had Sadiqi's remarkable combination of fiery coolness. And that was why Podesta just couldn't figure out what the hell his boss was doing bringing the young Canadian along to their interview with Clavreul.

The inspector sensed the storm of scepticism rumbling around the lieutenant. He'd noticed the furtive glances at Toni and the silence during the drive over. Usually it was impossible to get Podesta to shut up. Today, he hadn't said a word between the Luxembourg Gardens and the senator's apartment.

But justifying his decisions wasn't something Sadiqi had ever done in the past and he wasn't planning to start now. Whether Podesta could see it or not, Corrigan could help with Clavreul's interview; that was certain. For starters, she was the specialist they needed. She knew both the catacombs and Caron and she would be able to pick out any inconsistencies in the senator's words. She was there to help. To save time. Because the June 23rd deadline was very close. On top of that, despite the senator's righteous pandering to the religious right, he had quite the reputation as the ladies' man. Yet another example of his hypocrisy. Clavreul's first wife had been a *Playboy* fold and there had been a variety of unconfirmed rumors about his affairs with female parliamentary assistants. The cop suspected Toni's slim calves and plunging neckline would do wonders to loosen Clavreul's tongue. And that was the real reason why he'd asked her to come along.

"The senator will be with you in a moment," the maid said, showing them into the library then bustling off.

Of all the Paris districts, the 7ᵗʰ was the one Sadiqi liked least. He associated it with old money and hereditary distinction. It was a part of town filled with gilded ceilings and parquet floors but with little else to recommend it. There were no cinemas, no theaters, no good cafés and its few good restaurants tended towards over-priced classical.

But while Sadiqi felt defensive in this upper class haven and Podesta remarked to himself that the library was roughly the size of the entire apartment he occupied with his wife and two daughters, Toni couldn't help thinking she'd just caught a glimpse of heaven. When she was a kid, she'd dreamt of having a library. Her own. A real library. An entire room, filled with books, wall to wall, with a ladder on wheels that you could roll from one end to the other. And that's what this was. Straight out of *My Fair Lady*, only better because it was modern, with spotlights in the ceiling, sparkling white paintwork and brass railings. The room was enormous. It was built on two levels, with a small balcony around the mezzanine.

The opulence was tantalizing. If there was a library, there must also be dining-rooms, studies and possibly a conservatory or some sort of music room. The diversity of Paris would never cease to amaze her. Compared to her tiny bed-sit, Caron's apartment had seemed staggering by its wealth. But this was a whole new dimension.

"Do all politicians in France live like this?" she asked, gently sliding a leather bound first edition of Balzac's *Le Lys dans la vallée* out of its space on the nearest shelf.

"Only the ones who were born wealthy – which covers most of them," Sadiqi vented. "Most senators come from upper-class backgrounds: doctors, professors, lawyers. 15% of them are professional politicians and another 6% have no stated profession."

"No stated profession?"

"Landowners."

"Landowners running the country," Toni marvelled. "Wow. That so Old Europe."

"That's exactly what it is. Nineteenth century logic. Old money. Old corruption."

Toni raised her eyes from the book and noticed Sadiqi's arms drawn tightly across his chest, a look of loathing on his face. If they'd been alone she would have sidled up beside him to relieve some of the tension by running her hands over those gorgeous, strong arms. But that type of intimacy was out of the question with Podesta looking on. Instead she just tilted her head sideways and asked, "Is it all politicians you hate or just Clavreul?"

"There's a special place in hell for Clavreul," he said. This was a rich man who used the fears and frailties of the unemployed or underemployed to make himself richer. Clavreul and his party were tearing the country apart. Driving it to collective suicide. Creating contrived conflicts that circumvented the real problems facing the country by keeping the political aristocracy in place and making it impossible for the republican mechanisms to work properly.

Toni turned her attention back to the library. The dislike she felt for Clavreul was, no doubt, just as strong as Sadiqi's. But, unlike the cop, she wasn't ready to inflate her personal dislike into any apocalyptic generalization about the malevolence of wealth. On the contrary, opulence wasn't something she disdained but something she indulged in when given the chance. The gold leaf on the mouldings. The elegant furniture with luscious fabrics and gilt armrests. It was all tastefully indulgent.

Yet, although she recognized the signs of wealth, her attention was only lastingly ever drawn to the underworld. After checking a few of the volumes on the shelves she migrated towards a glass cabinet containing various military medals and paraphernalia along with some photos. Of course, it wasn't the medals that had caught her attention; it was the yellowing skull in the center of the display case.

Sadiqi wasn't sure whether he felt impressed or affronted by the way the Canadian made herself at home in the upper-class haven. Regardless, he realized that her open-mindedness made her more receptive to her surroundings. She could analyze without judging. Which was what he was supposed to be doing.

He ambled over to stand beside her and studied the objects in the glass case. "Probably some sick trophy from Algeria," he suggested, pointing at the skull. "The senator was a French commander during the Algerian War, when the colony fought for its independence. A lot of people think he may have exceeded his role as commander. There are rumors he was involved in torturing Algerian resistants." Toni could see why Sadiqi might think the skull was a souvenir from the senator's Algerian campaign; the shelf it was on contained a number of black and white shots that obviously dated back to colonial days in North Africa. Sometime in the late 50s or early 60s. Yet she wasn't convinced the skull was the same vintage.

Beside her, Sadiqi reached into his pocket for a nicotine candy but nodded to a photo stashed to one side. "That photo there – that dates back to Algeria."

Toni had already noticed the black and white image pushed to the back of the shelf. Despite his young age in the shot, she was easily able to pick out the senator. As in many of the color pictures at the front of the cabinet, Clavreul was once again surrounded by dozens of young soldiers. Except in these ones, *he* was in uniform, too. A clean crisp uniform that contrasted with the dusty fatigues the younger men were wearing. The aristocratic stance of the commanding officer, preparing to send his troops into battle was unmistakeable. But it wasn't the wretched inevitability of young death that struck Toni; it was the landscape framing the faces. The barren mountains. Dusty scrub. Rocks and boulders. Snowy peaks. A three-foot wide path running along the edge of an impossibly sheer drop. A minuscule path above a deep gorge.

By this time, Podesta had joined them in front of the cabinet and they were so busy examining the senator's mementoes that nobody heard the library door click open. It wasn't until a voice broke the silence that they landed back in reality.

"You're admiring the pictures of my youth," a gentle tenor resonated from a few meters behind. The three of them reeled. Everyone recognized the senator's face.

"Yes, we were looking at your pictures of Algeria," Sadiqi said flatly.

"Is that Chabet el-Akhira?" Toni asked.

If the senator disapproved of three strangers roaming around his library, he didn't say so. In fact, he encouraged their curiosity by congratulating Toni on her remark. "Very good, Mademoiselle. Not everyone is quite so talented at telling one rock face from another."

"I spent several months in Algeria researching my doctoral thesis."

The senator looked mildly impressed. "Do I detect a slight accent?"

"Canadian. I'm from Montreal."

"Ah. *La Belle Province.* I spent two years there myself."

There was no way Sadiqi was going to let his interview degenerate into a social call. "Rock is Madame Corrigan's specialty. She's our catacomb expert. I'm Inspector General Khalid Sadiqi and this is Lieutenant Rémi Podesta. UCLAT." The order he presented this information in was purposely ambiguous.

The senator didn't seem to notice. He shook everyone's hand – vaguely reminding Toni of a political rally she'd once unintentionally got caught in as an undergrad – then he waved the trio toward the Chesterfield sofa in the middle of the room. "I wouldn't have thought the quarries were a place for a woman." He didn't wait for the others to be seated but relaxed into a large armchair that would keep him safely separated from the *hoi polloi*.

"Why not?" Toni asked.

The senator gave a little chortle as if she'd said something quaint. "A little dreary for the gentler sex."

She laughed outright. Such an extravagantly sexist remark couldn't be anything but a conscious attempt to be provocative. "Women have always played an important role in the quarries. Their work under the Feuillantines stands as proof of that," she added, referring to the quarrying carried out by the nuns below their convent.

The senator stroked his Adam's apple pensively. "Yes," he murmured, trying to decide what to make of this 'catacomb expert'. Sadiqi and Podesta he had expected. Right down to the jeans and cheap suit – even if he would have assumed the officer to be wearing the suit and the lieutenant the jeans, instead of the current reversal. Having said that, what could be expected from a commanding officer with a name like Khalid Sadiqi? The girl, however, left him at a loss. Whoever she was, she was unlikely to be part of the UCLAT. Her general demeanor was professional enough but the ratty knapsack at her feet was more in keeping with a student than a police officer. "The catacombs are full of interesting stories. Pierre Caron taught me that. His knowledge of the subject was astounding."

"That was his job," Sadiqi commented, still slightly nauseated about having shaken this man's hand.

"If everyone knew his job as well as Pierre Caron, France would be doing much better than it is." It wasn't until he'd finished delivering this opinion that the senator unglued his eyes from Toni and turned his attention to Sadiqi with studied pathos. "I was sorry to hear of his death."

As much as Sadiqi disliked the man, at least his businesslike attitude was something to be thankful for. "Pierre Caron is precisely what I want to talk about, Senator. I'd like you to tell me how you came to collaborate with him?"

"Inspector," Clavreul said with a smile that lacked any warmth. "How many times do you need to hear that story? I know you've already asked my secretary the exact same question and I presume you spoke with Professor Caron about it yesterday."

"How do you know I spoke with Caron?" Sadiqi asked.

"He told me so himself."

The interview was starting badly. This didn't confirm what St. Cyr had said earlier. "Your secretary said you'd lost contact with the professor in recent months."

The look of indignant denial was quite convincing. "Not at all. It's simply that we had less reason to meet after our petition was unsuccessful."

"You're referring to the report you wrote together."

The senator nodded thoughtfully. "Professor Caron wrote the report. All I did was provide a name that would garner attention for his work." It would have been reassuring to Sadiqi to think that vermin like this man didn't garner anyone's support. Unfortunately, not only was the snake able to attract the attention of the press and the public, he even had the president's ear. Tibrac and Clavreul had grown so close over the past parliamentary session, it had been quite the talk of the media, as the president tried to win shares of the far-right vote by ingratiating himself to the senator.

"And why did you call him yesterday?" Sadiqi asked.

Any answer to this question was cut short as the maid came in and placed a platter with a silver coffee set on the table. The senator thanked her dismissively then held out the tiny espresso cups to the trio on the sofa. Although Sadiqi was in desperate need of a coffee, he didn't take one. There was no way he would drink anything offered by the senator despite the deep aroma that was drifting over. Full-bodied real espresso. Instead, he went for another nicotine candy, snapping it out of the aluminium with a loud pop.

After stirring his coffee, the senator returned to the previous question. "I didn't call the Professor. He called me. He was concerned about the events at Val-de-Grace. He believed the Prime Minister's death would rekindle interest in our report."

"And what did you tell him?"

"I told him that an accidental allergic reaction, be it ever so deadly, had nothing to do with the catacombs."

This simple comment accomplished its aim elegantly: to annoy Sadiqi. *Sly old bastard.* Officially the topic of the attack on de Chanterelle was off-limits. The information surrounding the PM was still classified. Clavreul wasn't supposed to be informed about the true circumstances of de Chanterelle's death. But Sadiqi knew the senator was bluffing. There was little doubt he knew exactly what had actually happened. Probably almost everyone in politics already knew by now. There was no way Sadiqi was going to stick to the official line and miss an opportunity to question this man. "I'm sure you're aware that the UCLAT doesn't investigate allergic reactions."

The comment amused the senator. "Then tell me, Inspector. What exactly are you investigating?"

There was a thin line to tread; Sadiqi had to say something without breaching confidentiality, especially with Toni sitting there. "Over the past week there've been several indications the catacombs are being used for terror purposes. Including events at Val-de-Grace. Professor Caron's death makes that situation all the more worrying. The quarries are under threat yet the leading quarry specialist is dead, depriving the intelligence services of a major source of technical and strategic support underground."

If Sadiqi had been expecting to rein in some of Clavreul's bluster with his comment, the plan backfired. The senator simply shrugged. "Nonsense.   Apparently poor Professor Caron has outlived his usefulness.   You have the charming Miss Corrigan to guide you, instead." As a politician, the senator had plenty of practice both at making inflammatory remarks and ignoring the ones aimed at him. Tasteless black humor was right up his alley. "Sadly, few people listened to Caron while he was alive.   Why should they pay more attention to him now that he's dead?"

"You're referring to the fact that the President chose not to act on the report's findings when it was circulated last winter," Sadiqi said.

The senator discarded his cup on the platter with an impatient clatter. "Inspector, it wasn't just the President who chose not to act. None of the people who read the report responded favorably.   The president was unmoved. I believe your own service saw the document and rejected it." Clavreul's voice had lost its congeniality. "Quite frankly, Inspector, I'm more than a little surprised to see the UCLAT chasing around asking about it now. It's a little late." And with that, his eyes strayed back to Toni.

When the inspector first arrived in the apartment, he wouldn't have thought it was possible to dislike the senator any more than he already did. He was now discovering a spectrum of emotions ranging from loathing to hate and possibly beyond that. The man's politics were bad enough without him criticizing Sadiqi's professional record. "I was never shown the report when it came out. If you'd like to show it to me now, I'd be happy to take the necessary steps."

"That train has gone, Inspector. I had the report shredded when the President declined to act on it."

"Shredded?" It was Toni who had spoken, her voice subdued but showing authentic surprise.

The senator's gaze lifted from her bustline to her face. "It contained some confidential information. Information that was too sensitive to leave lying around. The President ordered it shredded when he declined to act on it."

As she shifted forward on the sofa, her skirt rode a little higher up her thigh. "That sounds awfully contradictory," she said. "To claim it wasn't worth acting on but at the same time to consider it so delicate it needed shredding."

"Politics is filled with unfulfilled promises and shredded documents." The senator's gaze had once again migrated downward.

66

While Clavreul droned on with some generic complaint about political immobility, Toni slipped off the sofa and wandered back to the glass cabinet on the other side of the room.

In her quick examination of Trouvé's copy of the report earlier that afternoon, she'd seen nothing that merited having the written trace shredded. Which would explain why she hadn't thought much of the report when she'd first seen it back in November. Even assuming it *was* sub-chapter 4.6 that contained the most damning information, she still couldn't think what that information might be. Not that there weren't questionable things happening in the quarries. There were. But none of them had anything to do with potential terrorist weak links. She knew the toxic levels of water holes under the city were well above acceptable danger level. She also knew there were quarries that were unstable because they'd been injected with cement that was already flaking, only two or three years after the consolidation work. But Caron would hardly have denounced that type of problem because he was the one who'd ordered the shoddy work done in the first place. That kind of information she could definitely understand the authorities wanting to hush up. But it wouldn't have been the kind of thing Caron would be using to convince Tibrac to close the quarries. She knew Caron's approach. It was all that horseshit about the subterranean network being taken over by terrorists. People blowing up the city from below. But that wasn't possible. Nobody could carry out that type of attack without being noticed.

She bent closer to the skull in the cabinet and stared at it through the glass pane while in the background Sadiqi shifted the conversation away from the shredded document.

"While he was preparing this report, I believe Professor Caron took you to visit the catacombs." Glancing over her shoulder, Toni saw the senator nod. "He also took you to a gallery used by the

Freemasons.   Something called the *Chamber of Reflections*." Toni
noted the bluff.

"No. I don't believe so. I would have remembered a name like
that." The denial was crisp, almost indifferent

Which wasn't helpful.   If Clavreul denied knowledge of the
chamber outright, they weren't going to make headway with this line of
questioning.   There was no other way to find out whether Caron had
shown it to him or not.

Toni had no doubt Khalid was a damn good cop, or whatever the
hell it was he did in counter-terrorism. Unfortunately, she was a little
worried that his personal dislike of the senator was making him miss
some important details. There was no way she was going to stand by
and let that happen. She had some questions of her own. "I'm curious,
Senator," she said, barely loud enough to be heard on the other side of
the immense room. "But did Professor Caron teach you anything you
didn't already know about the quarries?"

The reaction to the words was instantaneous.   All three heads
reeled to stare at her. All for different reasons:

Sadiqi was annoyed. He hadn't brought Corrigan along to run the
interview; he'd brought her along to show leg and smile. No doubt he
should have defined that more clearly before roping her in.

Podesta was simply noting that this odd investigation had just got
a lot odder.

And the senator was trying to assess the meaning of the question.

Clavreul was the first to speak. "I beg your pardon."

"You already knew the catacombs before talking with Caron.
You'd been down before," Toni said, pointing to the skull.

This time there was a longer pause; the senator missed a beat as he
re-assessed the young woman. His hesitation was brief. Like any good
politician he attempted to cover his tracks with a compliment and a
lavish smile. The fawning politician was back. "You're very shrewd
Miss Corrigan. Both brains and beauty. A rare combination. Yes, I
thought you might notice that. A souvenir of youth."

Toni ignored the backhanded compliment and craned to get a
better view of the skull. She had seen too many of these to brush it
aside that easily.   "A souvenir of *cataphile* youth," she said,
emphasizing the significant word. And now a look of understanding
started spreading across Sadiqi's face as he realized that the skull he
had taken for some hideous war trophy was something very different.
One of the skulls from the Paris catacombs. One of the millions of
skulls of erstwhile Parisians laid to rest in the ossuary. "Stealing bones
from the catacombs warrants a 155 euro fine," she quipped.

"Oh Mademoiselle Corrigan, I doubt that bylaw even existed yet when I picked up that souvenir. It goes back to my student days. The catacombs were still easily accessible back then and quite a popular destination for parties." Clavreul smiled naughtily. Just one of the guys out for fun.

Sadiqi didn't like the senator's manner. He knew this man's charm was his weapon. He was one of the elite churned out by de Gaulle's military-political training school, the ENA. Despite his unsavoury side, the senator had been taught to be charming. Now he was paid to be charming. That was a source of his power. Seduction. And Sadiqi really didn't like him using it on Toni. "So why were you pumping Caron for information if you were already a cataphile?" he asked.

The senator remained almost jocular. "Inspector, I'm hardly a cataphile. When I was a student everyone used to go down into the catacombs. Things were very different sixty years ago. There were entrances all over the Latin Quarter. I guess I must have gone down half a dozen times. I couldn't say exactly. You know, sixty years later it's difficult to distinguish one outing from the next. We were just having fun. It was a good place to take girls to give them the shivers. To get them flying into our arms for protection. Of course, girls have evolved over the years," he said, running his eyes over Toni. "I guess that wouldn't work anymore."

The inspector was slightly disturbed to see just how effective his plan to loosen the senator's tongue with an attractive woman was working out. Clavreul could hardly keep his eyes off Toni. Which annoyed Sadiqi all the more because she wasn't showing any sign of outrage at all the sexist innuendo. Instead, she just kept prattling on with that perfect calm, intermingled with upward movements of her skirt. Almost as if she'd been filled in on Sadiqi's plan to use her. Except she hadn't.

"But your student days weren't your first contact with the catacombs, were they?" she remarked.

That's when the senator's smile faded. The sweet memories of youth evaporated. This time he was caught entirely off guard. "I'm sure I don't know what you mean."

"You knew about the quarries long before the '50s," she said. "From your earliest childhood."

Despite the senator's attempts to hide it, Sadiqi could tell Toni had hit a chord. Clavreul was fazed. His "no" was too forceful.

Corrigan looked on curiously. "I was thinking of the attack planned by the *Cagoule* on the Senate back in the 30s."

Sadiqi's mind whirled back to the conversation from the night before. He had no idea what she was talking about; whatever it was, he wished she'd mentioned this earlier. But then the previous night, she hadn't known about the case's incipient link to Clavreul. Even though he wasn't sure where this was going, the cop could at least watch with pleasure as the senator squirmed. There was still a smile on the man's lips, but the muscles were drawn and tense. "I was just a babe in arms when that happened."

"I realize that. But because it was a family affair, I'm sure there must have been whispers about it all around you during your childhood."

Unable to maintain the smile any longer, Clavreul's expression hardened into something more unsavory. He was doing his best to appear intrigued but in the depths of his eye there was a shade of something darker. "You're referring to my aunt's husband."

"In other words your uncle," Corrigan confirmed.

"Yes, my uncle by marriage. I really can't see what bearing a political incident from 80 years ago can possibly have on today's events."

"My point is that you'd probably heard about the catacombs quite early in life. They were part of your family's history. The kind of topic that comes up at family dinners."

Although the exchange gave Sadiqi the chance to watch the senator sweat, he needed to know what the deal was. He thought he knew the *Cagoule* narrative fairly well but he'd certainly never come across any reference to Clavreul in it. "I think you're going to have to spell it out for the senator," he suggested in an attempt to get Toni to fill him in without informing Clavreul he had no idea what all this was about.

Toni moved back to the sofa and regained her place beside the two officers. "Senator, your uncle was a member of the *Cagoule*. He was accused of participating in their attempted *coup d'état* on the Senate via the catacombs."

"He was pardoned in 1940," Clavreul stated forcefully.

"Yes," Toni agreed. "By the Vichy government. But the point is that you've been familiar with the catacombs for a very long time."

"The point is," Clavreul snapped, "I was a babe in arms at the time of the *coup d'état* and I was only 5 years old when my uncle was pardoned." The change was quite astounding. All trace of the unctuous charmer was gone. "I certainly wasn't old enough to measure the political importance of those events, or to understand the role played by the catacombs."

Podesta finished his espresso and placed the cup back on the tray, then reached for a biscuit and bit into it with a resounding chomp. This was turning out to be way more interesting than he'd expected. The girl certainly livened things up. "I have a five-year-old. She's very curious about the world around her. She's certainly aware what's going on in the family and who all her aunts and uncles are. And, believe it or not, she's even heard of the catacombs."

Clavreul was quickly losing patience. "Yes, except in 1940, children weren't as worldly as they are today. Nobody had time for rumors and gossip. There were more important issues at hand."

The senator's response was less an answer than an attempt to avoid the deeper subject, so Podesta kept going. "Those early years are formative. Not easily forgotten."

Toni didn't want to let this go. "Did you ever discuss the *Cagoule* with your uncle when you were older?"

"No. He left the country immediately after the war."

Of course he did, Sadiqi thought. *Because the Vichy pardon would have been overturned by the post-war government.* "And you never saw him again?"

"No."

"And nobody else in your family was an avid catacomb visitor?"

"No."

"Really?" Toni asked.

"Indeed."

"Hm." She shrugged. "That's too bad." Although the comment seemed ironic, her attitude was neutral. As if she honestly accepted the senator's words at face value. "Often you find whole families of cataphiles. Parents taking their children on visits. Grandfathers taking their grandson. Like Caron. I thought, maybe you'd shared a similar connection with your uncle."

Sadiqi observed the senator. It was interesting the way Clavreul had happily opened up about the skull and his cataphile past during his youth but then tried to deny prior knowledge through his family. Perhaps, he'd anticipated the questions about his student period. It was as if he'd laid out the clues – putting the skull in the cabinet. But he hadn't expected the reference to his uncle. He'd been knocked off balance by that. And now that he was a little shakier, Sadiqi decided to raise the stakes. "If we could return to the present. I noticed the photos in your cabinet. Many of those were taken on parade grounds with servicemen. I believe you're acquainted with someone named Paul Rossignol?"

Far from disturbing him, the senator seemed quite pleased to have a change of topic. "No, I don't believe so."

"A legionnaire. You met him last fall. At an award ceremony."

Again the senator shook his head, eyes slightly unfocused as if trying to place the name. "I meet a lot of people. I attend a lot of award ceremonies. I've been to Aubagne several times to meet our brave soliders."

"He received decorations," Sadiqi prompted. "The Medal of the Nation's Gratitude. He spent eighteen years in the Legion."

Clavreul gave a sharp nod. "Indeed. That's quite an accomplishment. But I'm afraid I really can't remember. I do remember going to Aubagne. Several men were decorated, when I was there in September. All of them for quite outstanding work."

It was another dead end. If there was more to learn about the connection between Clavreul and Rossignol, Sadiqi knew he was going to have to find it elsewhere.

All the cop could do now was play his trump card. He reached for the file he'd left on the coffee table and slid out a piece of paper carefully wrapped in a plastic zip bag. "We won't keep you much longer, Senator. I just have one last question. When Caron's body was found last night this was on his desk. Apparently he'd been in the process of answering a letter he'd received from you when he was murdered."

Of all the curve-balls the senator had been hit with over the past twenty minutes, this was perhaps the most unexpected. He frowned and held out his hand, almost grabbing the letter from Sadiqi. As his eyes darted down the page the well-composed elegance evaporated. "This is ridiculous. I never wrote that. It's a fraud."

The discomposure warmed the cop's heart. If he had to lay a bet on the letter's authenticity, without hesitation he'd say it was a plant intended to frame the senator. Clavreul was far too wiley to have left behind such a blatant link to himself. But that didn't necessarily mean he had no connection to Caron's murder. "That may be so," Sadiqi said soothingly. "But in that case, it's a very good fraud. It's written on official senate letterhead paper. It also has the same reference codes as your official correspondence. And there's a copy of it in your file at the Senate. Your secretary showed it to me."

For a moment the senator was speechless. Then an expression of shock washed across his face. "I didn't write that."

"Maybe not," Sadiqi agreed. "But then who did?" Under French parliamentary law the senator was entitled to total legal immunity. He couldn't be accused of a crime or detained for questioning. The immunity was his constitutional right (a right which encouraged considerable corruption within the country's ruling class). Nevertheless Sadiqi was optimistic the senator's inviolability would soon be lifted. The fingerprints on the letter had already been checked against the fingerprints registered on the senator's biometric passport. They were a match. And requests had already been filed for search warrants for both Clavreul's apartment and his senate office. Hopefully those would be issued before the day was out.

67

Podesta tore off his jacket and laid it on the roof of the Renault, a frown of disgust on his face. "Well, that was sort of entertaining, but basically a waste of time."

"If you say so," Sadiqi rumbled under his breath. He was still trying to get a firm grasp on what had just happened in there.

Not surprisingly, the senator hadn't been able to suggest anyone who might be trying to implicate him in Caron's murder. The interview had drawn a blank. But Sadiqi could see the shoots of an answer. At the very least, he was confident that he would have the eminently sickening senator in the VIP interrogation room of the Criminal Brigade within 72 hours.

In any case, the question at the forefront of his mind no longer had anything to do with Clavreul. He popped a nicotine candy and strode towards the driver's door, leaving Podesta and Toni on the sidewalk. "How did you know about his uncle and the *Cagoule*?"

Toni fanned herself with one hand and brushed her ponytail against the back of her neck with the other. Burning heat was radiating off the parked car. "You know me. I'm good with quarry trivia."

True enough. But that had been her least surprising contribution to the interview. "And what was that stuff about Chabet el-Akhira?"

"Chabet el-Akhira. The Gorge of Death." Her thoughts clicked back to the black and white photo in the cabinet. "It's in Kabylia."

Sadiqi's eyes dropped to the roof of the boiling vehicle. If there was one thing he couldn't stand it was being played for an idiot. "I know it's in Kabylia. What I don't understand is why you're so familiar with an obscure mountain region of Algeria."

She was standing beside the shotgun door, flashing that reassuring smile. "Like I said I spent a few months there when I was working on my thesis. The gorge is full of caves. It's an interesting place. I guess you'd call it tragic. That's probably why it stuck in my mind. The region's been wracked by war for over 200 years and people from local villages go and hide in the caves whenever trouble flares up." She had both cops' full attention. Her smile dissolved, as she considered the seriousness of what she was saying. When she resumed the story, the words came out with measured gravitas. "But the strategy often backfires. The military tends to smoke civilians out, or brick them in and leave them to suffocate – or die of thirst and starvation. There was one instance during the War of Independence when 1000 villagers, mainly women and children were asphyxiated by the French military in those caves."

Sadiqi's gaze dropped to the car roof. The vision was sickening. "War's never clean."

"No," Podesta agreed. "And I'm sure Clavreul can personally testify to just how dirty that one was."

Toni slipped her phone out of her backpack and started flicking through her messages. "Well, one thing's for sure. If he commanded troops in Chabet el-Akhira, he probably knows a thing or two about cave warfare." She spoke without looking up.

"Those weren't just lucky guesses back there, were they?" The inspector seemed to be making a statement rather than asking a question. "You know his background, don't you?"

She pulled a bottle of water out of her bag and took a sip. "Yeah sure. I was an undergrad during those two years when Clavreul was living in Montreal. He was the focus of several student protests."

"What was that stuff about him living in Canada? I thought he'd always lived in France," Podesta said, paying homage to the widespread disease of voter amnesia. "I don't remember him moving to Montreal."

"I do." Sadiqi remembered it well. It was a few years back. The senator had been accused of misuse of parliamentary funds. A million and a half euros of taxpayers' money had somehow been funneled into renovations on his personal apartment. It was the kind of thing all the newspapers screamed about for a couple of months then everyone forgot. Politics was just too boring for most people to remember any of the stories for long.

"He was mired in some political scandal. He needed to get away from France long enough to let the storm blow over." Corrigan's phone was now stretched out towards Podesta, an article summarizing Clavreul's exploits in Canada on the screen. "Anyway, while he was in Quebec, he was invited to give some lectures at UQAM – one of the big universities. The invitation caused an outcry. Questions were raised about his human rights' record."

Podesta barely glanced at the article. "Let me guess. You were standing outside the lecture hall chanting slogans against him."

The look she sent him could have turned water to ice. "Something like that." She took her phone back and started swiping from screen to screen. The lieutenant was considerably less impressive than his commanding officer and didn't merit her full attention. "Let's just say I'm not a big fan. Unfortunately, his brand of rightwing diatribe exports well. When hatred against the Maghreb and Islam is stoked in France, it spills over into the rest of the French-speaking world. There are no borders on bad ideas, especially not in cyberspace. A Parisian senator spews hate; an unemployed teen sitting in his bedroom in Chicoutimi decides to go out and buy a shotgun."

Podesta had no idea what the hell Chicoutimi was, but he was at least smart enough to know when he'd hit a nerve. The student had darkened measurably.

Attention to detail was what made a good investigator. Podesta was detail-oriented. Sadiqi, on the other hand, had always prided himself on being an exceptional investigator. He was unrivalled. Mainly because he not only saw the details, he saw the micro details. The minutiae. He read what was written on the page, but he also saw what was written between the lines. He listened to what was expressed verbally, while at the same time noticing the inflexion in the voice. He saw the body language and facial expression, but he also measured whether those movements were natural or studied.

What Sadiqi now saw standing in front of him was the image of the perfect student. How old was she? 25? Maybe 28. Helping him because she had nothing better to do with her day. Messaging her friends with lightning thumbs whenever she got bored... Yet there was something just ever so slightly askew with this picture. Something that didn't quite fit. "You know a lot of stuff. I thought the catacombs were your specialty, not the Algerian War."

"My specialty is structural weakness; my research is pluridisciplinary." It was a litany – repeated by rote. Probably the kind of meaningless outline she gave whenever she had to make small talk. "The catacombs are interesting, but there are other interesting things out there, too."

Which could mean absolutely anything. Or nothing at all. A little clarity would have been nice but after that excrutiating interview with the senator, the inspector decided to turn it into a joke. He needed a little relief. "Maybe I'll buy you that vodka martini next time we get the chance."

She didn't even bother looking up from her phone. "You flatter me, Khalid Sadiqi... my Immortal Friend."

The street they were on was three lanes wide, packed with busy traffic, yet Sadiqi suddenly felt the world go silent. All he could hear was the echo of those words in his ears. Not only had she pronounced his name with a flawless Arabic accent, catching the 'kh' at the back of her throat instead of snapping it on the palate like most Europeans, but she'd also provided the exact translation of the words. *Immortal Friend.* How would she know that? His name, translated. He was barely able to contain his surprise. Under other circumstances, he might have been intrigued. Coming out of the blue today, the idea just fuelled his budding apprehension. "You speak Arabic?"

As always, the student answered with an innocent smile and a lighthearted shrug. "Nahhh. I'm just really good with Google Translate." She slipped her phone back into her backpack. "So what's next?"

The 37° heat was suddenly more stifling and unbreathable than a moment earlier. Maybe it was just the weather or maybe it was the complexity of the case, but Sadiqi was beginning to worry he wasn't thinking straight. Who was this girl? He was thinking of Corrigan as an innocent little student. Someone who had handed him some useful information but whom, essentially, he felt he should protect. Someone fragile and vulnerable.

Except everything he had heard over the last half hour seemed to throw doubt on that analysis. Algeria. Arabic. Her mention of Clavreul's war experience. Surely that type of knowledge went well beyond the bounds of your average catacomb specialist. Wasn't it just possible that she wasn't the wide-eyed little post-doc she appeared to be?

And if that was true, then who was she?

There was trouble in the air. Maybe it was time to stop letting her tag along. It was time to go back to playing by the book.

It took a lot to shake Sadiqi, but she'd manged to knock him slightly off-balance. The movement was stilted as he waved his lieutenant toward the passenger seat. And he had to force his voice to stay even. "Podesta and I are going to see the Grand Master," he unlocked the car and slid in. "I suggest you try to keep out of trouble."

The lieutenant rolled down his side window and Toni leaned in. "Can't I come, too?" Silence hung in the air as the two officers ignored the question. "You're really going to dump me, after everything I've done to help?" The tone had morphed from playful to annoyed.

"Sounds like Barbie's mad she's not invited to the party," Podesta muttered just loud enough for everyone to hear. He was pleased to see his boss back to his usual rigorous self.

"*La ferme.*" *Shut up.* Sadiqi felt no pleasure in his change of heart. He fixed his eyes on the road, hit the ignition and shifted into gear. There was no point in dragging out the long goodbye.

After pulling the car out into the raging traffic he screeched in front of a delivery van.

"You're a little tense, *Chef.*"

"I thought I told you to shut up." Sadiqi tossed the magnetic strobe light onto the roof, activated the siren and tore into the taxi lane.

No amount of small talk was going to improve his mood. He was now entertaining the insane idea that maybe Ms. Corrigan wasn't really just a graduate doing research on the quarries. He felt there was something about her he'd missed before. Something hazy and opaque. *Perhaps some ideological inclination. Or a political agenda?* He leaned on the horn to warn the bus in front to get the hell out of his way. *Or the one they'd joked about: a sideline in intelligence work?*

No. That wasn't possible. He had to be over-reacting. Amélie always used to complain that he did that. That he was paranoid. That he saw bogeymen everywhere.

Maybe he did. He'd certainly built his career on his ability to anticipate every possible outcome. And that inevitably meant considering the most outrageous ideas alongside the most reasonable. So maybe this was just the craziest possibility along the spectrum. One he had to explore but that ultimately would be disproved. He would ask Dukrin to run a background check. Hell. Dukrin had probably already run the background check. She would have had all his new contacts from the previous day screened so that she could warn him if there was anything stalking up on him. And if she hadn't given him the heads-up, that probably meant there was absolutely nothing to worry about. Corrigan was just what she claimed to be – a student doing a research stint in Europe. Someone who had a lot of time for reading and research, and who knew bucketloads of trivia about all sorts of things.

It was probably nothing. But he needed to take a step back. There had been too much going on over the past 36 hours. Things would seem clearer if he focused on the job.

68

The Nightingale turned and followed the tunnel past the area the cops had been guarding then pivoted into an adjoining gallery. He knew the path by heart. Straight nine paces then left another twelve, then right at the fork. Another twenty meters along he reached the halfway point on the way to the dead end.

There he marked his halt, releasing the arm of the body he had in tow. The corpse joined the small pile of colleagues now lying against the wall. There had been no explicit orders to kill the men. The Nightingale's instructions had simply contained the details of the shifts under the Senate. But killing the guards had been the safest and easiest way of getting them out of the way. No challenge at all. He didn't know what sort of training a cop got but obviously it was sloppy because these guys had no idea how to protect themselves when flying solo. All they understood was working as a team. *Security in numbers*, he simpered. Sure, teamwork was important. But if something happens to your partner, you need to know how to protect yourself alone. These guys didn't. They'd let themselves be picked off one by one.

The Nightingale knew he could count on the same sloppy training to keep his mission from being discovered. At least long enough to avoid problems. The next shift would be arriving soon to replace this one. When they got to their posts they would think it strange that their colleagues weren't still on guard. That would miff them. But not having a radio or cell phone to contact their commanding officer on the surface, the new shift would fall into the same trap as the old. They wouldn't want to go above ground to signal their colleagues' absence because that would mean both abandoning their post and possibly getting their colleagues in trouble. So the new shift would check out the terrain by themselves. In their sloppy, blind way. And the Nightingale would be waiting for them.

So it would be several hours before anyone noticed (let alone confirmed) that something really had gone wrong. And by then the Nightingale would be comfortably installed in an Airbus on his way to the other side of the world.

Anyway, that was the plan. None of these thoughts were visible in the Nightingale's behavior. If someone had been watching him as he dragged the lifeless bodies down the tunnels all they would have seen was a killing machine. And when he began running his hand across the graffiti covered stone wall in front of him an observer might have wondered what the meaning of this strange communion of stone and human tissue was about.

But the redhead knew where the small indentations were and why they were so beautifully concealed. He would have to prop up the bodies in order to apply pressure to all the points at the same time.

If nothing else, the months he had spent working in the catacombs had taught him that these tunnels deserved all the awe they got. Not that the Nightingale was a sentimentalist. He knew when it was time to move on. His life in the catacombs was nearly over. Still, the knowledge he'd accumulated over the past months would serve to protect him.

He checked his watch. It was almost time. As soon as he had neutralized the new team, he would creep above ground to set up the fireworks. Then he would come back down and tidy up the loose ends by detonating the explosives. The strike points were intended both to shake the city as well as clear away every remaining trace of himself. There would be destruction and there would be death because that's what it would take to ensure nobody stopped this – neither the police nor anybody who might be trying to double-cross him. From here on in, the legionnaire was the only person with the full picture of what was about to happen.

69

The printout in front of her was nothing short of what Dukrin had expected. There were days like that – when things got worse and worse until they went into such a tailspin she felt nauseous. It wasn't that she wanted the world to be a horrible place. She didn't. Really. She loved those moments when she was proved wrong – when those sparks of humanity and kindness ignited around her. Sadly, those moments were too often outshadowed by blight.

She reached over to unlock the bottom drawer, pulled out the aging brown file and dropped it on her desk.

Unlike many people from her generation, Dukrin had no trouble following the tech side of her job. She'd studied computer programming in university. Of course that was a long time ago. It had all been fairly basic back then. Literally BASIC. Pascal. C. Languages that people hadn't even heard of today. The upshot of it was that she had no trouble understanding the computer geeks when they fed her their briefings.

And the briefing today was damning. Her eyes went back to the printout page.

She had asked IT to trace the origin of the Ng messages, which, miraculously they'd managed to do, quite successfully. The search for the source of the posts had revealed that the author was using a VPN to disguise the computer's IP address. Unfortunately for him, his VPN was leaking his real address. The WebRTC feature on his computer was divulging his real address.

Dukrin slipped the printout page into the file marked *Clavreul.*

The world was ruled by the rotten. But if you trailed those bastards closely enough, you could snare them when they tripped.

70

The dingy two-room apartment where the Grand Master lived contrasted with his majestic title. Sadiqi recognized the signs of an old boy's den. It was a sanctum ruffled neither by the decorating whims of a wife, nor the indelicate hands of neglectful children. There was no sofa, only two uncomfortable looking armchairs with straight backs and wooden armrests as well as a worn leather easy chair bearing a dented seat that indicated its evident rank of favorite chair. Even more unusual, there was a pack of cigarettes plus an ashtray and lighter on the coffee table.

The term *Grand Master* had conjured up the image of a sage with white hair and a long flowing beard. Nothing could have been further from the truth. Installing himself on one of the hard wooden chairs, Sadiqi reflected that, if anything, the man in the easy chair looked slightly younger than himself – probably because he'd managed to avoid the worry lines imparted by a frustrating job and a complicated personal life. Judging from the titles on the bookshelf, the time that most people devoted to family and career had been used by Bernard Malaisieu to explore the many facets of Freemasonry.

"Monsieur Malaisieu, I believe Cédric Trouvé told you about Professor Caron's death," Sadiqi began slowly. Starting an interview by evoking a close friend or relative's death was always tricky. Fortunately, Malaisieu seemed to be the solid, both-feet-on-the-ground type. He simply nodded, then waited for what was to follow. "I'd like you to tell me if Trouvé's call was the first news you had of Caron's death?"

"Yes. Absolutely."

"I believe you also received a call from Monsieur Trouvé yesterday. I'd like you to tell me about *that* call."

The man sat so still he reminded Sadiqi of a field mouse frozen into place at the sight of a hovering owl, preparing his defenses. Sure enough the words matched the attitude. "I don't see what that has to do with Pierre's death."

The only explanation the cop offered was silence.

After a few interminable seconds with nobody saying anything, Malaisieu shifted uneasily before offering a hand-picked choice of words. "You see, the three of us are members of the same group..."

The same group, Sadiqi couldn't believe these guys. Secret societies. Lodges. Passwords. Protecting Brothers. It was the stuff of fairy tales. He couldn't be bothered tiptoeing around the issues. "You mean you're all members of a Freemasons' lodge called *Pythagoras and Euclid*."

"I see Cédric's been talkative," Malaisieu responded coldly.

"No. Not at all." The inspector's tone was slightly more aggressive than he had intended. "He wasn't talkative. That's why I charged him with obstruction of justice and we've come to see you." A look of distaste spread across Malaisieu's face but Sadiqi ploughed on regardless. "I need you to fill in all the gaps he left us with. I'd appreciate it if we could do that without wasting too much time. I'd like you to tell us exactly what was said during that call."

The tips of Malaisieu's fingers pressed against his chair. "As I said, it concerned our lodge. I don't see how it's relevant to Pierre's death."

The endless stalling he was getting from these guys was exasperating. How much blood would it take before he got them to talk? "Let me read you something," Sadiqi said, pulling out his phone and activating the screen. "This is the transcript of one of the last phone calls Pierre Caron ever received. Cédric Trouvé left it on his answering machine last night but Caron never heard it." Sadiqi put on his best reading voice. When he'd finished sharing the message he looked up and let his eyes bore into Malaisieu as he recited one of the lines a second time: "*I've informed the Grand Master and he intends to take punitive measures.*"

"Yes. I thought we'd just been through that. You know Cédric called me."

If Malaisieu was playing dumb, he deserved a job at the *Comédie Française,* Sadiqi thought to himself. "Quite honestly it's a message that reflects poorly on your brotherhood. After all, Pierre Caron probably knew his killer – he willingly let him into his apartment."

The distaste on Malaisieu's face migrated to something closer to outrage. "Are you suggesting the lodge had something to do with Pierre's murder?"

"I'm not suggesting anything. I'm just trying to understand the message."

Malaisieu lifted himself out of his chair and started stamping back and forth in front of the two officers. "We don't kill our members for breaking the rules."

Sadiqi's knuckles went white as he tightened his grip on the wooden armrest. The Freemason stared back at him coldly. It was this type of stalemate that made working as a team both necessary and effective. It was up to Podesta to release the tension. "Mr. Malaisieu," the lieutenant said. "I believe the Masonic oath states that members shouldn't protect felons – whether they're brothers or not."

"But I'm not protecting a felon. That's what I'm telling you."

"Sir, in order for us to establish that, you need to answer Inspector Sadiqi's questions. We need to understand the exact reason why Professor Trouvé contacted you yesterday. The details."

Malaisieu sank back into his chair and propped his elbows on the armrests then spread his fingers open in a sign of capitulation. "Cédric thought I should know that Pierre had written a report for Jacques Clavreul in which he'd given away information concerning the initiation rituals of our lodge."

"More specifically something related to your Chamber of Reflection," Sadiqi offered.

His urge to drive the conversation forward only made the Freemason more defensive. "Did Cédric tell you that, too?"

"Cédric Trouvé said less than I would have hoped and more than he was comfortable sharing. Perhaps he didn't want to find himself with a broken neck, like Caron."

"Don't be absurd," Malaisieu sneered, picking up the pack of cigarettes off the coffee table and lighting up without asking whether it bothered anyone. "Whatever happened to Pierre, I can assure you it had absolutely nothing to do with the Masons."

The cloud of nicotine that wafted across the room immediately relaxed Sadiqi. He couldn't have been happier if the man had poured him a double whisky and offered him a winning lottery ticket. Edging forward, he hoped the Grand Master would be kind enough to blow a little smoke his way. "Perhaps," he said, taking a deep breath. "However, Trouvé did make the link between the report Caron wrote and an initiation ritual your lodge holds in the catacombs. Unfortunately he refused to give us the details of where exactly that ritual takes place."

"I should hope so."

Sadiqi's patience was waning. "Monsieur Malaisieu, you're being very unhelpful. Let me remind you that your friend is dead. We're doing our best to get to the bottom of his murder. You need to be more cooperative."

Only the sounds from the street broke the silence as Malaisieu studied the cigarette clasped between his thumb and forefinger. When he finally glanced up, Sadiqi rephrased his question. "Where is this chamber of yours?"

There was little room for manoeuvre. Malaisieu had to say something otherwise the inspector would never relent. "Our lodge is located by the Luxembourg Palace. Our Chamber of Reflection is in a nearby underground gallery."

It was an answer only pretending to offer clarity. "So you have some direct access route between your lodge and the catacombs?"

The Mason took another deep drag on his cigarette. The smoke swirled out from between lips so tense they barely parted. He wasn't happy sharing stories of the lodge's rituals but he understood that not speaking would probably be even more detrimental to the Brotherhood; if news of P&E's link to the quarries got out it would stir up a lot of unfavorable public attention. "In most lodges the Chamber of Reflection is in the lodge building itself. In our case, it's in the catacombs – not far from our lodge. Candidates are taken there to reflect alone before officially joining the lodge."

"So you do have a direct link between your lodge and this gallery?"

"Not directly from our lodge. No."

The words had been chosen carefully the better to obscure meaning. Like Trouvé, Malaisieu was being as enigmatic as possible. The only way to find out why this chamber was so important was to visit it. "I'd like you to show us exactly where that room is."

Malaisieu was concentrating on the very demanding job of coaxing the ash from his cigarette into the ashtray, all the time shaking his head vigorously. "That's out of the question."

The cop wished he had some magic device to compel witnesses to give information. "I've obviously not made myself clear. There's considerably more to this situation than Pierre Caron's death. It's highly possible that the catacombs are being used for terrorism."

The Freemason suddenly lost interest in his ashtray. His eyes shot up. "Terrorism," he growled. "Don't threaten me with terrorism. Politicians would have us believe the war on terror is central to our nation's survival. Yet, history has shown that today's terrorists are tomorrow's respected leaders. Gerry Adams. Yasser Arafat. The war on terror has itself become a form of terror over the masses. It's become an excuse for everything."

Sadiqi was in no mood for a philosophical debate. He knew the bleeding-heart diatribe by heart. He heard it on the TV, read it in the papers. "Call it what you like, Mr. Malaisieu," he said, his voice dangerously loud. "Personally, I don't go in for semantics. But I can tell you exactly why *I* use the word *terrorism*. I'm talking about organized murder on a vast scale. Pierre Caron isn't the only victim so far. Several people are dead. I believe the number could grow exponentially over the next three days. If you don't want to help me, if you'd rather wait for us to charge you with obstructing justice, then fine. I'll draw up the paperwork. But that will take time. Precious hours. And that wasted time could cost lives. Is that what you want? Blood on your hands for some stupid fraternity because you prefer the term *freedom fighter* to *terrorist?* Well let me tell you something: when the bodies start rolling in, either way, it's murder."

The man was too much of an intellectual to be moved. "Yes, yes. I'm familiar with the arguments," he rasped. "Still I don't understand how learning about our Chamber will help your investigation."

"Maybe it won't. But until I know more about it, I can't assess whether it is or isn't relevant. What I do know is that a few months ago Professor Caron wrote a report detailing possible terrorist scenarios involving the quarries. Over the past week, at least two of those scenarios have played out. My concern is that the next scenario is about to be put into action. Based on what Professor Trouvé said, I'm beginning to suspect that scenario may involve your Chamber of Reflections."

"That's absurd. Why would anyone want to attack us?"

"I can only speculate. But perhaps because prominent members, such as Professor Trouvé, express positions that are offensive to some opposing groups."

The Grand Master took a moment to collect his thoughts while he stubbed out his cigarette. When he spoke, his words were more subdued. His voice reasonable. "Our lodge is one of the oldest in the world. When Freemasonry first reached France, my forebears were initiated by English and Scottish Masons. That was before our present lodge building existed. Symbolically, the catacombs provided a place that corresponded to what was needed to act out the first part of our initiation ritual. Over time, the chamber has played an important part in our lodge's history. Its existence has weighed on French history."

Well that was just fascinating. Not to mention absurdly exaggerated. Sadiqi curbed an urge to slam the man against the wall. "Just tell me its location."

With pursed lips, Malaisieu gave a stiff shake of his head. "I've told you as much as I can. I can't break two hundred years of silence and have it on my conscience."

"But the information is in Caron's report anyway. All I have to do is read the report."

"No, Inspector. I don't think so. You're bluffing." The Mason had stopped fidgeting and had grown more confident. "According to Cédric, Pierre didn't go that far. He mentioned the Chamber's existence but he didn't give the exact location."

The effort that was being put into stopping Sadiqi from finding out which gallery their lodge used for their silly ritual seemed grossly excessive. "Why does it matter so much if people learn which of the galleries your lodge uses?"

"I have a duty to my lodge and my brethren," the Grand Master retorted. "In any case, our periodic use of the catacombs for certain rituals isn't really of any great interest. It's a well-known fact, documented in any number of books on the Paris quarries. The catacombs are used by secret societies. So what?"

Sadiqi wondered how anyone with the least bit of intelligence could be so indifferent to the risk of some major cataclysm being wrought on the city. He stared into Malaisieu's eyes as if he might find the information he wanted written on his retina. The link was broken when he heard a shuffle beside him as Podesta leaned closer to the Grand Master. "I think you'll find that when there's been a crime, the Law *does* expect you to expose your Brothers," the lieutenant said.

"I have nothing more to add," Malaisieu croaked.

The inspector rose and strode over to a window that opened onto a dank little courtyard. Leaning across the windowsill, he searched for a hint of a breeze. Although the courtyard had been sheltered from the sun over the past two weeks, the walls radiated heat and the scent of rotting fruit drifted up from the garbage cans below. It was depressing. Like this case. Sadiqi certainly wasn't going to waste any more time debating the merits and shortcomings of Freemasonry. He wasn't getting anywhere with this interview.

He brought his head back into the apartment and sat against the windowsill. "Do you know anyone called Paul Rossignol?"

The Grand Master shook his head.

"Jean Brune?"

Again, the same movement.

Grand Master. What a joke. An insignificant little man who had dedicated his life to a club. Perhaps he would be more concerned if he felt his club personally threatened. "We've also received a message that sounds like a warning," Sadiqi said. The quotation was etched in his memory: *"There will be fireworks above the Temple on New Year's Eve. Darkness will triumph over light. The songs will change to screams.* Do you have any idea what that could refer to?"

Rather than looking concerned, the words seemed to amuse Malaisieu. "I didn't know the police were expected to solve riddles."

Sadiqi turned his back on the man again and stared into the bleak courtyard. Belligerence wasn't working with this guy so he decided to appeal to the man's civic spirit, instead. "Mr. Malaisieu. I'm asking for your help. Do you have any idea what the message could mean?"

The Freemason took out another cigarette. Instead of lighting it, he simply tapped the tip on the edge of his chair. It was a few seconds before he shook himself out of a half-dream. "I really can't think of anything helpful."

"Nothing at all?"

"Perhaps it's a reference to June 23rd. Some lodges recognize the Feast of St. John as their New Year. As for the temple and the songs, I have no idea."

Partial confirmation. Sadiqi should have been happy. But he wasn't. So much was still missing. All he had was a date. That wasn't enough. If he didn't learn where the Nightingale was planning to strike, he wouldn't be able to stop him.

"For the last time, tell us where the chamber is."

"No."

Sadiqi rotated to face Malaisieu. "In that case, we're charging you with obstruction of justice. And if there's an attack you could be charged as an accessory." He caught Podesta's eye. "Read him his rights then call backup to take him in."

71

Being told she couldn't attend the interview with the Grand Master irritated Toni. But there was more than one way to skin a cat. If she couldn't investigate Freemasonry with the cowboys, she'd do it her own way. She was used to working alone.

After clicking her Velib self-service bike back into the stand at the top of rue Cadet she started down the narrow, cobbled street. The atmosphere contrasted with the crazy traffic she'd left behind on rue Lafayette. The noise and bustle of the Opera district dissipated into the calm of the ideal Parisian street, complete with barrow vendors selling fresh fruit and sidewalk cafés filled with people sipping *citron pressé* or Pastis under parasols.

In addition to these regular neighborhood fixtures, today there were also a number of musicians setting up sound equipment for the *Fête de la Musique*. According to the news report she'd heard that morning, for the past thirty-five years, the summer solstice had been marked in France by a nationwide music festival. Everybody and anybody could descend into the street with a beat box or a kazoo or whatever they chose, and play all night long. Judging from the amount of loud speakers and up-market sound equipment, the *Fête* was going to be loud tonight.

Not that Toni was paying much attention to the musicians. She'd come to rue Cadet to visit the museum of Freemasonry, housed in the Grand Orient lodge building, and her attention was focused on the street numbers. From Marco's explanations of the origins of Freemasonry dating back to the great cathedrals, Toni had imagined the lodge would be a magnificent domed temple with intricate carved stonework. But n°16 looked more like an office complex, than a reduced model of the Roselyn Chapel. Glass, concrete and ugly metal siding. The administrative appearance lent the building all the charm and mystique of a passport office. No stonemason had ever been anywhere near it.

The lack of beauty was equalled only by the lack of secrecy. She had psyched herself up for an unmarked door with a peephole that a sash-wearing concierge would slip open before hustling her into the lobby. Instead, the name was emblazoned on an outcrop of steel that ran the length of the building – *Grand Orient de France* – with the square and compass seal stencilled on the window. The unabashed openness was disappointing.

Inside, the Museum of Freemasonry was as unglamorous as the building it was housed in. And as sophisticated as a high school history fair. There was a wooden table at the entrance instead of a desk, and cardboard partitions separated one display from the next. Posters lined the walls, each covering an important stage in Masonic history. And glass display cases had been brought in to show off sashes and aprons that had probably been handed down by someone's grandfather.

The overall impression of dilapidation radiating off the displays told Toni she was wasting her time. This wasn't the kind of place she would find anything useful.

"*Vous êtes de la maison?*" the man at the entry desk asked. Toni was stumped trying to translate this. *Are you from the house?* No. That wasn't it. It took her a second to grasp what he meant: *Are you one of us? Are you a member?*

She was vaguely intrigued. "I didn't think women could join."

The man seemed to enjoy her gaffe. "The Grand Orient includes many female members," he said with a crooked grin that made him look like an old satyr.

"I didn't know that."

"I'm sure there's a lot you don't know about Freemasonry. Perhaps I can show you around." Toni knew the type only too well. Worldly-wise, confident, and on the look out for young flesh. The kind of guy who picked you up, offered to buy you a coffee and before you'd taken your first sip came straight out and asked if you were planning on sleeping with him. It was a breed often encountered at academic conferences. Not one she appreciated. But one she had learnt to domesticate. In short, she wasn't going to turn down a guided tour.

She followed obediently as he skipped the first aisle and went straight to one of the last posters of the exhibit. It was entitled "The Commune" and the display case housed two black and white photos of women in floor length dresses: one buxom and confident the other frail and hungry looking.

"The first women ever to be admitted into Freemasonry were French," her guide said proudly signalling the poster. "Maria Desraismes and Louise Michel."

Toni frowned. *Okay. This isn't sexist at all,* she thought. On top of her discomfort with her guide's assumption that she could only possibly be interested in female Freemasons, she was worried that he might not be giving her accurate info. According to Marco, women couldn't become Freemasons – and Marco was never wrong. In the two years she'd known him he'd never told her anything even vaguely misleading let alone incorrect. "I thought only men could join."

"Maria Desraismes joined the *Droit Humain* Lodge in 1881. She was one of the great humanitarians of her day. She fought for women's rights and women's suffrage." Toni noted the date. 1881. Obviously a woman ahead of her time; French women would have to wait another 63 years for the vote. "And Louise Michel was a contemporary of hers but more engaged in the fight for social rights."

This was the first Toni had ever heard of Maria Desraismes but Louise Michel was a fairly well-known figure. The Red Virgin. A strong-minded woman from the revolutionary heydays of the late 1800s. Still, Toni was unconvinced. "If women can join, then why was I told they can't?"

"Well, it depends on the lodge. Some lodges are strictly male. Others are co-ed. And some are entirely female."

"Ah." Finally, a little clarity. As well as confirmation of Marco's information. "So women aren't really allowed to join; they're put in an ersatz branch."

The guide looked as if he'd just been slapped. "It's not an ersatz. It's simply that the choice to allow women to join or not is left to the discretion of each lodge."

"In other words, to the men," Toni noted discordantly. "And because most men don't want them to join women are, by definition, left with an ersatz – cut off from the mainstream. After all, how could the women know all the secrets of Freemasonry if they've never been allowed into the full-fledged lodges?"

"Within certain circles it would be entirely feasible to transmit information from a male lodge to a female lodge." The guide was spiralling from the role of bored tour guide to defender of the cause.

As unconvincing as she found his arguments, Toni hadn't come all this way for a feminist debate. She knew that if she let the guide continue harping on about what an open-minded organization Freemasonry was, she would just waste time. Instead she put on her best dumb blonde smile so that the supposed free-thinker would believe he'd won her over. "Why don't you show me the rest of the museum?"

The illusion worked. Satisfied, he ambled towards the next poster with renewed confidence. "Ah yes," he said knowingly, reading the heading. "The Third Republic and Leon Gambetta." Toni winced. She hoped this guy wasn't just going to follow her around, reading out the posters. She didn't need help with that. What she wanted was extra insight. Something that wasn't plastered all over the walls.

"He was one of the presidents during the Third Republic, wasn't he?" she prompted, remembering the urn in the Pantheon holding this very man's heart.

The guide nuanced the concise biography. "Actually he was President of the Council – basically Prime Minister. But yes, he was deeply involved in establishing many of our greatest republican principles, like secular school and social equality."

Calling up her sweetest smile she added, "The Third Republic was also the period when the Pantheon was turned into a secular temple."

"Yes. A monument to the men who made France what it is today."

Toni could hardly argue with that description although she did consider adding that the building was a shocking mixture of Catholicism, mysticism and State as a divine entity, not to mention the almost total absence of women. But she wasn't that stupid. Better to keep the guide on her side. So she flashed an enticing smile and ambled on in search of something more useful.

It wasn't until she reached the back of the room, almost hidden behind another glass case, that she finally noticed a poster that called to her. "The Freemason's year." That sounded promising. Maybe she would find a mention of the New Year.

As she read the narration on the blue and brown placard a feeling of perplexity began to grow. "It says here that the New Year begins on the summer solstice," she said turning to her guide for clarification. "I thought it began on the Feast of St. John."

The guide rubbed his hands together. There was a renewed glint of playfulness. It was obvious he held the key to information that the cute brunette was looking for. The schoolboy with a secret was going to be able to tease and tantalize the schoolgirl. "You're right and you're wrong. It's true that the Grand Lodge year begins on St. John the Baptist's Day."

"June 24th."

"Yes. With the traditional agapes the night before. The 23rd."

"But either way that's not the summer solstice. The summer solstice is June 21st."

The grin on the man's face screamed out that he was basking in his intellectual superiority. "Today the dates are separate. Historically they were one and the same. You see, the summer solstice is a festival that dates back long before the Christian calendar and saints' days. Its roots are based in the most powerful pagan tradition ever: sun worship. From Ra to the Phoenix to St. John, the sun has always been an object of devotion simply because the sun is the source of all life. It provides heat to keep us warm and a natural clock to order our lives."

"So ancient man started worshipping the element itself: fire," Toni agreed. *Yadda yadda yadda.* She knew plenty about the tradition.

Back in Quebec, as a child she'd often gone out on mid-summer's evenings to watch the bonfires and fireworks.

"Yes. Across Europe, fire and the sun were honored in the pagan calendar when the sun was at its highest or lowest point in the sky; the summer and winter solstices." The guide looked at her inquiringly, as if checking whether all this information wasn't overloading her pretty little brain. "But when Christianity was introduced, there was both a strong theological need to get rid of these pagan superstitions and a strong popular resistance to removing them."

"In other words, the Church didn't dare scrap the old holidays, so they just gave them new names and slowly worked in the Christian rituals alongside the old pagan ones."

"That's right," he agreed, complimenting her on following so well. "You see the early Christian fathers were pragmatic. They knew they'd stand a better chance of attracting new followers if they hung on to some of the old rituals and holidays."

"People like holidays. I get it." When would this guy cut to the chase? "What I don't understand is why you call it the summer solstice if you're really talking about St. John's Day. June 24th is three days after the summer solstice."

A glint of raffish amusement sparkled in his eye. "They're not the same anymore..." and he paused for effect, "but they used to be. You see, we think of June 21st as being the summer solstice. The day when the sun is furthest from the Earth and therefore the days are longest. That wasn't always the case."

If this guy didn't spit it out soon, Toni was going to slap him. "But the solstice hasn't changed."

"The solstice hasn't changed; the calendar has. I'm talking about the change from the Julian calendar to the Gregorian calendar."

Toni plunged inward, desperately searching her memory for the relevant information. It wasn't there. Luckily, the guide was enjoying the opportunity to shine. "The Roman calendar continued to be used long after the fall of Rome and its empire. But even though it was fairly precise, the length of the Julian year wasn't quite right. By the time Gregory XIII became pope, the spring equinox had slipped to March 10th. The seasons were out of sync with the calendar. So Kepler calculated the length of the new calendar. In 1582, the Pope decreed that October 4th would be followed by October 15th."

Although the titbit was amusing Toni was struggling to understand what it had to do with anything. "That was 450 years ago. You guys are still using the old calendar?"

The more impatient Toni became, the slower her guide seemed to go. "Not really. The thing is, you have to understand the historical context of the change. The Pope made his decree, but there was a lot of resistance to it. The general population didn't like the new calendar because they thought they were being cheated (they'd paid rent for their houses for a full month and then eleven days disappeared into thin air). They thought it was just another plan by the landlords to get rich." Toni could definitely relate to that. "The Protestants didn't like it, either. The Reform was well under way by then and the papacy didn't carry the same clout anymore. A few deeply Catholic countries went along with the pope's decree – Italy, Spain, Poland – and a few others followed a year or two later. But the strongly Protestant northern countries resisted. Great Britain didn't accept the change until 1752."

The guide placed his hand on Toni's shoulder and led her to a display a few meters along. Theoretically it was the first poster in the museum but they'd been working backwards chronologically, so Toni had missed it. The information on it dealt with the origins of Freemasonry and talked about Anderson's rules. It stated that the Premier Grand Lodge of England, the first lodge ever, had been formed on June 24th 1717 and the First Minute Book of the Grand Lodge of England was dated June 24th 1723. Both dates came before the acceptance of the Gregorian calendar. "You see," the guide explained, "the summer solstice is a very important date in the Freemason's calendar. It's the very date when the Brotherhood was first forged. But it's the old solstice that we're attached to, for historic reasons."

"So despite the fact that the calendar's changed, you still link June 24th to the summer solstice. Even though it's really the 21st."

"You're a fast learner."

Although the compliment was given with more condescension than Toni was happy with, she was well beyond worrying about it. In any case, she wasn't even listening to her guide anymore. Her mind was struck by the fact that any non-Mason who had heard that the Masonic New Year began on the summer solstice wouldn't be waiting for St. John's Day. He would be celebrating it on the 21st. Tonight.

72

When the two officers returned to the car, they found a motorcycle cop waiting for them, standing rigid beside his bike, a slim black folder tucked under his arm. Sadiqi had a fairly good idea what that meant. Dukrin had something for him. Special delivery.

As Podesta checked his text messages, the inspector cracked open the protective leather case. *The Clavreul Report.* Sadiqi flipped straight to the fourth chapter, subheading 4.6. There it was! Maybe his luck was finally changing. As if in response, to this hopeful thought, Podesta lifted his eyes from his phone: "I've got some good news and some bad news. Which do you want first?"

Sadiqi scowled but played along. "Give me the good news; I'd like to think I'm on a roll."

"Philippe Desjardins has come out of his coma. It looks like the kid's coherent again."

"So what's the bad news?"

"We've got a new message from the Nightingale."

Sadiqi wasn't sure that was bad news. It could be the clue he was looking for. But before he could start rejoicing or believing that a good cosmic vibration had finally come his way, a text message pinged through his phone. One look at the screen told him his optimism had been misplaced:

Corrigan: **WRONG DATE. It's going to happen TODAY."**

73

Toni had been waiting at the meeting point beside the Opera for barely five minutes when Sadiqi's hatchback screeched to a halt beside her, siren blaring. She climbed straight in and was instantly thrown backwards with the car tearing away from the curb before she'd had time to pull the door shut.

"So where's Sancho Panza?" she asked, buckling up to avoid being flung from the car as they swerved around the corner.

"If you mean Lieutenant Podesta, he's following up some leads," Sadiqi explained cooly. "So what makes you think our deadline's been moved forward?" If Corrigan hadn't already provided him with several useful leads he wouldn't have taken her message seriously. But if their time scale really had just shrunk by two days, he needed to know the details.

Toni gave a concise rundown of the confusion of dates between the summer solstice and St. John's Day. "The point is," she added, "if someone who's not a Mason is writing the messages to make it look like the Masons are involved in this, it's just possible they got the dates wrong. They might have heard that the Masonic New Year starts on the summer solstice. If that's the case, they would be thinking June 21st. There aren't a lot of people around nowadays who still think of June 23rd or 24th as the solstice."

Sadiqi seriously hoped Toni was wrong. If he had another forty-eight hours he might stand a chance of figuring out what was going on. If the next stage of the attack was already imminent he was going to have one hell of a time stopping it. Unfortunately, what she was saying made perfect sense. "That would fit with the other part of the message," he agreed. "The songs turning to screams. It's simply referring to the *Fête de la Musique*. Which confirms the idea that this is going to happen tonight and not on the 23rd."

Eureka moments were supposed to be positive experiences but this one had the opposite effect. Sadiqi felt sickened by the horrific logic of the plan. If there was a madman out tonight, the terror he could wreak was enormous. Every year on June 21st, people descended into the streets to sing, play music, dance or just listen to the cacophony of musicians. The sidewalks would be packed with people from 6PM to 2 in the morning. There would be countless tens of thousands of people in the Latin Quarter alone. There was no telling how many.

As the car passed between the Tuileries Gardens and the Louvre, he looked at the groups of young people sprinkled along the sidewalks and squares, setting up loud speakers and tuning guitars. The *Fête de la Musique* was like Christmas shopping on December 24th except worse. There would be families out with babies in strollers; teenagers everywhere with special permission to stay out late. And tonight, because of the heat, there would be even more people than usual. People trying to enjoy a wisp of fresh air at the end of a sweltering day.

"Of course, the big question is 'What's the target?' Did you learn anything from the Great Master?" Toni asked, reaching for the nicotine candies on the dashboard. She snapped one out of the wrapper and teased it along the driver's lips.

As he navigated through near-saturated traffic at breakneck speed, Sadiqi glanced sideways at the girl driving shotgun. She still looked the same as this morning. Hell, she still looked the same as last night. Even better. After no sleep and a day of crazy.

And seeing her sitting there so cool, he had to ask the question: "Who are you? Any normal person would be terrified by what's happening."

She smiled. "I'm Canadian. We've got ice in our veins."

He turned his gaze back to the road. "Thanks. Just what I need: Another riddle." But he parted his lips and let her pop the mint in. Then he answered her question. "The Grand Master was unhelpful."

"So you banged him in prison with Trouvé?"

"A few hours behind bars gives people time to think. Makes them more amenable." Not that there was a lot of time to play with if Corrigan was right about the new timetable. "For the moment, all we've got to go on is a new message from the Nightingale. It says: *'Retribution will come from St. Genevieve.'*"

Toni barely needed to think about the words. The answer was obvious. "That confirms what I thought. The Pantheon *is* the target. The Pantheon was originally designed as a church dedicated to St. Genevieve. It only became a Pantheon after the Revolution. One of the streets that leads to the Pantheon is still called *'rue de la Montagne Ste. Genevieve'.*" *St. Genevieve's Hill.*

"That's one possibility," Sadiqi acknowledged. "The other one is Henri IV High School. Before it was turned into a school, it was a Genovefan monestary." She no doubt understood but he spelt it out anyway. "Genovefan. As in the order dedicated to St. Genevieve."

"So maybe Trouvé was right. Maybe the Chamber of Reflections is just a red herring. Nothing to do with the message. The killer's aiming for something high profile. "

"Maybe," Sadiqi conceded. *Or maybe there were two attacks planned: one near the Pantheon and one in the Chamber – wherever the hell that was.*

74

"So is that where we're headed," Toni asked, as they barrelled along the embankment beside the Seine. "The Pantheon?"

The cop gave a tense shake of his head. "Not yet. We're going to the hospital first. You remember that kid I told you about – the one raving about the Vauvert Devil." He shot a glance sideways just long enough to catch her nodding. "Well, apparently his condition has improved. I want to interview him. I thought I'd take you along in case his ramblings got a little too Technicolor cata-crazy for me."

As the car in front failed to get out of his way, Sadiqi slowed gears and reached into the back seat for the *Clavreul Report*. What he was about to do carried the risk of taking him somewhere he really didn't want to go. If the need to know hadn't been so strong, he wouldn't have done it. "And being as you're such a hot detective, you can do me a favor," he said, tossing her the document. "Read Chapter 4.6 and tell me what you think. Tell me what got Trouvé and the Freemasons upset. Find any information about anything in the catacombs that you've never heard before."

Toni looked so happy you would have thought she'd just been handed the cup of eternal life. "I thought this was confidential," she said, flipping through to Section 4.6 to see what new information was added compared to the version she'd already seen.

"It is." If he was making a mistake sharing this with her, then it was on Dukrin. She should have given him the heads-up. "I'm just assuming I can trust you."

*   *   *

Sub-chapter 4.6 was only eight pages long and Toni was a fast reader. It wasn't until she was about halfway through that she even slowed and that was only because a fluorescent orange Post-it was pasted across the middle of the sheet. She deciphered the message on the small rectangle then peeled it away, crumpling it silently between her fingers so that she had a clear view of the words below. With the cop silent other than the occasional profanity aimed at the heavy traffic, she was easily able to read all the material before they drove into the compound at Cochin Hospital.

"So, what did you learn?" he asked, pulling on the handbrake.

Toni wavered. Hope was pinned on what she was going to say. "Most of it's just Caron's usual scare mongering. *Yadda yadda yadda.* Turning shadows into threats. It's true that he names the lodge and that he lists several members. A couple of ministers. A few famous actors. Journalists."

Sadiqi sensed the tiniest hesitation. "But there's something else bothering you."

She glanced down at the pages, looking slightly nervous. She certainly wasn't as lighthearted as she'd been when he picked her up. "I guess. Yeah. It's not 100% Caron. Only 99%."

"So what's not right?"

"You're going to think it's stupid."

"That's never stopped you before."

Toni winced at the dig before pointing to a paragraph halfway down the page. "He goes on about how dangerous the unauthorized use of the quarries is. The risk of supposedly reasonable groups being infiltrated by dangerous extremists who then take advantage of knowledge acquired through groups like the Freemasons to wreak havoc on the city."

"The honorable Freemasons going over to the dark side." There was a tinge of disappointment in his voice.

"Yeah. That's exactly what he means. But that's pure Caron," she said, waving aside this first unimportant aspect of the report, her confidence returning. "The thing that's strange is that he refers to something he calls *the puzzles of history*."

"Very poetic. But what does it mean?" Sadiqi had noticed that, too, when he read the report before coming to meet her.

"That's the whole point." Her voice was more animated now. "Caron was never poetic. He didn't think like that. He thrived on engineering norms and administrative blueprints. On a good day, he might have given a few minutes' thought to architectural heritage or styles. But he would never, *never*, give a second's thought to stories based on folklore and rumors." Her finger traced the words on the passage. "Yet here he says:

> *'the puzzles of history have woven a fabric of impenetrable popular myths. Long before Rol and Von Choltitz discovered the protective attributes of the quarries, the revolutionaries of the Convention and the Commune exploited the portal. Thus, the urban warrior stepped through the looking-glass in order to escape persecution. If left unchecked, this shadow world could be used to destroy the city rather than preserve it. '*

Toni looked up. "The end is pure Caron. But the references to *the puzzles of history*, the *portal* and *stepping through the looking-glass* are something else."

Why did French intellectuals always insist on being so pretentious, Sadiqi wondered. Why did they always have to use so many words to say so little? So much time spent on form rather than substance. "What does it mean?"

"That's the problem." Her usual enthusiasm had disappeared below a blanket of unease. "It's pretty ambiguous. Caron wasn't usually wordy. He was concise. And never romantic."

"And the *portal*."

"Yes, the *portal* is particularly obscure." That was the strangest point of all. "Normally I would have said that it simply refers to someone gaining entry to the quarries. But if the Freemasons were all upset about this chapter, it must mean something more specific."

"Their Chamber of Reflection," Sadiqi suggested.

"Yeah. Or some hidden access used during the historic periods he mentions. If we piece it together with the message you just received it could be referring to somewhere under the Pantheon or Henri IV. They're both buildings that survived the Revolution and the Commune. Maybe there really are tunnels down there. A secret door linking up with the rest of the network." She was trying to be analytical, but excitement was creeping into her voice again.

"The puzzles of history," Sadiqi breathed a sigh of disgust. Even in death Caron got on his nerves. But of course, Caron had been vague for a reason. He'd wanted to refer to his damn Chamber without actually saying where it was. He hadn't wanted to annoy the Brotherhood. So instead, the damn fool had failed on both accounts: he'd managed to annoy the Brotherhood while at the same time missing the opportunity to leave a useful clue.

Desjardins was their last hope. Hopefully he could shed some light on things.

"Anything else in there you noticed?" the cop asked.

"No. That's it."

Sadiqi was really beginning to feel beaten. There was something else in the report she should have mentioned. He knew that because he was the one who'd left it there. By choosing not to mention it, she had just proven that she couldn't be trusted.

She was assuming he hadn't looked at the report before giving it to her. But he had.

If there was one thing he needed on a case, it was perfect trust in the people he was working with. She had just broken that circle of trust. His brain told him to boot her out of the car right there and then. His instinct told him to hold on to her. The layers of complexity in this case were overwhelming. And none of this stuff was his field of expertise. Despite the fact that she was adding an extra dash of confusion to everything, he wanted her to hear Desjardins' story. If nothing else, maybe she would be able to add a little clarity to whatever he had to say.

75

It wasn't easy getting Philippe Desjardins' parents out of his room. After waiting four days for their child to regain consciousness they weren't ready to abandon him that easily. Fortunately, when Sadiqi finally managed to hustle them out, he found the young cataphile's mental faculties much clearer than he expected, even if his nerves were still frayed.

"We were at a party under Val-de-Grace," Desjardins explained. "I was there with a friend."

"Quentin Asselin," Sadiqi said.

The young man was reclining in bed, his head raised on a pile of pillows. Despite these efforts to put him at ease, he was alive with ticks – outward signs of inward torment. His fingers had gathered together fistfuls of sheets that he was kneading compulsively. "You know about him?" His eyes flashed back and forth between Toni, who was sitting at his side and Sadiqi, standing at the foot of the bed.

"We know he's missing."

Desjardins' left eye-lid twitched. "He's not missing. He's dead. There was a guy with a gun. He shot Quentin and Quartz. I guess I got away," he added bleakly. Toni thought the young man should have shown more enthusiasm about being alive but Sadiqi recognized the dull monotone of survivor's guilt. The cop would give this kid a chance to exorcise some of those demons by describing what had happened.

"You'd better go back to the beginning. I'm going to need more details."

Desjardins' eyes ricocheted back and forth between his two visitors. "Me and Quentin have been visiting the catas together for nearly two years," he said. "We go down at least once a week, usually more. Anyway, last Friday there was this big party. Lots of tourists, but a few serious cataphiles, too." His words began quietly, barely a whisper. But with each sentence he seemed to draw a little energy. "There was this one guy: Quartz. A real legend. He knows the whole network inside-out. Anyway, this guy told us that he'd found a passage from the GRS to H4."

The young man's agitation suggested that not everything he said was entirely lucid. He was probably still suffering from some form of shock. Yet Toni couldn't hold back a sense of wonder. "It really exists," she muttered.

The young man nodded. "Yes, it really exists." He seemed so certain about what he was saying. "And Quartz took us there. I didn't believe it existed at first, but he leads us down a few corridors, then stands us in front of this dead end of solid wall and then he goes: '*Voilà!*'" As much as Desjardins longed to pass himself off as a quarry professional, Toni recognized the amateur's vague awe in the way he described the mysterious tunnels of the network.

"At first I thought, 'You're kidding, right?' I thought Quartz was having us on. All I could think about was getting back to the party but then Quentin starts running his hands over the crust of the limestone. The wall was a "bourrage": a dry stone wall." Toni knew exactly what this meant. Centuries earlier, a totally gutted, structurally weak gallery had been filled in with disused bits of stone and dust in order to stop the ceiling from collapsing. "It took Quentin a while to find the weak link. To find the stone that would unlock the tunnel. The ones on the right were wedged too tightly together. But he keeps going until he finds a big stone that comes loose. I couldn't believe it. Behind it there was an empty space. *Une chatière.*" Again Toni knew exactly what this meant. They had uncovered a cat flap. A narrow shaft leading upward above the loose stones.

"So we take out a few other rocks blocking the entrance and hoist ourselves up and start squeezing through. We had to crawl along on our stomachs, flat against the ground. The shaft wasn't very long; maybe three or four meters. And really narrow. But we didn't care. We were so blown away at the idea of discovering whatever was on the other side. It led to this other tunnel. Bigger, but still awfully tight. We weren't crawling anymore. We were on our feet. But we couldn't stand up straight. The ceiling was too low. But in front of us, it was huge. A perfectly straight corridor. Maybe 20 or 30 meters long."

The cop was glad there was no medical staff around because he knew he'd get thrown out for agitating the patient if anyone saw his current state. Desjardins had let go of his bedclothes and was now squeezing Toni's hand so hard her fingertips were purple. But the pain wasn't enough to make her want him to stop the story. Despite the terrified look in the young man's eyes, she was lapping this up. "Do you understand what I'm saying?" he stammered. "It was fantastic. It wasn't a quarry; it was a tunnel. A tunnel built for moving between the southern network and Henri IV." His eyes flew nervously from Sadiqi to Corrigan. Panic sprang into his voice. "I know you don't believe me, but it's true. Henri IV. Quartz had been there. He said the tunnel passed under the Pantheon. And then another shaft leading to an old isolated gallery. Then another shaft going to the school."

Toni used each of the details to draw the map in her mind. The tunnel he had seen must have connected with the potters' wells that used to run under the area. It was something she'd seen mentioned on maps before, but she hadn't thought they were accessible anymore.

The young man was reaching fever pitch. Toni caressed his arm. "Just relax," she soothed with more composure than she felt. What she was hearing went well beyond anything she'd ever imagined in her wildest dreams, no matter what she'd suggested to Sadiqi. "There's no hurry. Don't exhaust yourself."

Desjardins' body relaxed the tiniest bit. His hand slipped out of Toni's and his fingers went back to the sheets, gently massaging them again. When he finally spoke, his tone had calmed to the point of morbidity. "We never got to H4. Quartz and Quentin headed off down the passage, but I stayed behind. Just for a second. I needed to take a leak," he said, diverting his eyes from Toni, then adding almost apologetically, "All the beer from the party. So I fall back and wait for them to move ahead. It's while I'm pissing that I start to get a bad feeling. I start looking at the rock – at the way it's cut – and I see the problem. I'd never seen stone cut like that before. The marks were too rough and deep, as if the pieces had been hacked off in huge slabs. Some of the gauges were like five or ten centimeters deep. I ran my hands over the surface and the edges were sharp. It wasn't normal." He grabbed Toni's hand again, digging his nails into the soft flesh. "You know what I mean."

Yes. She knew exactly what he meant. The old quarries had been laboriously chiselled out by workmen using very basic implements. Their tools had left shallow furrows in the stone. If the walls of the tunnel Desjardins had seen showed deeper marks, it meant the stones had been torn apart by modern tools, and that no erosion or concretion had had time to occur. "The tunnel was a new creation," Toni explained for Sadiqi's benefit. "Made recently using modern equipment."

"Is that when you turned back?" Sadiqi asked.

The look of devastated sadness on the young man's face was answer enough. "No. I was still trying to figure it out. I look back at the opening we've just come out of and that's when I really get worried. Just below the shaft exit there's a strange, brick-shaped rock. Except it isn't a brick. And the color is all wrong. It's too dark. Not at all the same color as the limestone."

"Did you touch it?"

"Yeah. It was heavy. But when I squeezed it, my fingers sank into it. It was soft. Like clay."

Toni had a pretty good idea what that meant. She caught Sadiqi's gaze. "Semtex?"

A tiny shiver passed through Desjardins' body. "Yeah. That's what I figured. And that's when I started freaking out. I mean, I've known cataphiles to dig out tunnels. To carry rocks around. Even to carve out new tunnels and galleries. But not with dynamite or plastic explosives."

"What did you do?"

"It was too late. I wanted to tell the guys that something was wrong. But that's when I heard the shot. When I turn, Quentin is already on the ground. There's some psycho with a gun, trying to pick us off, one by one. He shoots Quentin. Then he shoots Quartz. Then he comes after me." There was panic in Desjardins' voice, his breath coming in gasps. His fingers dug into the bedclothes and his whole body went rigid, as if he were trying to push himself backwards into the oblivion of his pillows. "Except because I hung back I actually had a chance of escape. The guy's chasing me. But I have a head start. I get into the shaft. He shoots at me. But I have time to get away. At least out of sight. Then I hide in a hole I'd used once before to hide from the cops. But this guy won't let up. He spent hours stalking me; walking back and forth down the tunnels. Waiting for me to come out. He knew I was hiding somewhere and he wanted to be there when I finally came out."

The gist of the story left little doubt. This was confirmation that the niche with the backpack in it had been a hiding place used by the kid to duck the killer. That's how he'd survived. Sadiqi knew it was time to let Desjardins calm down before he freaked out completely. "The gunman was alone, right?"

"Yes."

"He never called for reinforcements or spoke with anyone else."

"No. There was just silence. I could hear his footsteps whenever he passed by the niche I was in. But that's all."

Sadiqi visualized this brutal Nightingale walking around in the dark with his night vision goggles, carrying out his solitary work like some apocalyptic angel of death. "Can you remember where that connecting shaft was?"

"Sure. It was under rue des Ursulines."

"Could you mark it on a map?"

"Of course."

Sadiqi pulled the stopper off the tube he'd brought from the car and handed the roll of sheets to Toni. She took the cue, producing the desired page and flattening it across Desjardins' knees. The young man had obviously never seen the dense detail of the IGC *Atlas* before. His eyes shot from one corner of the page to the other, trying to get his bearings. But then his trembling finger started tracing an imaginary line across the page before stopping on a squiggle that indicated a dead end. "It was there. Right there. Quartz said that it ran under rue d'Ulm then straight up to the Pantheon."

"That's not far from where we were yesterday," Toni said.

Sadiqi grabbed the map, thanked the kid and was out of the room before Toni had time to register he was on the move. When she caught up with him in the corridor, he was shooting instruction into his phone while practically bouncing off passing doctors and nurses.

"I need a special ops team in the catacombs. Make sure everyone's equipped with night vision goggles. No lamps no flashlights." It took a couple of minutes for him to run through his complete list of order.

Toni jogged close behind. "What do you think they're planning?" she asked as soon as he had clicked off his phone.

"You were right. He's going to blow up the Pantheon. It fits. He's going to blow up the Pantheon during the *Fête de la Musique*. The songs turning to screams. That entire area will be swarming with people for the festival; he wants to kill them all. The Freemason's temple of humanity. The Pantheon is the logical link between the GRS and H4." All the clues were connecting. "Semtex explosives. They're going to blow the whole damn thing sky high," he said, throwing open the hospital door and breaking into a sprint across the compound. It only took him a second to reach his car and climb in.

The student was right behind and equally fast climbing in. "Khalid, please, listen to me. Stop. That's not possible. They can't blow up the Pantheon. When I said the Pantheon, I meant that general area. Something in or around the building. Part of it maybe. But he can't blow up the actual Pantheon structure. That's crazy."

"This guy *IS* crazy."

"No. I mean blowing up the Pantheon – it's not feasible." If he would just listen, she could explain.

Instead he fired the ignition.

So she lunged for the key. The engine went dead. "Calm down and listen."

There was a look of such concentrated intensity in the man's eyes it scared Toni. "Give me the keys and get out." The tone was so harsh it was unrecognizable. This was a side of the man she hadn't yet seen. She wasn't going to risk finding out what would happen if she didn't comply.

"You've got to trust me on this," she murmured as she dropped the keys in his hand and slid out.

That was the problem. He didn't trust her anymore.

The door was still open and she was peering in. "Have you ever looked at the Pantheon?" she asked quietly. "I mean really looked at it. Do you know how solid it is? I know you saw the simulation photo on my laptop of the thing imploding, but it can't really be destroyed that easily. It's solid. It's enormous. You'd need roomfuls of dynamite to make the meters of ground between the surface and the quarries collapse. You couldn't hide that amount of Semtex. Someone would have noticed it. Ferry or some cataphiles. Hell, you probably couldn't sell that amount of Semtex without someone noticing. And even if someone did set off a tonne of explosives and weaken the underground structure, the building itself wouldn't crumble immediately. It's too massive. If the ground underneath were unstable, it would take days even weeks for the building to start showing signs of instability. First a crack would appear. Then we'd realize that the land wasn't stable. Then there'd be another crack. That's how it works. Slowly. Time measured in months or years, not minutes. You can't just decide, 'Okay, June 21st at 8PM I'm going to blow up the Pantheon.'"

Sadiqi grabbed the steering wheel and pushed backwards, shoving his shoulders against the seat. This case was driving him crazy. He smashed his hands into the steering wheel in a quick angry motion, the power of which shook the whole car. The physical release seemed to calm him. At least a little. "Look, I don't know how the hell he's going to do it, but I'm damn sure he's planning to blow something up around there."

"Maybe he can compromise the land's structural integrity; but he can't blow up the Pantheon."

Instead of giving him clarity, Corrigan was just making this worse. She was an added complication he didn't need. He should have ditched her as soon as they'd arrived at the hospital. This wasn't how he worked.

Except usually he wasn't working in the catacombs.

He grabbed the Zippo lighter and flipped it open and closed once, then shot it back into the tray.

He couldn't do this without her. On his own, without her input, there was just too much information missing. "Get in," he growled, not even looking at her but sliding the key into the ignition.

Toni took another step away from the car. "Get in. Get out. Get in. What is your problem?"

"My problem is that someone seems to be planning on blowing this whole fucking city sky high tonight. That's all I have time to focus on right now." He didn't want to have to worry about why the otherwise righteous Ms. Corrigan was messing with him. Because that's what was happening. She was messing with him. Not only had she not mentioned the Post-it that had been glued in the middle of section 4.6, she had been very dexterous at ungluing it and sliding it into her pocket when she thought he wasn't looking. Not only did she not want to mention it, she didn't want him to know about it at all. Which is why he would have preferred to keep her out of the investigation. There was too much other stuff going on for him to be wasting his time, looking over his shoulder, keeping an eye on her.

But his composure had returned. He pointed to the empty seat beside him. He needed her expertise. Without her, there were just too many details missing in his intel. "You're right. Get in. I need you. You need to help me figure this out." He was thinking out loud now. "If it's not the Pantheon then it must be the school. Desjardins said there was a tunnel to the school. I'm sending Ferry with a RAID team to look for Desjardin's passage from the GRS. I need you to find me a way into the catacombs from the other side. From the high school. From H4. Hopefully we can trap the Nightingale in the middle."

Toni raised her eyebrows but climbed in. "That school has been there for over two hundred years, without anyone ever finding a passage. How am I supposed to find one?"

The cop glued the magnetic strobe light to the roof and shifted into gear. "That's your problem, Ice Lady."

76

On the drive over from the hospital, Sadiqi had Toni on the phone to Ferry, feeding him the coordinates of the tunnel Desjardins had described so that the cataflic would know where to head with the special ops team. His group would have to find the tunnel from the south side of the Pantheon. In the meantime, Toni was supposed to find a way into the network from H4 on the north side.

Sadiqi's car blazed onto the square opposite the school and pulled to a halt in front of a group of riot police in full body armor who were trying to hustle a folk band to safer grounds. Far from being intimidated by the horde of cops, the budding musicians were squabbling to maintain their right to play at the *Fête de la Musique*. It was a losing battle. In any case, a rumble of thunder announced that nature was planning on ruining the party for everyone. There was a storm coming.

Shimmying a "police" armband onto his sleeve, Sadiqi raced past the rabble to where Podesta was waiting inside the school gates. By the time Toni caught up with them they were flashing police ID at the concierge and ordering the evacuation of the premises.

While Sadiqi was doing his Zorro routine, Toni pushed through the swinging door that separated the reception area from the school grounds. The sea of contemplative calm that unfolded before her contrasted with the bedlam that seemed to materialize around Khalid wherever he went. She'd often walked past H4, admiring the stately aspect of Clovis Bell Tower that dominated the narrow street but this was the first time she'd ever come in. Sadiqi had said the building was originally an abbey dedicated to St. Genevieve. The meditative atmosphere of the order was still palpable even in the building's current form as a high school. The space where Toni was standing was in fact a cloister and off to her right she could see a door labeled 'Chapel'.

As she looked around she became increasingly aware of the size of the task Sadiqi had set her. There was a lot of ground to cover. All told, the school occupied an entire city block. Across the cloister, there was an archway leading to another courtyard. And beyond that, yet another. She also knew that if the Genovefans had been anything like as enthusiastic about the quarries as the Carthusians, it was possible there were multiple routes from the buildings' basements to the limestone below.

Before she had time to finish taking in the surroundings, Sadiqi slammed through the swinging door with Podesta and a plain clothed officer in tow. "The concierge says the access to the basement is this way," he said, as he led them diagonally across the courtyard and through another massive archway, where they discovered a marble staircase framed by statues of saints and the Blessed Virgin.

With a marble Baby Jesus looking on curiously, Sadiqi vaulted over the stone banister and yanked open a heavy door that was niched behind. "I think this is it." A plummeting corkscrew stairwell had appeared. The architecture was promising as far as Toni was concerned – it had to be about 300 years old. On the other hand, judging from the modern electric lighting and the metal handrail, the passageway was probably regularly used by staff and students. That wasn't a good sign. If there really was a long-lost entrance to the quarries through the school, it was more likely to be well-hidden. Otherwise it would never have escaped the attention of two centuries of IGC inspectors and wandering students. Whatever they were looking for would be off the beaten path.

So, when only five meters below the surface the staircase ended in front of a plaster wall complete with a prefabricated door made of particleboard Toni figured the chances of finding any long-lost tunnel were pretty slim. The décor didn't exactly evoke the monks of past centuries. The sparkling white paint paid tribute to recent renovation.

Sure enough, when Sadiqi pushed down on the handle, instead of discovering a stone staircase leading to the quarries, they found themselves standing in a vast storage room cluttered full of objects that had passed from usefulness to limbo. Bric-a-brac relegated to obsolescence. Old blackboards. Discarded textbooks. Chairs that someone had thought might come in handy but then forgot about. Decades of refuse piled wall-to-wall, floor-to-ceiling. And, Toni noted, a shiny new linoleum floor.

"There's no way we're going to find an access point here," she said.

The cop turned to her. "There's an entrance somewhere. Desjardins said there was a passage. So let's find it. Just tell me what we're looking for?"

Toni shrugged. It wasn't that easy. It could be a lot of things. "A door in a wall, a trapdoor in the floor, a staircase, a shaft." Those were only some of the possibilities.

Sadiqi barked out more orders, assigning each person a perimeter to search. Toni was told to scour the center of the room. If anything, this was the hardest area to cover, because while the officers checked the walls for doors, she had to move piles of junk to see if there was a trapdoor or something hidden below, which meant pushing old desks out of the way and shifting crates piled with discarded textbooks. But each carton and crate that was shifted only uncovered the same disappointment. No well-hidden hatch. No shaft in the ground.

In his corner of the room, Sadiqi was a storm of perpetual motion. He knocked over tables and sent pictures crashing to the ground in a battle to discover what lay beyond. As his frustration mounted, he tossed aside heavier bundles, generating crashing sounds that echoed through the basement.

Toni's own exasperation was mounting too. Whether done gently or with machismo, she was pretty sure the ridiculous moving process was not going to uncover a link to the quarries. There was no sign of a passageway here. Not even the tiniest hint. She couldn't feel the presence of the quarries around her. Everything was against it. She breathed in. She could smell plaster, dust and whitewash. No earth.

The air carried the odour of mildew and heat from the world above, not the mineral pungency of the quarries.

Still, Sadiqi was convinced they were on the right track. And when, after less than half an hour he tipped a ping pong table forward and discovered a massive wooden door behind, his spirit soared. Although the surrounding wall was covered in fresh-looking plaster, the dark cracked aspect of the door itself told him this wasn't a recent addition to the school. Surely this was an old point of passage. Something that had been part of the original abbey.

He tried the latch. Nothing happened. On a calmer day he might have taken the time to work the lock with a skeleton key, but today he was too edgy. He stepped back a pace and took a mental picture. The wood was old. And years of silence had drawn the worms to the feast. The frame was half-eaten. It wouldn't resist. He concentrated his strength in his gut then lunged forward, sending the full force of a kick into the obstacle. For a moment he thought he'd underestimated the solidity of old craftsmanship. But when he turned and used his shoulder as a battering ram, bashing the full weight of his body against it, the wood crumpled.

Toni and the two other cops moved forward, anxious to see what he'd found. Half swinging on its hinges, half dragging its frame, the door creaked open. Unlike the room they'd just searched, which was lit by rays of natural light coming from clefts situated at ceiling level, the space beyond the door was engulfed in darkness. Sadiqi peered forward, waiting for his eyes to adjust to the dark. But Toni had already produced a Petzl lamp from her backpack and was shining it in the space.

"*Merde*," Sadiqi spat.

Instead of a staircase to the quarries, all they found was another storeroom, identical to the first, piled with more useless junk that should have been thrown out years ago. Objects that would need to be shifted and rearranged. And to complicate matters, this second room was entirely unlit. It would be much harder to scan than the first one.

Half an hour later, their hands grey with dust, the four foragers surrendered to the obvious. There was no passage to the quarries through the storage rooms.

A sense of fear was growing in Sadiqi. The elite RAID special ops team he'd sent off with the cataflics was already below ground. According to Toni's estimates, it shouldn't be long before they reached the passage Desjardins had told them about. In fact, it was possible they'd already found it. That meant they would be entering the tunnel under rue d'Ulm and approaching the Pantheon and Henri

IV any time now. Sadiqi's failure to uncover the passage leading from the high school left several dangers looming. If the legionnaire was still underground, the men from the RAID could find themselves alone in a dead end tunnel, with only the mercenary waiting to greet them. Or, the legionnaire might escape back into Henri IV, and he, Sadiqi, would fail to capture him as he left. Or, worse yet, whatever attack the Nightingale was planning down there would be set into motion before Sadiqi could stop it. Either way, it didn't look good. Either way, their Nightingale was free to continue carrying out whatever murderous frolic he had planned.

"*On est foutus,*" the inspector said as he stamped back to the entry way and up the staircase. *We're screwed.*

77

While the murmur of men made its way back upstairs Toni lagged behind.

As much as she knew time was short and they had to act fast, Sadiqi's door-smashing and general high-pitched intensity was starting to rattle her. He was action in motion but he was acting without analyzing properly. He was out of his element; out of his depth. It was probably the quarries that made him uncomfortable. She could understand that. It's just that she felt she should be doing more to help put him back on track.

She crumpled onto the bottom step of the staircase to collect her thoughts, the rhythmic beat of the men's ascending footsteps providing a note of calm.

The futility of their efforts in the storage rooms disturbed her. She had worked conscientiously moving things, but she hadn't been happy about it. It had been all wrong. There had been no chance of finding any link to the quarries in that newly renovated, plastered environment.

On the contrary, here, at the foot of the staircase, her feet firmly planted on the dirt floor and the smell of limestone oozing from the walls, her brain began to focus. Sadiqi was right. The quarries were close. She sensed them nearby.

She glanced at the door to the room they'd just left. No. They'd been off-track in there. Then she stood up and scoured the space around her. Unlike the storerooms, here, at the bottom of the staircase, the basement was built directly into the ground. The floor was beaten earth and the walls were naked stone. In front of her, the spiral staircase wound upwards, turning regularly around a central pillar.

That's when she realized. The central pillar. The stairs wound down to the right of the pillar and from where she was standing it looked as if the space on the left of the pillar was solid wall.

But it wasn't. She stepped forward and slipped her hand into the shadows behind the staircase. What had appeared like a solid wall from the stairs was in fact a square pillar, sheltering a narrow passage.

Toni swung her bag off her shoulder and took the cap lamp out again. Strapping it to her forehead, she squeezed past the pillar into the tiny cramped space behind. The walls around her were packed earth. Not stone. That could only mean one thing. Once upon a time, this space had been an entirely empty gallery. Then it had been filled in to reinforce the ground to support the buildings above. Over time, that earth had been packed together to give it the solid texture it now had. Advancing deeper into the passageway, she smoothed her hand along the wall, her lamp focused on the space ahead. Right at the end of the passageway, about a meter above ground level, there was a break in the wall. The wall didn't run the whole height of the space. There was a top ledge – a shaft.

It was easy enough hoisting herself up. The only snag was the dress. Stupidest invention ever, she griped as her knee caught on a stone and she felt the burning sensation of dirt rubbing into her flesh. She ignored the sting, focussing instead on her surroundings.

The space she was in was big enough for her to crawl along on her hands and knees but with only the headlamp lighting the way, visibility was poor. Yet the space was promising. After a couple of meters, the shaft widened then ended suddenly, giving way to a small cave. Here, she was able to stand in an almost upright position.

As she took in the full extent of what she'd just found, a restless voice rumbled down the shaft. "When I tell people to follow, I expect them to do it. There's no time for this crap." Despite the fact he was only a few meters away, the voice sounded distant.

She leaned into the shaft and bellowed her favorite line of cataphile literature. "*Ici je savoure les deux plus douces choses de ce monde, la vengeance et l'impunité[1].*" *Here I savor the two sweetest things in this world: vengeance and impunity.*

Sadiqi wouldn't like her answer. She knew the words would give him the itch to drag her out of the tunnel by her ponytail. But she also

---

[1] Spoken by the character Rousselin in the novel *Salons et souterrains de Paris*, Joseph Méry, 1858 Paris. Author's translation.

knew the text was long enough to provide an audio cue that would guide him to her. In any case, the anger wouldn't last long. After all, she had found what he was looking for.

She turned and moved to the center of the gallery then crouched down.

With the gentleness she might have used to stroke her lover's cheek, her hand brushed over the roughly hewn stone ring of the well's coping.

78

Sadiqi found her sitting on the edge of a circular stone ledge that stood out about a foot above the level of the dirt floor. Under the smudges of dust and limestone the expression on her face was triumphant. "It's an old well," she said, dropping a handful of pebbles over the edge. For several seconds the cop could hear scratching sounds as the rocks scraped against the sides, cascading downward before finally coming to rest on firm ground.

The girl was unbelievable. "How did you do this?"

"What do you mean 'How did I do this?' I followed the signs. I followed the stone. I followed the scents."

Again, his mind was going in circles, trying to figure out how she could have seen what nobody else saw.

"Come on. I'm pretty sure the shaft will take us down to quarry level," she added, throwing a leg over the edge and hooking her right foot into the first iron rung at the top of the shaft wall.

Even if she'd been wearing running shoes and coveralls, there was no way he would have let her in that well. Before she could begin her descent Sadiqi caught her around the waist and pulled her back. "You're not going anywhere. We're doing this by the book."

79

It took the inspector less than twenty minutes to round up a team complete with two officers and all the equipment they needed for their expedition: bulletproof vests, helmets and night vision goggles as well as climbing harnesses and ropes. They weren't going to clamber down the rungs, one at a time. They were going to rappel down.

While the cops checked their material, Corrigan glared at Sadiqi with the same controlled rage he'd witnessed the previous morning after revoking her quarry authorization. "All that kit is just going to block you. If there are connecting shafts down there, you're never going to be able to get through with all that stuff on." He was doing his damnedest to pretend not to hear. As the cops lowered their goggles, Toni made one final attempt to convince him. "Let me go with you. I can help." She allowed her fingers to hover over his arm, then glance against his shirt.

He didn't need to hear what she had already repeated several times. Nobody knew better than he did just how valuable her underground skills were. Even in the virgin territory of an uncharted area, Corrigan would have the reflexes to orient herself. That wasn't the issue. The problem was that Sadiqi didn't know what would be waiting down there. Or how she would react. If he had learnt one thing today it was that the girl was full of surprises. And that wasn't what he needed. Not in general, and certainly not up against the legionnaire. There was no way she was coming along. He just hoped that his instinct would be enough to navigate the labyrinth and ensure he rendezvoused quickly with the RAID men and the cataflic guides he'd sent to find Desjardins' entrance on the other side of the Pantheon.

Once everything was prepped, Sadiqi chambered the first round in his Sig Pro and put on the security. Then he leaned backwards and stepped off the rim of the well into the darkness. Mueller and Pecheron followed, filling the gallery with a whirring sound as the three cascaded towards the bottom, leaving Podesta behind to guard the area and make sure Toni didn't climb into the well behind them.

The obscurity they were heading into was both real and figurative. The tunnels below H4 were completely uncharted. The rungs that whizzed by in front of them were so rusted with age they blended in with the light beige of the surrounding stone. Whatever was waiting below would probably be suffering from similar disrepair.

Of course, the biggest threat was the possibility the Nightingale would be waiting for them. Surely that was what Message 4 meant. Retribution from St. Genevieve. The legionnaire was waiting below.

He had his den down there. That was why this expedition was so essential. They needed to find him and stop him. Which wouldn't be easy being as their adversary would be enjoying the home turf advantage, while Sadiqi knew neither the layout of the tunnels nor even their full extent.

The initial touchdown went smoothly. He gave two tugs on the rope to signal to Podesta that they were safe – that there was no ambush. And the first signs were reassuring: there really was a tunnel leading off from the foot of the shaft. With the inspector leading and the last man in the formation covering their tail, they snapped into motion, with calculated slowness for perfect balance on the uneven terrain, advancing with heel-to-toe steps. The greenish-brown spectrum of their night goggles was trained on the distance as they scoured the darkness for human forms. This was no place for the trigger-happy; they needed to be both attentive and cautious. Any shadow in the darkness might just as easily be the RAID team advancing from rue d'Ulm as it could be the Nightingale. But that didn't mean they should take their time. There was no room for indecision; the legionnaire would have lightning reflexes. Speed was of the essence.

Fortunately the layout was basic: There was just one straight tunnel with no perpendicular paths leading off. It was the smallest of mercies but at least they weren't going to get lost in a maze. Which would have been encouraging if Sadiqi hadn't had a lilting Canadian accent echoing through his head: "*Whether you build stone walls or inject concrete into the tunnels, the IGC has to be able to access the network to make sure the reinforcements remain in good condition. Water seeps into the quarries. Over time gypsum and limestone erode.*" This old, isolated network was worse than tired reinforcements. It was structurally perilous. The walls they were following were chiselled directly into the rock. There were no reinforcements, no sustaining walls and every few meters, Sadqi's shoes hooked against slabs of limestone that had collapsed off the ceiling – unmistakeable signs that the tunnels had never been checked by the IGC. And, again, the soft lilt crept into his mind: "*The dilapidation would be hidden from sight so nobody would know about it until one day, a sinkhole appeared.*"

Toni's lore helped him to notice the features of the surrounding landscape, but it certainly didn't reassure him. In fact, he felt a growing sense of disquiet. This quarry that had been hidden for centuries was still standing. That in itself might be considered either a miracle or a disaster waiting to happen. How old would it be? Two?

Three? Five hundreds years old? In a state of advanced disrepair. In other words, it could collapse any second. Or perhaps the fact it was still intact was more than a case of blind luck. Maybe the fact that there was no road or apartment building above – just an empty courtyard – had stopped the land from collapsing. There wasn't much pressure being exerted on the void.

Then again, what did he know? It was Corrigan who would be able to evaluate those risks. She would have known how to nudge the team in the right direction, nodding to the left or right, pointing out whatever he was missing.

And with each footstep, the deeper he advanced, the further her protective presence retreated while the Nightingale's shadow grew. The impression was so strong it felt almost as if the whole subterranean world was turning against Sadiqi – the corridors themselves were altering, becoming more inhospitable and hostile. He told himself it was just an illusion – his mind playing tricks. But it was no impression. When they'd started from the well shaft, the men had been able to walk upright. After a few short minutes they were bending at the waist, hunched over to avoid scraping their helmets on the ceiling, backs bent and heads strained forward to keep eyes fixed on the dangers ahead. The ceiling was lower than it had been a few meters earlier. Yet twisted into this Quasimodo-like position, they still had to make good time if they were going to catch the legionnaire before he carried out his plan – whatever it was.

And now, the specter of the legionnaire dug its claws deeper into Sadiqi's mind, whispering to him that this terrain had been specially designed to ensure the survival of just one man: Rossignol. Everyone else was a walking target – exposed and vulnerable. Uncertain where they were headed. Uninformed of the obstacles and dangers.

Every one of Sadiqi's senses was focused on his environment in order to pick up on the least sign of danger. Except what good was perfect concentration if there was nothing to focus *on*? His sight was restricted by the goggles, which had a limited scope, granting very little peripheral vision. As for hearing, the multiplication of his own scuffling and scratching sounds amplified around him, making it impossible to hear anything else. He could hear his shirt chafing against the nylon of the bulletproof vest as well as the crunching of his footstep on the earth, not to mention both his own breathing and the breathing of the man behind him. And whenever one of them stumbled against a piece of rock on the ground, the sound seemed to swell into a minor explosion. The previous day, all he had heard in the catacombs were Corrigan's words of guidance. Now he strained to hear a sound – any sound – that he wasn't creating himself. Worse yet, he feared that the sounds of his advancement were rippling towards the Nightingale, warning him of their approach.

Sadiqi tried to fight back his unease by conjuring up Toni's guiding presence. At the very least, he could use the lessons she had taught him. What he needed to find was the path to meet up with the other team. He knew he was probably looking for a recently pierced shaft. And he knew that passageway might be very small and concealed. In fact, he might be looking for little more than a shadow hinting at the existence of a passage.

It was hard keeping the group moving while at the same time carrying out a thorough check in the dark. His attention shifted from the walls to the blackness ahead then back to the walls.

But the exercise paid off. He soon caught sight of the mirage he was looking for.

Signalling to halt, he dropped to his knees to examine a lower segment of wall where the darkness was deeper than a simple shadow. As he suspected, the stone evaporated beneath his hand. The contours weren't solid rock; they were the crevices that flagged a crossroad. The shadow signalled a connecting shaft.

Although the mouth of the shaft was minuscule – nothing more than a space big enough for a man to crawl through lying on his belly – peering in, Sadiqi could see that a few meters along, it widened into what, in catacomb terms, looked like a spacious chamber. The existence of this larger chamber probably would have been enough to convince the cop this was the route he needed. But a second indication confirmed his choice. The narrow shaft bore a striking resemblance to what Desjardins had described. The cut marks in the stone were deep and jagged. The breach into the main tunnel's wall was recent and had been pierced with modern tools.

The cop lowered himself for a better view into the shaft. It would be feasible to crawl through with the vest on, but barely. Just like Corrigan had warned, the heavy protection was going to limit manoeuvrability and make it harder to keep his weapon trained on the space ahead as he snaked along. He signalled to the two men, silently telling Pecheron to follow him into the shaft and Mueller to hang back in the tunnel to cover them from behind.

Once inside the connecting shaft, their vulnerability was obvious to both he and the junior officer. Lying flat on the ground, their goggles and helmets scraping against the low ceiling, it would be almost impossible to aim effectively if someone suddenly emerged ahead.

Luckily, the distance was short. There were only about six meters until the wider gallery yawned open. Moving head-to-foot, the knowledge of their vulnerability provided the incentive to keep advancing smoothly. It wasn't until they were an arm's length from the bigger gallery that they paused again.

Just because the open gallery was unlit that didn't necessarily mean it was uninhabited. Someone could be waiting in the dark, biding his time until the cops offered themselves up like some sacrifice to the god of stupidity.

While Pecheron lay still, Sadiqi surveyed the chamber ahead for any sign of life. On one hand, the silence was total. There was no movement. The gallery looked devoid of any human presence. But the man they were up against would know how to lie patiently waiting for them to make the wrong move. He could be flattened against the wall just beside the exit shaft, waiting to strike.

Whether or not there was anyone in the gallery now, someone had been there recently. The earthen pit was Spartan but functional. There was a ground sheet in one corner, along with a small camping gas burner and digging equipment. A wheelbarrow was tipped up against the wall, and to the side lay a pick, and even a small pneumatic drill with a generator. There was no doubt about it. This was the Nightingale's nest.

Sadiqi writhed closer to the mouth of the tunnel and took one last look before throwing himself head first into the opening, rolling into attack position, his weapon poised.

But again, there was no ambush.

Sadiqi did a quick once-over of the gallery, top to bottom. Although the night goggles didn't pick up detail with much clarity, his primary concern could be eliminated: The gallery was empty.

While Pecheron squirmed through to join him, the inspector continued his assessment. The gallery was no more than ten or fifteen square meters. Yet the one thing the cop had been expecting to find was missing. There was no exit leading towards the main network.

But there had to be. There had to be another tunnel. There was one tunnel leading from H4 to this lair, but then there had to be another one leading from here to the main network. Desjardins' tunnel. The one Quartz had discovered.

It wasn't hard to locate the missing shaft, hidden behind the wheelbarrow. By the time the other man was out of the tunnel and on his feet, Sadiqi had also found the only other objects left behind by the Nightingale: A pile of cardboard tubes that had been stacked against the wall. Sadiqi picked one up. They were a clean cylindrical shape, topped with a flattish pointed cone. Each identical. When he pried the cone off the top, he discovered a fuse and a hollowed out space filled with tiny shards of glass.

Pecheron looked on as the inspector picked up another cylinder and shook it. The sound of broken glass tinkled inside. He repeated the same movement with three or four other canisters until he found one that produced no sound of glass. Sliding the top off he looked inside. The container was also filled with glass, but not shards. A fully intact form. Rotating it, he worked a small glass tube out of the center. It was made of thin glass with a layer of paper over its tip – like a test tube, only much more fragile.

The cop slipped the tube back into the canister and slid it into his pocket. He was tired of puzzles. What he wanted were some straight answers.

"I'll signal if I need backup." Then he was twisting himself into the next shaft, which, if anything was slightly smaller than the previous one, barely big enough for a powerfully built man to climb through. Barely. But just feasible if he squeezed his arms in first. It was a dangerous way of proceeding. The Nightingale certainly knew how to put his adversaries at a disadvantage. There was no safe alternative.

The suspense didn't last long. Advancing down the shaft, Sadiqi strained his neck to keep his eyes glued to the space ahead, aware of the potential danger at the other end. The fact that he couldn't actually make out the end of the tunnel only made the discomfort greater. Instead of an exit cavity, all he could see were more stones at the end of the shaft. Presumably, for some reason, the Nightingale had sealed the exit – or perhaps blocked it in order to make it harder to find from outside.

It was a reasonable assumption, but incorrect. As soon as Sadiqi reached the stone wall at the end of the shaft, he understood why there were still no signs of the RAID team. Following Desjardins' instructions wouldn't be enough to get them through the passage today. Today there was no longer a tunnel under rue d'Ulm, just a wall of rocks and earth. The passage had collapsed. Or, more probably, been dynamited.

Hopefully Ferry and the RAID team were on the other side of the cave-in, not under it. Sadiqi tried to convince himself that the explosion had happened before his colleagues entered the tunnel. He certainly hoped they weren't buried beneath the rubble.

This operation, like the whole investigation, was fubar. For the past two days, Sadiqi had constantly been one step behind the

Nightingale. Close, but only close enough to be taunted over his inability to stop him. Lying, pressed between the ground, the ceiling and the rockface in front of him, the cop felt the strain of his vulnerability. There was nowhere to go but back. It was a messy way of moving; wriggling backwards, pushing on his forearms while pulling on the toe holds. When the ground finally disappeared below his shoe, he gave a final thrust to catapult back into the hideout. Crawling out of the shaft, feet followed by knees, he rotated into the gallery.

It was then, as he shifted from his knees into a semi-upright position, that he realized things were far worse than he'd feared. Emerging in such an awkward position, he had to manoeuvre backwards onto his haunches. And as he tilted his head up toward his colleague's face, he noticed something he'd failed to see earlier. It was hard to distinguish the detail in the fog of the goggles. But right there, attached to the ceiling, were greyish brown bricks, slightly darker than the limestone, and held in place by a web of wires.

"Out!" His words rang through the chamber as he shoved Pecheron towards the passage to H4.

There was no time to explain. They just dived into the shaft. Pecheron first, Sadiqi shoving him forward.

He didn't know where the trip wire was. Or whether the explosives worked off a timer. Either way, the result was the same. An explosion shuddered behind them followed by a blast wave.

80

Sitting at the top of the well, Toni recognized the dull thud for what it was. God knew she'd been on enough building sites to know an explosion when she heard one. Without even thinking, her first reaction was to offer help. The groan of the blast was still echoing around her when she threw her leg over the well and hooked her right foot into the first rung of the ladder. But Podesta's reactions were just as quick. That part of his orders had been clear: keep Corrigan out of the quarries. Before she could plunge out of sight, he grabbed her arm and was pulling her back to the surface.

"That was an explosion; they could be trapped," she snapped.

Rémi Podesta had done several training courses with the bomb squad before moving up to work for Sadiqi and he didn't need the girl to tell him what he'd just heard. He also knew that if his colleagues had been buried underground, they would need more than good intentions to unearth them and tend to their injuries. Paramedics and digging equipment were required. With no cell reception, he had to get to the surface. "You stay here; I'll get help. And more climbing equipment," he said, locking Toni's gaze. He doubted her first instinct was to wait patiently for his return, but there was an outside chance that the promise of proper equipment might hold her off climbing into the well alone.

It was a reasonable assumption. Under other circumstances it might have been correct. But not today. As soon as he was gone, she straddled the edge of the well. There was no way she was going to waste precious minutes waiting for reinforcements. If the men had been caught in that explosion they were going to need emergency first aid. Immediately.

She glanced into the shaft to plan her descent. But that brief glance was enough to cut short the impulse. Because as soon as she looked down, the beam of her caplamp flickered against a reassuring sight – a familiar glimmer sparkled below. There was someone on their way up. The silver coolness of the word "POLICE" shimmered in the rays of her lamplight, bouncing off the reflective tape sewn to the back of a pair of cataflic overalls.

The vision of this figure rising towards the surface brought Toni both a sense of relief and one of apprehension. Relief because the man climbing the ladder showed no signs of injury in his easy movements. Apprehension because the crew cut hair hidden behind the strap of the infrared goggles didn't belong to Sadiqi. Her mind raced. Maybe Sadiqi was evacuating his officers before getting out himself. Women and children first, or whatever the police equivalent was. That was the best explanation she could think of. All the others were more pessimistic. It was possible that only part of the team had survived the blast. What if not everyone had escaped? What if Khalid was still trapped below? A sense of hopelessness was balanced only by her desperation to find out what had happened. "Are you guys okay?" she shouted down. "We heard an explosion."

"Yeah, yeah. We're fine," the cop called back as his hands gravitated from rung to rung on the upward journey. It was only a couple of minutes before he reached the surface, but each second expanded intolerably for Toni who wanted more than monosyllabic reassurance. It wasn't until the officer hoisted one leg then the other over the stone rim that she felt the weight begin to fall from her shoulders. Now she would get the full rundown. She shot a glance down the well, hoping to see the form of Sadiqi following behind or, at the very least, someone else. It was hard to see more than a few meters with the weak beam of her caplamp. But the shaft seemed deserted.

Her eyes darted back to the man standing beside her, worried that his reassuring words hid a more complex reality. "Where is everyone? Are they alive? Are they injured? Was there a cave-in?"

There was no answer, just a slight pause as the man in the overalls pulled off his night goggles. And in that split second, rather than being reassured, Toni's incomprehension doubled. When she'd seen the cataflic coveralls in the well she had automatically presumed they belonged to one of the men who had set off with Sadiqi. But the face in front of her was unfamiliar. No that wasn't true. It wasn't Mueller or Pecheron, but she knew this guy. She'd seen him somewhere before. Maybe it was a cataflic she'd come across before; perhaps one of Ferry's men who had come through from the GRS. Maybe they'd found the passage Desjardins had described and this was a guy from the other detachment. But that wasn't likely; and, in any case, she knew all the cataflics personally. So maybe it was someone she'd seen at Val-de-Grace the previous day. Somehow that didn't fit either.

Then she remembered.

And fear flooded over her. It came in a flash of photographic memory. Truly an image. That was it. She had never seen this face before in real life. She had only seen it on paper, on a photo. The image of the IGC authorization card out of Caron's file. This was Jean Brune. This was Rossignol. Toni was standing in front of the Nightingale. This was the man who had killed de Chanterelle, broken Caron's neck and injected anthrax into maternity wards across the city. It was at that precise moment that she also noticed the deep dark red stain on the coverall. Along the shoulder line. As if blood had seeped down from a higher point.

Her body tightened with fear. The police uniform had been taken from one of Sadiqi's team. Someone had been shot straight through the head.

Whether the Nightingale saw the realization dawn on her face or whether he had planned his next move in advance was irrelevant. Before she had time to consider what to do next, he had slipped the service weapon out of its holster with one hand and grabbed her around the neck with the other. There was no mumbled threat. No brutal shaking to call her to heel. There was no need for it. This man was a professional. Nothing she could do would save her. His hold was firm. The gun was placed so that any false move would kill her.

There was no point begging for mercy. This man didn't know compassion. Her mind raced for a solution – an avenue that might save her. But when he pulled her down onto her hands and knees and started dragging her across the rocky shelf towards the staircase she realized he didn't want to kill her. At least not yet. He wanted a human shield. She was the poor helpless female he was going to use to get out of this safely.

Her existence depended on getting away from this man. Yet self-preservation told her she had to keep up with him. So she scrambled along, sometimes beside him, sometimes half crushed under him, the sharp stones of the ledge cutting into her hands and knees. And in that instant when the physical pain began to obliterate the emotional pain, a sound floated up from behind: the sound of footsteps echoing on the rungs of the well. Just as she and the Nightingale reached the edge of the shelf and tumbled down towards the staircase, Toni glanced back into the hidden gallery. The beam of her lamp bounced off the rim of the well providing her with a vision of Sadiqi's face surfacing over the edge.

He wasn't dead. He was behind the Nightingale. Whatever the explosion she had heard, it hadn't killed Khalid.

The vision was there and gone in an instant. With the gun still pointed at the base of her skull, the Nightingale hauled her to her feet, scraping her head against the wall and knocking off her lamp.

With the loss of the lamp, the vision of Khalid vanished. All she was left with was the brutal reality of the Nightingale racing up the stairs to the surface, holding her in a firm body lock, his arm clenched around her waist, her arms immobilized by his steel grasp.

81

Panic wasn't something Sadiqi engaged in. What he felt was more like a sickening anxiety caused by his total lack of control over the endless sequence of horror that was unfolding.

When the explosion went off, he and Pecheron had found themselves caught in a minor rockslide, half buried. Luckily, only small pieces of limestone had dislodged around them, but the two men had been left swimming in dust and pebbles, their movements obstructed. And the heat and sweat produced from the physical effort necessary to extricate themselves only served to fog up their night goggles, making the underground nightmare even more surreal.

But it was the shadow that erupted at the mouth of the tunnel while they were submerged in the unearthing process that proved more deadly than the rockslide. Pecheron didn't notice the Nightingale until the irreversible had happened. The volley of bullets let loose in the tunnel was unforgiving.

Sadiqi had sensed from the beginning that the narrow shafts were designed for ambush. Assuming defensive positions was impossible. The prognosis was tragically accurate. Pecheron collapsed, his crumpled body forming the only obstacle that saved Sadiqi from the legionnaire's bullets.

Lying flat, the inspector listened for the receding footsteps of the legionnaire before undertaking the macabre exercise of digging himself out from behind his colleague. Both the limestone and the cop's clothing were soon soaked with blood as he thrust the dead man forward, pushing toward the end of the shaft. The energy he was able to call up as he fought his way out of the blood and horror was drawn solely from the powerful urge to kill the man who had done this. As he raced up the well a few moments later, that hatred expanded, screaming to be let free.

Yet when he reached the top of the shaft and caught that glimpse of Toni with a gun against her head, the lust for revenge transformed into something greater.

Sadiqi had lived through more terror scenes than he cared to remember – the preps, the aftermaths and the live shows. They were moments so surreal and disconnected from normal life, that his mind and body would click into a cold, unthinking survival mode. Everyone's survival. His, his colleagues', the victims'. But while panic never clouded his professional vision, he could feel it creeping into his emotional being. Today things had just got personal. Sadiqi always put his partners' safety above his own. He had taken the lead in the tunnels, telling Mueller to hang back, and it had cost the officer his life. He had thrust Pecheron into the tunnel to protect him from the blast, and it had cost him his life. He had told Toni to stay safely outside the unknown tunnels… And the Nightingale was now using her as his ticket to freedom.

Seeing the legionnaire dragging her away, Sadiqi felt a pang of actual physical pain, as if some palpable bond between him and Toni were being wrenched apart. Any doubts he had about this woman were gone. All that mattered was getting her back.

The cop jumped out of the shaft into the basement then tore up the stairs. *Merde. Merde. Merde.* Where the hell was Podesta? The man's instructions had been simple: guard the well, take care of Toni and make sure the Nightingale didn't escape. What the fuck was he doing? Why had he left her alone? And where the hell was the Nightingale planning on taking her? Surely he couldn't escape from such a tightly-guarded perimeter. Sadiqi had posted dozens of men around the schoolgrounds. Surely they'd caught the bastard.

Just as the questions were pulsing through his mind, Podesta barrelled into the Prophet's staircase where the inspector had emerged. "You're okay."

Sadiqi heard the relief in his colleague's voice but didn't take the time to explain that Pecheron and Mueller had been less fortunate. "Where are they? Where's the legionnaire?"

Podesta pointed at a spot beyond Sadiqi, up the staircase past the statues. "He's headed for the roof."

A shot of adrenalin fired into the cop's bloodstream. "Cut the bastard off from the street," Sadiqi bellowed as he raced up the stairs. "Clear out the pedestrians. And make sure he doesn't get away."

82

By the time Sadiqi reached the roof, there weren't many choices open to him.

The thunderstorm that was brewing had turned the sky a mixture of purple and orange, casting curious shadows across the buildings and making objects difficult to discern. But in the shadow of the Pantheon's huge dome, the Nightingale was escaping across the quadrangle roof, with Toni tightly wrapped around his shoulders, fireman-style. They were already nearing the opposite side of the school buildings, separated from the cop by a distance of nearly 50 meters.

Sadiqi raised his weapon and took aim. But instantly lowered it again. There was no way he would risk taking a shot. If he missed, there was no telling what the legionnaire would do. And if the bullet hit its target, the potential consequences were just as lethal because the Nightingale would crash to the roof. Which meant he would let go of Toni who would find herself hurtling down the smooth steep incline, mercilessly earthbound.

There had to be some other way to stop him.

Although the roof sloped in its lower portion, the top was almost flat, so it provided a relatively stable surface. Sadiqi began sprinting across the buildings, ignoring the possible consequence of a misplaced step, his feet crashing against the hot zinc.

What he couldn't figure out was where this guy was headed. What the hell did he have in mind coming up here? It was a dead end. It was suicide. The school buildings were set up in cloister-like box formation around courtyards. Where was the Nightingale headed? Round and round in circles? Or was he planning on ducking back into the building via one of the skylights built into the roof? Was that possible?

Lugging less excess weight than his adversary, Sadiqi was gaining on the Nightingale who was slowed by the burden of the girl's protective body. The cop accelerated, pushing his own body faster. And as he closed in on his target, he observed the layout of the buildings extending out in front of him. That's when he understood what the legionnaire was doing. He wasn't going to head back into the building. He was going to climb down to street level. The Nightingale was headed southward because the courtyard at that end was full of plane-trees. He was going to climb down through the branches then lose himself among the crowds of music lovers roaming the neighborhood.

Barrelling along the rooftop, Sadiqi had reduced the distance between them by several meters. And as he drew closer, he projected himself into the legionnaire's mind: Rossignol would continue to the edge of the roof but before starting down, he would have to pause – maybe just for an instant – to change his grip on Toni, to redistribute the weight for the descent... During that pause, Sadiqi would get his chance to neutralize him. He would fire at the man's legs... praying all the time that Toni would have the reflex to catch hold of something as she fell. Before she slid off the roof.

It was a good enough plan – as far as any improvised plan can be good. But there was one major problem. Sadiqi had almost predicted the Nightingale's escape strategy. But not quite. Sadiqi had missed one essential detail. Although the redhead really did plan on going over the edge of the building and using the trees to swing back down to street level, he wasn't planning on stopping to rebalance his load. In fact it was the complete opposite.

The girl had outlived her usefulness. The Nightingale could see the cop gaining on him and guessed his intentions. The descent would be easier without the girl's deadweight.

As he approached the southwest tip of the rooftop, instead of slowing to balance his center of gravity, the legionnaire accelerated. He started sprinting towards the emptiness of the tree-lined courtyard. And in that same flash of speed, he flung Toni off his shoulders before plunging down the final slope of the zinc roof towards the tree.

In response, Sadiqi ground to a halt and pulled the trigger, sending four rounds into the combined haze of the Nightingale and the tree beyond. He was focused on the target only long enough to see it slump and miss the branch. But then his attention shot back to the other form hurtling groundward.

Toni was still tumbling down the edge of the eaves, desperately grappling to catch hold of the disastrously sleek zinc roof.

The scene had that surreal feel of imminent horror. Even though he knew it was pointless, Sadiqi broke back into a sprint. There was no way he could close the distance. Running like a madman wouldn't change this. All he could do was watch as a surge of dust and leaves rippled over the edge of the rooftop, and Toni plummeted toward oblivion in their wake.

83

The knowledge that he was four storeys above the ground had deserted Sadiqi long ago. Sprinting along the final meters of rooftop, it felt like he'd been condemned to watch the world through some hideously enchanted lens – witnessing his lover's death in slow motion. As she toppled over the eaves, she seemed to pause, magically suspended in mid-air by some grotesque, taunting destiny. She didn't fall. She just hung there. And he knew that wasn't possible. This moment couldn't last. He couldn't reach her in time. He was powerless to help.

Except he was still moving forward, and she was still dangling there.

It wasn't until he skidded down the final meters towards the edge, that he realized what had really happened. Somehow she'd managed to catch herself on the drainpipe or her dress had snagged on the roofing or something. It didn't really matter. All that mattered was that instead of falling over the side she was clinging to the edge of the eaves, one leg hanging in nothingness and the other scrambling to gain a foothold, one elbow trying desperately to bury itself in the drainpipe.

The burning zinc roof scorched his skin through his layers of clothing as he threw himself down and wrapped his hand around her wrist. If he had taken the time to think about it, he might have worried about the risk of losing his own balance. There was nothing to anchor himself to. But he wasn't thinking; he was doing. In any case, he knew how strong and lithe Toni's body was. It wouldn't take much force to provide the extra leverage she needed to pull herself up.

Sitting on the roof edge, he hooked his heels into the drainpipe, tightened his grip and hoisted backwards. The soft metal bent under the pressure, then began to creak as she managed to gain a toe hold. Then a knee-hold. Then she was up, stretched out flat on the roof beside him.

His senses were so heightened, the brief moment carried with it more information than a normal day. He could see the heat rising off the roof, he could smell the wind, he could hear the promise of rain.

More importantly, he could feel her heartbeat.

She was alive.

Still sitting with his heels fixed in the drainpipe, he noticed the weals scorched into her hands and legs from the heat. There might be other injuries too. He would have to get her off the boiling zinc and inside to see if she needed treatment.

"You okay?" he asked, putting his hand gently around her waist.

She nodded several times but didn't speak.

"We'd better get you inside."

Maybe he should have held her. Really held her. But he didn't. His feelings had taken control too many times already today. He wasn't going to let it happen again. That's how he kept his job doable. That's how he kept his life bearable. By keeping the emotions separate from the job. Maybe by keeping the emotions separate from everything.

Coolness wasn't, however, the reaction he was expecting from Corrigan. He waited for her to turn to him, gasping for breath and trembling. Instead, she shifted onto her knees, like a marathon runner trying to catch her breath. Then she laid the palm of her hand flat against his chest. "I can't feel your heartbeat."

That's what he was waiting for. The confusion. The blurred perception. "It's okay. It's just the vest." He slid her hand up to his neck, where a solid drumbeat was pulsing madly through his carotid.

The deep breath she took might have been a sigh of relief, or possibly just meant to steady herself. He half expected the sigh to transform into a flood of tears. Again, it didn't. Instead, her hands slipped away from his neck. "You're injured." She had straightened up and although her voice was shaky, her eyes were focused on the front of his coverall, and the stains from the blood that had drained from his colleague.

He prodded her gently towards the flat of the roof, away from the sloping edge. "No. I'm fine. It's Pecheron's blood."

Again, her reaction was unexpected. There was no appaled look of horror. No tears. She scrambled upward, stopping and turning only when she reached the central ridge. He caught up and placed a hand on her shoulder, somehow trying to steady her against both the wind and the craziness of the past minutes. "You're shaking. You're probably in shock," he said softly. The calm tone was something he had had far too many opportunities to practice.

At first she just shook her head.

"I'll carry you if you like." He tightened his arm around her waist, ready to lift her.

Her hand was instantly on his, removing it from her waist. And – magnificently – there was the tiniest of smiles on her lips. "NOBODY is carrying me across any more roofs today." She raised his hand to her lips and brushed it with a kiss. "No, I'm fine. We're both fine. I'm just shaking from the effort. But I'm fine. Did you get him? Is it over?"

Sadiqi knew what people in shock looked like. He'd seen it often enough. And this wasn't it. The shaking was already abating. The pupils seemed normal. Her touch was warm and she was flushed, not ashen.

He tightened his fingers around hers, as if testing to check whether the flesh below was truly human. If she was steady on her feet and able to continue, there was serious business that needed tending to. His other hand reached into his pocket for his phone and pinned in Podesta's number.

The lieutenant's calm tone told Sadiqi that their battle with the Nightingale was over.

"He's dead," Podesta confirmed. "We can't find a pulse and he's bleeding massively from his leg. You must have hit his femoral. Thank God he fell on the school side and not into the street. It's berserk out there. There are masses of people." Sadiqi didn't need to be told. He knew what the *Fête de la Musique* was like. Evacuating the perimeter around the school would be an impossible job tonight. People flocked to the Latin Quarter for the celebrations. You couldn't just close it off at the last minute.

"Anything on him? Have you got his phone?"

"There's no phone."

"There's got to be."

"There's nothing. No phone, no ID. Nothing." That truth was left hanging in the darkening sky. The fact that Sadiqi rang off without even pushing Podesta to make one last effort to find it was proof he felt beaten.

"He's dead," Toni repeated. "And you don't know why he did this."

The expression on Sadiqi's face was confirmation enough. "The problem isn't that I don't know why he did this," he said, staring at the crowds of people gathered in the streets below. "The problem is I don't know what the hell else he had planned."

"You think there's more? This isn't over?"

"Just because he's dead, that doesn't mean this is over." The tone was bitter. "We know he was planning another attack tonight. Until we find the trace of that attack, we don't know it's been shut down."

"But I heard an explosion."

"Sure, there was an explosion," Sadiqi agreed, locking away the memory of his dead colleagues in a corner of his brain where it couldn't affect him. "In fact, there were probably two. It's a mess down there."

"But that's got to be what the *fireworks* message refered to."

Sadiqi shook his head. "No. There were a few bars of Semtex taped to the gallery we examined. Enough to blow out the tunnel, to cover the Nightingale's tracks, perhaps to get rid of DNA. But not enough to blow up the Pantheon. And, there was another tunnel connecting from the Pantheon to the GRS that was blown out, too. But neither of those exploded *over* any temple."

Toni considered this. "Maybe there is no temple. Maybe you're taking the messages too literally. Maybe there is no deep symbolism. But if he's set off two detonations below ground, he's done some serious damage to this neighborhood, even if we can't see it yet from up here. If he blew out the tunnel connecting the school to the GRS then he's compromised the land under us." Toni could see the crowds of people in the square below, milling around. "You need to evacuate the whole area around the Pantheon and down rue d'Ulm. The explosions may not have ruptured the surface yet, but if heavy traffic keeps rolling over those tunnels, the vibrations will weaken the substrata. It won't take long for the upper layers to collapse. The danger is there. Until those tunnels have been consolidated this whole area is one big sinkhole just waiting to happen."

Sadiqi called up Podesta's number again and gave the order to evacuate the vicinity and cut traffic. Then he placed his hands on the young woman's shoulders, half guiding her towards the skylight, half bracing the two of them against the increasingly powerful gusts of winds announcing the approaching storm. His words were distant, as his mind raced to figure out what was going on. "Rossignol may have created a rift underground by setting off those explosives, but that can't be what the *fireworks* message means. All the other messages announced specific things. St. Genevieve was the source of retribution; his hideout is down there. Evil is definitely being administered from below ground. And I'm pretty damn sure there are going to be real fireworks," he said, slipping the narrow, slightly crushed, cardboard tube out of his pocket. "These."

Toni's hand was still trembling but she reached out to examine the object. "An actual firework?"

"That's right. Quite literally. We found a pile of them down in the tunnels." Sadiqi took the cap off the cylinder. The glass tube inside had been crushed. "The casing has been modified; there's an extra element in the center. This one's broken now, but it was a test tube. Given our legionnaire's past history I'd say the extra tube is designed to disseminate something lethal." He moved the firework through the air as if he were a boy playing with a toy rocket. "Possibly a little anthrax. Powdered all over whatever unsuspecting crowd is watching this fireworks display."

Another gust of wind blew in from the west.

The air might be clearing, the temperature cooling, but there were still some serious questions to answer.

"You think these can be set off even if the Nightingale's dead."

"It's a possibility I can't ignore."

"So if these are the fireworks, filled with anthrax or whatever, then where's the temple? Where's he going to set these off?"

Sadiqi's eyes were concentrated on the skylight ahead and the relative safety of the school building. "You tell me."

84

Just when she thought she was getting a sick form of clarity, things got more opaque. Dukrin tossed the brief from IT onto the desk. She'd thought she had a clear lead on this case. But that would have been too much to ask. No. Three messages sent from the same device. But, of course, Message 4 had to come from somewhere else. The only good news was that at least it had come from Paris.

So much for the clear link to Clavreul. As far as she could tell, the message didn't trace to any of the devices she had linked to him. Not that that excluded him completely. Maybe he had a new device she didn't have eyes on. Either way, the process of trying to track down the source of that last message was going to be much longer than she had hoped. Tricky. Messy.

Worse yet, the failed link between Message 4 and the previous three raised the question of the message's authenticity. Was the author simply sending the messages from different devices, or were they sent by different people? Possibly even some sort of copy-cat messenger – although that seemed unlikely. After all, the messages were posted publicly, but there had been no official statement linking them to de Chanterelle or any of the other crimes. Official concern over the messages hadn't been released to the press, so in principle there was no motivation for a copy-cat.

So what was going on?

85

By the time Sadiqi got to the courtyard, the paramedics were already doing clean-up detail. This guy wasn't going to be resuscitated.

There was no pool of blood around the body. The parched ground had soaked up any liquid spilt by the Nightingale's lifeless body. Sadiqi squatted down, first checking the back pockets in the pants, then flipping the body to get to the shirt pockets. All he wanted was a phone. Surely that wasn't so much to ask.

"There's nothing. No phone. No papers. No wallet. Nothing," Podesta said from behind.

"There's got to be a phone. Everyone's got a phone."

"Not this guy. At least not here."

Sadiqi caught the Nightingale's chin in his palm and rotated the face so that he could look into the frozen eyes. There probably hadn't been much more life in those eyes even when they were alive. No. The cop didn't regret killing this piece of shit.

But he did regret the fact that the bastard had taken all his secrets to the grave.

Podesta watched as his boss stepped over the body and grabbed the navy blue ballerina pumps lying in the dust before heading back inside.

86

Air was not Toni's element. Earth was. Sitting, waiting for Sadiqi at the foot of the marble staircase, the bracing earthiness of the quarries wafted up from the tunnels below, spreading its reassuring presence. Nonetheless, when he returned a few minutes later, carrying her shoes and looking grimmer than usual, it was a stark reminder that this day could still get worse for a lot of people. "I'm really sorry about your colleagues," she said.

The cop slumped down onto the step beside her, leaving a wide berth between them. "I don't want to talk about it."

She slipped her hand onto his thigh.

He lifted it off and dropped it back on her knee. Even though he realized it was already a done thing, he didn't want her to get into his mind. At least he didn't want her burrowing any deeper. Then again, how much deeper could she burrow?

Again she tried to reach him. "You might not believe it now, but it was actually a good thing you were down there. If nobody witnessed the explosions, we wouldn't have known that the land was weakened. That's always the biggest danger underground. The unknown. That's when we end up with sinkholes. When we're caught off guard. When we have no warning there's a problem."

"My men are dead," he growled. "And I don't know how many more people are going to die tonight. I can't delude myself that things are fine."

The pent-up rage silenced her. Unable to lighten the unfathomable inspector's load, she observed the swarms of cops and emergency workers trailing past them on their way down to the basement. Bomb squad, paramedics, whoever else they needed from special branches to reinforce the tunnels and extricate the victims. It was a grim scene. She turned to her bag for distraction. She'd slipped downstairs for it while waiting for Sadiqi. And now she unzipped the front pouch and pulled out her phone. "So what have you figured out about the fireworks? Where are they going to be set off? The Pantheon?"

Maybe he should have just shut up. But sometimes it was helpful to revisit the details. More than once he'd figured out a case by running through the questions and answers routine with colleagues. Except she wasn't a colleague. But then there was nobody else handy. "Unlikely," he mumbled.

As he pulled off the cataflic overalls, he watched her thumbing messages into her phone at lightning speed. Sadiqi used his phone all the time. But he just couldn't type that fast. Not with the two thumbs going in rapid fire. It was a generational thing. And, as if to highlight that generational chasm, she spoke without even looking up from her device – like so many millenials did. "Why the change of mind? At the hospital you were convinced the Pantheon was the target."

"There are two messages, two targets. Retribution from St. Genevieve – in other words, what he did downstairs. And the fireworks above the temple – what we're still waiting for. The two aren't the same."

"How can you be so sure?"

"For starters, I'm certain there are going to be real fireworks. And there's no fireworks display planned anywhere near here tonight. We've checked."

"That doesn't mean that the reference to the temple isn't the Pantheon."

"I think it does." There was certainty in his voice but no enthusiasm.

Toni suspected Khalid had a very dark side but she didn't want him going there now. "Why?" she said, looking up this time.

"Over the past two days everything has been a balance between the Nightingale's messages and the *Clavreul Report*. Everything has developed in line with that double register. Even those explosions under the school. That was 4.7 – what you call the Von Choltitz plan. Set up explosives underground – compromise subterranean structures. Except, we managed to avoid the out-and-out worst-case scenario. Like you said, because we know what he's done, the IGC should be able to reinforce the tunnels before they collapse and create any irrecuperable havoc on the surface. Which mitigates the damage. Unfortunately it also increases the probability that whatever the *fireworks* message refers to is also outlined in the *Report*. In other words, whatever we're waiting for has something to do with section 4.6. And, by association, something to do with the Masons and what the Grand Master said."

Even though it shouldn't have, that riled her. The way he said it, as if she should remember the meeting with the Grand Master. "Except you booted me out of the car, remember? So I don't know what he said. And in any case, the *Clavreul Report* doesn't mention any temple." Between what she'd read in the car and the office, Toni had scanned through the whole document. "Why are you so sure the tunnels under H4 aren't the 'portal' Caron mentioned, which would make the Pantheon the temple?" Sadiqi's gaze had wandered to his discarded kit on the floor, topped by the bloodstained coveralls. *Not healthy, not helpful,* Toni thought, reaching out with her toe to flip the pile of fabric so that the blood spattered parts were no longer visible.

Apparently his adrenalin high had passed and now Sadiqi was in some sort of withdrawal. He ditched the bulletproof vest then leaned his elbows on his knees, head drooping. "That well shaft has nothing to do with the secret chamber Malaisieu and Trouvé were worried about." His calmness bordered on morose, as he took the sham cigarettes out of his pocket and popped a candy. "The passage Malaisieu told me about is supposed to be part of the main network. He said that before their lodge building was built, the catacombs were the obvious place for their rituals. They hung on to the tradition even after the real lodge existed. But, either way, the lodge has been using the GRS tunnels for the past two centuries. The tunnel downstairs, on the other hand, wasn't connected to the GRS until the Nightingale pierced it, a few weeks or months or whatever ago. It's like Desjardins said. All the digging work has been done recently. The tool marks on the stone are new – deep and jagged." He broke off as Podesta came jogging in holding a small plastic baggie for the student. An offering of ice from the school kitchens to relieve her blistered skin.

The inspector watched as she thanked the junior officer then picked out an icecube and started massaging her welts. But his thoughts were concentrated on sorting through the tangle of information that had been thrown at him over the past hours. *What had been said by whom and when? What had Corrigan heard? What might she have missed?*

"And Malaisieu wouldn't tell you anything about where this place is," she prompted. "Nothing?"

"He said it was by the Luxembourg Gardens," Podesta offered.

Toni's raised her eyebrows and breathed out. "That hardly narrows it down. I mean that could even mean H4 or the Pantheon."

"No," Sadiqi was shaking his head. "He said the Luxembourg Palace, not the Gardens. So definitely not the tunnels under H4. No. I'm sure of it. Messages 3 and 4 refer to two different locations – two separate attacks." There was nothing solid to go on other than the fact that Caron's report read more like a blueprint for the past days' murderous rampage than an outside expert's opinion. "Why can't we figure out where the temple is? Simply because it is the great unknown. Because it's linked to this big secret nobody wants to share. That's why we need to figure this out. Once we learn the Chamber's location we'll be able to understand what the fireworks and the temple are."

That was the longest spiel Toni had ever heard Khalid deliver. Which made it all the more powerful. If he was convinced this Chamber was the key to the riddle, she would try to figure this out. "What else did the Grand Master say?"

Although his eyes were turned towards the delicate motion of the young woman massaging her legs with the ice, Sadiqi's gaze was floating in the void. "He used a lot of mumbo jumbo to justify not disclosing the tunnel's whereabouts."

"Like what?"

"Garbage about how its existence had weighed on French history," Podesta offered.

Toni placed the icecube between the palms of her hands and pressed down lightly, making tiny circular movements while she closed her eyes to visualize the map of the quarries. "Yeah," her voice was thoughtful. "Caron talked about the same cryptic stuff in his report, too. What was it? The *puzzles of history,*" she said, half-answering her own question.

"The Convention and the Commune," Sadiqi added.

She nodded, silently trying to fit the pieces together. Until now she'd been concentrating her theories around the Pantheon. But now she let her speculation drift a few blocks west. *The quarries. The Masons. The Convention. The Commune. And the Luxembourg Palace.*

From one to the other, the links multiplied in her mind. Since the Luxembourg Palace marked the northern extremity of the GRS, the network around there wasn't very dense.

It was, however, rich with history. Connecting ideas multiplied. The map. The stories. The physical appearance of the tunnels. Toni laid them one on top of the other... until it all came together.

Her eyes shot open. "The Odeon," she exclaimed in a combination of amazement and desperate frustration, digging her fingers into Sadiqi's arm. "Of course it's not here. It's the Odeon. The actual Odeon Theater." Her words trailed off as the multiple queries and unknowns suddenly began linking together into some coherent whole.

Sadiqi knew the look on her face. It was the same passion he'd seen the previous day when she told him stories of Philippe the Pious or the Cagoule. And it was seriously misplaced among all the bullshit going down today. The cop rocked to his feet, pulling away from her grip. "How do you figure that?" The fatigue in his voice screamed out his reluctance to chase yet another phantom lead.

"This Chamber of Reflection. It's not simply a spot in the network that's used by the Masons. It's an actual hidden gallery. A secret passage. Something that nobody from outside the lodge could possibly know about."

"That's impossible."

"No." The voice was slightly calmer. "It's improbable. But it's not impossible. In fact, it's the only thing that makes sense. It's a secret gallery and it leads to the Odeon Theater."

The cop didn't want to listen to another anthology of ghost stories. "Secret tunnel," he hissed, turning away. Hadn't she understood yet? This was the real world. He wasn't looking for fables or myths. He was looking for something real.

But there was no stopping Toni. All the elements were there. She could see them. "According to all the maps there's no link between the Odeon and the quarry network. Except there are loads of stories about a secret entrance. Stories that go back hundreds of years. I know it's sort of 'out there' but it makes sense. At least as far as any of this makes sense." The inspector was standing with his back to her. Closed. He didn't want to believe what she was saying. But he was going to hear it anyway. "The land around the Odeon used to belong to the royal family. There was the Petit Luxembourg Palace on one side, then across the road there was a smaller palace that belonged to Monsieur le Prince, Louis XVI's brother. Just before the Revolution, the palace started getting rundown so the prince decided to have it torn down and a theater built in its place. But Monsieur insisted the theater be built on a slightly different spot from the original building. Rumor had it that the change was made so that the prince could cross directly from his living quarters in the Petit Luxembourg to the theater without having to go outside. The two buildings were said to be linked via the underground network. Don't you see?" Toni was speaking with feverish intensity. "It fits with Caron's reference to the *puzzles of history*. The reference to popular myths. I couldn't figure it out. It seemed so unlike Caron. He would never have mentioned anything as frivolous as a rumor. That wasn't his style. But now it makes sense. He mentioned the passage because he knew it existed. He'd seen it himself. It was real. These aren't fairy stories. This is reality. This is what you're looking for. I'm sure of it."

Sadiqi was tired of this bullshit case. This wasn't what he did. He didn't chase fairytales. He didn't untangle riddles. He stopped terrorists. He followed Salafist networks. He investigated S-fiches who were at risk of turning into lone wolves. On a weird day, he might even check out rightwing extremists attacking mosques. He did NOT run around looking for secret passages based on urban legends.

But there was no stopping her. "And it fits in with the Convention and the Commune – 19th century revolutions. I can't remember what exactly it was that Caron wrote but there was something about the revolutionaries of the Convention and the Commune exploiting some sort of portal. All that garbage about urban warriors stepping through the looking-glass. It might sound crazy, but even that fits with the Odeon. You see, during the Revolution, the Odeon became the *Théâtre de la Liberté*. Public meetings were held there. Public meetings that tended to get out of hand. Once, during the Convention, the government sent guards to the theater to close down a meeting being held by insurgents. When the soldiers arrived on the square in front of the building there was a huge crowd blocking the entrance. It took the government soldiers a while to beat a path to the theater but when they finally did get in, it was empty. The insurgents were gone."

Podesta, who had been leaning against the banister listening, looked unconvinced. "So what? The insurgents took advantage of the confusion on the square to creep out the back way and avoid being guillotined."

"Maybe," Toni conceded, "except the exact same thing happened again during the Commune. In 1871 the theater was used as a rallying point by revolutionaries. When government troops stormed the city to quash the uprising, about 100 communards took refuge in the Odeon. Again the troops surrounded the building while the communards fought from the windows. But ultimately they couldn't hold out against the government troops' superior manpower. Only, the thing is, when the soldiers did finally break open the doors and storm in, the building was completely empty. Everyone was gone. And this time the insurgents couldn't possibly have escaped out the back way, because the theater had been surrounded the whole time."

Podesta was beginning to soften. He glanced back and forth between Sadiqi and Toni, wondering if, like him, the inspector was ready to take the hook. "So you figure they escaped through the catacombs?"

Before Toni could reply, Sadiqi interrupted sharply. "There are hundreds of cataphiles down in those tunnels every day. And you're telling me that in the space of 200 years none of them has ever noticed this tunnel."

"That's the whole point, isn't it? That's what makes it so believable. There isn't any entry point marked on any maps. But there have been rumors about it for centuries. Ever since the theater was built. It's just that nobody has ever found it."

There had been so many bad leads over the past hours, it would take more than a couple of strings spliced together to convince Sadiqi that this was more than another story like the Green Monster and the Vauvert Devil. "Aren't you forgetting one thing? What about the Nightingale's messages? The Odeon's a theater, not a Temple. It was never anything else. The message talks about fireworks above a temple."

The spark in her eyes glinted stronger. "No. Even that works. But only tonight." The water from the melting ice was dribbling through her fingers as she rubbed her hands together with growing tension. "You know there was a big conference at the Senate today. The one organized by Trouvé." She paused to check that Sadiqi remembered. "The closing ceremony is being held at the theater. The Odeon Theater. They're having a big musical evening in honor of the *Fête de la Musique*. A performance of Mozart's *Magic Flute*." The announcement fell flat. Apparently Sadiqi and Podesta weren't opera buffs. "It's also known as *The Freemasons' Opera*. Most of the opera is set in the Temple of Trials." There was a glacial silence in the hallway. "You do realize that Trouvé's big conference is strongly linked to the Freemasons? 30VNG, the group organizing the event, is basically like scout camp for Mason babies."

Damn, Sadiqi thought, *the crazy train really was calling at all stations today.* Suddenly this sounded like a serious possibility. "Wait a minute. Didn't Trouvé say Tibrac was invited to the gala evening?" His eyes flashed back to Podesta for confirmation.

But it was Toni who was nodding. She was the one who had been sitting in the office on Boulevard St. Michel listening to Trouvé and Marco plan this conference for the past year.

"This isn't terrorism," Podesta said. "It's political assassination."

"It's both," the inspector answered. "Tibrac isn't alone. The Odeon seats over a thousand people and there's a plan to powder all of them with some type of poison."

There was nothing more to say. Sadiqi was already twisting his orange "Police" armband around his bicep and running across the courtyard. *Why had it taken so long to make the link to the Odeon?*

Why indeed? Because all these friggin Masons were doing their damnedest to keep the police out of their affairs. Trouvé could have helped tie all these threads together hours ago.

Pushing through the school gate and into the street he began barking instructions over his shoulder to Podesta. "I need a perimeter cordoned off around the theater and a police escort to evacuate any VIPs from the building. We need to get the president out."

87

On a normal day it took less than ten minutes to walk from H4 High to the Odeon Theater; five minutes at a run. But this was no ordinary day. As soon as Sadiqi, Podesta and Toni stepped out of the high school, they realized that a steady pace was not going to be attainable. During the two hours they'd spent in the school, the number of people in the area had increased exponentially. The streets were seething with movement. Teenagers, couples, students, babies in strollers. It was a mid-summer festival with participants paying homage to the gods of music, late evening sunshine and Bacchanalian pleasure. In her ten months in Paris Toni had never seen the streets so dense with people. The roomy squares of the Latin Quarter had drawn a disproportionate number of both bands and onlookers for the festivities. Sadiqi cursed himself for waiting until after the explosions to start evacuating the perimeter. His colleagues' efforts to direct people away from both the Pantheon and rue d'Ulm were only adding to the confusion, making it more difficult for him to beat a path to the Odeon. Pedestrians had overflowed onto the roads. Traffic was moving slower than walking pace. For once the cop didn't bother recuperating his car; driving would have been even slower than walking. He shoved ahead, unapologetically breaking through the linked hands that anchored children to parents or connected couples.

It was impossible to break into a sprint; at jogging pace they were already knocking into people. "*Imbécile de flic*," someone yelled, bouncing off Sadiqi like a human pinball. Perhaps in a different country his "Police" armband would have made the crowd part like a human Red Sea, but in France signs of authority only made people aggressive.

It was the scene that greeted them on arrival at the Odeon that was the hardest to face. The limestone building rose up majestically above a cobbled stone square, which was saturated with yet another dense congregation of music aficionados – this one swaying to the rhythm of a salsa beat. Getting the president out was going to be a logistical nightmare. There were people everywhere; it was going to be nigh impossible getting a car anywhere near an exit door, let alone a motorcade. Until they got rid of this crowd, the cop wasn't sure how in sweet hell they were going to evacuate the president let alone empty the building.

He did a quick survey of the security detail on the square. At the foot of the arcade, a motorcycle squadron was lined up. Above them were two rows of riot officers in full body armor guarding the doors. In other words, the entire perimeter around the building was swarming with gendarmes, which wasn't good for Sadiqi. He would have happily taken charge of a dozen police brigades; but working with gendarmes was trickier. Cops were civilians; gendarmes were military. They might all be doing the same job, but he knew he was going to have trouble getting gendarmes to follow his orders. It just wasn't the same dynamic as working with colleagues from the same clan.

If that wasn't bad enough, the nail in his coffin was the GSPR – the president's personal protection unit. Those guys were trained to take orders from nobody except their direct superior. They weren't likely to give two shakes what some cop had to say.

Sadiqi slipped his phone out of his pocket and swiped to Dukrin's number. As soon as she picked up he gave her the run down. "This place is crawling with the Mobile Gendarmerie and the GSPR. This'll be easier if you can get a message through to the Ministry of Armies. Otherwise these guys might not take my word for it when I start telling them what to do."

"There's not time for that. This thing is getting worse by the minute." Sadiqi had known Dukrin for his entire career, which was long enough to learn how to recognize her tone. It was the voice of dispassionate reason, in its purest form. "I've just been told we've lost track of six officers under the Odeon."

"What?"

"Two of Ferry's teams patrolling under the Senate have just been reported missing. That's all I know. When the guard was changed, the old teams weren't where they were supposed to be. That could mean they've wandered off a little too far. It could also mean something has happened to them. Either way, we've had no contact with them for over four hours." Sadiqi knew those clipped sentences meant danger. Real, total, undefined danger.

All that was left to do was for Dukrin to send him off with a final battle cry. "That fucker's killed too many people. If you're right about what he's planned, you've got to stop it. Do whatever you have to."

The specters of all the Nightingale's victims were far too fresh in Sadiqi's mind: De Chanterelle and Caron, of course. More importantly

Pecheron and Mueller. The six cops under the Senate. And possibly others in the tunnel below the Pantheon.

"I'm on it." He hit the red button and shoved the phone into his pocket. He didn't need Dukrin to spell this out for him. If the Nightingale really had planted poison in that theater, this was potentially a new 9/11. A 9/11 in which almost all the victims would be 20- to 30-year-olds. And that threat awakened the cop's worst ghosts.

The French Touch. These bastards always took aim at the most vulnerable.

88

The steps that led up to the theater were lined with music lovers using the extra height offered by the arcade to get a better view of the band in the center of the square. As he forced a passage to the top, Sadiqi slipped his ID card out of his pocket while scanning the rows of gendarmes for the officer who looked most likely to be in charge.

All those years back, when he'd first joined the security forces, career advancement had been measured by the amount of gold braid an officer wore on his shoulders. Today it was gauged by the cut of the jacket. The cop straightened his shoulders and headed for the guy dressed in the most expensive suit, knowing that the unbuttoned Armani hid both a body trained in hand-to-hand combat and a Glock 26.

"Khalid Sadiqi, Special Operations, UCLAT," he clipped, lowering his voice pitch just enough to send out what he hoped was a signal of dominance, and flashing his card. "I'm here to evacuate the building. We believe an attack is under way. There may be poison and explosives inside. The President needs to leave. NOW."

The dark glasses the GSPR officer was wearing made him look like something out of a bad 1990s TV series. When he spoke, his words struck Sadiqi as equally idiotic: "The theater's been surveilled since yesterday. I have a list of everyone who's been in or out. They've all been checked. The perimeter is secure."

"That's because the people you checked went in through the front door. It's likely someone has gained access through the catacombs."

The gendarme twisted the right side of his mouth upwards into a half-smile as if he'd just heard a tasteless joke. "There is no link between this building and the catacombs."

"That's what I was told, too, but it's starting to look like that information's inaccurate."

"I have that information from the highest catacomb authority…"

"The highest catacomb authority is dead. As are six of my colleagues who were patroling the tunnels below the theater," Sadiqi said, raising his ID again, encouraging the bodyguard to take a closer look. "I suggest you send that information on to your point man."

Having had time to inspect the ID, the gendarme now looked considerably more concerned. If the threat was real, there was no time to lose. "Code black. Get him out," he grunted. The words weren't intended for Sadiqi. They were aimed into the agent's mike and transmitted to his team. Immediately the other bodyguards on the steps were on alert, assuming their formation to escort the President out.

As the GSPR man turned and retreated towards the theater doors, Sadiqi took a step forward. But already a new bodyguard had appeared to take the place of the first. Again Sadiqi lifted his card. "Inspector General Sadiqi. UCLAT. We need to evacuate the building."

"We're evacuating the President first, Sir. There's a strict protocol and my orders are simple. No one enters until the President is secure."

Sadiqi could tell this new man was less senior than the previous one. His words had the whiff of phrases memorized from a handbook. "Then don't let me in. Just get everybody else out."

"Evacuating the building precipitately would create panic and confusion, putting the President's safety at risk."

"And not evacuating the building immediately could cause the death of everyone sitting in there." The muscles between Sadiqi's shoulder blades tightened and he could feel a tingling in his fingers inviting him to think with his muscles rather than his brain. Unfortunately, even if he knocked this guy flying, there were about four-dozen other bodyguards ready to take his place. Beside him, he could feel Podesta's anger rising, too, while on the other side, Toni was snapping out an impatient message into her phone.

Sadiqi turned to her.

The intensity of her gaze suggested the dozens of ideas racing through her mind, trying to find some solution to this problem. "I was trying to get my friend Marco," she explained. "He helped prepare the conference. He'll be in there. But he's not answering." The cop had no idea who the hell Marco was, but he was hardly surprised to learn the concert-goer wasn't picking up his phone. Opera buffs didn't text and facebook during a show. Which, in this case, was unfortunate.

The cop could feel the shroud of death closing in. All he could do was make one final attempt to convince the GSPR man. "You know as well as I do what happened at Val-de-Grace yesterday. The same thing is going to happen here on a massive scale if we don't do something." Sadiqi was working on the assumption that this guy had heard the rumors about de Chanterelle, which was likely given the GSPR's proximity to the president. And sure enough, the man's concentration on the messages running through his headset cracked slightly. "Check with your commanding officer," Sadiqi prompted. "My boss will be trying to get word through right now. We've just found a gallery under H4 stockpiled with explosives. The person who put them there also planned to attack this theater. Getting the president out isn't enough. We need everyone out." Sadiqi took a step forward.

But as if he'd been asked to dance, the other officer shifted forward to block his path, arms tensing and inching upwards as a lead-in to some defensive move. "Inspector, my orders are to ensure the president's safety. Either letting unauthorized people in or evacuating the building precipitately could threaten his safety. If you want access to the building, help us to make this go faster. I suggest you assist us in evacuating the square."

Sadiqi had had a lifetime's experience of being talked down to. Usually he would have told himself that defending his position in the pecking order wasn't worth a fight. But never before had the potential consequences of someone else imposing their agenda on him been so monumental. He leaned forward with the intention of forcing his way into the buiding.

Except he was held back by a hand sliding against his arm and squeezing it for attention. "We're talking in circles. There's another way in." She caught his gaze. "Do you still have the key from Caron's office." Sadiqi's hand slid to the pocket where he'd placed the iron key several hours earlier. He nodded. "Then we'll just have to find Trouvé's entrance." And with that Toni pivoted on her ballerina heels and beat a path through the crowd and away from the theater.

89

Once they'd rounded the corner and were out of sight of the bodyguard, Toni broke into a sprint. Unlike the square, Rue de Vaugirard wasn't a prime spot for bands or crowds. The sidewalks were still packed, but they were easily able to weave between passers-by.

"Where are we going?" Sadiqi called from behind, falling into single file to duck traffic.

"There's a door to the catacombs just around the block."

She said it very convincingly. Yet if Sadiqi had been able to look inside her mind, he would have realized there was a hitch. Whatever happened in the next couple of minutes would depend entirely on an uncertain calculation. That morning, when they were in Caron's office going through his papers Khalid had taken the key out of the desk. She was pretty sure that key was the same one Caron had used a few months earlier when he had taken her catawalking under the Senate; the 'B' on the keychain certainly looked like the same one that held the key that unlocked the IGC quarry entrance in rue Bonaparte. But she wasn't entirely certain. She put the probability at about 95%. The key sure looked familiar. But then, one wrought iron key was pretty much the same as the next. And if she was wrong about this – if the key didn't open the grate in rue Bonaparte – she was 100% sure Sadiqi would go berserk. His patience had been waning. If they were talking probabilities, she figured there was a 99% chance Khalid would never speak to her again and perhaps a 30% probability that he could strangle her on the spot if the key didn't work.

None of these doubts showed on her face. She played her bluff beautifully. Two blocks over from the Odeon, she swung into a small courtyard and led the way to a heavy grate door on the far side of the cobbled quadrangle. And when she turned the key in the gaping lock, the grind of cogs echoed across the courtyard.

The relief Sadiqi felt as the door cracked open would have been greater if he hadn't been so furious with himself for going along with Corrigan's gamble. Increasingly she struck him as a risk-taker rather than a cool-headed analyst. As a general rule, he liked to know exactly where he stood with collaborators, yet there were enough mixed signals floating around Toni to confuse a cryptograper. If only he'd had a better solution, he would have gone with it. Except with the normal entrance route to the theater barred, he had no hope of getting into the building other than to follow her.

And he was going to have to follow her very closely because his night goggles were still lying at the bottom of the Prophet's Staircase back in the high school, along with the rest of his kit. Corrigan's caplamp was the only light available and nobody had a bulletproof vest. Not the best situation walking into a zone where several cops had just been killed according to Dukrin. Sadiqi wished he'd at least held on to the glasses, if only to ensure some autonomy.

Dependent or not, he wasn't going to leave Corrigan in the frontline. When they'd met up that morning in the Luxembourg Gardens, the light muslin dress had floated against her legs with a combination of sensuality and simplicity. Nearly ten hours on, her appearance had altered almost beyond recognition. Her dress was torn and dirty, covered in dust from the quarries and splatters of blood picked up at the hands of the Nightingale. Her face was smudged and her once artistically messy ponytail was grungy with limestone and sweat. She looked like a castoff from a Tim Burton movie. "You're going to give directions from behind," he said, reaching for her caplamp as soon as they hit quarry level. "If we run into a patrol of gendarmes we're going to get shot with you in the lead. Just point me in the right direction."

It was a good call. Two minutes later, a beam of light dazzled them. "Freeze and put your hands on your heads." The voice had none of Sadiqi's calm. Whoever was behind it was deeply strung out.

The inspector and Podesta cautiously raised their hands into the air. "Khalid Sadiqi. UCLAT. I need to pass."

"Don't come any closer or I'll shoot." The man in front of them was both young and twitchy. Perhaps he'd caught wind of the news about the missing officers from down the corridor. Reaching the theater through the quarries wasn't going to be easy if every twenty meters Sadiqi was stopped by high strung patrols.

"There are three of us," Sadiqi said with a tone designed to sound commanding not cordial. "I have orders to cover the sector at the top of Rue de Vaugirard."

"If you come any closer, I'll shoot," the voice repeated.

Sadiqi had given in to the GSPR man. He wasn't going to do the same here. The kid was visibly uncomfortable in this subterranean ambush zone – no doubt he was straight out of training school. Rather than appealing to a colleague for help, the cop opted for the steamroller routine. "*Ecoutez-moi mon bonhomme*," he said, laying a thick layer of contempt into his words, "if you can't authorize me to pass you'd better go and find someone who can. You have your orders. I have mine.

And if we spend all night arguing I'm sure as hell not going to get my work done."

Toni could tell by the silence that followed that the young cop was weighing up the pros and cons of obeying Sadiqi. It didn't take him long to surrender. "Wait here. I'll go get my commanding officer. But don't move..."

"No," Sadiqi corrected, "you'll escort us to your commanding officer."

* * *

The commanding officer okayed their passage and within a couple of minutes the group had been escorted to a spot under the Odeon Theater. The gendarme then saluted and headed back to his post below the Senate – taking with him the beam of his flashlights, and leaving the other three reduced to their single lamp. It was sub-optimal. Although they were geographically where they wanted to be, they were also plunged into almost total black.

On top of that, whereas normally Toni would have been happy to blaze a trail, at the moment she was still trying to figure out her next move. For the third time in two days, she wasn't quite sure where exactly she was headed or what exactly she was looking for. Sure, there was a passage somewhere nearby. Unfortunately, only Trouvé knew where to find it. And he was nowhere near. The past two days had been a succession of enigmas and Toni was beginning to worry her luck might be running out.

But Sadiqi hadn't let himself be dragged twenty meters below ground just to waste time wavering about whether or not it was the right choice. There was a theater full of people above their heads listening to an opera that was poised to end with everyone from the diva to the guys mopping the floors in Intensive Care. It was time for Corrigan to sniff out this famous portal. "So where's the passage?" The light from his lamp cast a glow over the two faces. The look of uncertainty plastered across Toni's was not encouraging.

If this was another dead end there were going to be massive human consequences.

He didn't need to say the words aloud. Toni was fully aware what was at stake. "It must be this way," she said, moving out of the surveillance tunnel and ducking into a narrower corridor. With the map of the network etched in her memory, she knew the secondary tunnel ran the length of the theater and therefore it offered the most likely spot for a connecting passage into the building. "The tunnel we need goes back to the earliest days of Freemasonry. Which means it pre-dates the consolidation works."

Up until now Toni had always prided herself on her knowledge of the quarries. She knew every tunnel in the GRS. This was a fact not an exaggeration. She had been down this tunnel previously, both on her own and with Caron. During her months in Paris she'd been meticulous about visiting every single corridor and taking every turn open to her in the network. So she was vaguely ashamed at the idea that she'd never detected what she now knew lay hidden somewhere around here. She'd walked by the Mason's secret passage without sensing what was hiding there. Which left her with one disquieting certainty: For this to have stayed hidden so long, the entry she was looking for had to be almost imperceptible.

As if that wasn't bad enough, their lack of equipment was going to slow them down. Although in cataphile terms the tunnel they were now in was minuscule (barely twenty meters long), in logistical terms, it presented a lot of surface to inspect. And Sadiqi's impatience was complicating the search process. The second they turned into the tunnel he started charging ahead without lingering on any given spot. Which was understandable given the urgency of the situation. Except every time he turned his head in a different direction, the light beam on his caplamp disappeared from Toni's point of focus. And that was a problem, because clearly the cop wasn't looking for the same type of clues as her. "What exactly are you looking for?" she asked, as he rumbled along the corridor, the beam of the lamp glued to floor level.

"Any sign of the Nightingale."

The cursory answer struck Toni as unhelpful but it seemed to satisfy Podesta, who pulled his phone out of his pocket and switched on the flashlight.

Toni, on the other hand, had no idea what sort of traces the Nightingale would have left behind. She would have to do this her own way.

With a click of her wrist, she also pulled out her phone and turned on the flashlight. While Sadiqi and Podesta concentrated on scouring the floor, she knew the best place to look was up.

Raising her head and the flashlight beam, she first made a quick assessment of the basic structure of each wall panel. Crazy as it sounded, presumably they were looking for a secret passage. The obvious corollary was that any secret passage was unlikely to be cut directly into the limestone. It was more likely to be part of a reconstructed segment of stone panel.

She moved swiftly down the corridor toward a wall made out of layers of carefully laid stones. The next step was to look for the traces of time on the walls. Those would be visible at the top of the walls, not at the bottom. So while she directed the lamp with one hand, the fingers of the other hand scuttled from left to right then back again along the upper ridges of stonework in search of an indentation in the rock or a ledge – anything but solid stone.

As Sadiqi advanced down the corridor in a rumble of, "*Merde, merde, merde,*" hanging back, Toni found what she was looking for.

To most people it would have been unnoticeable. To the student, who was used to the wear and tear of the quarries, it was a blatant discrepency. There was a gap. It wasn't glaring. That's why she had never noticed it before. Yet, in a corner of the quarries where the upper rock strata had been pressing down on this same wall for centuries, theoretically there shouldn't have been any gap at all between the wall and the stone ceiling. That gap should have been compressed by the slowly descending layers above. If anything, the stones at the top of the wall should have been cracked or shattered by the weight of the city pressing down on them. Instead, there was a space. A tiny space. Barely half a centimeter. But if that space existed, it was because for some reason, the wall wasn't supporting the weight of the limestone above. That was because it wasn't a wall at all. It was a door.

"The top of the wall. Look. It must be here," she called. Despite the urgency of the situation, she felt a tremor of wonder.

The cops were beside her and nodding confirmation before she'd even finished speaking. They weren't, however, looking at the same clues as her. While she was looking upwards, Sadiqi was on his knees beside Podesta, both with their flashlights pointed at a smear of brown at the foot of the wall. There was no doubt. "Blood," Sadiqi said. "And it goes under the wall. This wall has moved recently."

90

With the rays of Sadiqi's cap lamp aimed strategically, Toni started evaluating the structure's solidity. It was like many of the other walls in this sector, with medium-sized stone blocks carefully mortared one to the other. Perfectly even. There was nothing to distinguish it from a similar wall a few meters further along other than the bits and pieces of graffiti covering it. It was also massive.

It was Podesta who voiced the question on everyone's mind. "So how do we get in?"

The impossible question. Presuming this was really the *portal* mentioned in Caron's report, how were they supposed to get that door open? The answer had to be somewhere in the jigsaw puzzle of identical stones. So they all began scrambling – searching for something that would distinguish one of those blocks from all the others. Toni's heart speeded up. It was insane. Could there really be a latch or a release mechanism? How could anything like that possibly be hidden here in this area so often traveled by cataphiles? How could there be a secret passageway in the middle of a fair sized tunnel and yet nobody had found it in hundreds of years? It was crazy.

And yet, just when she had convinced herself that it was impossible, she saw it. A tiny engraving. About the size of a tangerine. Around knee level, slightly to her right. Although the lines of the engraving had been worn by time and partially obscured by the layers of spray paint injected by innumerable graffiti artists, the motif was unmistakeable. Leaning closer, she could make out a shape chiselled lightly into the stone: a triangle.

"Look, there's a symbol." She pressed on it. Nothing happened.

Podesta shone his light on the spot. "That's just a triangle."

"Yes, but I'm pretty sure the equilateral triangle is a Masonic symbol," she answered. The cop leaned closer and tried pressing on the form, but still nothing happened.

Sadiqi, who was on his knees examining the lower segment of wall, brushed his hand against a stone near the floor, flicking away a thin layer of dust. "There's another one, here."

"Maybe we need to press both at the same time." Again nothing happened. Before they had time to feel a sense of disappointment, Sadiqi found two more engravings.

"There's another one here. And here," he said, pointing to the parallel pair.

"Four triangles forming a square," Podesta said impatiently. "The Masons have a cute sense of humor." He and the inspector were already pressing on the four points but still nothing happened.

But it was true. It was almost a square. Looking on, Toni could see that the engraving Podesta had found was directly above the one Sadiqi had pointed to at the foot of the wall. Toni's symbol was near the top of the wall, but only slightly off-center compared to the other two.

With the cops hunched at the foot of the wall, she stood back to leave them room to work. *Four triangles forming a square,* she repeated to herself. Her eyes roved upward to a spot above the two men's heads. That's when she saw it. "No," she said. "It's three squares forming a triangle." Starting from the four points Sadiqi and Podesta had picked out at the base of the wall, Toni was easily able to reconstitute the rest of the diagram.

Podesta scoffed. "I might not be great at math, but it's definitely a square. Not a triangle."

But he was wrong. Toni's eyes were focused higher. "Maybe, *that* is," she said nodding at the lower quadrant, but that's only part of it. There are two other squares higher up," she said, pointing at the upper segement of the wall. "That's definitely three squares forming a triangle. It's Pythagoras. Their lodge is called Pythagoras and Euclid. And that's the Pythagorean theorem." She tapped successively on the nine small engravings. "Three squares forming a squared triangle."

The math theorem was hardly a mystery for anyone who'd taken eighth grade math. "Nine points."

Anything was worth a try. "Okay. So let's do it. We all push at the same time," Sadiqi ordered. "Both hands plus a foot. Let's go." There was another scramble as phones were shoved back into pockets and each of them lurched for three points in what was beginning to seem like some strange underground Twister game.

"Now," Toni called out, simultaneously pushing down with her full strength on her hands plus a knee. The fingers that had been extended, searching their way across the wall now came together to concentrate their force into a tiny area. The student held her breath, every inch of her body tensed to see what would happen next.

The deep rumbling that followed chased any other thoughts as the center of the engravings sank into the wall.

91

A shower of dust sprinkled down from the ceiling, setting off a fit of coughing. Although Toni knew there was a direct link of cause and effect between their pushing on the stone and this mini-earthquake, a sense of unease rose up inside her. Collapsing stone walls were every underground explorer's nightmare.

But the fear didn't last long. The mortar was still holding the stones together and the ceiling was intact. Nothing was falling down. On the contrary, the wall was sliding away in a smooth inward motion. The stone wall had transformed into a doorway.

Despite the urgency to get up into the theater, standing in front of this newly created opening, Toni felt a page of history was revealing itself to her. And the beauty of the moment was somehow enhanced by the shimmering ray of light from Sadiqi's lamp and the shadows it cast into the alcove. She leaned forward, squinting into the darkness, trying to see what lay ahead in this never-before explored corner of the network. It was Sadiqi who entered first, easing into the rocky chamber, his pistol raised. But the darkness was still and empty.

The cop took three steps into the gallery, his beam bouncing off the surfaces. The rocky cave was furnished, like some subterranean troglodyte dwelling. A wooden chair and a table had been placed in the corner. On the table was an unlikely collection of objects including a statue of a rooster, an hourglass and, in the corner, a human skull. And on the wall there was a banner with the word "VITRIOL" written on it. The fabled Chamber of Reflection.

At any other time, it would have been a curious world to examine. Today it was nothing but a nightmare. If the light in the cave had been better, the cop might have noticed Toni staring at the scene, willing herself to lock that image away, the same way she had observed Sadiqi locking away the memory of his dead colleagues. Whatever she'd expected to find in the secret passage, it wasn't this. She certainly hadn't been ready for the vision of carnage. Heaped on the floor beyond the table was a tangle of quarry police jumpsuits covering a mass of lifeless corpses. Hands and shoes sprawled out of the pile. But none of the heads had been left intact. Only their uniforms made it possible to guess who they were.

Podesta eased past the table and knelt down beside the bodies, running his hand along a neck in search of a pulse. Pointlessly. They'd been missing for hours. They'd been dead for longer. There was no doubt this was the Nightingale's work. Sadiqi recognized the style. A single shot straight through the head. Fast and effective.

The guy had had no limits.

God only knew what was about to happen in the theater.

Sadiqi glanced around the Chamber. "How do we get upstairs? The fireworks are up there. Not here." There was no sign of a staircase or a path upward. The gallery was tiny. It was also a dead end.

Toni had promised him a passage to the Odeon. So where the hell was this historic portal? A dead end under the theater was of no use to him. He rounded on the academic, half-expecting to find her looking at him with a quizzical expression, encouraging him to enjoy the riddle. Instead he found her squinting at a small shadow just behind his knees.

Dropping to the ground he ran his hand over the shelf of dust and rubble. What he discovered was the same mirage he'd observed at H4. An opening where a minute before he'd imagined a solid wall.

With only cursory precautions, he crawled into the hole. It wasn't a long shaft like at H4. This time, the hole opened directly onto a tiny gallery. In fact, the stifling cylindrical room it led to was so small that once he'd crawled through, Sadiqi's feet were still in the doorway while his face was almost pressed up against the wall. There was no space to advance. He was immured in a tiny cell.

But he knew how this worked now. Tilting his head upward, the beam of his light shot twenty meters higher through the darkness.

Fastened to the stone walls was a ladder that would take him where he needed to go. And the metal of the rungs was shiny and solid looking – very different from the aged, rusted rungs that had cut his hands in the well under H4. Obviously having Caron as a member of their secret society had had its advantages. The equipment in the Mason's chamber was in sparkling condition.

92

The way the music and voices swelled around him in the shaft, Sadiqi could tell he was very close to the stage. As he moved upward, the sounds became more vibrant.

Although he didn't know enough about *The Magic Flute* to recognize the three boy sopranos announcing the final trials of Tamino and Pamina, he could tell the performance was building towards a climax as the voices mixed more and more densely with the instruments. The countdown was speeding up. The grand finale was drawing near. Presuming the fireworks hadn't yet gone off, they probably wouldn't be long in coming.

By the time the inspector hit the top rung of the ladder, he had a feeling the hysterical sounding female now shrieking out her fears on stage must be warning him of what he was about to find in the theater. Combing the place was going to mean a whole hell of a lot more surface to cover than a couple of empty tunnels below ground.

Finding the release mechanism for the trap door was easy. The Freemasons had used more ingenuity designing complicated ways of hiding the passage from non-believers on the outside than making it complicated for the initiates to escape from within. A moment later Sadiqi was racing across what looked like a storage room for props and old costumes, then up to stage level, where he burst into the wings.

* * *

The cop knew he was standing on a time bomb, but the calm of the backstage area only emphasized the fact that everyone else in the building was enjoying a quiet evening of music. He'd expected the wings to be seething with life; instead he found emptiness. Obviously a slickly run show didn't need dozens of people hanging around behind the curtain. Everyone had a job to do and everyone was elsewhere performing that job. Even on stage, there wasn't exactly a crowd. Just a man in an elegant Edwardian suit made of apple green velvet being escorted in an operatic promenade by two armored guards who looked more like something out of *Blade Runner* than a piece from the Enlightenment.

Sadiqi moved toward the only other person in the wings – a young man dressed in a black jacket and tie. "We need to stop the show and get everyone out."

As the man turned to shush the cop, Toni and Podesta came barreling into the wings.

Outrunning a slightly breathless Podesta by an easy margin, Toni spoke urgently. "Marco. You've got to help us. We've got to evacuate the theater." Sadiqi hadn't immediately recognized the person in front of him, but now he realized it was the student who he'd seen in the office at *FranceTech* the day before, his features darkened by incomprehension. "There was a message online," Toni continued. *"Fireworks above the temple. The songs will change to screams."*

Sadiqi was already pulling the cardboard canister out of his pocket. "I think they're going to use these. There's a test tube in the middle. I'd say they're designed to contain some sort of toxic material.

They'll need a shock to make them airborne. Something to shatter the glass and blow the contents over the audience."

The look of confusion on the young man's face mutated to concern.

"Fireworks over the temple…" Toni repeated.

Marco's gaze darted from one face to the other. Although it sounded outrageous, the fireworks scenario fit perfectly with the show. "The trial of fire. At the end of the opera. There's a pyrotechnics display integrated into the scene. There are casings all around the stage for fireworks," he nodded towards the set. "They look exactly like these."

This was confirmation of Sadiqi's worst fears. By integrating the attack into the show, the outcome became potentially more deadly. If a bomb were set off, at least the survivors could make a run for the exits. But if the attack looked like it was just part of the evening's entertainment, the audience would sit tight enjoying it as the whole area became contaminated and poison filtered into their bloodstream. They would all be infected before anyone even realized what was happening. Set off in an enclosed area, the consequences would be devastating.

The canisters had to be disabled. "How are the pyrotechnics controlled?" Sadiqi snapped.

Marco's face was a blank. "I've no idea. I saw part of the dress rehearsal but I don't know anything about the technical side."

Like everything else today, they were just going to have to wing it. "Podesta, you organize the exits. Make sure everyone gets out." Sadiqi turned to Toni. "I want you out of here. Go dance around that jerk from the GSPR so he realizes there really was another way into the building. You," he said signalling to Marco. "You come with me. We have to get people out. The audience will recognize you. Tell everyone to leave."

93

Despite his Italian elegance, Marco looked more like a little lost terrier than a man in control of his destiny as he strode out on stage alongside the inspector. It was perhaps this lack of conviction that worked against them. Rather than helping to get things moving, their presence simply produced confusion. The microphones hanging ten meters above the stage were there to amplify the choristers' song, not to pick up an isolated voice in the sea of sound. So when the cop raised his voice to maximum pitch and called out: "The show's over. Please make your way to the closest exit," the order was inaudible above the singing. Perhaps in another theater, the presence of a man with a police armband accompanied by someone in black tie might have sparked the audience's curiosity. But the opera had been transposed into a sort of dystopic futuristic world. The setting was modern. More importantly, the costumes were modern. Nothing on stage could surprise the audience.

Engrossed in the spiralling chords, the conductor hadn't noticed that the two latest people to take center stage weren't part of the cast. Only a couple of spectators from the front rows who had recognized Marco were beginning to wonder what was going on. To the best part of the crowd, Sadiqi looked like nothing less than a slightly dishevelled cast member in his plain-clothed cop get-up – clashing artistically with the young Italian's tuxedo.

Nobody was moving. Sadiqi had been confident that once the first people started leaving, it would create a snowball effect with everyone crushing towards the exits and gendarmes ushering the crowds to safety. That wasn't happening. Everyone was still sitting firmly nailed to their chairs. And to make matters worse, the orchestra was still blaring and the diva screeching.

*   *   *

Fortunately for everyone, the young Canadian had a taste for insubordination.

While Marco's reflexes were slowed by what was happening around him, Toni's were sharpened. So, when Sadiqi had told her to follow Podesta to the nearest exit, she nodded compliantly but remained standing exactly where she was. Watching from the wings, she easily saw the cop's attempts to usher the audience to safety were backfiring. Nobody could hear what the hell he was saying.

There were probably several sensible, even-headed solutions to the problem. But Toni opted for the one that came to her first: A fire alarm switch.

An ear-splitting screech tore through the building. Above the combined cacophony of the music still rising from the stage and the wail of the alarm, Toni was just able to catch the words of a stagehand screaming after her: "Pauvre folle" – *crazy bitch.* She didn't stop to discuss his choice of words or sentiments.

There was a tiny staircase leading from the edge of the stage to the front rows of the audience and she belted down the steps two at a time, each footstep bringing her deeper into the darkness of the stalls. No doubt she looked like a crazed shadow, hovering against the light of the stage, but she made her presence known by leaning into the second row and shrieking: "Fire. Evacuate the theater. Please move to the nearest exit as quickly and calmly as possible. This is not part of the show."

Combined with the bits and pieces the audience had picked up from the cop, the message was gaining clarity. The tension in the air spiked noticeably as people began rising to their feet. Yet the absence of any obvious smoke or scent of fire kept them calm. Possibly too calm.

* * *

Squinting against the spotlights, Sadiqi watched Toni scramble back up onto the stage while behind him, the final words of the aria spiralled upward:

> *Going gladly hand in hand into the temple.*
> *A woman unafraid of darkness and death*
> *Is worthy and will be consecrated.*

The soprano who should have answered these words was now headed towards the emergency exit. As the show ground to a halt, the confusion rising from the orchestra pit was accompanied by a more than parallel surge in the sounds coming from the audience, alternating between disgruntled and concerned.

But the evacuation was still moving much slower than the inspector would have liked. Rather than flowing out onto the square, the people seemed to be stuck at the doorways. Probably Tibrac wasn't out of the vicinity yet and the gendarmes wanted him safely whisked away before they let more people onto the adjoining streets. Or maybe the crush of bodies on the square was just too dense to accommodate the extra thousand theater-goers. *Let that not be the case.* If they didn't hurry, a free road for Tibrac would mean death for the people left behind in the theater.

But, Sadiqi couldn't cover everything at the same time. From here on out, Podesta would have to take care of the evacuation. The inspector had other things to deal with, namely making sure the fireworks didn't harm anyone – starting with Corrigan.

* * *

Once she'd climbed onto the stage, Toni had raced over to the closest pyrotechnics casing. Sure enough, inside there was a glass holder sitting atop the firework. And inside that glass, she could see a fine white powder.

Sliding her hand down into one of the cylinders, she pressed her index and middle fingers flat against the glass' smooth surface. Smooth was the key word. The glass was too smooth. Her fingers slipped against the covering as she tried to caress the tube out. There was only enough room to fit one finger on either side between the metal casing and the glass tube and the fact that her hands were sweating didn't make the manoeuvre any easier. The metal tore into the webbing between her fingers as she stuffed her hands deeper.

But the pain of the extra effort was worthwhile. Her hold on the glass was better this time and she started to shimmy it out. In fact the tube was nearly within reach for her to grab when a hand came crashing down on her shoulder, causing her grip to slip. "I told you to get out," Sadiqi boomed.

"Yeah, because you were doing such a hot job evacuating the theater," she snapped. "In any case, you're going to need my help with these. You were right. The glass tubes are in the fireworks, and there's definitely powder in there."

With a single motion he dropped to his knees and pushed the girl aside before shoving his fingers into the cylinder. "Get out," he repeated with an authority that might have sounded threatening if mere survival weren't her sole priority.

But rather than proving his self-sufficiency, his attempt to distance her simply demonstrated just how indispensable she was. The cop was grappling for the fireworks but couldn't get a grasp. He tried dislodging the slippery tube but his fingers blocked its passage. His hands were just too big. They were perfect for hand-to-hand combat and firing weapons with a strong recoil but not so good for the delicate operation of slipping a fragile object out of the tiniest hole. His attempts to coax the tube out were a series of fumbles.

In all the roles that Toni had seen Sadiqi perform over the past two days, this was the first time she'd seen him so obviously beaten. It was a fluke of nature. A question of anatomy. For once her long, aristocratic fingers were actually going to prove useful. "I've got this. Let me do it," she said, easing herself back down beside him. "Go find the central switch that controls the fireworks. I'll get the tubes out."

She shifted towards the casing and slipped her fingers into the hole where they slid down the side of the metal cylinder and gripped the tube.

"I can't let you do this," the cop repeated. Yet he was standing there, letting her do it.

Before the words had even finished rolling off his lips, Toni had eased the first tube out and was holding it up to the light. Sure enough, inside, a snowy white reflection was visible. "I get it. It's anthrax. It's dangerous."

"It's not dangerous. It's deadly."

She'd already moved to the second hole. "Weapons grade no doubt, if it's a gift from your charming legionnaire." Toni understood that Khalid wanted her out and safe but that didn't make any sense if he was in here with this poison. "This goes off and everyone who hasn't managed to get out those doors is dead. I get it."

Sadiqi glanced at the back of the theater where hundreds of people were still either staring at the stage or pressed against one another to get to the exit. He knew she was right. The only way to save the people still blocked in the auditorium was to make sure the fireworks didn't go off. "I'll go find the control booth to make sure this doesn't blow."

From the stage, he pinpointed the light and sound booth at the back of the upper balcony. If anyone in the building could tell him how to disable the pyrotechnics, they would be up there.

94

The cop knew better than to aim for the main staircase. It would be impenetrable with a jam of bodies. So he headed for the wings instead. Not quite so big a crowd, but still too many people, straggling towards the exit.

The electric energy of his ascent contrasted with the public's leisurely descent. Below, he could hear Podesta calling to people from the lobby to move faster, but no one was paying attention. The obvious absence of any real fire was keeping everyone way too calm, creating a huge static obstacle. Sadiqi had to fight his way upwards through the hordes, forcing against the tide, leaning into the banister for extra leverage to help swim against the current.

While his body struggled to find a path through the crowd his thoughts circled to all the remaining questions. Some of the answers seemed clear, others not. The Nightingale must have planted the tubes of poison earlier that afternoon – which explained the six dead quarry officers. He must have entered the theater through the secret passage to plant the fireworks, then gone back to H4.

But how did the rest fit together? The fact that they hadn't found so much as a telephone on the Nightingale's body was a huge setback. It was going to make it almost impossible figuring out who he'd been working for. There was no way the legionnaire had orchestrated this attack. If it had been his idea, he would have left a message somewhere; a recording or a tweet explaining who he was and what he was seeking to accomplish. That's what the ideologues always did – propagate their message. But this guy hadn't done that – the four retribution messages had been obscure. A taunt for police, not a claim of responsibility. No. The legionnaire was just the gun-for-hire, not the mastermind.

So who was behind all this blood? Could it really be Clavreul? Was that possible? For all his faults, it seemed unlikely the senator would attempt to kill a thousand innocent people. And yet. So many of the clues fit. Including the information about the secret passage to the Odeon. After all, how else would the Nightingale have learnt about the chamber he'd used to access the theater? If Clavreul had learnt about that passage from Caron he could have handed on the knowledge.

So what was the deal? If this was Clavreul's plan, what could he possibly be hoping to achieve? To kill the president? To shake up the Freemasons? To create a new strain of terrorism that could somehow serve his political manoeuvrings?

A trickle of sweat formed on the cop's forehead, as much from his angst as the physical effort of fighting his way up the stairs. With the Nightingale dead and nothing to connect him to anyone, there was little chance of confirming who was behind the plan... Sadiqi didn't regret killing Rossignol, but he did regret the fact that he was dead. He should have tried to take him alive. Shot him earlier. By delaying his strike, the cop had simply made the ultimate unravelling worse. He should have shot him in the legs while he was still carrying Corrigan across the roof. She would have found some way of getting away. She would have figured out how to stop herself from flying over the edge of the roof, even if it had meant hanging on by her teeth.

No. That was unfair. Surely the way she'd survived the fall at H4 had simply been dumb luck. Her dress had got caught on the gutter.

And yet. Here she was again. The first thing Sadiqi saw when he raced onto the balcony beside the light booth was Corrigan in the distance, fighting to squeeze the fireworks out of the casings. There was no way she should be doing that. Anyone with a drop of good sense would have been trying to get as far away from the theater as possible right now. Except there she was. Digging out anthrax tubes.

He wasn't sure whether he should be impressed with her level-headedness or appalled by her recklessness.

Either way, he'd have to worry about it later.

Dashing into the sound booth, he found the tiny technical hub empty. Abandoned. At least someone had the sense to get out while they still could.

The cop glanced around. There were knobs and buttons and sliding level indicators everywhere. The gadgetry was unfamiliar. Only one thing was clear. The technicians had left everything the way it was. Perhaps they hadn't wanted to cut the stage lights for fear the fire alarm was some sort of hoax and the show was really going to continue. And once they'd gone off to check, it was too late to come back and cut the power. So the lighting on stage was still the same as it had been when the cop first arrived. Which was a good thing: the lights weren't shifting. Which must mean that the systems were all operated manually. There would be no automatic changes. More importantly, it also meant that the fireworks, too, would have to be set off manually.

The inspector looked down and saw Toni bent over a casing on the far right of the stage. The mess of glass tubes on the floor beside her was growing. There were probably over a dozen already.

From the booth he had a view of the layout. In all there were eighteen casings arranged in nine pairs, forming a v-shape working backwards in twos from the center front of the stage to the back. Toni had been working from left to right and she was already nearing the end. At most, there were four tubes left to remove. The job was nearly done.

The cop suspected that the best policy would be to do nothing. If he didn't touch the controls in the booth, everything would be fine. In a couple of minutes Corrigan would have all the tubes out – and the alert would be over. The main thing was to make sure that nobody set off the fireworks manually while she was still working. And that wasn't going to happen with no technicians around.

He stepped out of the booth and moved down to the railing that ran the length of the balcony. Things were looking up. They'd stopped the Nightingale's plan. Okay. It was far from a perfect day. They didn't know who was behind this. But Sadiqi was willing to accept the small mercy that all the people in this theater weren't going to be poisoned. Leaning forward over the rim of the railing he called out, "Hey Ice Lady. We're good. The fireworks need to be triggered manually."

His voice was only just audible over the continued wail of the fire alarm, but Toni noticed the movement on the balcony. For a fraction of a second she saw Khalid's relaxed figure leaning over the railing and she smiled her thanks.

At least that was the brief moment of calm before the world went insane again.

* * *

The flash of light registered before she heard the crash so it took her half a minute to realize what had happened.

The technical booth had just exploded.

The ease with which Sadiqi's body arched over the railing then plummeted down to the dress circle made the strong muscular body look like a flimsy patchwork doll.

There was something in the fluidity of that motion that suddenly woke Toni to the full realization that they were in deadly danger. Just as Khalid's body had been thrown from the balcony, so too, she knew it would take only a fraction of a second for her to be powdered with anthrax and have all her endeavors blown into the sweet hereafter.

Apparently the remaining spectators still in the hall were drawing the same conclusion. The screaming started the moment after the explosion. The orderly evacuation began degenerating into panic.

As the last shards of glass and metal tinkled to the ground from the destroyed booth, Toni rose to her feet. She threw a quick glance around the auditorium, desperately trying to assess what would be the fastest path to the balcony.

But before she could make her choice or break into motion, a slight movement in the dress circle cut short her calculations. At first it was just a vague form, but then an outline surfaced.

He staggered to his feet, shaken. Possibly injured. But Khalid was alive. The fact that he'd been propelled over the railing by the blast meant that he was thrown clear of most of the glass and burning wire that shot out of the booth.

"Don't move," she shouted over the layers of noise. The glare of the spotlights made it difficult to see exactly what was happening. "I'll come and help you."

Sadiqi stared upwards, in the direction of the shattered light booth, but was unable to see it. Everything was very confused. He wasn't sure how he had ended up two levels down from where he'd started. But looking around at the pieces of wire, glass and wood on the floor, it all fell into place.

He reeled towards Toni. "No! Get out! Get out, now," he yelled, waving his arms so she would understand even if she couldn't hear over the noise. This was it! This was what he'd feared.

As if in answer to his signal, on stage a flash flared out of the two tubes at the front of the stage. A clue to help her understand. Toni whirled in time to see the shower of sparks. The fireworks. Khalid had said the fireworks could only be set off manually. This wasn't supposed to happen.

She wasn't moving. Sadiqi tried screaming louder but he wasn't able to match the volume of the panicked crowd and the alarm. There was also a searing pain in his side, making it harder for him to fill his lungs properly and project his voice. His back stung, too. Probably lacerations. But hell, if he could feel them, they were minor. There was a bigger problem: Some sort of override system had just been triggered on the fireworks. The Nightingale had made his plan foolproof. No matter what happened, the anthrax had been set to go off. The legionnaire's plan didn't depend on the lighting engineers triggering the fireworks. If the pyrotechnics weren't set off manually by a certain time, the lighting booth blew and the fireworks followed automatically. There must have been a timer in the booth with a bomb. Every possibility was calculated.

Sadiqi looked down at the stage and saw Toni's face still turned towards him.

"Get out," he yelled, much louder this time, ignoring the flare of pain in his side. This was the second time today he'd seen this woman staring death in the face.

Her gaze shifted back to the scene at the auditorium door, where there were still at least a hundred people pressing forward, struggling to exit. More on the upper floors.

The audience was emptying in drips and drabs instead of pouring out onto the street. No doubt the square was still saturated with music lovers not to mention hundreds of gendarmes with their vehicles blocking the roads. Getting an extra thousand people onto the square was proving hopeless. The result was a confused bottleneck. It was clear to Toni that even if she made a dash for the back of the theater, it wasn't sure she'd be able to get out before the last casings blew. And if those last fireworks exploded – the four she hadn't had time to empty yet – the anthrax would be airborne, meaning death to anyone still in the theater – and probable contamination well beyond. Even if she tried to get out like Sadiqi said, she would probably just find herself at the back of the theater, pushing against the other people fighting to get out when the last fireworks went off, along with the anthrax.

It wasn't a risk she was willing to take. She fell back on her knees. The other tubes had come out easily; these last ones would, too. She had mastered the technique. She was going to get this done. Stopping would be more dangerous than continuing.

In answer to her boldness an almighty explosion nearly made her lose her grasp on the tube she'd just pulled out. She watched as a sea of red flame spit from the stage floor to the ceiling above. Damn damn damn, she thought. Two more fireworks had just gone off.

The only good news was that this wasn't going to be over with just a single explosion. There was going to be a succession of blasts. Apparently the firing sequence was simple. The casings were arranged in pairs and each of the blasts released a single firework. The center pair had gone first, and then the other pairs worked successively backwards from the curtain line towards the background, with each set in the V exploding simultaneously. Which meant Toni was safe for now, but not for long. Another explosion sounded. There would be just four more before the sequence reached the cylinder she was working on. She still had two last holes to empty.

Even as she dove towards the seventeenth casing, two more fireworks exploded. Three more to go.

She closed her mind to everything except prying out the deadly tubes. A whooshing noise sizzled close by as another pair of fireworks spluttered upwards in streams of yellow and orange. She hadn't expected that one quite so soon. Pushing her fingers down again she tightened her grip. Her hands were so damp with sweat that the glass nearly slipped out of her fingers. Another flash, closer this time. She wiped her palms against her skirt then thrust her fingers back into the cylinder. Just as the tube began to slip out she heard a sizzling in front of her. Doubling her speed, she wrenched out the thin vial then leaned away from the casing just in time to avoid a wave of fire as it rocketed upwards, spitting out so near she could feel the heat of the sparks against her face.

Only one left to go. Corrigan's body was taut with fear. Without thinking, she slammed her fingers into the last casing. How long did she have before the final volley? Would there be a hiatus or would it follow immediately? Things had got complicated quickly today. Her eyes dashed up to the dress circle, but Sadiqi wasn't there anymore. Hopefully he'd got out safely.

It was too late for her to do the same. There was a better chance of removing the final tube than there was of escaping. In any case, if the anthrax was going to kill her, it was probably better to have the damn thing explode in her face and get the lethal dose directly.

Her sweaty hands slid against the edge of the glass. *Come on, please, come on*, she begged the air. Perhaps the tube heard her plea because it inched upward. But not enough to draw it out completely. She needed it. *Come on!* And as if in answer to her plea, the tip of the tube peaked out above the rim of the cylinder.

Her hands cupped the top ridge but in that same instant she felt the tiniest tremor below. Then that tiny tremor grew into something ever more powerful with a sea of flames engulfing her. As she lost her balance and tumbled backward onto the floor, the delicate glass tube of death slipped from her fingers.

95

It was so absurd. All that work for nothing.

Toni lay on the stage, her eyes pressed shut against the glare of the fading light from the fireworks. She'd been so close to stopping this. The tube had been right there in her hand but for some reason she hadn't been able to hold on to it. She'd let go. And the delicate glass must have shattered around her at its first contact with the floor. The virus was probably already in her blood. She could feel her body growing weaker. How potent was anthrax? What were her chances of surviving spores at such close range? She thought of herself as a lucky person. Maybe not that lucky.

She wasn't the machine she was pretending to be. Why had she done this? To save people she didn't know? To save herself? To save Khalid? What was the point now? It was over. She'd dropped the tube. She was as good as dead.

It was with that sense of fatal certainty that she pried her eyes open to observe the pure brutality of life, as a cloud of smoke settled around the stage.

Instead, what she saw framed in the aura of shimmering light and smoke, was Sadiqi. On his knees beside her, holding the last tube. Intact. And he was smiling.

It was the first time she'd seen him with a full, radiant smile.

There was no explaining this guy's reactions. *Maabol.* He was her very own personal crazy man. "Who are you and what have you done with the inspector? Khalid Sadiqi never smiles."

"Yeah. And the Ice Lady feels no fear." He combed the wild strands of hair out of her eyes. "We all have bad days."

When he wrapped his free arm around her shoulders he clenched her so tightly it almost hurt.

96

"One thing's for sure, this is one crazy country," Toni said, squeezing closer to Sadiqi on the side of the ambulance while a paramedic disinfected a cut on his back. "Soldiers planting bombs under schools. Presidential assassination attempts with 1000 bystanders as collateral damage. You know, in Canada we think it's big news if an MP accidentally bangs into a colleague in the House of Commons; you guys are in a whole other league."

Sadiqi wrapped his arm around her shoulders but he wasn't paying much attention to what she was saying. It was enough to know they were both still alive. In addition to the simple sensual pleasure of feeling the young woman pressed up against him, the cop was enjoying the intellectual pleasure of watching Podesta wonder what the hell was going on between him and the girl. She was draped against him so tightly, the paramedic could barely uncouple them long enough to cleanse their wounds and check for broken bones. Just when Podesta had convinced himself his boss never thought of anything but work, Sadiqi had managed to introduce an element of surprise.

In any case, the lieutenant could think whatever the hell he liked. Sadiqi was glad to be in one piece. The same couldn't be said for all his colleagues today. He was sure as hell going to indulge in every scrap of human pleasure he could scrape out of this miserable day.

Every scrap, minus the time spent on inevitable work. Dukrin's ring tone announced a final dose of unpleasantness.

"Just leave it," Toni said, as he shifted away to reach for the phone.

"No. I've got to take this." The various messages that had been sent back and forth over the past hour needed clarifying.

There was seldom chitchat with Dukrin. The fact that today she actually bothered to ask how he was doing only highlighted just how severe their losses had been. "I've been told your injuries are only minor."

"I'm fine. Two of my men are dead." The paramedic had outstayed his welcome. The inspector waved him away and buttoned his shirt. Then he moved the phone to his left hand so he could hold Toni in the right.

"I know." Plus the six under the Odeon. The worst had been averted at the theater, but at a significant price to the force. Dukrin knew that there was no point in making this any harder on Sadiqi by reminding him of the body count. He was going to be flagellating himself over his losses, telling himself that if he had made different calls, those men would still be alive. The only vaguely good news was that the officers that had been sent out to find the tunnel under the Pantheon hadn't been in the shaft when it collapsed. It was the smallest of mercies: she couldn't afford any more losses. "We're going to see if we can track down anyone who knew Rossignol and might know what he was up to. Every cop in the country has a photo of him. And the picture has been transmitted to the media." De Chanterelle's assassination had been covered up; the attempt on Tibrac's life was already making the headlines. "Don't make any plans for the weekend. I'm going to need you on this."

The prospect was less than enticing. It wasn't the first time Sadiqi's weekend had been screwed over by work but if he was going to be doing overtime he would prefer not to spend it trawling through public feedback inspired by pixelized photos. An hour after the photo was flashed on the late night newscast, he'd be wading through tens of thousands of dead ends called in by concerned citizens whose neighbor with the noisy motorbike had a mole behind the left ear, just like the suspect. It was a complete waste of time. "Rossignol was just the hired hand. That's all he ever was. A mercenary. Working for whoever was willing to pay him his stipend." Nestled in the crux of his arm, the student was listening with rapt fascination to both sides of the call. "And the guy who hired him isn't going to be reaching out to us."

Although Dukrin didn't have eyes on her inspector's indiscretions with his new lover, she was, nevertheless, keenly aware that telephones were unreliable devices. She might be at the top of the intelligence hierarchy and, as such, the person calling the shots on whose phonecalls were bugged in their great Republic, that still didn't mean she was certain this line was secure. Fortunately she and Sadiqi had been working together so long that they understood one another implicitly. Dukrin knew he was referring to Clavreul, so there was no need to say the name aloud. In any case, if there was one politician whose ideas were so nauseating you could complain about him without raising too many eyebrows, it had to be the man on Sadiqi's mind. "By reaching out to the public, we might come up with some new leads. For the moment our only evidence is circumstantial and inconclusive."

"Inconclusive maybe. But there's plenty of it. We've got an IP connection to the retribution messages. We know Caron received a letter from the same person just before he was murdered. We know he met Rossignol. Most importantly, he was one of a very limited number of people who probably knew about the existence of the tunnel under the theater – which in itself may be the strongest link."

"Possible link. Your words." Dukrin was willing to admit Clavreul was the obvious suspect. There were several suggestions he was mixed up in this in some way. She just wasn't sure he was the one pulling the strings. "Unless you have conclusive evidence, I suggest you avoid closing yourself into one specific scenario. This is an unprecedented episode. We've already had messages claiming responsibility for this from three different Islamist groups. We need to check all the leads. I don't want to run the risk of making incorrect accusations that could undermine the UCLAT's reputation and stop us from bringing in a conviction." More importantly, it would bring her position at the head of the DGSI into question if she lunged for one suspect only to have his name cleared by some damning piece of evidence they'd missed due to sloppy investigating.

Not that Sadiqi was overly anxious to pursue a case around a sitting senator. As a general rule, he tried to keep as far away from politics as possible – his sole concern in that field being to make sure his department's budget didn't get cut back any further. No. The further he could stay from politics, the less sullied he felt. But it was impossible to ignore the fact that more and more clues were pointing to the senator. Even if there wasn't any incriminating evidence yet, he knew the best way to substantiate any potential link to the legionnaire would be to follow the money. "Rossignol wasn't a religious warrior being funded by jihadis. He was a mercenary bankrolled by someone with lots of connections. And if he was a mercenary then, by definition, he was being paid. Find me the bank accounts. Find me the transfers."

It was a valid point – one Dukrin intended to pursue. "I have people exploring that angle." In contrast to Sadiqi's pessimism, she placed a tiny amount of hope in the fact that Clavreul had been messy. She wasn't sure whether the senator's mistakes had been caused by hubris, laziness or stupidity, but she was starting to have a neat pile of clues connecting him to Caron's death. And from Caron, there was a lot to link him to everything that had happened in the quarries, from de Chanterelle to the Odeon. So maybe they really would be able to turn up the money line.

Overall, she might almost be starting to feel serene about the chances of closing this case if there weren't so many pieces that didn't fit. Ironically, as more and more clues poured in pointing towards Clavreul, Dukrin was growing more reluctant to believe he was the sole force behind the legionnaire. To begin with, the fourth retribution message was linked to a different IP code from the other three – nothing to do with the senator. More importantly, there was the question of motive. She couldn't see what the senator would stand to gain from something as outrageous as killing the president and taking out nearly a thousand innocent bystanders in the process. "At the same time, I don't understand what incentive he could possibly have to do anything this unconscionable. Rossignol was probably a psychopath who just wanted to watch the city burn. But if your suspect is the right guy, he would have to have a solid strategy. An aim. We're not talking about a little rabble rousing. This is terrorism on a massive scale."

The doubt left Sadiqi unmoved. *Why did anyone do anything like this?* Twenty years in counter-terrorism and he still hadn't come across a satisfying answer to that question in any of his cases. Terror was the warped belief that by hurting other people, the terrorist made his own cause stronger. The cop had seen kids blow themselves up, somehow believing that their death (along with that of any bystanders) would give meaning to their lives. He had seen people from seemingly promising backgrounds try to wipe out kindergartens or shopping malls. Twisted though it was, most of the time the decision had something to do with power – increasing one's power in the community, increasing the power of the movement they believed in. This current case seemed a million miles away from Sadiqi's usual Islamist extremist terror cases, yet somehow it jigsawed with those same incentives. "You know I'm out of my depth on this case. But I'd speculate that he saw the attack as an opportunity to reinforce his reach. Presumably he was looking to make political gains." Dukrin was invariably better informed than the inspector about the latest power struggles. "You tell me." Clavreul hated the Freemasons, and the conference at the Odeon had overt links to that community. Perhaps the attack was an attempt to eliminate a vocal faction of his opposition. Make him stronger by slimming the opposition.

But for Dukrin, that's where this lead fell apart. "This was also an attempt on the President's life," she reminded him. Even if Clavreul was trying to reinforce his political base, why kill the President? The suggestion that the senator would do that was untenable. After all, the two politicians had grown thick as thieves over the last parliamentary session. The president's increased affinity with Clavreul's party had been one of the big news stories of the past year.

Sadiqi knew this was true. Tibrac had been schmoozing Clavreul. Reinforcing the narrative of the dangers associated with immigration and cultural diversity. By associating with the senator, the president had simultaneously made Clavreul's loathsome policies appear more mainstream and his own policies more attractive to voters who felt disenfranchised. That didn't, however, necessarily mean the senator was entirely under the president's thumb. "Political back stabbing is nothing new – and it doesn't matter how close politicians get, they're hyenas, ready to turn on one another if they think they've got something to gain. The truth is, no matter how close they were, Tibrac's death would reinforce the far-right. If Tibrac had died in there, the country would have been thrown into chaos." Not only was Tibrac a cornerstone of politics, he had also spent the past year singing Clavreul's song – fuelling popular fears about terrorism and insecurity. If he had been killed in a terrorist attack, his death would have fanned those flames and the country would have turned to the other vocal Cassandra of terrorism: Clavreul. "His death would have created a void. I know exactly who would have stepped in to fill that void." It was the explanation that made the most sense. It was exactly the type of scenario Clavreul had wet dreams about: A new Evil, created straight out of thin air. Sadiqi could see it perfectly. The senator on the evening news spouting: *I've been warning you for years. We are no longer safe in our homes, our streets, our public places.* "The threat of evil would have been used to legitimize populist lies."

The idea had already crossed Dukrin's mind but she wasn't convinced. Then again, she had had more time to think this through than Sadiqi – the advantage of working from a desk, as opposed to the firing line. "I'm not sure you're reading this right. The attack planned at the Odeon goes beyond a little political backstabbing; the person who organized this belongs in the annals of infamy, right beside Pol Pot and Hitler."

"This guy is already on the wrong side of history. He couldn't care less so long as his power base is solid and growing." All Sadiqi could see was a man, with a single aim – to become stronger, no matter who he hurt, no matter how many ethical or legal rules he violated.

"And spend the rest of his life in jail?" Dukrin protested.

"If only," Sadiqi murmured. "He's impervious to the judiciary." Year after year, the senator had grown accustomed to his political immunity. None of the charges ever brought against him had stuck. And there had been several: negationism, defamation, misuse of parliamentary funds, assaulting various civil servants and private citizens, misconduct... Clavreul believed he was above the law. So did the entire political class as a monolithic whole, as far as Sadiqi could see. Although this was far bigger than anything he had witnessed before, it was just the logical conclusion of a political system that had come unhinged. The list of politicians involved in questionable legal dealings was extensive. Out of all those people only two men had ever been sentenced to any time in prison. Most of the accused were given suspended sentences and didn't even lose their mandate.

In any case, before members of parliament could even be investigated and charged, they needed to have their parliamentary immunity revoked, and by the time that was achieved nobody ever seemed interested in pursuing the case anymore. Clavreul was safe committing murder quite simply because nobody was going to have the balls to pursue this. Despite all the suspicions linking him to the legionnaire's action, nobody was going to want to touch this case. Voicing this type of accusation publicly would be professional suicide. For Sadiqi. For Dukrin. For the judiciary. "Let's face it, at best you're going to come up with some trivial corruption charge. Possibly traffic of influence, or conflict of interest for the work done with Caron."

There was nothing quite like Sadiqi's brand of dire pessimism, Dukrin mused. "I'll take what I can get. They got Al Capone on tax evasion. At least he was behind bars." She didn't need the lecture. She knew the statistics better than her associate. Given how hard it was to make lightweight charges like breach of trust stick against politicians, she wasn't overly optimistic about the prospect of attempting to pursue a terrorism case against a senator, if that was indeed what all this boiled down to. The prospect was far too ambitious. Very few politicians were ever held criminally responsible for anything in France. Politicians taking advantage of their parliamentary immunity was nothing new. But this wasn't a speeding violation they were talking about. If Clavreul really was involved in these attacks, he had reached a whole new level of malfeasance. This was murder. On a massive scale. This was beyond Machiavellian. "Don't think that I'm not pursuing this. I am. The warrants have come through on the senator. I've got officers in his home and his office right now seizing documents." On a more practical note, she circled back to the facts that had been the reason for her call in the first place. "I've already put a team together to go through the papers, looking for anything else to connect him to Caron or Rossignol. I'm hoping to have him at Quai des Orfèvres by tomorrow evening."

The vision struck the inspector as miserably inadequate: a roomful of trainee recruits falling asleep as they tried sifting through page after page of the senator's parliamentary papers. "Why even bother?" His voice was thick with disgust. "Are you actually even hoping to bring charges or are you just going to do the razzle-dazzle three-ring circus. Bring him in for questioning so that it looks like we're doing something, then let the whole thing fizzle out on some technicality."

As much as Dukrin understood the harshness of Sadiqi's words, she also knew the corollary: If Clavreul really was behind all this, their proof would need to be more than rock solid. It would need to be bloody titanium. "I'm not yet ready to make this a one-scenario investigation. No doubt there are other leads that need investigating. We'll have to see what we find in his papers."

"He's a bastard, not an idiot. We're not going to find anything in his papers." Clavreul wouldn't even lose his seat in the Senate. He'd barely get a slap on the wrist.

Listening to Sadiqi's rantings was worse than listening to the voices in her own head. As her anger deepened, so too did Dukrin's voice. "You want blood from a stone…"

Sadiqi felt like he had been through hell. "I want justice."

Her silence might have hidden an ironic smile. Or perhaps quiet despair. "We're both too old to believe in justice," she clipped. What else could she say? Sadiqi took it all so personally. Just like she did. "Try to get some rest. Sleep in late tomorrow, if you want. Then I need you back on top of this. This isn't over until we've found who was paying Rossignol – and whoever else you want, so long as you bring me the proof."

*   *   *

When the line went dead, Toni barely dared move. She felt like a rabbit that had mistakenly wandered into a fox den. In addition to a sense of unease, what she'd just heard added a layer of complexity to the way she viewed Sadiqi. As for the woman on the other end of the line, she wasn't sure whether her attitude showed iron authority or administrative impotence. "That was insightful," she managed to whisper, with only a tinge of sarcasm. "You guys work for the justice system but you don't believe in justice."

Sadiqi ran his hand over his right abdomen. He hoped the ribs were just bruised and not fractured. The paramedic had told him to go to Cochin for an x-ray but he was damned if he was going to waste his night sitting in the ER. In any case, the pain was strangely bracing. Sort of like a stiff whisky. It helped to ground him – to make this feel more like reality and less like insanity. "My job is to maintain law and order. It's fairly straightforward." His voice an earnest rumble. "Justice, on the other hand is spatially and temporally variable."

This enigmatic response struck Toni as even more unexpected than the phone call. She straightened to face the inspector. "So you're a closet philosopher. Tell me, what temporal and spatial variables will affect the outcome of a case against a person who tried to poison a thousand innocent civilians?"

The only way to avoid eye contact was to find something else to do. Being as he had nowhere to go, Sadiqi began swiping through his phone messages. "Where the attack took place, the people targeted, the people attacking, not to mention the ambient legal definition of what is or isn't considered terrorism at the time of the attack."

More than simply surprising her, the answer disturbed Toni. "I hope you're not saying what I think you're saying. Because it sounds like you're suggesting that since it might involve a white, high level politician this case won't be given the same attention it would receive if the attacker were a working class jihadist."

Sadiqi's eyes were glued to his phone. She'd summed up his thoughts elegantly. There was nothing he could add.

Toni waited for a denial. It didn't come. That set her off. "What about Lady Justice blindfolded for impartiality. I thought your boss said she was making an arrest. Maybe even tomorrow."

Sadiqi knew that the most sensible thing he could do was to keep quiet, but there was something about Corrigan's constantly searching eyes that made it almost impossible for him to hold back information. "No. She said he would be taken in for questioning. Which means the Criminal Brigade's VIP interrogation room." He kept flipping through his messages. "He'll be very comfortable. And he'll be out again within a few hours."

From the corner of his eye, the inspector was vaguely aware of Podesta, who had been typing messages into his own phone while occasionally lifting his head to listen to the conversation. Rather than looking more and more concerned as the gravity of the debate developed, he was looking increasingly entertained, with a smile now plastered across his face.

Which was deeply annoying. "What are you laughing about," Sadiqi snapped.

The lieutenant strained to reign in the growing smile. "Sorry, *Chef.*"

"What the hell is wrong with you?"

"It's you. You're back."

"What are you talking about?"

"A few minutes ago, I saw this guy, sitting on the back of the ambulance. Holding a beautiful girl. Letting the paramedics bandage him up. Happy that the Apocalypse wasn't for tonight. And I was watching and asking myself: 'Who the hell is this guy?' He looks so…" The lieutenant searched for the word he wanted. "I don't know. Maybe detached. Just acting the same as everyone else – at peace with all the bullshit simply because there's no other choice. But now that guy's gone. And you're back. So I'm smiling, *Chef*. Because everything's back to normal. The world is bad. You're unhappy. Order is restored to the universe."

The words were probably meant to wind Sadiqi up. Get a reaction – liven up Podesta's evening. The plan backfired. For some reason the comment simply drained all the inspector's energy. Instead, he let his hand glide over Toni's back. He didn't need to exert much pressure to cajole her back to his side. With the other hand, he held down the off-switch on his phone.

Podesta was a clown but like all clowns there was an element of truth in most of what he said. Except, unfortunately, it was unlikely order had been restored to the world that evening. On the contrary, a major disturbance had been created in Sadiqi's life when he met Toni. And he, in turn, had created a disturbance in hers.

A peel of thunder cracked deafeningly above them.

The storm was very close now.

A drop of rain fell. Then another.

97

Deep in the suburbs Swart watched the screen on the café wall showing the President's car roaring into the courtyard of the Elysée Palace in a cavalcade of motorbike gendarmes and worried looking security men. The footage had been filmed earlier. It was followed by a soundbite of Tibrac standing in front of the official Elysée lectern: "The attack on the Odeon was more than simply an attempt on my life, it was an attempt on the lives of the hundreds of young people assembled in that theater. In response to this unprecedented threat, a heightened state of emergency is now declared. We are moving to Vigipirate Acute Warning Level Crimson."

There was a volley of flashes from cameras and an avalanche of questions from the press. The one repeated the most often was: "Do we know who was behind this attack? Has anyone claimed responsibility?"

Tibrac stared menacingly into the camera. "The person behind this has been neutralized. But there are still questions that need to be examined. This is something new. Something insidious."

The anger coursing through Swart was red hot. His resolve was only reinforced by his frustration. *Neutralized.* His friend had been neutralized. He had always known this was a dangerous game, but Swart had been certain Rossignol would survive. Clearly he'd miscalculated.

He was going to have to avoid making the same mistake.

98

A heightened state of emergency. Vigipirate Acute Warning Level Crimson. Dukrin felt like spitting as Tibrac's well-trained voice was replaced by the drone of a journalist's political analysis. Dukrin didn't need the commentator's insight. She had 20/20 vision when it came to observing political manoeuvring. There was no such thing as Acute Warning Crimson. She should know. For the past nine years, she'd been a member of the committee that defined the terror alert levels. In other words, Tibrac had just created a state of emergency that he alone defined and controlled. *Ex nihilo.* Sadiqi was right. Politicians like Tibrac and Clavreul weren't going to miss the opportunity to harness a new threat to increase their own powers. Their impunity was insufferable.

The head of intelligence slipped past the TV screen nursing a whisky and went to stand in front of the window. Regardless of the rain pouring down, the view was one of the most stunning the city had to offer, second only to the panorama from the co-pilot's seat of a helicopter. Her apartment was nestled in Montmartre and from her living-room window she had a view of the entire storm swept city. It was quite a vision, she thought as she downed the dregs of her Nikka Coffey Grain. A beautiful city silently hiding its moral cancer beneath its jewelled exterior.

Dukrin stifled a yawn. The past few hours had been busy. The day had been hell. The fact that Sadiqi had killed the Nightingale at least meant Tibrac would be off her back for a little while. But incidents like the anthrax and the Odeon meant debriefings. The night wasn't over yet. The week wasn't over. The shit never ended. *Weekend* was a *non sequitur*.

She turned back to the television screen where Tibrac had stood a few moments earlier. Tibrac. She hated him. She hated the way he made her beautiful country look like a banana republic. She knew he was rotten. Past experience had proven that. Her personal knowledge of his nefarious dealings was extensive. She'd been watching him for years. Following his financial misdealings. Watching him end colleagues' careers. Studying how he muzzled the media. But most of all, he was the one who had allowed Clavreul to grow into a rabid titan.

Dukrin walked over to the bar, poured herself another shot and downed half of it. She didn't drink often. Her size 6 figure wouldn't have survived. But today she needed that contradictory effect. She needed that bitter jolt combined with the gentle numbing. Because today she was facing eternity. She was standing in front of her legacy. She had been keeping files on Clavreul for years, waiting for him to make a fatal move that would allow her to expose him. She had been patient. She had seen a lot of shit. And she had collected a secret file on him the length of his Belize bank account. There was plenty of material to tuck into. So far, he had always managed to cover his tracks, ensuring no accusations of wrongdoing ever stuck. It was nothing less than the smooth running of the well-oiled political machine. Between his parliamentary immunity and his senatorial immunity, Clavreul had been above the law for nigh on forty years. Before that, of course, there had been the military amnesty.

Dukrin put the empty glass down on the mantelpiece and opened the speckled blue porcelain box sitting beside it. She slipped out one of the cigarettes, lit it and took the deepest breath her lungs could contain. What could you expect in a country where, 200 years after the Revolution that was supposed to have overthrown the aristocracy, an incestuous little elite ran the country like its own personal country club, with one set of rules for the *hoi polloi* and another for the politicians – no matter how poisonous their antics became.

No. There was another revolution coming. There had to be. She would bide her time preparing for it.

As she opened the window to release the smoke into the other collected toxins of the city sky, her muscles were tense. The whisky had helped dissipate some of the cold fear, yet the days ahead were sketched out with perfect clarity. She was walking a tightrope and she would have to be pretty damn careful where she stepped. After all, there was a tradition in France of whistleblowers prematurely coming face to face with eternity. Whoever had been willing to kill all those people in the Odeon, wouldn't think twice about getting rid of her if he suspected she was on his tail.

And the idea of being discovered in some abandoned lot with a bullet through her head did not fit in with Sasha Dukrin's plans.

Epilogue

The rain hammered against the window in Toni's tiny studio. After nearly two weeks of everyone complaining about the unbearable heat, it would only be a matter of hours before people began complaining about the rain.

The drop in temperature caused by the downpour should have helped Sadiqi to sleep, but the soreness of his various injuries had woken him. Somehow he'd managed to ignore the pain during the night, losing himself in the sensual intoxication Corrigan brought. But now that his body had relaxed and cooled, the various lacerations, not to mention the bruised ribs, were bothering him. Sitting position was marginally more comfortable than lying down so he pulled himself to the foot of the bed and reached for his phone.

It must have been the noise that woke her. The rumble that shook the building had the cop on high alert in an instant, his head raised to attention, seeking to gauge the direction and intensity of the blast.

But the voice that sounded behind him was serene. "It's just thunder." A second later, he felt the tip of her toe brush against the nape of his neck, then the arch of her foot caressed his shoulder blade before passing over his deltoid. "Come back to bed."

He rotated his head and grazed the soft skin of the inner arch with the lightest of kisses, then let his gaze drop down to the pile of abandoned clothes on the floor.

He was tired. Exhausted. Disturbingly tired. Physically. Mentally. Yes, even emotionally. Maybe he should take a painkiller to help him sleep.

The foot passed across his back and glanced over the other deltoid. Again he turned his head and imparted a small kiss as it glided by.

And then she was sitting behind him. Her cheek pressed against his back.   Her arms hooked gently against his bruised rib cage. "You're a good man."

"Yeah, well. One good man working against a shitload of crazy isn't enough."

Five kisses across the cusp of his shoulders. A slight hesitation. Then a sixth. "'Goodness is stronger than evil.'"

The sigh escaped him before he could stop it. "That's bullshit."

He couldn't see her face, but he knew she was smiling; he could hear it in her voice when she spoke. "No. Actually it's a prayer:

> *Goodness is stronger than evil;*
> *Love is stronger than hate;*
> *Light is stronger than darkness;*
> *Life is stronger than death[2]."*

Sadiqi was too tired for sentimental crap. The growing exhaustion was made worse by the opposing voices fighting in his head: one telling him to just shut up and enjoy the suspended animation of the past hours, the other telling him to face the truth. The easiest solution probably would have been to leave but he had never been a fan of easy solutions. There was a messy question that needed addressing. He so wanted her to come clean without prompting but clearly that wasn't going to happen. Not quite able to find the courage to tackle her head on, he took the roundabout route. "I know a prayer, too. It goes like this:

> *Je reconnais devant mes frères*
> *que j'ai péché,*
> *en pensée, en parole, par action et par omission.*

The worlds jolted Toni out of her amorous languor. As far as early morning experiences in the arms of a new lover went, this one didn't bode well.   Her father was Irish Catholic and she easily recognized the Confiteor.

> *I ask my brothers to bear witness that I recognize*
> *I have sinned,*
> *In thought word, deed and by omission.*

---

[2] Desmond Tutu

Nothing good was likely to come from this type of conversation. "I wouldn't have figured you for a Catholic," she said.

He pivoted slowly so that he could at least face her for this. "I'm not. But I've been to a few masses. I put my kids in Catholic school. It was my wife's idea. I went along with it because I figured they'd get a better education."

Her reaction was immediate. What she needed was a thick enough barrier to keep out the news. She flopped onto her back and slid the folds of her inner arms over her eyes. "Okay. I get it. We're going to do confession."

"So do you still think I'm a good man? Lying by omission."

"Jesus. You really would make a good Catholic." The arms slid away from her eyes and she locked the intense green eyes on him. "Are you still married?"

"Divorced."

A shrug. "Then what am I supposed to say? We met two days ago. I can't resent you for having a life."

The girl was too laid-back. He was looking for a bigger reaction. He was trying to make a point. "I could have told you sooner. I could have been honest before we slept together."

She rolled her eyes. "We're not children. You were honest. I didn't ask; you didn't say. It's not a big deal."

Her pardoning nature was strangely incendiary. It didn't help. He wasn't looking for her indulgence. He just wanted her to do what he was doing: to state outright the things she'd been keeping to herself. "So that's how it works." Despite the comprehensive nod, there was irony in his voice. "You never ask; I never say. I never ask; you never say."

The morning was degenerating into something more tense than Toni had hoped for. Wrapping the sheet around herself she pulled her knees into lotus position, straightening her back so their eyes met on the same level. "I don't get it. Do you want me to get angry? Is that it? Would you feel more alive if I did the big jealousy scene?"

He turned away and reached for his jeans.

Which only annoyed her more. "Ah come on. You've got to be kidding. You're not leaving already."

"My ex is away for the weekend. The kids are with their grandparents. I should go and see them before Dukrin hauls me in for the weekend." He was standing now, the jeans buttoned, kicking the other clothes around in search of his t-shirt.

"How old are they?"

"14 and 16."

This was so ridiculous Toni didn't know whether to get angry or laugh. For some reason, she was getting angry. "It's fucking nine o'clock on Saturday morning. If your kids are anything like semi-human they're not going to be out of bed for another two or three hours." She could have moved closer. Touched him – just to defuse the tension. But somehow the atmosphere had reached such a critical mass she knew she would get burnt if she crept too close. Instead her voice rose. "What's your problem?" The past two days had been stressful, but wasn't that another reason in favor of him staying a little longer and unwinding. "You're acting like you can't wait to get away. Like I've done something wrong. Jesus. You're the one who lied to me."

The way he froze in mid-motion, abandoning the search for his shirt, gave her forewarning. Then the oddly disturbing movement, as he swaddled his phone in her t-shirt and tossed the bundle into the bathroom, made her even more uncomfortable.

"Am I?" he asked, pulling the washroom door closed, cutting himself off from the device.

The bitterness in his voice had a de-escalating effect. The fact that he was concerned that his phone might be listening to them knocked her completely off balance. "What are you talking about?" she whispered, suddenly much less confident.

He wanted to sound strong but he thought he probably sounded pathetic, standing there in the middle of her room, half-dressed, looking for his clothes, scared of his own phone. "Maybe I'm not the only one who left out part of the truth. Maybe there's something you haven't told me..." He bent down and picked up the dress he'd unzipped her out of a few hours earlier. The fabric was delicate and translucent so it was easy to feel the small wad of paper through the folds. He found the pocket and reached in. "Like why you took this out of the Clavreul Report," he said, dropping the dress back on the floor and unfolding the Post-it that had been glued in the middle of section 4.6 the day before. It was pointless the way he turned the bright orange rectangle towards her so she could see the words. She already knew what it said. *Corrigan probably doing intel acquisition for Canadian Intelligence.* Signed with SD for Sasha Dukrin. "Why is this here instead of in the report?"

She was a smart woman. The realization dawned instantly. The message from his boss she'd found in the Report had been planted there purposely. Sadiqi had wanted her to see that he knew she was working for the intelligence services; he had wanted to see how she would react.

(And what had she done? She had ripped it out and made him doubt her honesty. Not a good move.)

She hadn't seen that coming. Certainly not after the last few hours they'd spent together. The Wonderful Khalid Sadiqi Roller Coaster. It moved so fast, you never knew whether you were up or down. Her first reaction was purely professional, coolly analytical; she had just learnt something new about how Inspector Sadiqi worked. "That's not very fair play. I wouldn't have expected you to go in for entrapment." She was also a little disappointed with herself for having fallen for it without even thinking.

"It's not a game."

That, on the other hand, grated. The words rang hollow – more like a weak accusation than a factual statement. After all, hadn't he been playing her? He had already seen the message long before she took it out of the report. She might not have been entirely forthright, but he wasn't much better. "It sure seems like a warped little game. You get your boss' message, but instead of acting on it, you show me the report anyway." Not only that, they had spent the night together, as if everything were hunky dory. Then all of a sudden, bam!, he brings this out. "Why did you show me the damn thing if you knew I was a security risk?" She might equally have asked, *Why did you fuck me all night if you were just planning on walking away?*

Sadiqi crunched the Post-it between his fingers and shoved it in his jeans' pocket. "I wanted to see how you'd react... And I saw." If he had spat out his usual angry rumblings she could have ignored them. It was the pain in his voice that doused her anger. The quiet disappointment. Her fair skin flushed ever so slightly. "I'd already read the report," he added. "I figured there wasn't much in there you didn't already know. Possibly something I'd missed but that you would see. Which you did." In any case, it wasn't like she was working for the Russians. The Canadians were supposed to be allies. Almost as an afterthought he added, "If Dukrin had been worried, the message would have been more direct. She would have told me to break contact." Spotting his shirt on the floor he lunged and rummaged for a nicotine candy. "So what is it? Industrial espionage? Cyber spying?"

His anger had disappeared and the fatigue was back. One step was all it took to reach the desk. Why did everything in his life have to be so complicated? Espionage was messy. Corrigan might get thrown out of the country for this. By Monday she could be on the other side of the Atlantic. At least, that's what would happen if he passed on the information she had just confirmed. There was a pain in his chest other than the one caused by the bruised ribs. He didn't want her to go. He didn't want to turn her in. Sinking into the chair, he realized that this was what had been bothering him most – the possibility of her leaving.

She brought beauty to his world. His thirst for her was ineffable.

An atmosphere of suspended uncertainty now hung over the room. Toni watched as Sadiqi dropped his head into his hand; looking battered.

Only the right words could mend this. That was obvious. But it was definitely worth mending. "It isn't anything like that. It's Clavreul," she murmured. He glanced up, and was caught by her gaze boring into him. Challenging him. "I was supposed to use my contact with Caron to learn more about the senator." She could understand his disappointment but how could he possibly question her actions if they both shared the same aim?

The cop could feel the exhaustion pressing down. His usually straight back wilted over the desk. "Please don't feed me any more bullshit."

"It's not bullshit."

"Why the hell would Canada care about Clavreul?"

Reality was so much more difficult to explain than fantasy – it was so much more complicated and therefore much less logical. So much harder to make it sound convincing. She would try anyway. "Clavreul isn't a French problem any more than Daech is a Syrian problem. He may have started here, but his ideas are spreading around the world. Like I said yesterday, some red flags went up while he was living in Montreal. He used his time there to grow his international network." If she didn't keep this simple it would sound crazy. "Clavreul is the driving force behind several right-wing extremist groups implanted in Canada – particularly in the French speaking areas, where there's a growing immigrant population from North Africa. His expanding reach is a big problem; his brand of racism threatens Canada's multicultural ideal. If his influence continues to grow, he could have a destabilizing effect on domestic affairs." Judging from Khalid's look of complete exhaustion, this explanation wasn't improving his mood. As a last ditch attempt to pacify, she threw in a brief summary anyway. "I was supposed to find out more about his network. His contacts. His collaborators. Make sure his influence didn't seep back into Canada."

"You don't seem to have your story very straight." His disbelief, she had expected. The bitterness in his voice she hadn't. "You say you were supposed to use Caron to learn more about Clavreul, but then what about Algeria? Are you trying to tell me that you weren't already doing some sort of intel when you went to Chabet el-Akhira two years ago?"

The Good Inspector was certainly paying attention to all the details. It would almost be flattering if it wasn't so pathologically cop-like. "Yes. You're right. But it was still all about Clavreul." Despite the urge to come clean, she wanted to make this as brief as possible. If she ranted for too long, she would only end up annoying him more. In any case, some things were just better left unsaid. "I've collected info on both his past and present. My research incorporates history and politics; I don't focus on the purely technical aspects alone. Caron hated the approach, but it's what makes me a good operative. I can look into just about anything without raising suspicions. At least that's what I'm told." With the exception of the Good Inspector, up until now she'd always been able to move around below everyone's radar. "I can gather intel under cover of the research. But you're right. My trip to Algeria was a perfect chance to find out exactly what Clavreul did during the war. I was told that if I uncovered war crimes it would stem the growth of his movement." Sadiqi wasn't even looking at her, which wasn't a good sign. His eyes were closed, head in hand. She hadn't meant for this to happen. It was as if she'd pushed him to some emotional knife's edge and now she was scrambling to stop him from falling over the brink. "I don't know. I was told that greater clarity on his past would discredit him. Possibly even lead to a war crimes' tribunal over what happened in Chabet el-Akhira."

Maybe it had made sense to her when her handlers had fed her the bait, but it sounded like crazy talk to Sadiqi. His head was ready to explode. Nobody was going to send Clavreul to the Hague for war crimes in Algeria. Not sixty years after the fact. And in any case, why would anyone want to even try to drag this up? "Why do you care what happened 2000 kilometers away before either of us were even born?"

Having wanted to pacify, this last comment now angered her. Surely he couldn't be serious. Not after what he'd said to his boss. "Why do I care? How can you NOT care?" Although she felt a little repentant about the deception, she certainly wasn't going to apologize for her actions. The knowledge that the walls were paper-thin forced her to lower her voice to a hiss rather than raising it to a scream. "You say you want justice, but somewhere, deep down inside, you don't want to believe Clavreul was behind what happened last night, do you? You think: *It's too horrible. He's rotten, but he's not that rotten.* Let me tell you. He is that rotten. What he tried to do last night, he already did the same thing sixty years ago." The words were flooding out with passion. "You think I'm stupid to be wasting my time on war crimes

from sixty years ago. Is that the deal? Well, I can tell you, I might
have thought it was a waste of time when I first started trying to find
out what happened in Chabet el-Akhira, but I don't anymore. Do you
want to know what Clavreul did in Algeria? No? Well, I'll tell you
anyway. He had his troops round up over a thousand villagers: men,
women and children. Children," she repeated, her voice almost a
scream. "Do you know why? Because they were suspected of
belonging to the nationalist movement. Suspected. Not proven guilty.
Suspected. Then he got his men to drag those people into caves and
light a huge bonfire outside." Her voice was hypnotic, with its rapid
flow of questions and answers. "It was quite hard to find confirmation
of those events. You know why? Because most of the families from
the region had been decimated. I was able to find an old man, who had
been a child at the time. Who even remembered the name of the man
who had organized the cull: Colonel Clavreul. As a six-year-old, this
poor man had managed to run and hide in the hills – to escape from the
soldiers. Hiding in the bushes he survived. But sixty years on he still
has nightmares about the screams of his family and friends being
suffocated. His mother. His father. His brothers and sisters. Cousins.
All killed by *Colonel* Clavreul." As she enumerated the list of victims,
her outrage flared across the room. "Do you know how Clavreul was
punished for that family's murder and all the others in that town?"

Sadiqi was familiar with the punishment Clavreul would have
suffered for war crimes against 1000 civilians. His sense of collective
shame was so great he could barely manage more than a whisper. "The
'62 Evian Agreement." Not one of the more glorious political moves in
French history.

"That's right. Practically the day after the war ended, France
decreed a total amnesty for all the soldiers who had fought to keep
Algeria French, no matter how horrible their crimes. 'Decreed'. They
didn't even bother to pass the vote legally in parliament, they simply
decreed it. He was also awarded several medals, including the Legion
of Honor and the Cross of Valor. So, you ask me why I care, I'll tell
you. The French authorities have never shown any interest in wanting
to know what exactly happened in Algeria or holding Clavreul, or
anyone else accountable. I was doing the research because you guys
just weren't interested."

The last accusation was left hanging in the thundering silence that
followed the tirade. *You guys.* The world was divided into 'us' and
'you'. How many times in his career had Sadiqi heard someone
complaining about how it was 'us' against 'you'? And so often it had
been true. But not this time. It couldn't be. He didn't want to be

exiled into the team of the 'yous' against Corrigan's 'we'. Why should he? After all, he had no doubt the story of Chabet el-Akhira was true. North Africa was awash with so many other identical stories.

It was all starting to make some form of sense. He could almost believe her story... At least he could understand her reasoning. If only there weren't so many other lies making the tiny bits of truth so much harder to swallow. "Why weren't you straight with me?"

And now here they were; full circle back at their starting point. "I could ask you the same thing," Toni said, the calm returning to her voice. "Why didn't you tell me that de Chanterelle had been assassinated? Or that Montaigne school had been sprayed with anthrax?" Her voice was flat and dispassionate. "You know the answer as well as I do. Because you weren't at liberty to share that information. The same goes for me. France doesn't like to talk about its colonial past. News of foreign investigations into Clavreul might have been badly received. There might have been a backlash. I might have been labeled *persona non grata.* Whatever. There were lots of potential problems," she ended, seemingly having run out of steam to spew any more fury.

He shook his head. It was just the tiniest of movements, almost lost because his face was pressed into his hands, elbows dug into the desk. Right now he didn't care about Clavreul or politics or anything beyond the room. "That's not what I mean. Why did you take the message out of the report? Why did you try to hide it? Why did you lie to me?"

It only took her a moment to cross the room and wrap her arms around his shoulders, burying her face in his hair. She hadn't meant for this to happen. Okay, so maybe it was true that when he had made that stupid joke at dinner the other night about journalists and grad students making good spies, she had found the urge to test him irresistible. But the stupid, juvenile game hadn't lasted. She wasn't exactly sure when the change had happened – when she had stopped messing and started caring. All she knew was that she liked Khalid. She liked him a lot. He was a beautiful person. She had taken the Post-it out because she had known just how threatening that information was to their entanglement. But she had never meant to hurt him. "I'm like you," she said. "I never asked to do this. I was told to do it. I was told my links to Caron would facilitate access to Clavreul. I was serving my country."

The mantra called to him. Like him, there was something in her profile that had drawn the authorities to her, making her a good recruit. Mechanically, almost against his will, his arms slipped around her waist. How had this become so natural so quickly despite all the half-truths? "That's not the only lie. You're always avoiding questions. And you said you didn't speak Arabic."

"I don't. Only a few words. *Yes. No. A coffee, please.*" Her hand gently grazed his cheek, carrying with it the mingled scents of both their bodies blended into a powerful intoxicant. "I was moving in intellectual circles. I could get by on French, English... Google Translate."

Google Translate... What intelligence service had ever sent its operatives off with Google Translate? The lie was absurd but he didn't have the energy to fight any more. It was too difficult unravelling what she was thinking. She was so hard to read. Her gaze was always so steady. Almost too steady, as if she were trying to figure out what he wanted to hear rather than the truth. "You know, I just find it ironic that all this – your investigation, or whatever the hell you call it – started in a place called Chabet el-Akhira?"

The crystal gaze. "The Gorges of Death?" *The innocent incomprehension.*

"That's not really the right translation, though, is it? The word is more complicated than that."

At first, he thought she was going to step down. That she would claim she didn't know what he meant. Yet for some reason she gave him what he wanted. "*Akhira.* Yes, I guess it is sort of complicated," she agreed.

"So how would you translate it?"

The answer didn't come spontaneously. Her fingers slipped behind his ears, carefully kneading away some of the knots she herself had caused. "It's been a while," she said thoughtfully. "Algeria was a couple of years ago. You're an Arabic specialist. You know this stuff way better than I do."

"Humor me."

She raised her eyebrows ever so slightly, tilted her head, then focused the green gaze on a point somewhere over on the floor in the corner of the room, searching her memory for the details. "The way I understand it, *akhira* is sort of like a combination of *afterlife, hereafter* and *final judgement* all rolled into one." *If I understand right. Damn, she was good.* Usually Sadiqi wouldn't put up with lying – not from the people he worked with, not from the people he loved. But there was a perverse elegance in the way she delivered her lies. Every facial movement was studied; every inflection of her smile was practiced and perfected. It was like watching a wonderful actor on stage. She made him want to believe the show was real. "In Islam, when a person dies, their deeds are weighed by Allah. He decides whether that person's *akhira* lies in Heaven or Hell."

It was precisely the definition he had been waiting for. She certainly was an outstanding student. "So is that what this is all about? Is that what you're doing? Playing God? You're going to decide where Clavreul's *akhira* lies? Weigh the crimes of a lifetime."

She twisted away and flopped onto the edge of the bed, a new wave of frustration rising over the room. "This isn't as stupid as you're making it sound." Sadiqi recognized the tone of her voice. It was so familiar. It was the same tone he used with people all the time. The one that meant *don't-talk-to-me-as-if-I-were-an-idiot.* "History creates bridges to the future. Crimes against humanity need to be punished because if they're negated they fester and generate payback and more violence. Immunity and statutes of limitations only serve to give the criminals licence to keep on committing their crimes. Clavreul got his taste for blood long ago. If he hadn't been pardoned, he probably wouldn't have killed again."

. She wanted him to share her indignation. Even though they didn't view the events of the past days through the exact same lens, surely she and Sadiqi were both looking for the same outcome. A deep breath helped her regain her calm. "I realize what I'm saying may sound abstract and idealistic, whereas you want to address something raw and real," she said, gently. "You lost two of your men yesterday. Other colleagues, too. You wanted the Nightingale dead. I get that. But he wasn't the one who killed Pecheron and Mueller. Not really. It wasn't his idea. He may have pulled the trigger; but it was Clavreul who paid for the ammo and loaded the gun. The bastard's been handing loaded guns to people all his life. So, okay, fine. I'm nobody. I have no power over Clavreul's *akhira* but maybe – just maybe – I can help make sure he faces some form of justice here and now."

That was the point of no return. That was the moment when Sadiqi knew he wouldn't do anything to stop her. It was also the moment he understood why he had been drawn to her from the start: the way she believed she could change the world. It was one of the more elegant flaws of youth: that almost fanatical belief each generation holds that they will do better than the generations that have gone before. It was outrageous – it was a tenet that was systematically disproved, generation after generation. Yet, at the same time, it was a beautiful illusion. More than that: it was the definition of hope itself. He had been like that once, long ago, when he had started in this game. He had shared that hope. It seemed like ages now. So long ago that he wasn't even sure when he had lost it. Yet the knowledge that she still had that drive helped to crystallize their connection.

Opposites didn't attract. Like attracted like. That's why he was here, in her room. That's why he couldn't bring himself to leave. That's what held them together so inseparably. Even though she hid it so much better than he had ever been able to, she was dark. Very dark.

It was unrealistic to hope the senator would be pursued for what he did in Algeria all those years earlier, but together, they might be able to get him for what had just happened in Paris.

The past twelve hours had been exhausting. No. The past forty-eight hours had been exhausting. When he stood up, his intention had actually been to head for the door and go home, but the fatigue had finally caught up with him. He was drained; there was no strength left in him. Instead of leaving, he went and sat on the bed beside her. "Can I stay a couple more hours? Just to sleep. I need to sleep."

It was an absurd question. Of course he could stay. She only had one pillow but she grabbed the quilt out of the closet and folded it so he wouldn't have to lie completely flat. The paramedic had said he would be more comfortable if he kept his back elevated.

The set-up was passably satisfactory. The second he closed his eyes he would have been asleep if she hadn't spoken: "I've said too much."

That was absurd. She had told him barely anything. And of the things she had said, he only believed a fraction. "You haven't said enough. But you've said more than I want to hear," he murmured, not certain whether he was speaking loud enough to be understood.

There was a moment's silence. He wasn't sure quite how long because he was already falling towards sleep. It may have been very long or very short. Then there was another question. "Are you going to brief your boss?"

His hand stretched towards her, coming to rest against some undefined source of warmth. "No." Nobody needed to know what she was doing. They were both on the same side. They were both trying to get Clavreul. Nobody would care about her sniffing around some third rate politician. On top of that, nobody knew about her sideline in intelligence acquisition. Not Dukrin. Not anyone. "I wrote the Post-it. Dukrin doesn't know. Nobody else knows." It was their secret. Just him and Corrigan. And Corrigan was very good at keeping secrets.

Which probably should have worried him even more than it did.

Author's note

FranceTech does not exist. Although there is an engineering school on the corner of the Luxembourg Gardens, any link between the school and Freemasonry is entirely fictional.

Likewise, Chabet el-Akirah is fictional. It is intended to serve as a marker of several different massacres that took place in Algeria throughout the colonial period, most notably the caves of Dahra (1845) in which hundreds of villagers were suffocated by colonial troops (accounts range from 600 to 1000 dead), the massacres in Constantin in 1945 (with several thousand Algerians estimated dead), as well as other alleged massacres perpetrated between 1954 and 1962. It was the events of May 9th, 1945 outside Kherrata that provided the inspiration for the name 'Chabet el-Akhira'. The actual incidents took place near Chabet el-Akra, where villagers suspected of instigating nationalist resistance and unrest were rounded up by French troops and taken to the Kherrata gorges, where they were executed and thrown in the ravine.

Acknowledgements

Thank you to everyone without whose help this book wouldn't exist.

To those who read the initial version and encouraged me to keep at it. Geneviève, Jacek, Dorthe, Sergio, Astrid, Jean-Christophe. It's been a very long time. I'm sure there were others. That initial validation made me think it was worth continuing.

To those who read the second version and still encouraged me. To John for man-splaining my book to me. To Alison for saying the manuscript was better than the commercially published stuff she'd read the same month. To Moira for her enthusiasm. To Chris, for not hating it. To Elisabeth for throwing out Dukrin's Chanel and making her dress in YSL. To Françoise for not liking the president's name. All those comments helped make this project feel like it actually mattered.

To everyone who supported me when I decided to self-publish. To Mixie who liked the Facebook page and spread the word. To Jeanette who followed Toni on Twitter as well as buying the paperback. To the friends and colleagues who clicked to download. Thanks to you the search engines know this book exists (even if no one else does).

I especially have to thank everyone who read both versions and still dared to criticize. Many thanks to Shirley whose tireless comments helped make the characters so much more likeable. To Jill for taking Sadiqi's cigarettes away from him. And to both Shirley and Jill for all the typo corrections. To Mum and Dad for believing that writing was a useful way for a grown-up to be spending her time. To Sacha for not minding his mother talking to him obsessively about people who don't exist. To Antoine for saying the story should start with the young engineer, not the jaded middle-aged men.

And, of course, to Pascal, for telling me to stop constantly changing the book every time one of my friends made a comment.

Thank you, everyone. I hope you can share some of my pleasure at seeing this story become an authentic, physical reality and not simply a figment of my imagination.

ABOUT THE AUTHOR

C.H. Dickinson was born in Canada but has spent most of her life in Paris, with lengthy stopovers in London and Prague. She holds a doctorate in Economics from Pantheon-Sorbonne University and teaches in French higher education. She has published two novels and is currently working on the sequel to *City of Dark.*